BLACKWOOD INSTITUTE #3

DESECRATED SAINTS

J ROSE

Copyright © 2022 J Rose
Written & Published by J Rose
Edited by Nice Girl Naughty Edits
Proofreading by Lauren at DarkbyDesign
Cover Design & Formatting by Books and Moods
First Paperback Edition July 2022
All rights reserved. This is a work of fiction. Any names, characters and events are used fictitiously. Any resemblance to persons living or dead, establishments or events is coincidental. This book or any portion thereof may not be reproduced or used without the express permission of the author, except for the use of brief quotations in the context of a book review or article.
www.jroseauthor.com

*For the younger version of myself, too afraid to speak up.
You've found your voice now.*

TRIGGER WARNING

Desecrated Saints is a why choose, reverse harem romance, so the main character will have multiple love interests that she will not have to choose between.

This book is very dark and contains scenes that may be triggering for some readers. This includes self-harm, graphic violence, psychological torture, and strong mental health themes including psychosis, trauma and suicidal ideation.

There is also explicit language used throughout and sexual scenes involving blood play, breath play, knife play, asphyxiation and mutual self-harming.

If you are triggered by any of this content, please do not read this book. This is a dark romance, and therefore not for the faint of heart.

Additionally, this book is written for entertainment and not intended to accurately represent the treatment of mental health issues.

Grab your tissues and get ready for a wild ride. The end of Brooklyn's story is finally here!

"Someone begging for their humanity to be acknowledged can sound an awful lot like rage."
- Kalen Dion

PREFACE

Here at the journey's end, we begin again.

The years of trauma and self-destruction have passed in a blur.

Time has healed some wounds, while rubbing salt in those left gaping wide open.

I thought that forgiving you would free me. Allow me to rise from smoke and ash, a scarred phoenix, determined to fly once more.

Nobody tells you that true forgiveness can only come from within. Relegating the monsters of the past to mere shadows isn't enough.

Pain remains.

Clinging.

Destructive.

Poisonous.

At the end of this road, the truth is painted in blood and wasted tears. I see it so clearly now. Victimhood is a choice, not a death sentence.

I choose to forgive myself.

I choose to live the life I deserve.

I choose to let go.

Now, I take my first steps into the future.

PROLOGUE

SEVEN - 2016

Be Invited - The Twilight Singers

Straightening my pressed blue shirt and matching pinstripe tie, I give my reflection a decisive nod. It's time. No more skulking around, stealing the odd stack of papers or eavesdropping behind locked doors.

I need proof.

The world has to know what goes on in here.

Leaving the safety of my comfortable office behind, I slip down the thickly carpeted corridor of the prestigious Blackwood Institute. This is my place of employment, and a source of constant worry for the past six months. It's far from the romanticised dream I'd built up in my head.

"Doctor Farlow?"

Freezing, I plaster an impassive mask in place.

For fuck's sake.

Miss White's designer pumps sink into the soft carpet as she joins me, dragging her eyes over my muscled chest. Her flirtation has only increased in the time I've worked here, reaching unprofessional levels that make me uncomfortable.

"What can I do for you, Warden?" I smile politely.

"Please, Jude. How many times must we discuss this?" Her red-painted nails scrape over my bicep. "Call me Elizabeth. I just wanted to see how you're getting on. I heard you had a difficult time last week."

I match her smile. "Naturally, working in an environment like this poses its challenges. But don't worry about me. I can look after myself… Elizabeth."

Her tinkling laughter grates against my skull.

"Oh, Jude. You do amuse me. I'll leave you to continue with your day, but should you need anything… you know where to find me. No matter the hour."

With a final lingering look, she retreats in a cloud of sickly sweet perfume. I watch her return to her office down the corridor. I have no doubt that her thick lashes and pouty lips hide a multitude of sins.

The incident she's referencing involved a patient who had a complete psychotic breakdown in the group session I was facilitating, and it drew a lot of attention to my traineeship. I can fend off their questions and pretend to be unfazed, but truthfully, that session was the final nail in the coffin.

I knew the patient, Lucia, had been struggling for some time. Her regular clinician is a dinosaur who refuses to discuss his treatment methods with me, but he also happens to be my boss. I've had to tread very carefully as a result.

There are a lot of unusual things about Blackwood.

And many unanswered questions.

Scanning my ID badge, I let myself into the gloomier corridor that leads down the winding staircase. The solitary wing is my least favourite place in this gothic museum of insanity. I avoid it by necessity. My work

DESECRATED SAINTS

does not concern those incarcerated in Professor Lazlo's basement, but Lucia has been missing all week.

I'm done lying to myself about Blackwood's involvement in her deterioration. Inching past locked cells and occupied signs, I pause to read the names printed across the paperwork attached to each door. By the end of the corridor, I've yet to find Lucia's name.

She isn't fucking here.

What now? Think!

With a glance at the ever-present CCTV cameras, I throw caution to the wind. I won't unravel this mystery by playing it safe. Passing Lazlo's office door, I take the next staircase down. This one is lit by faint bulbs that cast the entire world in uncomfortable shadows.

The temperature drops even further as I emerge on the lowest level of the basement. Expecting more solitary confinement, I'm unnerved by what I find instead. These aren't the padded cells equipped to handle the sickest of patients I've seen in Manchester and Clearview.

I'm staring at torture chambers, blood-stained and windowless.

With my heart threatening to shatter into terrified shards, I inch inside the closest room. The door is ajar to air out the scent of industrial bleach. A rusted bathtub sits in the centre, boasting medieval-style shackles that make my stomach turn. I have to cover my mouth to ensure I don't throw up.

The bathtub is full of crimson, bloody water, as if the occupant sliced a vein, exposing them to the cruel justice of death. Peering around the chamber, I note the scratch marks and dents scattered across the concrete walls. Someone was locked in here.

No, not someone. An animal.

Whatever remains of a person when you strip the humanity away.

"Doctor Farlow. Fancy seeing you down here, son."

Jumping out of my skin, I turn to find Professor Lazlo lingering in the doorway. With his arms crossed and wire-framed spectacles hanging around his neck, he grins at me.

"Finally opened your eyes, did you?"

"What is this place? Where is Lucia?" I demand.

"No need to raise your voice. We're both professionals, are we not?"

Gesturing around the chamber, I laugh. "You call this professional? Where is my patient?"

"Lucia is my patient, Jude."

"I have the right to enquire about her welfare!"

Lazlo sighs. "Fine. You want to see Lucia? Be my guest."

Turning on his heel, he stalks off down the murky corridor. I follow, shivering from the sub-zero temperature and something far worse—real, tangible fear. I suspected foul play, but nothing like this. I'm out of my depth.

Lazlo pauses outside the final locked door, rust-spotted and made from thick, impenetrable metal. Retrieving a black swipe card, he waves it over the hidden scanner and the squeal of old hinges fills my ears.

In those brief seconds before the interior is revealed, I consider running. Actually running. But it's no use, as two of his personal guards have joined us and now box me in on both sides. My unease triples.

"Five? You have a visitor," Lazlo singsongs.

Choking on my panic, I glance into the damp cell. An old-style cot rests in the corner, boasting a familiar bag of bones, strapped down with heavy restraints. Blinking at me with no recognition, Lucia's mouth opens and shuts without a word.

"Holy shit," I breathe.

"As you can see, she is acutely unwell and must remain here."

"What on earth are you doing to her?"

Lazlo chuckles behind me. "Reconditioning."

Before I can defend myself, sharp pain blooms in the back of my head. I fall to my knees, my vision blurring. I'm surrounded by brutes with tasers. I scream at the electrical current, jerking and thrashing until the torture ceases.

"You should have stayed upstairs," Lazlo says simply.

"You w-won't... get a-away... with this!"

Peering down at me with his spectacles replaced, his dead orbs of sick human curiosity scare the living daylights out of me. Lazlo smirks, taking in my still-twitching form, before turning to his two guards.

"Call Augustus on the private line. Tell him to come and collect; I have two new acquisitions. Bring the sedatives too. Let's prep them."

Sparing me a final glance, Lazlo shakes his head.

"You'll wish you never stepped foot in Blackwood Institute."

1

BROOKLYN

Died Enough For You - Blind Channel

Stretched out on the sandy hill, a steep slope leads straight down to the thunderous crash of waves. Part of me is tempted to throw myself over the edge rather than face the people behind me. Instead, I watch the sun sink on the horizon.

On all sides, nothing but ravenous ocean waves surround us. The nearest town is miles away, with a total population of fifty this far up north. We arrived a few days ago, moving under the cover of night. The plan was executed to utter perfection.

I spent the first couple of days unconscious. My body had shut down on me. I wish I could go back to that oblivion now. As I turn my back on the sea, the deep hole I created with my bare hands waits for me. It took me almost an hour to dig. I'm weak from months of imprisonment.

According to Kade, it's been four months.

I hardly believed him at first.

Humans are fucking resilient. Our bodies kick in and keep us alive, even when our minds have checked out. The last few months are a blur to me, punctuated by regular doses of horror. The devastating stares of all four of the men I left behind affirm the truth.

I was Patient Eight for a long, long time. Now, I don't know who I am. Brooklyn West is gone, Patient Eight too. Someone else remains. A broken creature, born of blood and pain.

"Blackbird?"

Glancing back, I find my family waiting for me. All of them look at me with equal parts relief and guilt. I fucking hate it. Crouching down, I retrieve the journal from my discarded leather jacket.

"You don't have to be here for this," I mutter.

Tentative footsteps approach.

"We want to be," Kade says gently.

"You don't. None of you can stand to look at me."

I catch Phoenix's flinch as he runs a hand over his odd, natural-brown hair. He doesn't look like the person I remember. Fuck, none of them do. My guys are gone, just like their girl is. We're drowning in the unknown, lost at sea without hope of rescue.

Stepping forward to join his brother, Hudson's gaze is too intense to bear. It's like staring into the sun, full of fire and brimstone, fury and devotion in equal measure. He holds the entire group's strength now.

"That's not true and you know it," he insists.

"We had to get here before the authorities could catch up to us," Kade adds. "It wasn't for any other reason, Brooke. You were exhausted too. We wanted to let you rest."

I look away from them all, returning to the journal that's somehow followed me for all these years. I was surprised to find they brought a bag of my belongings with them when we escaped Blackwood. Identifying the items that used to mean the world to me is an impossible task.

DESECRATED SAINTS

I cared so much back then, before my entire being was deconstructed, piece by fucking piece. Now, my memory is bruised and scarred from months of abuse. Flicking through the journal, countless dark entries assault me, along with the names of my lost family, immortalised by ink.

The battered polaroid photos that I entered Blackwood with are still tucked away in my bag. I can't stand to look at them. With a final glance at the heavily laden pages, I drop the journal into the hole in the ground. There are no words to be recited at this funeral, no eulogy or emotional speech.

I'm the only one left alive to mourn Logan's ghost.

I feel so alone without him by my side.

With his blonde ponytail and warm, humoured eyes, he was always ready with some retort to take my mind off the onslaught of torture. It feels wrong to mourn the dead. Why should we? It's the living who suffer, the ones left behind to wade through the fallout.

"I'm sorry I forgot about you. I couldn't have asked for a better big brother. I hope that wherever you are… you're at peace. I know I won't be until I see you again."

Eyes closing, I find Logan's imaginary face waiting.

You have nothing to be sorry for.

Forgive yourself, kiddo. Let go.

You have my permission to move on.

I crouch down, shoving wet sand back into the hole. Wild, desperate sobs wrack my entire body. Hudson quietly joins me on his knees. I instinctively dodge the arm he tries to wind around my shoulders, letting out a low growl.

"It's just me, baby," he murmurs.

"Please… I can't be touched right now."

Nodding, he silently helps me fill the hole in. By the time we're done, my journal has vanished from sight and Logan disappears too.

He's just another ghost now, one of many that haunt my life. I find my feet and turn to face the guys, scrubbing away my tears.

"He died protecting me," I admit roughly. "When our mum's delusions and paranoia got worse, she would beat on me and smash shit. Logan always stood between us, until he didn't."

"What happened?" Kade asks carefully.

There's no point in sugarcoating it.

I have far worse to tell them.

"She murdered him when I was ten years old. My father helped to cover it up. Even then, he was afraid of losing her. They were both victims of her sickness, one way or another."

No one knows quite what to say to that. I tried to explain my hallucination to Hudson, the phantom that kept me company for many lonely months. A person I'd erased from my memory until Augustus pulled him from the depths of my traumatised brain.

"What was he like? Your brother?" Phoenix asks.

"He was alive."

There's nothing else to say. I can't delve into the toxic waste of the past yet. It's too painful, the knowledge of all I've lost along the way. It feels like Logan has died all over again, leaving me alone in the world.

"Come inside," Hudson orders, his hand outstretched. "We all have questions. I'm sure you do as well. No sense avoiding them any longer."

"I can't. I need... space."

His arm drapes around my shoulders. I can't help but fall into his warm embrace. Hudson winces as he jolts his injured shoulder in the process, another reminder that the last few days really happened.

"You've had enough space. We need you now."

"No. You don't."

He stares deep into my eyes. "I fucking need you, alright? Stop arguing. I'll throw you over my damn shoulder if I have to, fuck the gunshot wound."

Studying the other three, they all seem equally desperate for something from me. I'll tear strips off myself without blinking an eye if they need something to hold on to, even if the girl they're in love with is long dead. Yet somehow, I'm still here.

The breath I've been holding since leaving Blackwood whooshes out of me. It isn't a trick, we actually escaped. Left our lives and convictions behind to begin again. But it isn't that easy—our demons have followed us. The unresolved suffering of many months apart won't be ignored.

"That won't be necessary," I concede.

Phoenix visibly deflates, leaning on Eli by his side. My curly-haired twin flame stares at me with such intensity, I feel like my skin will peel back from my bones and reveal my darkest secrets. He's barely left me alone since our reunion, trapped in his own terrified bubble. We've returned to a world he hasn't seen for a decade.

When I woke up here, he was there.

Watching. Studying. Waiting.

I've seen the deep, vicious slashes across his arms. Much like Kade's weight loss, Phoenix's brown hair, and Hudson's newly scarred knuckles, it's undeniable proof that time has passed while I dwelled in Augustus's mental prison. Their lives continued in my absence, however painfully.

"Hudson?"

"Yeah, blackbird?"

Cupping his unshaven jaw, I force myself to smile.

"Thank you for saving my life."

My monstrous sinner sacrificed everything to save me from the darkness, to atone for all his inhuman deeds in the past. Despite everything, I owe him my life. What remains of it, at least.

"You're the one who saved us, baby."

2

BROOKLYN

Out Of The Black - Royal Blood

Hands clutching a mug of tea, I settle into the sofa beside the empty fireplace. It's late summer, but the temperature is cold up here. Soon, we will need thicker clothing and logs to burn. If we are to remain here for the rest of our days, we have to prepare.

There's nowhere else for us to go. We're outlaws now. Even more than we were before, far beyond the constraints of society. As I look around the cottage that Kade's mum organised for us, I realise it can't last. We've been missing for almost a week already.

They will come for us.

What we did to escape won't go unpunished.

In the kitchen, Kade and Sadie chat in low, urgent tones. She accompanied us up north with no preparation. The presence of Seven—or Jude, as she calls him—changed everything. I have a feeling the temporary peace is about to explode.

"Firecracker?"

Hesitating with a beer in hand, Phoenix looks longingly at the empty space beside me. I sigh and pat the cushion for him to sit.

"You don't have to ask."

"I didn't want to assume."

"I'm not made of glass, Nix. Just sit the fuck down."

He curls up by my side, tentatively resting his head in my lap. I hesitate before stroking his brown locks, sifting the strange hair with my fingertips. It looks so wrong, this colour. Like the person I knew has also faded away.

It doesn't take long for Eli to approach like a silent sentry. He doesn't bother asking permission, burrowing into Phoenix's side so the three of us are curled up in a dog pile. Their familiar scents wrap around me, slipping beneath my skin and warming the empty shell of my heart.

"You feel so fucking good," Phoenix whispers.

I swallow the lump in my throat. "You do too."

"I didn't think I would ever see you again. None of us did."

Eli lets out a rumble of agreement, but no words. He hasn't spoken since we found each other in the ashes, communicating with little looks and deep frowns.

"Yeah," I say lamely.

"Did you miss us, Brooke? As much as we missed you?"

I flex my spasming fingers, fighting to regain control of my extremities. His question has me feeling all kinds of fucked-up. Eli grabs my hand. I meet his green gaze, shining brightly beneath the nasty bruises he gained in the riot.

"I had to… put you guys aside to survive," I admit.

"What does that mean?"

"There's stuff you don't know. If I remembered you, I wouldn't have survived what Augustus made me do. Losing myself was the only way to make it through."

"What did he make you do?"

"Christ, Nix. Lay off."

His head lifts from my lap to pin me with a glare. "We deserve to know. Do you have any idea what we've been through in the last four months? Fuck, Brooke. You're not the only one that barely made it through."

I find the entire room listening to our argument. We're a sorry sight, all covered in bruises and lacerations, bandages and pained grimaces. Kade and Sadie are seated at the cluttered kitchen table, while Hudson rests against the countertop. Every single one of them is staring at me.

"Don't shut us out again," Phoenix begs.

"I can't do this right now."

I shove him off my lap and retreat to an empty corner. I can't have any of them touching me while I still have one foot in that basement. There's a slither of Patient Eight alive and kicking inside of me. She's below the surface, a violent force pumping through my veins.

"Show them the pictures," Hudson orders.

Kade's hazel eyes bore into me, already seeking forgiveness. The entire room falls away as he turns his laptop around so everyone can see. Each hazy photograph shows a different slice of hell. My blood freezes as I watch.

The Z Wing.

Solitary confinement.

Isolation chambers.

Bathtubs and shackles.

Empty syringes and straitjackets.

"What the actual fuck?" Phoenix walks over for a closer look. "I don't remember seeing all this shit when I was in the hole."

"This isn't the hole, it's something else entirely," Kade surmises.

He doesn't break eye contact with me, not once. It's unnerving. He's demanding the truth without mercy. I don't have to confirm it. He can see the photos are real from the way my body shakes.

"I took these on my way down to find her." Hudson knocks back his beer. "It was like a fucking horror show down there. Mariam helped us to free some of the patients being held."

"We turned them over to the authorities for protection," Sadie speaks up for the first time. "I don't know if they made it out alive. Incendia's reach is further than we can comprehend."

Approaching the safety of my corner, Hudson's footsteps ring out like gunshots. The tension carved on his face warns me of what's to come. His gentle handling is about to expire.

"Tell us what we need to know," he demands, hands on his hips. "We've danced around each other for well over a year now. None of us have walked away. Tell the truth and don't you dare leave anything out."

"Hud," Kade warns, frowning.

"Stay out of this. We need to know what we're dealing with."

"Are you sure you're ready for it?" I counter.

Hudson's expression hardens. "You can't scare us off."

"What if I told you that I deserved to be left in that basement? I've done things these past few months… things I can never tell you. Some I can't remember. We were Augustus's… brute force. Me and Seven."

"What does that mean?" Sadie interjects.

Sinking further into the corner, I wrap my arms around my bony legs. "He needed people that he could control. We had no choice but to obey, no matter what he ordered. Refusal resulted in punishment."

Phoenix fists his brown hair. "Like in these pictures?"

All I can muster is a nod.

Turning his back, he seethes through gritted teeth, angrier than I've ever seen him. My head is spinning with confusion. They're all so different. I feel like I don't know them anymore and it's killing me inside to think that. I can't get back all of the lost time.

The fact is, none of us survived Blackwood.

We all died in that riot.

Only scraps of our souls escaped.

"Let's all just cool off a bit." Kade closes his laptop. "We've got a lot of evidence to trawl through and we haven't managed to access Augustus's hard drive. This is going to be a long process."

I shiver, not cold, but fearful of the invisible threads in my mind that pull taut at the mere mention of Augustus. Dead or not, his sharp claws remain inside of me.

"Plus, the data I stole from Incendia's headquarters," Sadie supplies.

The mental image of the security guard's final moments jumps into my mind. Sadie doesn't need to know what me and her brother did to the poor motherfucker. I can still see his throat gaping open in a red, dripping smiley face. Worst thing is, I enjoyed it.

"What did you get?" I ask neutrally.

"Mostly records of stakeholders and shares, basic corporate stuff. It'll take time to decode it all."

"I have copies of my father's files. We should collate the evidence and start from there." Kade absently cleans his glasses. "If we can trace Incendia back to him and Augustus, we're in business."

"I, uh, met him."

I fight the urge to slap my hands over my mouth. I didn't mean to say it out loud. Kade looks at me with confusion creasing his brows, like he's piecing together a puzzle that's fighting him at every turn.

"My father?"

I manage a jerky nod. An odd kind of darkness passes over Kade, his expression morphing and changing. There are shadows in his eyes that never used to be there.

"When?" he barks. "Why didn't you tell me?"

"It's... complicated. I was on a job."

His next words become a jumbled blur as ringing fills my mind. All I can do is stare at Kade while acid churns my stomach, noting all the similarities between him and his father. I can almost taste Martin's warm, sticky blood in my mouth. It soaked my entire body after my bullets tore him to shreds.

I don't realise I'm hyperventilating until Sadie approaches me. I read the words on her lips. *Breathe. In for four, out for four.* My nails dig into my skin as I scrub my face, trying to remove the awful feeling. I'm still covered in blood. I can fucking feel it.

The guys helplessly watch me fall apart. It sickens me to leave myself so vulnerable. I've maintained my thick shields for months, pushing the hysteria down to stay alive. It won't stay buried anymore. Sadie's words finally begin to resonate, and I grab hold of the distraction.

"Repeat after me... what day is it?"

"Tuesday," I bite out.

"What time?"

Checking the clock above the fireplace, I recite the time.

Sadie tries a calming smile. "Good. What's your name?"

"I... I... I don't know."

Her warm hand slips into mine, squeezing so hard it hurts. I try to ground myself with the feeling, working on taking the smallest breaths to relieve my lungs.

"I know," she replies. "You're Brooklyn. Okay? Nobody else."

"Nobody else," I whisper in a small voice.

"Brooke, I need to know. Jude... was he with you? On these jobs?"

"We worked as a team."

"Doing what, exactly?"

I finally meet her bleak gaze. "Whatever Augustus wanted."

The tension in the room reaches a breaking point. Kade tosses his glasses aside to rub his temples, while Hudson curses and storms into the kitchen. Phoenix is bouncing on his feet like a live wire, in complete opposition to Eli, who silently shuts down in the corner.

I know it must hurt them, the fact I blocked them all out while relying on another man. Desperation is a cruel mistress. It doesn't bargain or leave you with easy options, only the impossibility of putting one foot in front of the other.

"What happened to him?" Sadie whispers.

There's a sudden chorus of loud banging, like explosions are destroying our temporary home. We all look at the partition door, where the bedrooms lay beyond. The sound of a struggle filters through and something tells me it isn't Two or Five making such a racket.

We all knew it was coming.

He's awake.

"You didn't tie him down again?" Hudson bellows.

Sadie's face contorts with pain. "I just… I want to talk to him, even if it's just for a moment. We can't keep him sedated and locked up like an animal."

The door crashes open. Tall, gangly, and wild-eyed, Seven stands unsteadily on his feet. He's dressed in a borrowed pair of Hudson's sweats, leaving his scarred, bruise-laden chest bare. I can still see the healing marks from the electrocution that nearly killed him.

He takes one look at us and goes on the offensive. A blur of bare feet and tangled brown hair, the animal that kept me company launches himself across the kitchen. Hudson intercepts him before he can attack anyone. The pair tumble to the floor, exchanging powerful blows.

"Stop! Let him go!" Sadie shouts.

With the pair wrestling and snarling like wolves, I don't think anyone expects Seven to come out on top. Hudson's the burliest of the group, carved from muscle and bad decisions. But they don't know Seven like I do. Even with one hand, he's a ruthless killing machine.

I quickly grab a knife from the kitchen block, dancing past Kade. I don't need his protection. Seven slams his one remaining fist into Hudson's face, becoming frenzied at the sight of fresh blood. Before he can kill the man I love, I throw myself at him.

We collide and roll across the hardwood floor, the sharp press of the blade trapped between us. One wrong move and we'll both bleed out. Seven's still weak from being half-starved to death, so despite his adrenaline rush, I manage to gain the advantage. I end up straddling his chest.

Hudson swipes blood from his mouth. "Grab her!"

"Wait! I can calm him down!"

Seven growls gutturally, but his eyes are wild with terror. Underneath the rage, he recognises me. His movements slow slightly. I press the knife to his throat, my teeth bared. He almost smiles before bucking and slicing his own skin without caring. He wants me to kill him.

"Seven! Stop it! You're safe!"

The pain doesn't register in his expression as his throat begins to bleed. Hudson looks ready to drag me away by my hair, so I throw the knife across the room and watch it embed in the floor right next to his left foot. He jumps back, giving me several precious seconds.

I grab Seven's bleeding throat and begin to squeeze, easily crushing his windpipe. He stops fighting, succumbing to my bruising grip without complaint. His inherent trust in me is dizzying.

"Sev?" I repeat, softer. "You don't need to be afraid."

"His name is Jude," Sadie barks.

"Is that really relevant right now?"

Staring into Seven's eyes, my nails dig deep into his flesh. Blood begins to weep from the wounds. He'll pass out soon. I wait for a trickle of awareness to return, keeping him on the edge of consciousness. I won't abandon the man who kept me company when we had nothing but endless screams for comfort.

"It's me, Eight. I'm not leaving you."

When I loosen my grip a little, Seven gasps. His head crashes against the floor, his entire body going limp. He's drained of the rage consuming him and surrenders completely. When his amber eyes meet mine, there's a tiny flicker of awareness.

"Where are we?" he rasps.

"You're free, Sev. No more Augustus. Consider us even now."

The thinnest smile dances across his lips before it fades.

"We're never free, princess. He's in our heads."

Too far gone to stay awake, Seven passes out. I quickly let go of his rapidly bruising throat, brushing a strand of limp hair from his forehead. Shoved aside in a split second, I'm replaced by Sadie, who cradles his body and checks his pulse.

"What was that for? You hurt him!"

I struggle to stand, wrestling with my urge to punch her indignant face. Violence has become my default, so turning it off is harder than anticipated. Grimacing, I let her see the fury beneath my human mask.

"Hurting is the only thing we understand."

She flinches, holding her brother tight, but I'm not done.

"Augustus starved us, beat us, broke us into pathetic pieces, and sent us to fight a war against our will. If we didn't kill in his name, he sent guards with whips and fists."

"Brooke…"

"I'm not done. Seven—fucking Jude, if you insist—was electrocuted at least once a day, usually when they caught him talking to me. That was before they took his hand too."

Hudson tries to put his arm around me again. I shove him hard, ignoring the pain that lances across his face when he collides with the kitchen cupboards. I'm far too angry to be touched, even by him.

"Blackbird, please—"

"Stay back!"

I want to hurt them all. My fucking family, but the sight of them is just another reminder of the person I've become. I want to beat them, bruise them. Drench us all in innocent blood. It used to be us against the world. Now, I'm locked in my own hellish purgatory and not even they can reach me.

"Augustus wanted to take our humanity, and he succeeded."

"We need to talk ab—"

"Fuck off, Sadie. You have no clue. None."

I storm back outside and let the front door slam behind me. I can't look at any of them right now, not while Augustus's ghost is breathing down my neck. He lives on in my head, reminding me that no matter how far I run… my mind will always belong to him.

3

KADE

Give - You And Me At Six

Standing on the wrap-around porch that surrounds our rural retreat, I finish smoking my cigarette and pull the burner phone from my pocket.

Mum called last night, reassuring me she had packed her things, ready to move to a safe location with Cece. She's filed for divorce from my father. Once she realised his involvement in Blackwood's operation, it was a done deal. Even though we both had to play along for months, plastering on fake smiles to give us the faintest hope of escape.

The door clicks open behind me, disturbing the early morning. Brooklyn is shoving her ash-white hair up in a ponytail. Dressed in one of Hudson's t-shirts, she looks too fucking perfect. I want to say something, anything, but she takes off to begin her jog.

I watch her go, struggling with the exercise. Her legs are like pins, dangerously thin and weak. There's no ignoring all she's been through.

It's a constant reminder of my failure. I may have gotten us out, but by then, it was too late. The damage had been done.

Now, I don't know how to fix it.

When Brooklyn returns, she leans against the porch, gasping for breath. I study her silently for several seconds, hating the way she seems too afraid to meet my eyes. Her secrets are suffocating us.

"What do you want, Kade?"

"You should be asleep. It's six o'clock."

"I can't fucking sleep. Get off my case," she snaps.

"You want something useful to do?"

I'm rewarded by a flicker of the person I used to know, her grey eyes dragging over my body. Uncrossing my arms, I inch closer, itching with the need to touch her. Even if she screams bloody murder.

"What did you have in mind?"

"We need supplies. I'm going to drive into town." I drag a single fingertip along her bare arm. "I could use a hand with making a list and shopping for everything we need."

Her smile turns me to pathetic mush. Seeing her again, alive and breathing, fuck. It will never get old after being left in the dark for so long. I could watch her forever and die a happy man.

"I'll throw some clothes on," Brooklyn decides. "Don't leave without me."

"Ten minutes. Try not to wake anyone else up."

She cuts me a small grin. "Yes, sir."

Leaving her to head for the room she's sharing with Two and Five, I return to the bedroom I'm bunking in with Hudson. The girls are still out of it. Sadie gave them some more stolen meds in the middle of the night. Their screaming could wake up the Devil when their nightmares hit.

I throw on some sweats, leaving the two shirts I managed to flee

DESECRATED SAINTS

Blackwood with untouched. I don't need to be that person here. Hudson shifts in his twin-sized bed, moaning in his sleep. He passed out after polishing off a bottle of vodka with Phoenix.

I should establish some house rules.

Too much freedom could be a bad thing.

Returning to the country-style kitchen, complete with a farmhouse stove and huge bay window with a view of the surrounding woods, I listen for any other signs of movement. Phoenix and Eli are asleep in their own room, while Sadie and Seven share another.

"You ready?"

Emerging from the hallway, Brooklyn's located a pair of yoga pants to go with Hudson's stolen t-shirt. She flicks her gaze over my outfit, humming with appreciation.

"Can I help you with something?" I ask cheekily.

"Nope. You look good, all casual and shit."

"Well, there's no one to impress out here in the woods."

Grabbing her leather jacket from the back of a chair, Brooklyn snorts. "Maybe this bullshit has taught us something after all. You never needed to impress anyone."

"Only you."

Pausing to take a deep inhale of the worn leather, I catch the faint smile that graces her lips. Before I can, she picks up the notepad and pen I left on the counter to scribble things down.

"Do the girls need anything?"

Brooklyn shrugs. "More clothes, I guess."

"Have they spoken to you?"

"Barely. We should sit them down and talk."

"Are you sure that's a good idea?" I frown.

"I probably have a better shot than anyone else at getting something out of them." Brooklyn scans an empty cupboard. "Seven knows them better than me, but he isn't capable of talking to anyone. Sadie has him sedated again."

"She's going to run out soon."

"He'll come around."

"Do you really believe that?"

Her gunmetal-grey eyes meet mine, carrying a heavy burden that I can't hope to understand. None of us can undo all the damage that's been done, no matter the control freak in me demanding that I try.

"I have to believe that," she admits. "If I don't, then what would be the point? If Seven can get better, so can I. We can leave the people we became behind."

I capture Brooklyn's hand as she heads for the door, pulling her close. She comes reluctantly at first, still struggling to accept comfort, but eventually relaxes against my chest.

"You're still you, love."

"I'm far from me. I don't know what's left, after everything…" Her voice trails off. "He didn't leave me with much. I'm just grateful to be alive, I suppose."

"It's ironic, don't you think?"

"What is?" Brooklyn sighs.

"A year ago, would you have thought you'd ever be grateful to be alive?"

She surprises me with a chuckle. "I suppose not. If you're trying some gratitude therapy, I'd advise you to give up. I'm never gonna be grateful for all we've suffered."

"Neither am I. But we're alive, Brooke. That's something."

"You're right. It's something."

Scribbling a note for the others, we head for the Jeep that Mum left for us to use. Brooklyn hops into the passenger seat and I fire up the engine, pulling out onto the forest-lined dirt track that leads back to civilisation. We travel in comfortable silence, both lost in our thoughts.

By the time we reach the quaint, cobbled streets of the nearest Scottish town an hour later, the sun has risen. I can hear Brooklyn's stomach rumbling from here. We'll both be chewed out for leaving when we return, so I'm going to make the most of this moment.

"Wanna get breakfast?" I waggle my eyebrows.

"I thought we were keeping a low profile."

"Doesn't mean we can't have some fun. How long has it been since you were out in the real world, unsupervised? The Christmas trip doesn't count."

Brooklyn studies her bruised knuckles. "Two years, I guess. I can't remember, it's been so long."

"Exactly. What do you want to do?"

"I don't know, Kade. Anything."

"You have a choice for the first time in your life. We can do anything, be anything." Pulling into a parking space, I face her sad smile. "Come on, love. There must be something."

Biting her lip, Brooklyn nods to herself.

"I want to cut my hair."

"Your hair?"

"It's too long. I hate it. When I look in the mirror, I don't want to recognise the person looking back at me. I want to be someone else."

"That can be arranged, but I happen to like who you are."

I draw her lips to mine in a gentle kiss. Brooklyn reciprocates, her tongue sliding into my mouth, reclaiming my damned soul for her own. I'd forgotten what she tastes like, hatred and rage in a softened shell. The kiss deepens, and she grabs a handful of my t-shirt, seeking more contact.

To hell with it.

I grab her by the hips and drag her over the console, uncaring about the public street around us. It's deserted at this hour. Straddling my lap, her delicious weight presses against my erection. I surrender control to her frantic lips, content to lose myself. All that exists is the feel of her skin on mine.

"Kade," Brooklyn breathes.

"Yeah?"

"I need you, right now."

I brush my nose against hers. "We're in a car park."

"Nothing makes any sense. I can't look at the others without feeling like the worst person on the planet." Her eyes scour over me. "I need to know why I'm here, and not six feet under."

Skating my hands under Hudson's t-shirt, I find her bare breasts. Underwear is on the long list of essentials to buy, but I'm not complaining. Her nipples are rock hard and begging to be touched.

"Are you not wearing panties either?" I murmur.

"Why don't you find out?"

Lifting from my lap, her hand dips inside my sweats to find my hardened cock. I hiss out a breath as she takes a handful, stroking my length. When her hand cups my balls, I let my eyes roll back in my head. Nobody's laid a finger on me since we last slept together and it shows.

"Fuck, love. You better stop before I blow my load like a damn kid."

"I want to see you come for me," she goads.

Checking to make sure the coast is still clear, I snatch her hand from my sweats and pin it to the steering wheel. Brooklyn's eyes widen in surprise. She doesn't fight back as I work her yoga pants down to expose her bare cunt, begging for my attention.

"You're not the one in charge here," I growl at her. "Did you forget that you're my dirty little slut, huh? Do I need to remind you how this works?"

She bites her juicy bottom lip. "I need reminding."

Sliding my hand between her legs, I find her soaked pussy. She's wet for me already, so easily wound up. I push a finger inside of her before swirling my thumb over her sensitive nub. Adding another finger, I lean in to bite her lip myself.

The steering wheel at her back traps us close together, with no room to escape. Losing patience with my toying, Brooklyn shifts and removes my fingers from her wet heat. Her cunt is pressed up against my dick, inches from salvation. As I wait for her to make the final move, she hesitates.

"What is it?"

Insecurity flashes across her expression. "Has there... been anyone else?"

"You're kidding me, right?"

"It's fine if there has been... hell, I don't know why I'm asking. It's been months. I don't expect you guys to have waited. Forget I said anything."

Stroking her painfully sharp jawline, I force Brooklyn to look at me again. She's anxious and uncertain, the vulnerable girl beneath all her icy layers stripped bare for the world to see. Her many personas are dizzying, but I love that I can tease this version of her out.

"Not even for a second," I answer without hesitating. "None of us. Not even Phoenix and Eli were together. We don't work without you, love. You're our centre."

Brooklyn looks pleased with my answer on a primal level. Before I can offer more assurances, she guides my cock inside of herself. I groan, seizing her by the hips to guide her movements. Shoving my hands aside, she pins me with a fierce look, reaffirming her control.

"I'm disappointed I don't get to kill anyone who's touched you."

"You sadistic little bitch."

The corner of her mouth lifts up. "*Your* sadistic little bitch."

Moving to meet her thrust for thrust, I'm barely able to speak as heat burns through me. She's hugging my cock so tight. After months of taking very long showers with nothing but the memory of her scent, I'm not going to last long.

Brooklyn doesn't care, taking every frantic thrust. We can hardly get enough of each other, our tongues battling and teeth clashing like animals. When a car drives past, she ducks down low but continues to grind on me despite the possibility of getting caught.

I hold her head to my chest, plastering on a neutral expression for anyone passing. If anything, it makes this even hotter, marking my property for the whole world to see. Maybe I should take a leaf out of Eli's book and carve my initials into her ass. It'd certainly teach the rest of our fucked-up family a lesson.

With an evil laugh, Brooklyn cups my balls again.

"Fucking hell, love," I grind out.

"Let them catch us. Why not?"

"This isn't Blackwood. We're breaking the law."

"You care about that?"

"Like hell I care. Fall apart for me, Brooke. Show me how pretty you are when I pour my come inside of your tight cunt. I want to see it dripping out of you."

"Goddammit, Kade."

Coaxing my release to the very edge, she slams herself down on me and I'm shoved into the awaiting abyss. I can feel her walls clenching around me as our orgasms collide. Biting down on her lip to silence her mewling, I let her milk every last drop from me.

In the sweaty aftermath, she slumps against my chest. We both fight to catch our breath before bursting into near-hysterical laughter. We're literally in a public car park, getting off like horny teenagers.

"Did we just fuck in your mum's car?"

"She technically did buy it. So, I suppose we did."

"Well, what she doesn't know won't hurt her."

Stroking loose blonde hair from her face, I trace the seam of her mouth. "I'd forgotten how incredible you look while falling apart. I want to fuck you again later, where everyone else can hear how much you love my cock."

Her eyes widen. "Jesus, Kade. You're a filthy son of a bitch."

"Hey, I've been celibate for four months. Prepare for more of this."

Lifting Brooklyn back into the passenger seat, I give her some privacy to clean up. By the time we climb out of the Jeep and begin walking into town, she seems content for the first time since we escaped. We walk with our arms wrapped around each other, studying the perfect, early morning scenery.

"What do we need to get?"

I glance at the scribbled list. "Clothes, fresh food, and long-life cupboard shit that will last. Medicines, first aid kit. Toiletries. Booze. Cigarettes."

"Booze and cigarettes?" She laughs.

"We can't get any medication without being discovered. At least three quarters of our group takes it for various reasons. Booze is my short-term solution."

"So Phoenix can drink himself out of a manic episode?"

"If necessary."

"We're totally fucked, aren't we?"

I peck her cheek. "Totally fucked, but free."

We lapse into silence as the town centre approaches. The closer we get to civilisation, the more Brooklyn's good mood evaporates. Her eyes bounce about anxiously, and I can feel the fine tremor creeping over her. It's worsening by the second.

"You good?" I ask worriedly.

"Fine."

Surrounded by the high street, countless shops are starting to open. More cars park as people begin their weekend chores. The cacophony of noise blurs together, a slice of normality amidst the carnage we've been conditioned to. It's unnerving.

When a young man throws open the window to his cafe, the loud blaring of his radio is the final straw. Brooklyn's hand is ripped from mine as she abruptly stops. Crouching down in the middle of the pavement, her hands slam over her ears.

She tries to make herself as small as possible, curling up in a tight ball. It nearly breaks my heart in two. I wave off the concerned cafe owner and kneel beside her.

"Love? You're safe. I'm here with you."

"I c-can't do this, Kade."

"Talk me through it. Tell me what's happening."

"It's too much! I can't fucking breathe."

She battles against the panic attack, following my quiet instructions. We sit here for ages while the world wakes up around us. Several bystanders offer to help, but I quickly make excuses and tow her away before we arouse more suspicion.

We flee into the cafe, sliding into an empty booth. The owner immediately turns off the radio when I throw him a thunderous look, retreating back to the kitchen. With the safety of cracked plastic seats surrounding us, Brooklyn finally opens her eyes.

My heart stops dead in my chest. She isn't looking back at me with those devastating grey eyes. My girl is gone. Her face is slack and emotionless. Before I can react, she pounces on me. Her hands clench around my throat with surprising strength.

I grab her wrists, trying to prise her hands away from my windpipe. Brooklyn shoves me from the booth, and we go tumbling to the hardwood floor. I manage to roll us before her fist connects with my jaw and knocks me off balance.

"Brooklyn! Stop!"

Without responding to her name, she dropkicks me into a nearby table, which smashes. I gape in shock as she grabs a broken table leg, snarling at me again. Yelling her name does nothing to prevent her from striking me with it until blood is pouring from my forehead.

"It's me! Brooklyn, please—"

Snarling like a rabid animal, I have to grab a handful of her platinum hair to regain the upper hand. She lands beside me, and I crack her head against the floor for good measure.

"Stop fighting me, dammit!"

The pain barely registers. She's like an empty shell. Her nails rake down my cheek, narrowly missing my eye. Bleeding and running out of steam, I go for the nuclear option. Pain isn't getting the message across. I need to force out whatever monster is running riot in her head.

Managing to scramble back and grab another barstool, I test the weight of solid wood. If I can knock her insane ass out, I'll have time to formulate a plan that doesn't involve us both landing in a prison cell for assault and criminal damage.

"I'm sorry, Brooke. Forgive me."

Running at full speed, I smash the barstool into the side of her head. Brooklyn drops in an instant, clinging to consciousness. She's still writhing and beholden to invisible voices. I pin her arms down with my spread legs, cupping both of her cheeks to force her to look at me.

"Patient Eight."

In an instant, Brooklyn goes limp.

"You will stop fighting me."

Like a mindless machine with the plug pulled out, staring up at me is an empty vessel ready for its next command. I'm terrified by the gaping void inside of her; it's so clearly visible. The person I know was gone in an instant when this beast seized full control.

Before she can attack me again, I mutter another apology and punch Brooklyn straight in the face. Her head smacks into the floor as she's knocked out cold. Keeping her pinned down, I take stock of the destruction around us just as the cafe owner reappears with a phone at his ear.

"Please don't call the police," I blurt.

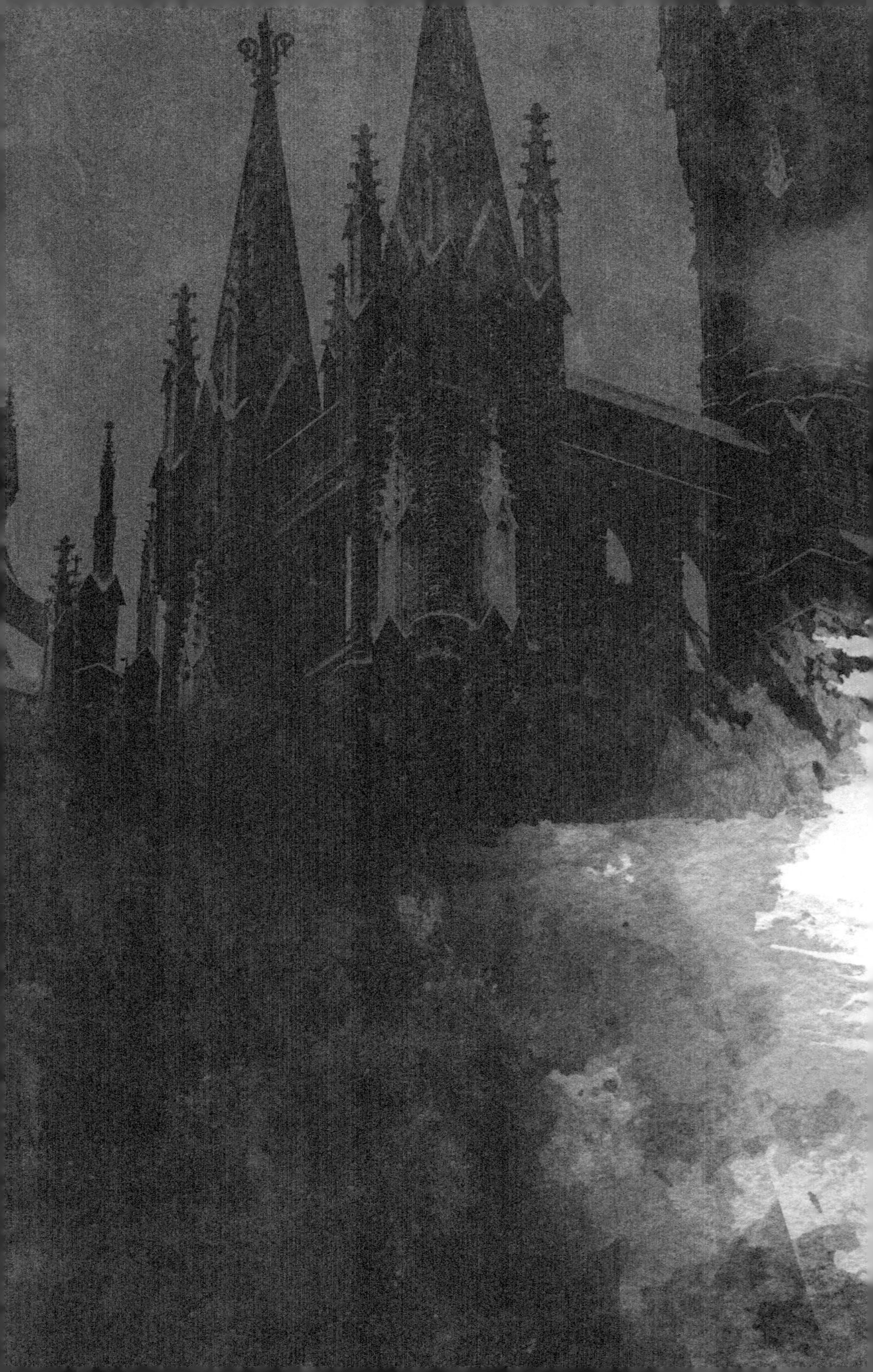

4

BROOKLYN

Crazy - Echos

Hands braced on the bathroom sink, I stare at myself in the mirror. I'm sporting a colourful black eye and swollen face. Kade didn't pull his punch yesterday. I let my fingers trail over the sore flesh, proof of what he claims happened. I can't remember a fucking thing.

I lost my shit and the world disappeared from sight. She took over. Patient Eight. I'm inhabiting this body with another person now. The result of careful calculation and experimentation. She's made her home in the desolate wasteland of my sanity.

Ignoring the sound of Hudson and Kade bickering about another supply run, I turn the shower on. Neither of them is willing to leave me after my performance in town. I've refused to come out of my room since, unable to look at Kade now that he's had a glimpse of the real me.

The girls kept their silence, and I didn't bother to break it last night. None of us have the answers we need; talking about all the shit still to resolve feels futile. Under the beat of scorching water, I let the frustrated tears flow.

I must stand beneath the spray for an hour without moving, trying to scrape some control together. I still feel freezing cold, despite the hot water. The chill of my basement cell refuses to thaw, no matter how far from Blackwood I am.

When the shower door slides open, I flinch.

"Kade, I swear to God—"

Peering over my shoulder, I find someone else waiting. Eli stands with his acid-wash t-shirt dangling from his hands. Adorable, chocolatey ringlets frame perceptive eyes that are full of questions he can't vocalise.

"Not now, Eli. I need to be alone."

He doesn't budge.

"Are you just going to stand there until I say yes?"

Eli nods, smirking.

"Fuck's sake. Just get in."

I turn away as the door clicks shut, then his heat is at my back. Slender, heavily scarred arms wrap around my waist. We stand in silence for the longest time, surrounded by steam and the scent of fruity body wash.

"Did they send you in here to sort me out?"

Eli bites down on my shoulder in response.

"I'm fine. You should all stop worrying so much."

Spinning me around to face him, Eli's eyes bore into me. I wonder if he can taste my lies, if they weigh on his tongue like the acrid flavour of smoke. I study his body, weirdly relieved to find it the same. Some things haven't changed.

The burn scars still cover his entire torso, thick and gnarly like tree bark. Running my hand over the fresh cuts on his bicep instead, I ask a silent question. They can't be more than a week old and they're deep;

brutally so. His dark eyes answer me, laden with secrets.

"Phoenix says you haven't spoken to him in months."

A head tilt, as if to say *so what?*

"You had a life before me. Why did you shut down and walk away when I was gone? You were all alone. Hurting yourself. Struggling. I want to know why."

With water clinging to his impossibly thick eyelashes, his eyes scrape all the way down my skeletal frame. With the briefest whisper of his fingertips, Eli traces the shiny, healed scars that mark my left hip. Remnants of a time long passed, and the eternal promise we sealed in blood.

Donec mors nos separaverit.

"Until death do us part," I whisper.

Eli offers me a sinister smile, his thumb caressing the precise knife marks made by his hand. I find his own matching scars, tracing each word to answer my question.

I get it, better than anyone. Existing is not the same thing as living. We've survived without each other, but lost all that we had in the chasm that separated us. Death didn't part us. Life did.

"The girl you loved is gone, Eli. She didn't make it out alive."

Cupping my cheeks, he wipes the curtain of falling tears aside. His raspy voice still refuses to make an appearance, but he doesn't need to speak for me to know exactly what he's thinking.

"We can't play this game. I'm not worth it."

Turning off the shower, Eli raises his eyebrows and steps out for me to follow. I'm engulfed in a thick towel, disappointed that he didn't bend me over and show me exactly what he's thinking in that complicated brain of his. My core clenches at the thought.

Jesus, Brooke.

Chill the fuck out.

After so long apart, my sex drive is going crazy. Drying off with the soft cloud of brushed cotton, I wrestle with my libido and emerge to find Eli waiting with an electric razor in his hand.

"What are you doing?"

He gestures towards my soaking wet hair.

"Oh, the haircut. We didn't get a chance to do it before my brain decided to go cuckoo." I fist handfuls of long, blonde hair. "Just get rid of it all."

Taking a seat on the closed toilet lid, Eli grabs me by the hips and deposits me in his lap. He plugs the razor in and frowns while attaching the correct blades. Excitement runs down my spine at his crooked smile.

"Do your worst."

Eli sends his agreement in a toe-curling kiss that has me slick between the legs all over again. I close my eyes, holding my breath as the razor meets my scalp. He works slowly and methodically, his fingers tilting my head every few seconds. His throbbing erection presses up against me the entire time.

It feels like an eternity has passed by the time Eli finishes. He clicks off the soft vibrating of the razor and presses a kiss to my temple, signalling his approval. I find him watching me with so much intelligence it makes me want to run away screaming.

"Please don't look at me like that."

His brows furrow with confusion.

"I don't want you to see inside of me anymore. It's pretty fucking dark in here, Eli. Too dark even for you to handle. I'm scared of losing myself again."

Lips skating down the expanse of my throat, he answers me in featherlight kisses, reaching the swell of my breasts. Teeth tugging on my hard nipple, heat gathers in my core. I can feel his dick beneath me. Wriggling on his lap, I can almost get in the right position to—

A loud bang on the door has us jumping like guilty teenagers.

"Fuck off," I shout.

"Family meeting!" Hudson hits the door again.

"We're busy, you wanker."

"Stop canoodling and get your asses out here. It's an order, not a fucking invitation."

Eli's forehead falls to my chest, his curls tickling my skin.

"We should go before he breaks the door down."

Running a hand over my freshly shorn head, Eli nods reluctantly. We stand and face the foggy mirror together. With the moisture wiped aside, I gape at my new look.

"Well… you left some hair."

Eli studies my short, platinum-blonde pixie cut, hair shaved high on the sides with the top section left messy. He turns me around, tucking a wet strand behind my ear while his raspy voice threatens to stop my heart for good.

"Beautiful."

I scoff. "Hardly."

"Y-Yes."

I twirl my arms around his neck, bringing our lips together for a kiss. "I wondered why I made it out alive. I understand now. It was so I could hear that perfect voice every day for the rest of my life."

Eli's lips twitch, an almost smile.

I grab my towel and flee before he can argue back. We dry off and get dressed in matching *Highly Suspect* t-shirts from his collection, exchanging grins before heading for the kitchen. The entire group has gathered in tense silence, Two and Five included.

Hudson spots me first, lingering in the kitchen with another beer in hand. His lips part on a sharp inhale as he takes in my new look. He's staring at me like he's a starving man and I'm his dinner. The thought of him fucking me against the countertop while everyone watches briefly crosses my mind.

"Damn, blackbird."

At his words, the other two turn and their mouths fall open.

"Looking good, firecracker."

Kade grins. "Agreed."

"I needed a change."

I steal Hudson's half-empty beer and deposit myself in one of the armchairs. Sadie spares me a look as I pass, but doesn't say a word. I'm still fuming after our argument about Seven. Curled up on the nearby plaid sofa, Two and Five are clutching each other tight.

I meet Five's timid gaze, offering her a nod of greeting. Her mousy-brown hair is so long, it must brush her butt. She's pretty, beneath the emaciation and bruises. Meanwhile, Two's hair has been buzzed to the scalp, showing off the misshapen lumps of her skull.

"Thank you for getting us out, Eight."

The guys all scowl at the use of that name.

I return Five's shy smile. "I wasn't going to leave you there after everything that happened. Seven either."

"Where is he?"

"Sleeping," Sadie answers.

Five presses a kiss to Two's shaking hand to try to calm her. The guys relax enough to take seats around the room, all nursing their beers despite it being barely lunchtime. Alcohol is needed for this conversation, even if Kade is glaring at Phoenix for drinking.

"Do you both have names?" I finally ask.

Two tilts her head at the sound of my voice, giving me a direct view of her scarred eye sockets. "Not that I can remember. I was one of Augustus's first projects."

It's the first time I've heard her speak.

I'm surprised by the vitriol in her voice.

"It took him a while to figure out what worked," she continues. "He put me in the tub first and electrified the water. Then sensory overload, just like you. I used to listen to you scream at night from my cell. I'm guessing you learned to follow orders like I did."

All of the oxygen seems to leave the room.

I fight to clear my throat. "Something like that."

"Sensory overload?" Kade frowns.

"Using waves of noise to torture compliance out of you," Two supplies. "No rest or sleep. You just lay there and let your ears bleed. There's no running from it."

The heat of all their gazes has sweat beading on my forehead.

"We've seen pictures of the tubs," Hudson hedges.

Two swallows. "Electricity was his favourite, after freezing, sub-zero water. There was another patient, but I can't remember his name. He lost several toes from being submerged for too long."

"Seven told me that Three, Four, and Six are dead," I manage to whisper.

Kade writes that down in his notebook, his gaze wary behind his glasses. This is just the tip of the nightmare iceberg. I don't want them to know what happened in the dark. Pictures are one thing, the truth is another.

Fishing for a change in topic, I glance at Five. "What about you? Got a name?"

"I remember," she answers reluctantly.

Releasing Two's hand, she wraps her arms around herself for comfort.

"My name is Lucia. I was a model patient at first. Anything to keep him happy and avoid the punishment if I didn't follow orders. When I first met Two, I was broken. Alone in the dark. She gave me hope."

Two smiles at Lucia's words, wrapping an arm around her shoulders to pull her in close. When their fingers interlink, I realise what Jefferson meant by his words in the basement. They rebelled by simply living the only way they knew how.

"Can't get distracted by pleasures of the flesh without any eyes," I vocalise the threat Jefferson levelled me with months ago.

Lucia snorts. "Jefferson rolled that bullshit out to you too?"

Ignoring the looks the guys all throw at me, I reach out and take Two's hand, careful not to startle her. Lucia watches me closely, still on full alert. I get it now. Two's her girl to worry about.

"You should know, I removed Jefferson's eyes before I cut his throat," I inform them. "He screamed and begged for death in the end. He won't hurt anyone ever again. I made sure of it."

"A-fucking-men to that," Two declares.

Hudson grins at me, the sadistic fuck. The memory of jamming my blade into Jefferson's eye sockets offers me some satisfaction. I would've preferred to skin his sorry ass alive and stretch it out over several hours, cutting his body away piece by piece.

A girl can dream, right?

"How long were you both under Augustus's program?" Kade asks, all business.

Two shrugs again, unable to provide an exact answer. Judging by what she's told us, several years at a bare minimum. She was Augustus's guinea pig from the very beginning. He afforded her zero privileges for that honour, taking her eyes instead.

Lucia fiddles with her long hair. "I was admitted to Blackwood in 2016 for attempted assault while off my medication. That's the last date I remember."

"Six years?" Sadie exclaims.

"Within a few months, I caught Lazlo's eye and he began the

sessions. Once his work was complete, I lost all control and never left the Z Wing again."

I begin to pace the room, ignoring the weight of apprehensive gazes watching me. Despite all I endured at the hands of Blackwood's demons, the mention of Lazlo is enough to set me on edge. He was where it all began, this dark and winding path descending to my own personal hell.

While Augustus was the architect, Lazlo was the pioneer.

I hope his corpse is rotting at the bottom of a fucking lake.

"There's something else you should know," Lucia begins nervously.

Kade offers her a reassuring smile. "Go ahead."

"I worked on many jobs for Augustus. Sometimes alone, sometimes not. Patient Seven… well, he was Augustus's favourite. We were inducted around the same time, but he was more successful than the rest of us. Pure, unadulterated evil."

Ignoring Sadie's sudden fascination with her shoes, I wait for the punchline. Lucia clenches her hands into fists, bashing one against her forehead to blow the cobwebs free. Her next words are forced out.

"Before I was taken to the basement, I met another clinician."

Sadie quickly perks up. "You knew him before?"

"Yeah. Doctor Farlow was nice, genuinely interested in helping patients. He did his best to make life at the institute more bearable."

I watch the tears fall down Sadie's cheeks.

"I did a job for Augustus a while back… an employee was leaking information to the outside," Lucia explains. "I was instructed to execute him. Seven, he was there too. He pummelled the poor man to death with his bare hands, didn't even break a sweat."

"How did Doctor Farlow become… that?" Phoenix inserts.

"Lazlo gave him to Augustus. We were taken together, drugged and tied up."

"To another facility?" Kade prompts.

"I guess so," she answers. "We came back to Blackwood a while ago, although the institutes all look the same. A prison is a prison, no matter where you go. That's when I met Two. Our cells were next to each other. Her voice kept me alive."

Digesting the new information, we fall silent. Everyone looks equally unnerved and sickened. Sadie is worst of all, silently sobbing as she's forced to reconcile Jude's fate with the birth of the man I know—Seven. It can't be easy for her childhood memories to be so thoroughly desecrated.

"Sadie, is it?" Lucia asks softly. "I know you're his sister."

"What about it?"

"I just wanted to say… I'm sorry for what happened. Your brother was a good person, but Seven has killed more people than the entire Z Wing program combined. Augustus loved to boast while prepping me for treatment. I did a fraction of jobs compared to him."

"They told me he went away," Sadie hiccups. "Even produced a fake letter, travel documents, the lot. Nobody believed me. All along, he was there, being slowly chipped away."

"I know it's hard," Lucia offers kindly. "But the truth is, Jude… Doctor Farlow, is gone. If any of us are going to survive, we should lock Seven away for good and throw away the key."

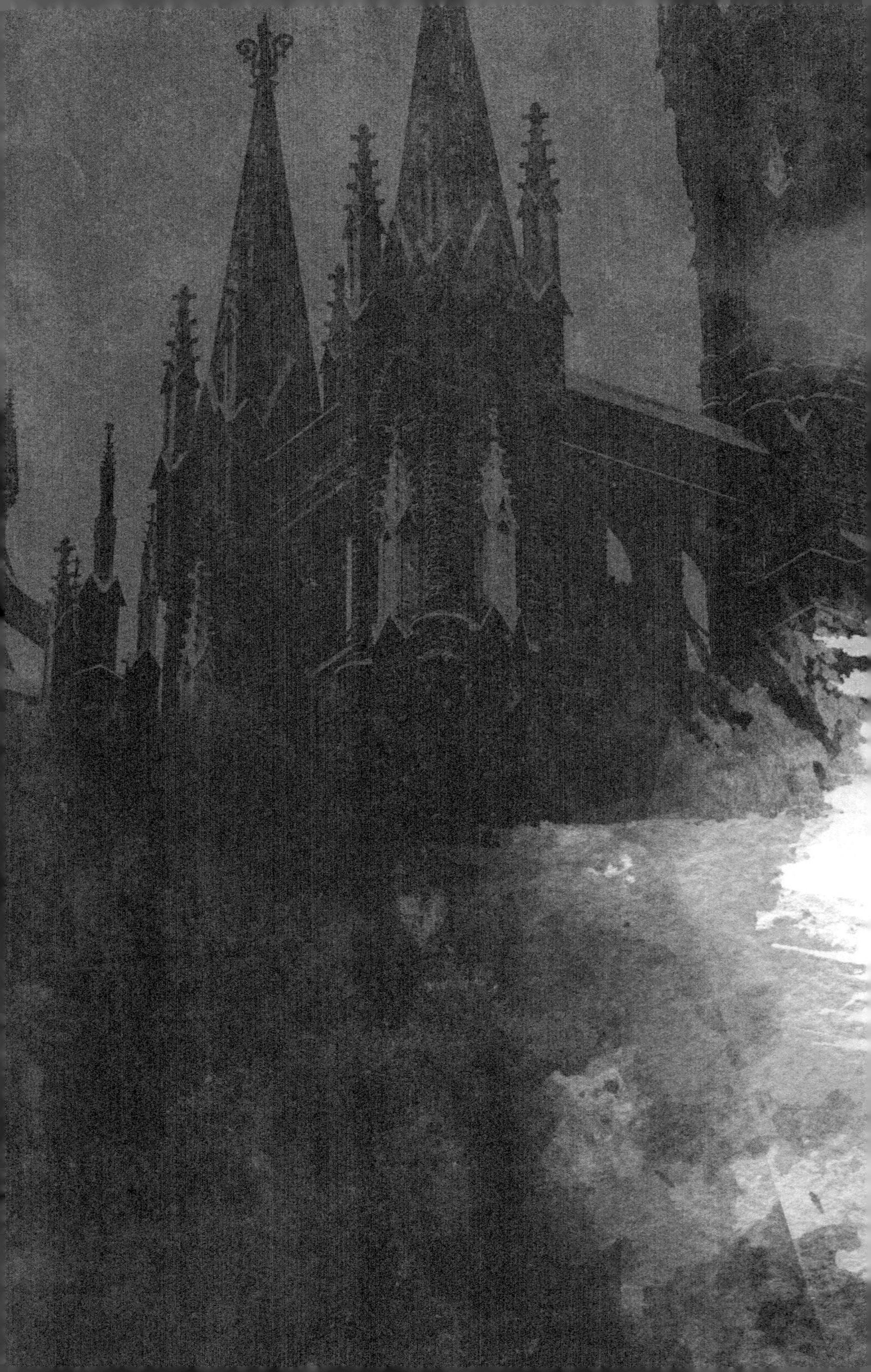

5

PHOENIX

Time Changes Everything - The Plot In You

After unpacking the food and shoving it into every available space, I declare the job done. Kade is scowling at my messy organisation from behind his laptop. I offered to make the run, leaving him and Sadie to continue working on Augustus's hard drive.

"Did you really have to buy that much alcohol?" Kade sighs.

"Well, it is an essential."

"Just watch it, Nix. This is a small house with a lot of people in it. We don't need any more issues than we already have because your drunk ass can't help but pick a fight."

Slamming a beer down in front of the miserable asshole, I help myself to a bottle of rum. We've been incarcerated for over a year, some of us for several years. It's time to live our lives and figure out who the fuck we are outside of Blackwood.

"I'm not trying to be a dictator," he adds. "We both know things have been... delicate, the past few months. Without meds, it's only going to get worse. Just be careful. I'm not running a rehab centre."

I brace my hands on the cluttered kitchen table. "The meds never worked anyway. I've scraped by since Brooklyn was taken away, no thanks to you. So if I want a drink, I'm going to have one. Got it?"

"Just don't expect me to pick up the pieces."

"No one but you ever does."

I head outside to hunt down Brooklyn and Hudson. It's been a tense week living in close quarters with so much shit going on. I'm not sure any of us have stopped to take a breath yet. She's been avoiding us too, still stuck in her stubborn ways. I'm determined to bring my girl back.

In the generous garden that stretches all the way back to the nearby woods, the late summer sun is sinking on the horizon. It bathes the overgrown jungle of a lawn in brilliant, warm light. The sound of an axe splitting wood draws my attention to Brooklyn.

Working on a pile of firewood, I watch her grab a small log and violently rip it apart with her bare hands. I can see her fingers are bloodied and splintered from here. Hudson watches helplessly, still nursing a bandaged shoulder from the gunshot.

I trail over, a peace offering of rum in hand. "Need any help?"

"Nope," Brooklyn snaps.

"Well, I come bearing gifts."

Sinking down on the grass next to Hudson, I deposit the huge bottle of rum in front of him. He lets out a grunt of appreciation and takes a much-needed swig.

"That's good shit."

"Tastes like freedom, my friend."

He rolls his eyes. "I'll go grab some food. Watch her?"

"Don't need a fucking babysitter," Brooklyn grumbles.

I offer Hudson a salute. "Go, I got this."

DESECRATED SAINTS

Reclaiming the rum, I watch Brooklyn finish her angry, lumberjack routine. Her bad mood clearly hasn't dissipated as she glowers at the campfire, lighting some old newspapers to ignite the wood. She finally collapses beside me and stretches her legs out.

"Nice shorts," I compliment.

She shoots me an unimpressed look. "Your choice, I presume?"

"Hell yeah. I should've been a personal shopper instead of a junkie."

"Hilarious. You realise it's cold here?"

"Don't worry, I'll keep you warm."

"Gee, my hero."

Brushing my fingertips over her ripped denim cut-offs, I caress her inner thigh, determined to coax a smile out of her. Since we're planning to hole up here for the foreseeable future, I picked up enough basics for the whole group and other essentials, using the stash of cash Kade's mum left us with.

Brooklyn steals the bottle of rum and takes a swig, cringing at the taste. "For future reference, I like tequila. You should know that."

"I remembered. It's inside."

"Wait, you did?"

"How could I forget? Jesus, Brooke."

We fall into uncomfortable silence, passing the bottle back and forth while watching the fire grow. I fucking hate that I don't know what to say to her anymore. Hudson eventually returns with armfuls of biscuits, chocolate bars and marshmallows, chucking the bags at Brooklyn.

"What are these for?"

"S'mores, obviously," he deadpans.

"What the hell is a s'more?"

We both gape at her. "You don't know?"

Hudson seizes a bag of marshmallows and loads up three skewers with giant bites of yumminess. He hands them out before sticking his in the fire, carefully turning to avoid burning it. Brooklyn copies, watching with open-mouthed fascination.

It's fucking adorable. When we're done, we sandwich the marshmallows with chocolate and biscuits. Hudson watches Brooklyn with a cheesy grin, counting down from five before we all stuff them in our mouths.

"Holy shit," she groans.

"See? S'mores!"

Hudson is already loading another one up, looking calmer than I've seen him in a long time. While Eli hid himself away and I battled with Kade for any drugs, Hudson spent the past four months beating on anything and anyone. He's got the new scars to prove it.

"So, what's the plan?" Brooklyn pipes up.

My good mood evaporates in an instant.

"There isn't really one."

"Surviving," Hudson supplies.

"And when Incendia comes looking for us?"

I stare into the fire, turning another marshmallow over while deep in thought. Those six institutes have left us in hot water. We all thought we were running off into the sunset, when realistically, we've just pissed off our captors by wiping out one of their prime locations.

"They won't," I answer, but it doesn't ring true.

Brooklyn scoffs. "Denial isn't going to help us, Nix."

"Neither is worrying about something that hasn't happened yet."

"Burying your head in the sand as usual, huh? Real smart."

"Enough," Hudson chastises. "I have spent months doing nothing but worrying about Blackwood. Scrap that, the past two years. We are going to eat s'mores, drink rum, and get pissed. Tomorrow, we figure all this shit out. Got it?"

I spread my hands in surrender. "Loud and clear, sarge."

Hudson pins Brooklyn with a look. "You going to cheer the hell up?"

She smirks. "Come over here and make me, *daddy*."

I'm gonna finish in my goddamn pants if she says that again. Hudson tosses her a heated look, full of dark promise. Hell, I'd pay to watch that shit. Even if he's the one fucking her before finishing all over her gorgeous face for the world to see.

"Truth or dare?" I suggest with a wink.

I half expect Hudson to punch me in the face. We all know he struggles the most with our unconventional relationship, despite the show he put on with Kade all that time ago. Instead, he passes me the bottle and silently lights a cigarette.

"You first," she pushes.

"You're mean, firecracker. Fine, truth."

"Kade said that none of you have been with anyone else."

I choke on a mouthful of rum. "No messing around, huh?"

"Is that a question or a statement?" Hudson adds tightly.

Brooklyn ignores him, watching me. "A question."

Rather than answer, I grab her wrist and drag her closer. Slamming my lips against hers, she soon gets over the shock and melts into the kiss. My teeth sink into her bottom lip, seeking the promise of fresh blood. By the time we separate, I'm hard and she's gasping for air.

"Does that answer your question?"

Brooklyn makes a non-committal noise.

"For fuck's sake," Hudson grunts. "None of us fucked anyone else. Of course, we didn't. Now take the bloody bottle and say truth, because I have questions too. I'm sick of waiting."

Chastised by the grumpy dickhead, Brooklyn snuggles up to my side and retakes the bottle. Hudson's stare is full of anticipation and barely restrained annoyance. Something serious is eating away at him. I have a feeling our playful game is about to be hijacked.

"Truth," Brooklyn concedes.

"I want to know what the deal with Seven is. No lies."

The crackling fire is the only sound in the silence his question brings. We're trapped in an infinite moment as everything rests on her answer. Brooklyn takes a swig from the bottle, which should indicate that she's passing. Instead, she pulls up her t-shirt to reveal her back.

I stare without blinking, sickness churning in my stomach. Hudson's string of curses would make the most hardened criminals wince. On the expanse of her milky skin, there are rows of vivid, striped scars. All the way down her visible spine, every inch of flesh is viciously marked.

"Who did this to you?" Hudson spits out. "I'll tear them apart and make a fucking hat out of their broken skull."

"You've never seen a whip mark before?" Brooklyn attempts at humour. "Beat you to it. I wonder what Incendia did with Jefferson's eyeballs. I sure hope they didn't put them back in."

Hudson traces a finger over a nasty scar, causing Brooklyn to shiver. She soon pushes him away, dropping the t-shirt back down before he loses his shit for real. I watch the shutters fall over Hudson's face at her rejection.

"Augustus was recruiting a new technician," she explains. "I later found out it was a trap, and this idiot was a mole sent looking for information. I refused to cut off his finger to mail back to his wife as leverage."

I try to drag her into my arms, but Brooklyn shuffles even further away. Neither of us are allowed anywhere close. She clearly can't stand to be touched while recanting this tale.

"Augustus didn't like my disobedience. He ordered Jefferson to beat me until I agreed to do as told."

"Fuck, firecracker."

DESECRATED SAINTS

"By the time I broke, the job was already done. Seven cut the son of a bitch's whole head off to send to the wife instead. He slept in his blood-stained clothes for a week. Augustus loved to dehumanise him even more."

Hudson looks set to explode in a torrent of rage. I watch him stand and promptly punch a tree. If he could go back and murder Augustus's psychopathic ass all over again, I have no doubt that he would. Brooklyn watches him with resignation.

"I was put back in my cell," she continues. "What they didn't know was that I'd slipped a knife into my sock, stolen from Jefferson's belt. I got it back without being discovered. I could barely move after the beating; my back was shredded, and I hadn't eaten in days. I couldn't go on any longer."

Flashbacks threaten to overwhelm me, still raw in my memory despite the time that's elapsed since I found her half-dead. The thought of her alone, back in that awful place, threatens to finish me off. I feel like a fucking failure for giving up on her.

"Firecracker—"

"No," Brooklyn interrupts. "Don't give me all that pitying bullshit. Hudson asked a question. The answer is this: when I had no one, Seven was there in the pitch black—a complete stranger who owed me nothing. He spoke to me through the air vent, talked me down. I could've slit my wrists, but I didn't."

Hudson stares at his bleeding fists, listening but not really present. The tree has matching dents in the rough bark now. He's slipped back into his angry, volatile haze, and can't be reached. I watch as he takes off, stalking into the nearby woods without a word.

"Probably just needs to clear his head." I wince.

"It's fine. I get it."

"He loves you. That's why he's upset that he couldn't be there."

"I know you all think that Seven is the bad guy." She sighs. "I'm not blind. He is the bad guy, but he's also the reason I'm alive. It's down to him that Hudson found someone resembling a person in the basement, not a rotting corpse."

I have so many pointless one-liners to roll out, but none of them will fix anything. He was there and we weren't. For that reason alone, Seven can remain alive. I don't like the guy, but I can accept his existence if it's inextricably tied to my girl. He's earned that much.

"Dance with me," I blurt.

"What?"

Scrambling to my feet, I wobble and realise I'm drunker than I thought. Freedom is doing my sobriety no favours. Offering Brooklyn a hand, she stares at me before letting me drag her up.

"There's no music," she complains.

"Do you need it?"

Hesitating, her arms twine around my shoulders until we're flush together. I gently rest my hands on her hips, teasing the sliver of exposed skin from her low-rise shorts. I can feel her heart hammering against mine, two racing engines set to implode.

"I guess not. Although we look like lunatics."

I grin at her. "Firecracker, we are fucking lunatics."

Beginning to sway my hips, I ease Brooklyn into it by holding her against my body. When she begins to relax at my touch, I twirl her in a slow, romantic waltz. I meant to lighten the mood and make her laugh, but I wasn't expecting this thick, intense atmosphere between us.

It feels like an ash cloud is raining on us both, sucking the very air from our lungs. I'm suddenly nervous. Shoving my insecurities aside, I take Brooklyn's hand and spin her outwards. She ducks beneath my arm before twirling back and colliding with my chest.

"You can dance!" she gasps.

"I'm full of surprises, didn't you know? I'll add dancer to my growing resume."

There's no space between us. I can almost feel the razor-sharp edges of her soul slicing my skin like barbed wire. We're magnetised together, an asteroid on a collision course, set on destruction. Her lips seal on mine and I kiss her slowly, gently, with all the emotion I've never been able to express.

"I'm glad you're still alive," I admit in a low whisper. "Even if another man had to hold you together when I couldn't. I don't give a fuck if he's what you need. I'll take whatever portion of you I can get."

"Phoenix…"

"No buts. If that means sharing, I'll share. Whatever it takes."

"It's not like that," she rushes out.

I slide a finger under her chin. "Isn't it?"

Brooklyn flushes. "I don't know, Nix."

Swaying in the light of the fire, we dance to no music. In all the madness, this is the first time I've been alone with Brooklyn. Anxiety wraps around my lungs as I realise exactly what I want to say, something I regretted never telling her in those long, lonely months.

"Brooke?"

"Yeah?"

Running a hand over her short hair, my thumb brushes her bottom lip. I silently curse my nerves. What's wrong with me? I've seen the world without her, and it isn't worth sticking around for. Tomorrow isn't guaranteed. I want to live for today and spend every second worshipping her.

"I'm in love with you. I want you to know that."

I don't look away or back down. I've spent my entire life running from commitment and emotions. I'm done. She's it for me—every step I take from this day out, it's with her by my side. Brooklyn bites her lip, looking oddly innocent as she mulls my declaration over.

"What about Eli?" she finally says.

I stare into her irises, lit by the flames. "What about him?"

"You love him, Nix."

"So do you."

The corner of her mouth lifts. "How does this work? I love all of you. I'm not afraid to say it anymore; it's time I grew up. I'm in love with every single one of you. I can't exist in this world without you guys. I refuse to."

"No one ever expected you to choose," I offer. "From day one, we fell into this messy, fucked-up family without coming up for air. We need each other to survive. It's that simple."

"But how is this fair?"

"We get you. That's enough. We get you, and you have us in return. None of us want to live without this family. We've all been lost and this… this is what it feels like to be found. I love you, and Eli and my brothers."

Despite everything, Brooklyn manages a laugh.

"Generous."

"Shut the fuck up, firecracker."

"You started it."

I bend my knees, dipping her low to the ground, before I sweep her back onto her feet. Brooklyn squeals, a brilliant smile blossoming on her lips for the first time in days. It takes my fucking breath away.

"I'll prove it to you," I whisper in her ear.

"How?"

"We'll burn the whole world and every last motherfucker in it to ashes if that's what it takes to get our revenge. I don't care anymore. Fuck everyone else. They will hurt like we do."

"You promise?"

"I promise. We'll take Incendia down or die trying."

Before she can say anything else, I seal the promise with a final, heart-stopping kiss. Everything I have is poured into the declaration, a goddamn irreversible stamp on my heart that I will proudly boast for the rest of my life.

Somehow, I'm grateful for Blackwood.

It taught us to grow up, and it showed me the truth. While the pain is temporary, family is forever. No matter what happens next, we'll go down in flames… together.

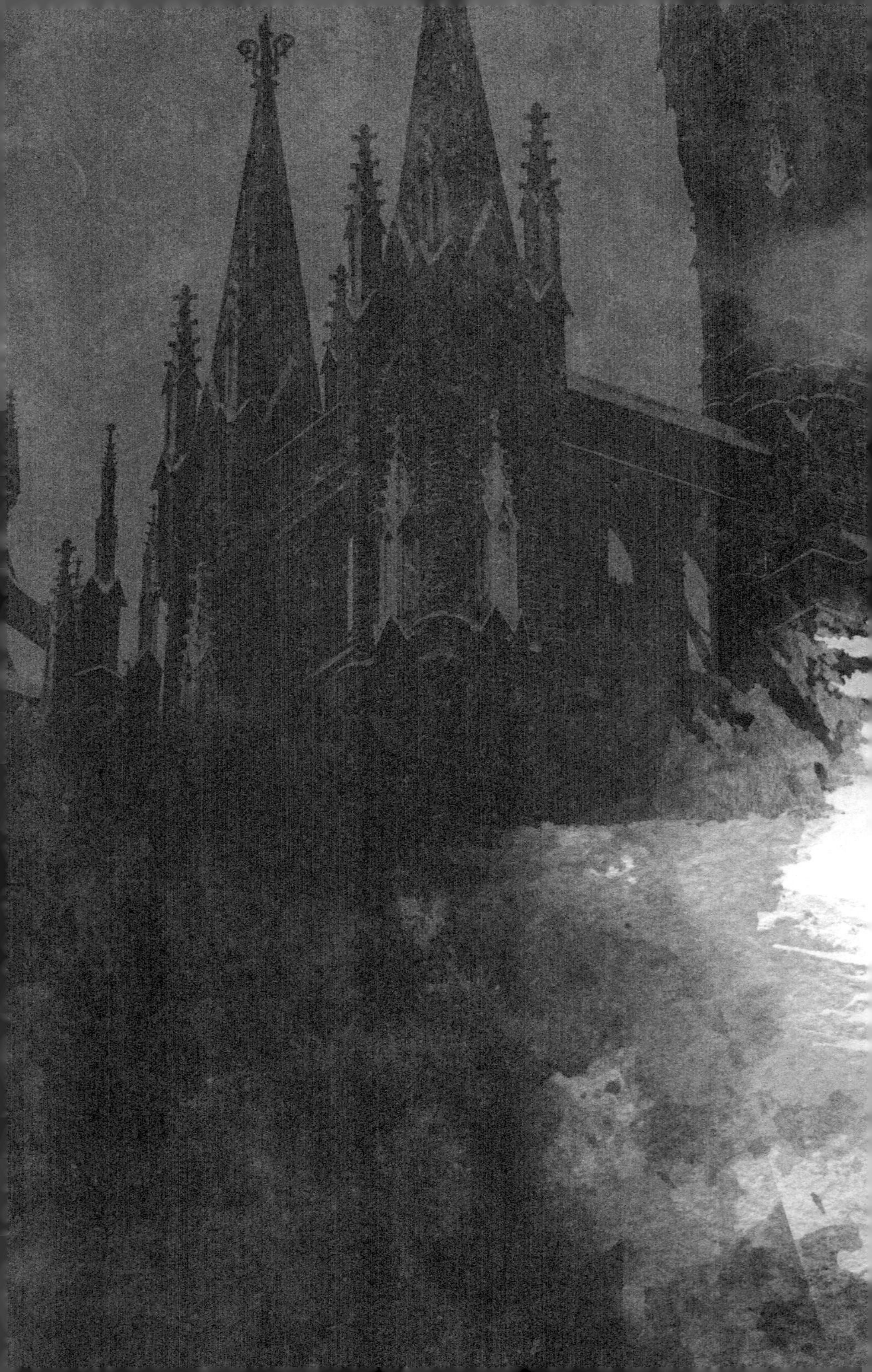

6

BROOKLYN

Doomed - Bring Me The Horizon

Leaving Phoenix and Eli spooning in the double bed, I throw a discarded shirt over my head. Watching them as they sleep for a moment, I smile to myself at the sight.

Phoenix is stretched out on his back, chest bare and arms folded behind his head. Eli is curled up by his side, head splayed across his pectorals and leg hitched high on his waist. He still sleeps in a t-shirt to hide his scars, even from us, but they both look so at peace with each other.

Padding into the kitchen, I hit the switch on the coffee machine. The sun has risen, but no one else has stirred. Kade is asleep at the kitchen table, drooling on his stacks of paperwork. He and Sadie were up late again last night.

Going to grab a blanket from the living room to drape over him, I startle when I realise someone else is awake. In one of the armchairs, huddled in a quilt and staring out the window, I find a pale, skeletal shadow of a man.

Conscious.

Blinking.

Breathing.

I stop dead, startled.

"Morning, princess," Seven mumbles absently.

"Jesus... Sev. You're awake."

"You lot have run out of drugs to use on me."

"Us lot?"

He spares me a blank look. "The pink-haired woman."

I sure as hell am not starting that deep dive into family history without being caffeinated. Instead, I watch him while returning to the open plan kitchen and filling two mugs with coffee. His intense gaze doesn't tear from me as I linger over the sugar pot.

"How do you take your coffee?"

"I have no idea," he answers.

Fixing it the same as mine, I tread carefully around Kade so as not to wake him. Taking the armchair next to Seven, I offer him the steaming mug. He wraps his one scarred hand around it. The healed stump on his right arm is tucked into the pocket of his sweats.

I have no idea what to say to him in the cold light of day. Our conversations were reserved for the shadows, a land beyond this world where labels didn't apply. At the mercy of demons and death on a daily basis, we clung together to survive.

Where the fuck does that leave us?

I don't know what we are in the real world.

Seven swallows a sip of coffee. "This is good."

"You remember it?"

"Just the taste. No idea where it's from."

"Anything else?"

Uncertain caramel eyes meeting mine, I'm taken aback to find a person resting there. Glimpses of the man he used to be stare back at me, someone who whispered to me in the dark and coaxed the knife from my grasp with mere words alone.

"Flashes. It comes and goes," Seven admits in his gruff voice. "I heard what they've been calling me. Jude. Was that my name? Before… everything?"

I don't answer at first. His calm exterior begins to falter, the cracks showing a hint of the madness that's battling to break free. I watch his gaze harden.

"Don't lie to me, Eight. We agreed to always tell each other the truth."

"Your name was Jude. Before Augustus. Before everything."

Placing the mug down, Seven brushes his unruly brown hair back to reveal his sharp, angular features and strong jawline. The mop on his head has fully grown out and touches his shoulders. He almost looks like a pirate, in a rugged, sexy-as-hell way.

"I see."

"What do you want us to call you?" I ask softly.

"My name isn't Jude."

"It was."

We follow the voice to where Sadie has emerged from the bedroom. Her sweetheart face and gentle gaze are full of exhaustion. She helps herself to a coffee, pausing to kick Kade's chair. It's like she needs backup while facing us unstable patients. I fight the urge to bare my teeth at her.

Breathe, Brooke.

No killing today. Yet.

"Care to take over, Sadie?" I ask tiredly.

"If you're going to drug me again, I'd advise against it," Seven adds.

We both tense as she passes us, taking a seat on the sofa. I inadvertently shift closer to Seven, driven by an unconscious need to protect him. Sadie doesn't miss a trick as she glances over to Kade for guidance. He's barely awake, sliding his glasses into place and stumbling towards the coffee pot.

"I'm not going to sedate you."

"Only because you ran out." I scoff.

"No." Sadie shoots me an exasperated look. "Because we can't dance around this any longer."

"Dance around what?" Seven utters.

Looking him in the eye, she declares, "I'm your sister."

Preparing myself for Seven to flip out and lose his shit, I'm even more surprised when he remains silent. He just stares at her like she's an alien invader, a crease marring his thick eyebrows. Sadie stares right back. I hate the way she seems almost afraid of him.

"Do you remember me?"

"Your hair used to be dark blonde."

Her mouth drops open. "A long time ago."

"Why did you dye it?"

Wiping away tears that spring free, she takes a breath. "Every time I looked in the mirror, I saw your eyes staring back at me. I wanted to see my reflection without being reminded of my dead family."

I'm sitting on the edge of my seat, prepared for things to change at a pin drop. I know just how volatile Seven can be. Despite everything, he seems to trust Sadie on an unconscious level, even if he doesn't know why.

"Do you remember our parents?"

He draws to his full height, a towering six foot three that dwarfs my small frame. I can still take him down if needed. My lessons in brutality were taught by his violence and bloodthirst. He walks over to the window and stares outside.

"No, I don't remember them."

"They both died," Sadie blurts.

"How?"

Taking a gulp of her coffee, she uses it as an excuse to wipe more tears aside.

"A plane crash when we were young. Grandma took us in, but she died a couple of years before you vanished. The last time I saw you was a week before my seventeenth birthday. We had dinner in the city to celebrate. After that… nothing."

Seven's forehead collides with the fogged-up glass. I watch his eyes slide shut, blocking the whole world out. His shoulders slump beneath the heavy weight of realisation, and my dead heart almost breaks for him.

"How long?"

"Six years. I've been looking for you ever since. It took me a long time to track your movements. I studied before applying to the first place you worked at. The rest is history."

"I don't understand," Seven murmurs.

Kade interrupts by stepping into the living room, looking much more awake. "Maybe we should take a break. We don't want to overwhelm him with too much, too soon."

"Wait, Jude—"

Seven spins, his expression shutting down into familiar, breathtaking anger. I step between him and Sadie on instinct, watching the way she quickly backtracks towards Kade.

"That isn't my fucking name!" Seven yells. "Eight, tell them."

"That isn't her name either," Kade combats.

"You wanna bet, asshole? Maybe I know her better than you think."

Kade pumps up his chest. "Try it, Seven. I was here first."

Fighting the urge to facepalm, I swim through their metaphorical lake of testosterone and stand in the middle with my hands outstretched.

"Can we compare dick sizes another time, please? Sadie, call him whatever the fuck he wants. And Kade, does it really matter if he calls me Eight? Really?"

"Yes! It does."

"Princess, step aside," Seven hisses. "Let me break this bastard's fucking skull."

"She's not your princess," Kade hits back.

Marching up to Kade, I glare until he grudgingly backs off. Unlike Hudson, Kade's anger usually has an off switch. Though I wouldn't be opposed to smashing their heads together for good measure.

"We're on the same side, so let's discuss this like adults." I look between the two infuriating men. "None of this possessive, alphahole bullshit. You both hear me?"

"He started it," Seven objects.

Kade glowers at him. "I should've left you to burn in that damn institute."

"You know, I once skinned a man alive. Want me to demonstrate?"

"Seven!" I bellow. "Cut it out. I'm going to strangle you both."

Sadie shakes her head at us. "We're doomed."

Needing some air, I storm back to my bedroom. The girls are still asleep, bundled together into one cramped bed. They've been quiet since the family meeting, but no longer look at us with bone-deep terror.

By the time I get dressed and have regained a sense of calm, the argument has broken up. Kade is outside talking on the burner phone, while Seven and Sadie sit in silence. Rather than dive back into that cesspit of complications, I step outside to check on Kade as he hangs up.

"Everything okay with your mum?"

His expression is bleak. "Get everyone up. Right now."

"Trouble? Are we safe?"

"For now, but we need another family meeting."

Cursing the universe for hating our delinquent asses, I head for Phoenix and Eli's room and force them out of bed. I'm much gentler with the girls, coaxing them to come out for coffee. My lungs are being squeezed by an impending panic attack when I reach the final bedroom.

"Hud, get up. Kade wants to speak to everyone."

He throws a pillow at me. I dodge and jump on the bed instead. Grabbing me by the ankles, Hudson yanks until I fall into his tattooed arms. He traps me beneath him, his eyes half shut. He's looking too grumpy and hot for my libido to take.

"Is it urgent?" he grunts. "I was dreaming about having your sweet pussy wrapped around my cock. I'd rather skip the meeting and go back to that, please."

My mouth is suddenly dry. "I, uh, have no idea."

"Then he can wait while I fuck you until you scream my name for the whole house to hear, right?" Hudson paws at my clothes. "I want to paint your body in my come, blackbird."

"What is it with you guys acting like animals today?"

"You don't usually mind."

"I've had one cup of coffee and already broken up a pissing contest. Don't make me even crankier, Hud. I'll stab you for my own satisfaction and dance in your blood to celebrate."

"Sounds hot," he purrs. "I'm yours to kill, baby."

Smashing a pillow into his face, I extricate myself from his body and escape before he can tempt me further. In the kitchen, the room has filled up with more sleepy, disgruntled men. I consider my options carefully, taking the space next to Seven on the sofa. I don't miss the way Kade's glare intensifies.

"You good?" I whisper under my breath.

Seven's nostrils flare. "Fucking peachy. When can we go home?"

"This is your home now. Not that cell."

"The cell was bloody quieter, princess."

"Just keep it together, ignore everyone else."

"You mean your boyfriends?" Seven says acerbically.

I rub between my eyes, a headache brewing. "I'm the only one in this room capable of beating the shit out of you. He broke us together, side by side. So don't underestimate me. I'm running very low on fucks to give this morning and my coffee has run out."

Seven sinks back into the sofa, carefully studying the room. He's every inch the violent, mindless soldier that Augustus trained him to be. Kade paces in the kitchen, his fingers flying across his phone while yelling at Hudson to hurry up. My stomach flips pathetically when Eli brings me a fresh coffee.

I catch his hand. "Thank you."

He shrugs, returning to stand by Phoenix's side. Lucia and Two have set themselves up in a safe corner, leaving Hudson to stumble out, dressed only in a pair of skin-tight, black boxers that leave little to the imagination. My mouth falls open before I wrench it shut again.

Kade grabs the TV remote. "You all need to see this."

"What's this about?" Hudson drawls. "Some of us had a crappy night's sleep with all the nightmares and screaming going on in this is fucking cottage." His eyes pointedly stray to me.

"Just shut up and listen."

Flicking over to a national news channel, we all fall silent as breaking news flashes across the screen. There's a familiar video playing that chills my blood. CCTV footage of the main building in Blackwood, burning to the ground. Several headlines run beneath the video, emblazoned for the entire world to see.

Prestigious Institute Suffers Mass Riot & Escape.
Tragic Night At Secure Mental Institution.
Blaze Claims The Lives Of Twenty Patients & Staff.

I reach for Seven's hand as the screen changes, showing fire trucks dousing the flames. Police escort shell-shocked patients into awaiting vehicles to be transferred, dosing them up with medication and restraining a few too freaked out to comply. The sight of body bags has acid burning my throat.

"Why are we watching this?" Phoenix demands.

"Because of this," Kade answers grimly.

Switching to a live conference, the newscaster falls silent. The camera shot is somewhere in London, framed by the famous skyline. Surrounded by glass monoliths and decadent high-rises, the opulence of a wealthier district is clear. I can see Kade clocking all the details.

There must be dozens of reporters lined up. They all stand and begin shouting when the doors to a grand, blacked-out skyscraper slide open. Flanked by security guards, an elderly man takes a stand behind the microphone, tapping it for their attention.

Smoothing his perfectly fitting, pinstripe designer suit with matching diamond cufflinks, his cold, expressionless face is wrinkled and worn beneath a smooth coiffe of silvery hair. His eyes are the most unnerving thing. I feel like he's staring straight into the windows of my soul.

"Who the hell is this prick?" Phoenix grumbles.

I gasp while reading the caption.

Sir Joseph Bancroft II.
Founder & President of Incendia Corporation.

"Motherfucker," Hudson curses.

"A fucking sir?" I exclaim. "You see that?"

Everyone falls silent when Kade waves for us to shut up. The well-bred asshole on the screen clears his throat, smoothing the snake-like expression off his face and plastering on a smile that screams of grief and sadness. I want to fucking puke.

"Twelve days ago, my beloved son and head of our clinical division, Doctor Warren Augustus, passed away. In an act of malice, he was attacked by the very patients he so passionately fought for. My son was murdered by those he swore to protect."

Son?

What the living fuck?!

The clicking of cameras and journalists scribbling notes punctuates Bancroft's words. His identity has shocked everyone here into silence. I swear the son of a bitch fakes a tear that he brushes aside with an embroidered, silken handkerchief worth more than my life.

"This act of violence will not go unpunished. We have been treating the mentally unwell in our private institutes for thirty years. Blackwood Institute will be rebuilt, and we will bring those responsible to justice. Several patients escaped during the riot and remain at large."

Seven's grip on my hand tightens involuntarily, creaking my bones. All of the guys have moved closer, unconsciously closing ranks around us.

Bancroft stares into the camera. "We are working with the police to track down the escapees. I came here today to warn the public and ask for your assistance in locating these criminals. They should be considered extremely dangerous."

Several photographs are plastered across the screen, taken straight from our ID badges. All of my guys are there, bar Seven. He's supposed to be dead, so they can hardly broadcast his picture. The final image that fills the screen stops my heart. My chest burns from holding my breath for too long as I study it.

"Son of a fucking bitch," Kade utters.

Plastered across the screen in merciless, high-definition horror, is my police mugshot. I have no doubt they chose this on purpose to scare the public. I'm blood-splattered and gaunt after the police caught up to me, before I could throw myself in front of a train. I barely recognise the ghost staring back at me.

"That's me alright," I grit out.

Bancroft flashes back on the screen. "Their ringleader, Brooklyn West, was one of Blackwood's most infamous patients. While she may have escaped our care, we endeavour to recapture her and bring her to justice for the atrocities committed. Miss West is a criminal and an inhumane monster."

The corner of his mouth tilts up in the tiniest way. He's staring straight through the camera, into the pits of my murderous soul. His direct eye contact is no mistake. Bancroft knows I'm watching; this conference is for our benefit.

"It is clear her rehabilitation has failed. We will not rest until she is back behind bars, where she belongs for the rest of her life. I will not be taking questions at this time."

Striding away from the roar of frantic voices demanding more information, Bancroft is followed by security before climbing into a blacked-out SUV. I catch the flash of two people waiting inside, but the cameras can't capture their faces.

Kade relaxes ever so slightly. "At least my father didn't make an appearance. He's getting butchered by a media shitstorm for our involvement in this, so that's something."

Hudson snorts. "That'll keep him busy."

I sit unblinking, the conversation around me melting into insignificance. All I can hear is white noise, growing louder and louder as the broken part of my brain unfurls. Stretching its limbs as if awakening from a long nap, thick, tar-like shadows begin to leak down the walls.

Inky droplets swallow the TV screen whole, blotting the room out. I can feel the cold from the basement around me, leaching into my bones, and the bite of handcuffs searing my wrists. Augustus's sound machine blares in my head, leaving nothing but terror behind.

I start to tremble, a heady current coursing through me. Something flickers to life in the corner of the darkened room, birthed from the shadows. A ghost has risen from the dead to walk amongst the living.

"Please no," I whisper, but it's too late.

The bloodied, hallucinatory face of Doctor Augustus stares back at me, his charming smile spread wide. He rests against the TV console, grinning while smoothing his crimson, brain-splattered suit. Even his glossy black hair is clumped with blood and deathly fluids.

Thought you'd gotten away with it, Patient Eight?

I told you before.

Blackwood is your destiny. It's inescapable.

I escape the hallucination by running at full pelt. Voices try to sneak into my stuttering mind, but I shove them all out, flying past the guys without stopping for a breath. Running until I trip over myself, I stumble into the garden, cutting my hands on thorny bushes.

The Devil follows me, guided by the invisible cord that binds us together. No matter how much I scream and beg to be left alone, he lives in that gaping chasm in my chest, carved by his sick will alone. Augustus kneels beside me, studying my state of distress.

Why do you run from me?

You never learn, Patient Eight.

Your mind belongs to me. It always will.

"Leave me alone. You're dead!"

Squeezing my eyes shut, I will him to go away. A cold breeze on the back of my neck answers my plea for mercy, sending more suffering instead. I'm too scared to look, but force myself to anyway. The swarming shadows twist through the air and give way to another skeletal figure.

"Not you," I whimper uselessly.

Logan isn't here to protect me from her anymore. Beautiful face burned from the air bags that did nothing to save her life, Mum's tumbling blonde hair is drenched in blood. Her smile is still the same beneath her soft exterior, predatory and ice cold.

Come home, Brooke.

Back to Blackwood.

You were born for the program, and you'll die for it.

Staring into the empty eyes of my hallucination, I'm trapped. Frozen by fear that I was stupid to think I could outrun. I've held them at bay since escaping, stuffing the voices deeper and deeper into oblivion. Despite everything, I knew I couldn't run forever.

Someone wraps their arms around me, attempting to shake me from my stupor. I think someone else is shouting, but it's no use. I still can't breathe. Can't think. Can't exist on this hellish plane, where ghosts walk in the skin of the living and haunt me even when I'm not asleep. I should've died in that basement.

"Brooklyn—"

"Get out of the way. She needs me."

"Fuck off."

"I'm the only one that can pull her back!"

Their voices sneak through the constraints of my fading lucidity. My traumatised brain recognises the gruff, pained tenor of my lone saviour. He's whispered to me many times in my darkest moments.

A rough hand cups my jaw and I stare into a pair of molten eyes, burning like wildfire. Matching horror and suffering stares right back at me.

"Breathe, Eight. Just breathe for me."

Seven grips my face until it hurts, demanding my brain to follow orders. Even with his best intentions, it's no use. I can still see her over his shoulder. She crooks her index finger at me. Mum won't go back to her shallow grave, content to continue ruining my life.

Devil child.

Couldn't even protect your brother from me.

You should have died a long time ago.

"You killed him, not me," I yell at her.

Seven looks over his shoulder to follow my gaze. I take the opportunity to punch him in the face. If I can get into the woods, maybe the hallucinations will leave me alone. Attempting to run, my feet are quickly swept out from underneath me. I end up with a face full of dirt as Seven pins me down.

"Jesus, princess. You're making me look sane!"

"Fuck you," I spit. "Let me go, Augustus!"

"It's me! He can't hurt you. Come back."

"Please... l-let me go. Mum's after me."

"She isn't real," Seven shouts. "Look into my eyes, Eight. Nowhere else."

He strikes me so hard, my lip splits in the process. I hear someone raging in the distance, but nothing exists beyond my line of sight. Only Seven's wide, burnished eyes, coaxing me back to reality. I taste the hot, metallic flow of blood slipping between my lips. It helps to latch on to the pain.

"That's it, Eight. Just us, no one else."

"Augustus—"

"Is dead," Seven finishes.

"And we'll be next."

He strokes my sweaty hair as I greedily suck in air. I can see the guys gathered on the porch, none of them daring to take a step closer. Kade is holding a seething Hudson back, while Phoenix and Eli cling to each other for strength, both looking terrified.

"Don't look at them," Seven orders. "Do as you're told for once."

"I c-can't do this, they're going to come for me…"

"You think any of us would let them?"

Seven offers me a tiny, threatening smile. I peer around apprehensively, but the shadows have abated. He's holding me in this plane of existence, keeping the madness in my veins from poisoning the world again.

"You got me out of Blackwood. I'm going to keep us out."

"How?" I whisper brokenly.

His grin turns savage, dripping with violent rage.

"I'll kill them all, princess, and bring you their heads on fucking stakes."

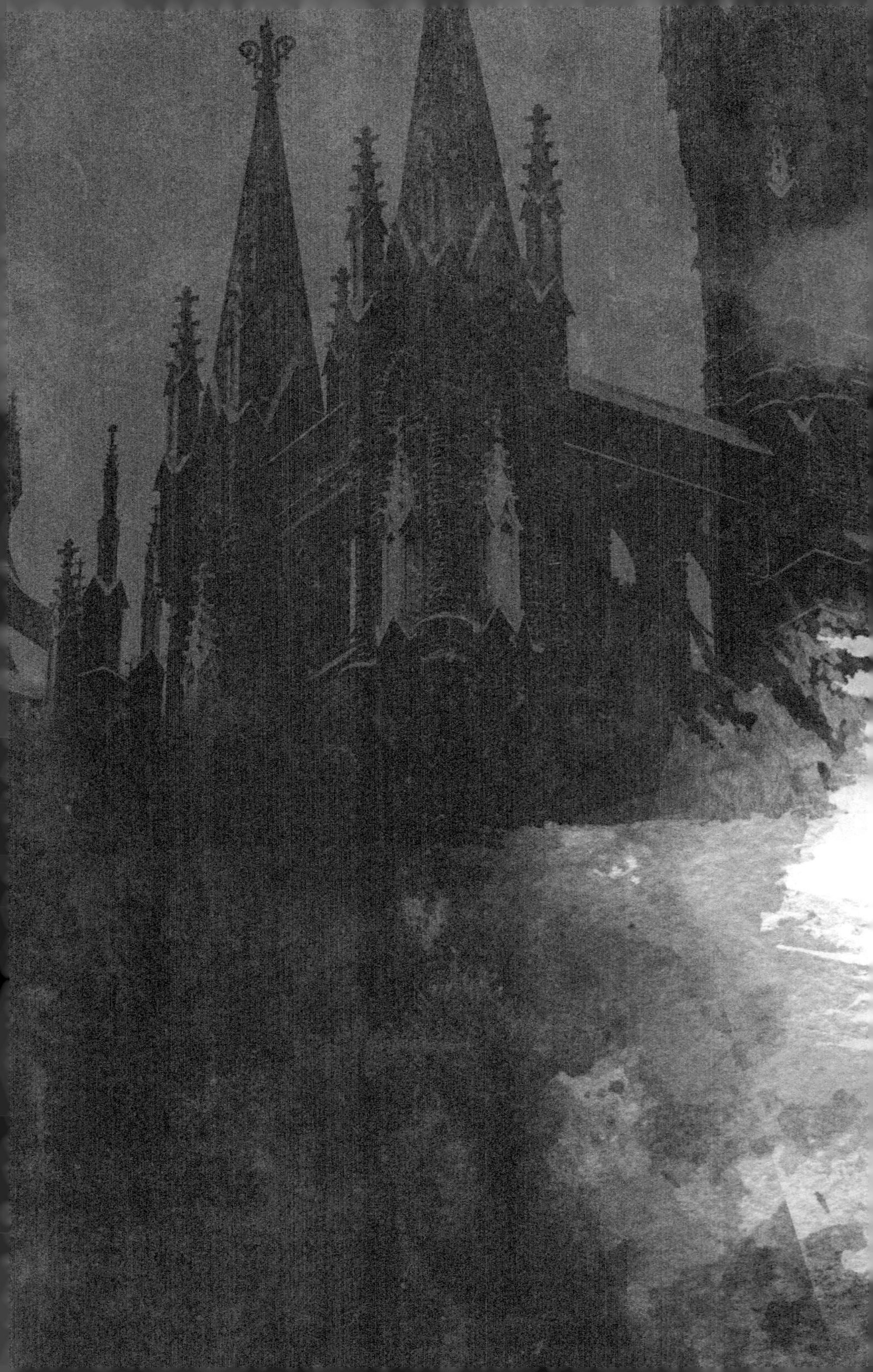

7

BROOKLYN

Left alone - Zero 9:36

Ducking through the oppressive woodland, I feel myself relax. I'm more at home in the darkness than anywhere else. I need the space to gather my thoughts. We've been hiding out here for another week, ever since Incendia decided to drop a nuclear bomb on our heads.

With few options, we had nowhere else to run. The guys have been worse than ever, refusing to leave me unaccompanied. It only got worse when I wouldn't discuss the whole losing my mind and becoming a complete fruit cake thing. I've been drowning myself in our dwindling supply of liquor instead.

"Blackbird! Jesus, slow down."

I run to escape Hudson chasing me through the forest. After two weeks of forcing myself to eat, I'm still weak and unable to get far before his long, powerful limbs catch up.

"Leave me alone, Hud."

"Can't a guy go for a harmless run?"

I shove him away and brace my hands on my knees. I can feel him glaring beneath his shock of unruly black hair and shining eyebrow piercing, his angled jaw clenched. Every inch of well-honed muscle is on display in his running shorts and tank top.

"What do you want?"

He shrugs. "Just jogging, that's all."

"Run somewhere else."

"You really think you should be out here alone right now?"

I fix him with a cold stare. "I don't need a babysitter. Least of all you."

"What's that supposed to mean?"

With rage steeling my spine, I prowl forward until he's backed against a nearby willow tree. It's still weird to see Hudson surrender to me after so much pain and misery inflicted by his hands. His aquamarine eyes are lit with amusement, like he's enjoying the show I'm putting on.

"You, of all people, know I can handle myself," I explain angrily.

"That doesn't mean you have to. We're all just trying to help you get through this, but you're pushing us away and trying to hide from what's happening back out in the real world."

"I am not!"

"Lies. You're being a fucking pussy, Brooke."

Before my fist can connect with his jaw, Hudson snatches my hand. I wrench it from his grasp, snarling like an animal. No one will find his body out here, right? I'll be doing the world a favour by slitting his throat.

"I'm a pussy? You've barely spoken to me since you stormed off like a baby last week. I'm not the only one in denial here. If I'm a pussy, you're a coward."

"You take that back," he utters.

"You first, dickhead. Don't start a fight if you aren't prepared for the truth."

Hudson tries to grab me by the throat, but I block him and slam my fist into his gut instead. Doubling over, he grabs my waist and pulls me with him. We both tumble to the moss-covered ground. Writhing and attempting to claw his face, I let out a hiss as he straddles my body.

"We're dropping the pretence then, yeah?"

"Fuck you," I growl. "Let me go before I really hurt you."

"I'm not done." Hudson grips my throat. "Yes, I have a problem with the way Seven looks at you. You're my fucking blackbird, you hear me? Mine. I share your ass with three other men already, and you want to add a fourth into the mix?"

Managing to get a punch to the face in, Hudson barely reacts as he's knocked off balance. I take advantage of his surprise and turn the tables. With my legs wrapped around his torso, I hold him captive beneath me and headbutt him straight in the nose.

"Fight me all you want." He glowers through the blood streaming down his chin. "I'm not afraid to put your infuriating ass in the ground. Try another punch, see what happens."

Curiously, I dip my index finger in the stream of hot blood coating his face. Hudson watches as I swirl the moisture around my finger, before bringing it to my mouth and consuming every last drop.

"Nobody said anything about adding a fourth person or whatever you're insinuating, you controlling, egotistical bastard. I spent months watching Britt trail around after you like a bitch in heat. Now you know how it felt."

Staring up at me, Hudson lets loose a laugh.

"Jesus Christ. What are we doing?"

"You missed this, admit it."

"I missed you. Not your temper."

Leaning close, I peck his lips. "Who did I learn my temper from, Hud?"

He grabs a handful of my short hair and drags my lips back to his. Teeth clashing, I forget how to exist while Hudson makes it his mission to invade every inch of my mind. He forces everything out, kissing me like the sky is falling down around us and this is our last moment on this earth.

The steady stream of blood running between our lips makes everything messy as hell. Like a red flag to a bull, my remaining self-control is obliterated. Seizing his sweaty tank top, I break the kiss to rip it over his head, revealing his inked torso and healing shoulder. The bullet wound is still swollen and inflamed.

"I used to dream about killing you myself, after you left me behind at St Anne's." I trace the injury with my finger. "Never thought I'd be the one standing between you and death when the time came."

Hudson chuckles. "Clearly, you're the only one allowed to take me out. If I'm to die, the least I can do is give you the satisfaction of taking my pitiful life."

"What would the fun be in that?"

I bite his plump, inviting bottom lip. Hudson retaliates by gripping the hem of my loose t-shirt. Tearing it over my head, he makes short work of tossing my sports bra aside too. My breasts are exposed to the damp air, contrasting the heat of his mouth securing over my hardened nipple.

Gasping, I grind myself on his lap. His erection is pressing up into me, demanding attention. Rolling the other bud between his fingers, Hudson pauses to glance up at me.

"You know, I've been thinking. Since you slit Britt's throat, it's only fair that I put a bullet between the one-handed psycho's eyes. Equality and all that shit."

"Seven isn't a psycho, and don't pretend like you're doing me a favour by hating him."

"You're seriously defending him?" he replies incredulously. "The man who decapitates people, skins them alive, and broke Phoenix's fingers yesterday for changing the TV channel? He can barely move his hand."

"So what? Seven likes the Discovery Channel. It calms him. Phoenix should've minded his own business."

"Stop deflecting," Hudson snarls.

"That man saved my life. He's far from perfect, but I owe him a debt that I intend to repay. I'm not going to break my promise just because your fragile ego can't handle a little competition."

"Competition?!"

Curling his hand back around my throat, Hudson squeezes right above my pulse point. His eyes look like two shards of ice, ready to slice me open and spear my heart with their rage. I can't fight back as he flips us so I'm back beneath him, slamming me down on the forest floor.

"There is no competition," he hisses. "I love your infuriating, crazy ass. I'll kill you myself before letting anyone steal your attention from our family. Strangle you until you're blue and make you watch as I break that son of a bitch's neck. Maybe I'll even fuck you next to his cold, dead corpse."

"What the fuck is wrong with you?" I choke out.

"As we've established, a lot. Don't believe me? I'll prove it to you."

He rips my yoga pants off before seizing my panties. I suppress a shiver when he brings the damp material to his nose, breathing deeply. When the first droplets of rain hit my bare skin, I try to escape again. It's getting heavier, penetrating the thick canopy of trees to soak the ground.

Hudson growls at my movement, shoving my legs open even wider until my pussy is exposed to the elements. I feel utterly vulnerable, hating the way his gaze eats up every last inch of my most private place.

With a hand splayed across my lower belly, he drops between my legs. My back arches as his tongue meets my folds.

"Keep still or I won't let you come."

"Lay one more finger on me and I'll break it," I warn, hating the way my body betrays me. He's always held this invisible power over me, even in the darkest days of our relationship.

"You don't wanna be my little whore, hmm?"

"Nope. I'm done."

Hudson ignores me like usual. I groan against the back of my hand as he slides a practised finger into my slit. I'm worried that someone is going to stumble across our secret tryst and see how toxic this shit is.

"What about now? Still don't want your daddy to touch you?"

"God fucking damn you to hell, Hudson Knight."

Curling his finger deep inside my pussy, my orgasm explodes out of me. We're both getting soaked in the storm, but it doesn't stop Hudson. He flips me over so I'm lying face down on the wet earth. His hand cracks across my butt cheek.

"Hud!" I attempt to claw myself free. "We're done here."

"We're not leaving until we get a few things straight."

"We can't—"

"Shut the fuck up, blackbird, or I'll make you."

"You're not listening—"

"I said shut it, you disobedient slut."

He spanks me so hard, I can't help crying out. I'm forced into a doggy position like a puppet on strings, beholden to the cruelty of its master. We're drowning in the heavy summer rain and my hands dig into the wet mud, covering myself in dirt as I battle to escape.

Hudson refuses to let me go. He knows exactly what he's doing to me. Trailing a wet digit over my asshole, I bite back a groan of pleasure. My body is betraying me all over again, ready to submit to his every possessive demand, whether my brain wants it or not.

"You pretend like you don't want to be owned and fucked like an object." Hudson buries two fingers back in my pussy. "But you thrive on having your choice taken away. You love it when I fuck you like the whore you are. Don't you?"

"You're a fucking asshole."

"*Your* fucking asshole, blackbird. Forever and always."

"Fuck your forever. I'll kill you long before then."

Hudson's fingers disappear and the tip of his cock presses against my tight opening. I'm caught between trying to escape and letting him fuck me. He's right; I grew up in pain and sickness, and now it gets me wetter than a fucking nun with her crucifix. The sadistic son of a bitch knows me too well.

Trapped amidst the storm that surrounds us, Hudson's thrusts mirror the beat of my traitorous heart. He fucks me just like he used to, all raw aggression and hatred, lost in our mutual need to hurt one another. Pummelling my pussy, he growls his annoyance at the lack of hair on my head to wrench.

"Tell me you're mine and I'll let you finish," he commands.

"Is that what you want to hear? That you still have your sick, twisted claws stuck so deep inside of me, I couldn't walk away even if I wanted to?"

"Yes."

"Well, I guess that means I'm yours."

Delivering another bruising smack to my ass, Hudson's tempo increases until I feel like I'm going to explode. Alight with sensation, the tension in my belly twists into a rising crescendo. I decide there and then that he can't get the last word. Not this time.

We can both play dirty.

I'm done being his victim.

"Plus Eli's and Phoenix's," I add, savouring his sharp inhale. "Kade's too. I've fucked them all, you know. Every single one of your friends has had their cock inside of me. How does that feel, Hud?"

"You're digging your own grave," he warns.

"Maybe I could be Seven's too. I'll make you watch while he bends me over and takes me for the first time, just to prove my point. You saved my life in that basement, but that doesn't mean it belongs to you alone."

Hudson's too far gone to withhold my release for pissing him off. The coiled spring deep within me snaps, pushing me off the deep end. I moan through the orgasm that threatens to swallow me whole. He manages another thrust before grunting his release, his heat spilling into me.

I shove Hudson away before he can collapse on me. We both sprawl out, covered head to toe in gelatinous mud and fallen leaves. Panting for every breath, my gaze collides with the two sparkling, oceanic jewels greedily taking me in. I'm surprised by the reluctant acceptance I find there.

"I dragged you out of that basement for myself." He flashes me a warning look. "But also for my family. Don't underestimate what I'll do for them, Brooke. I've given up the one person I care about to make them happy."

Hudson throws my sodden clothes at me, watching without shame as I quickly cover up. Now that we've both said our piece, the electric tension between us feels calmer, more settled. Before my brain kicks in, I tuck myself into his arms.

"I'm glad you found your home, Hud."

His fingers tilt my chin up to meet his eyes. "You're our home, blackbird."

Vulnerability shouldn't scare me anymore. I've lost everything, but I've also regained the most precious thing in the world to me. A family.

Hiding from them isn't helping anyone. I can't spend the rest of my life running away from my feelings.

I watch rain cascade down Hudson's face. "I love you."

He offers me a crooked, satisfied smile. "I love you too. So much it scares me."

Dragging a finger over his bloodied nose, already bruising from where I headbutted him, I feel a matching smile play across my lips.

"Even when you're a masochistic dickhead who should be locked up for the rest of his days."

Hudson smirks. "At least I'm consistent."

"Consistently aggravating, sure."

"That's probably the nicest thing you've ever said to me."

With an eye roll, I take his hand. We set off in a slow jog, my energy sapped by our frantic fuck fest. By the time we reach the cottage, my teeth are chattering. We thud up the carved wooden steps to the wraparound porch, listening to the sound of shouting inside.

My clothes are completely ruined. I'm only wearing my stained yoga pants and sports bra, covered head to toe in dirt and swirls of blood. Hudson doesn't look much better, bruised, bleeding, and shirtless. The moment we step inside, Phoenix's and Eli's eyes land on us.

"Fucking dammit!" Kade yells. "It's gone."

"What's wrong?"

He slams the lid of a laptop shut hard enough to send papers flying. "Augustus's hard drive was wiped by remote override. I've been trying to get it back, but there's nothing I can do. Incendia are on to us."

Hudson grabs a bottle of water from the fridge. "Not to point out the obvious, but we know they're on to us. Our fucking faces play every night on the news."

Kade glances at his brother and spots our state of disarray. His eyes widen, trailing over us both in a comical way. "What the hell happened to you? Did you get mauled by a bear out there?"

"I fell over," I lie easily.

Snuggled up on the sofa with a movie, Phoenix throws an arm around Eli's shoulders. He's staring intently at my bare skin on display while trying not to laugh. Eli's grinning at the pair of us, his shoulders shaking with silent laughter. It's painfully obvious why we're both covered in mud.

Kade looks exasperated. "Why is your nose bleeding?"

"We both fell." Hudson grins ear to ear.

Phoenix waves his two broken fingers that are strapped together. "I fell too, right into some asshole's fist. Funny how often that happens around here, isn't it? Very coincidental."

"You should know better than to mess with Seven's television schedule." I dump my ruined running shoes. "He's now obsessed with the cooking channel. I think he got bored of the nature shows. Wait until he finds the porn."

"Are we moving on from the fact our one lead has been destroyed?" Kade exclaims.

Ignoring him, all three guys stare at me.

"What? Six years in a locked basement makes for a lot of curiosity," I say innocently. "Who can blame him?"

Kade dismisses us all with a colourful curse. I catch the dusting of pink across his cheeks. He's got the dirtiest mouth of them all, and somehow, he maintains this innocent-as-fuck exterior.

"Is there really no way to get the hard drive back?" Hudson returns to the topic at hand.

"Nope, I tried everything. We're toast."

"We'll figure something out. That wasn't our only lead."

Tossing my wrecked t-shirt in the bin, I'm intent on a hot shower to ease the ache between my legs. The pair of jungle cats cuddling on the sofa are watching me closely. I don't break eye contact as Phoenix whispers something in Eli's ear.

Before we have a chance to investigate how many people can fit in the shower, the partition door slams open. Sadie struggles out with a duffel bag, her shock of pink hair tucked into a dark beanie. She startles when she sees us all.

"Going somewhere?" I break the silence.

"I'm leaving while Seven is asleep."

"We've discussed this, we're not ready," Kade rushes out. "There's still too much we don't know. We lost Augustus's laptop, but I'm working on a profile for Bancroft and…"

Sadie raises a palm to halt him. "This is precisely why I have to leave. The sooner, the better. Incendia will catch up to me when they find out I'm related to Jude. We're all in the firing line."

"But why are you leaving?" I demand.

Sadie seizes the remaining stacks of paperwork from the table to avoid answering my question. I grab her arm before she can turn away. There was a time when I considered us something akin to friends. Now, I'm not sure where her true loyalties lie.

"I'm sorry, Brooke. I have a job to do."

"What job? Who are you really?"

"I vowed to bring Jude's killers down. Augustus is dead, but the real monsters are still out there. Five more institutes. Incendia didn't build itself. They killed my brother and I want justice."

"Your brother is here. Alive. He needs you."

She shakes her head. "Jude isn't coming back. I belong out there, doing what I was trained for. I trust that you'll take care of him. Hell, you know him better than I do now."

"Trained for?" Hudson chips in.

"I've come to understand that Sadie was assisted in her search for answers," Kade answers for her. "Her employer enabled her to hide her true reason for being in Blackwood."

"Employer?" I repeat.

"She already blew her cover during the riot," Kade continues to fill in the blanks. "Now, she's planning to infiltrate Harrowdean Manor under a whole new identity to find more evidence to corroborate our stories."

The room explodes with disbelief and countless questions. Sadie seems uncomfortable, avoiding looking at us now that the truth has been revealed. I always found her presence too convenient, but this takes the biscuit. She's a fucking spook.

"Is Sadie your real name?" I blurt out.

"Does it matter?"

"Well, if we don't know you or your employer, who can we trust? Seems rather convenient that they're able to simply slip you inside a secure institution, no questions asked."

"You're suggesting I actually work for Incendia?" Sadie splutters.

"They could be on their way right now."

"So after sneaking into Blackwood under a false name, helping you stage your escape, killing Augustus, breaking out several patients and burning down half the institute, you think I work for the people that did this to you?"

I reluctantly admit defeat and back down. Even if I don't trust her as far as I can throw her, there was no faking her pain when she realised Seven was still alive. All of this is far too elaborate for one of Augustus's lackeys to pull off.

"Who do you work for?" I try again.

"That's classified."

"Why are you going back inside?" Hudson questions.

"Augustus's laptop was linked to an external server that's controlled by Incendia. The information I stole from that server is with my team, but it's heavily encrypted. Without that, all we have is some grainy phone footage and a story that no one will believe."

Her team. I file that information away. She's a lot more than she has let on. I feel like we've been living with a stranger for the past three weeks.

"You're saying no one will believe us," Phoenix surmises.

Sadie nods. "We can't bring Incendia down with our stories alone. They have more connections than you know. Investors, private sponsors, government authorities protecting them."

"If the government is protecting Incendia, who's your employer?"

"I'm sorry. You already know too much. This is for your safety, as well as mine. I'm under strict orders."

Kade rubs his temples, looking defeated. He isn't accustomed to not being in control. Weeks of work have yielded no results and we're back to square one.

"Incendia is looking for us. We're public enemy number one," I point out.

"Which is why I have to do this alone."

"Not exactly," Kade speaks up.

Sadie rounds on him. "Absolutely not. It's too dangerous! We just got you guys out. There's no way I'm letting you go to London. I'm handling this alone."

"We lost our one lead. Let us help."

"No!"

"That's not your decision to make."

"What's in London?" I interrupt.

"I've been speaking to someone on the dark web," Kade answers. "Blackwood is a hot topic right now. They claim to have evidence about what went on inside. I proposed we meet to discuss."

He stares at me with defiance, daring me to protest. The thought of diving back into this toxic wasteland of secrets and subterfuge holds zero appeal, but we're sitting ducks here. Freedom means nothing when we're still running for our lives.

"Who exactly is this contact?"

"We have no clue! That's why it's too dangerous," Sadie snaps.

"You're playing your part, let us do ours," Kade insists. "We can't hide forever. I want us to live. That can't happen until our names are cleared."

"You're wading into a war you don't understand."

"If Sadie can get into Harrowdean Manor under an alias and prove what's going on, we have a chance at bringing Incendia down." I look at her. "Let us help. Tell your employer to draft us in."

There's a chorus of nods from the guys. They're all on board with my plan. I don't trust Sadie or the people that she represents, but that doesn't mean we can't use her.

"How can I trust that you're safe to be out in the real world?" she asks acidly. "Or that neither you nor Jude will start butchering people? I can't take that risk."

She seems to regret her words immediately, lips parting on an apology that never quite makes it out. I stare, letting her see all of the agony and self-hatred that's been building beneath the surface, choking me to death.

"I can't sleep," I reveal in a harsh whisper.

"Brooke—"

"When I close my eyes, I see their faces. The people he made me hurt." I look away, shame burning my cheeks. "Not even killing Augustus fixed what he did to me. But watching his empire burn to ashes, ensuring nobody will ever go through what we did… that's worth risking it all for."

"You're gambling with your lives," she says grimly.

"And that's our fucking choice. Make the call."

With a curse, Sadie pulls out a basic burner phone. She taps on one of three names in her contacts. The name begins with *H*. Her voice is resigned.

"Wait here. This isn't my decision. If you wind up dead, that's your responsibility. I hope you know what you're doing, Brooke."

I swallow hard. "Yeah, me too."

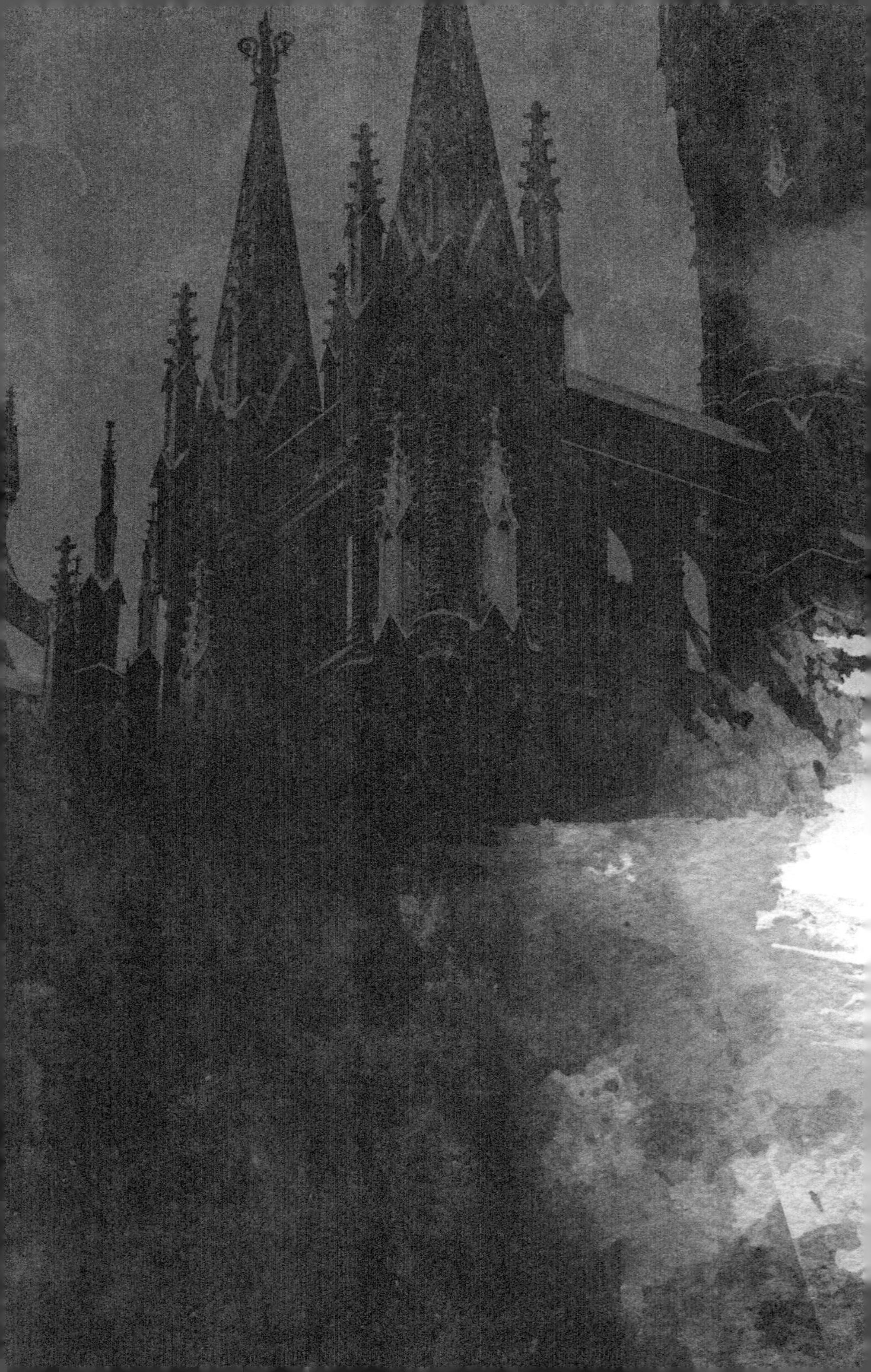

8

ELI

You Are Everything - Holding Absence

Kade and Hudson sit up front in the Jeep, watching Brooklyn yell at Sadie. They're standing outside the second-hand car we picked up on the way out of town.

Seven is sleeping off his vodka-induced hangover in the other car. Phoenix keeps a wary eye from the passenger seat, blowing cigarette smoke out the window.

"We should level with her, she'll understand," Kade insists. "This is the safest option."

Hudson glares daggers at Seven's sleeping form in the back of the car. "She'll kick our asses in the blink of an eye when it comes to that bastard."

"Look at what happened on the supply run. Separating them is just a precaution, in case something goes wrong on the way down south."

Kade's words enrage me, but I swallow it down. Treating Brooklyn differently will further alienate her from the group. She's pulled away from us as it is. Seven was the only one who could talk sense into her last time she had a breakdown. Whether they like it or not, he's part of this now.

"The further she is from that freak, the better," Hudson growls. "We need to keep them apart."

"While we're travelling, I agree it's best to ride separately. But you can't kick him out of her life forever. She needs him too."

"Fuck off, Kade."

"Just saying, brother. Time to face facts."

Hudson exits the car, which rocks from the force of him slamming the door shut. He marches over and stands between the shouting pair, ending the fight with a few brief words. Grabbing Brooklyn by the scruff of her shirt, he drags her back and throws her in.

"Brooke—"

"Shut the hell up," she barks.

Casting me a despairing look, Kade fires the engine and waits for Sadie to pull out onto the main road. Phoenix gives me a three-fingered wave as they pass, leaving us to follow into the fading light.

"Whatever game you're all playing, it's childish," Brooklyn says acerbically. "This is either some bullshit pissing contest or plain jealousy. Both are unnecessary."

"Sadie can handle her brother without your assistance, blackbird."

"Did you put her up to this?"

Hudson draws an invisible halo over his head, attempting to lighten the mood. With a sour look, Brooklyn crosses her arms and stares resolutely out the window. He isn't going to win this fight with her.

We've all been on a knife's edge while preparing to leave the safe, woodland retreat in Northern Scotland. After three weeks of something resembling peace, all too soon we're back in at the deep end, desperately trying not to drown.

"Have you heard from Lucia and Two?" Brooklyn asks.

"They checked in an hour ago, back at the cottage," Kade answers while turning onto the motorway. "They'll be okay. You guys should get some sleep. We have a long drive ahead."

Hudson shakes his head. "I don't feel good about this."

"We have no choice. Can't hide in the woods forever."

"Enough already! Quit being all wise and shit."

Kade suppresses a snort. "Maybe we should've left your miserable ass behind too."

We had no choice but to drive to London. With no passports and the entire country looking for us, flying wasn't an option. I can't help but feel like we're retracing our steps back into the lion's den. The aim of the game is to keep a low profile, pass under the radar and not get killed. *Easy peasy.*

"You good?" Brooklyn breaks the silence.

I ignore her searching gaze, attempting to control my breathing. I'm doing a crappy job of pretending like I'm good with this plan. The world passes in a blur of motion on the busy road, every mile back to civilisation serving to increase my anxiety. I haven't been outside in a decade, even longer than Seven.

"Shut your eyes, Eli," she murmurs. "I've got you. Lay down."

Reluctantly, I rest my head on Brooklyn's shoulder, and she entwines our fingers together. I don't belong in this strange world and want nothing more than to slice, stab, and punch my way out of the limelight, back into the safety of society's trash heap.

We drive through the night, the bleak stars our only companions on this road trip to hell. Kade and Hudson swap over somewhere around Sheffield, not bothering to disturb our tangle of limbs in the back. I don't sleep at all. I'm content to listen to Brooklyn's breathing while trying to keep my shit together.

As the dawn glow spreads across the darkened sky, the fuel light flicks on. Kade lets out a curse. We pull up at a petrol station ten minutes later and Brooklyn unravels herself from me. There are only two other cars—a red truck and a transit van. We study the vehicles, weighing our options.

Kade sighs. "I think it looks quiet enough."

"We're too exposed out here," Hudson argues.

"I agree." He switches off the engine. "But we're out of good options. Help me fill some canisters, then we can avoid stopping again. I'll text Sadie and get her to meet us."

Leaving the brothers to deal with the fuel, Brooklyn climbs out and stretches. We passed Sadie and the others a while back. I can see the worry on her face as she urgently scans the passing road for the other car. Separating the group was a shitty idea in my opinion, made worse by Hudson's insistence on being an asshole.

"Come with me to get food?" she offers.

I stare at her, unblinking.

"We should stick together."

She's right, but that doesn't stop the panic swarming through my limbs. The taste of ashes and battery acid is so intense as it crowds my mind, I nearly double over from the intrusion. The flavours have been calmer for a while, but everything about this situation is triggering me. Old habits die hard.

"I'll be with you the whole time," Brooklyn reassures. "You should ease back into the world, Eli. Hiding won't make it any easier."

Her outstretched hand beckons me. Those storm-cloud eyes are filled with hope that threatens to devastate me worse than any panic attack. Making my numb legs move, I climb out and flip my hood up to cover my face.

"Stick with me," she mutters.

"Okay."

Her grin is worth the pain of speaking aloud. My throat aches from just one word. Brooklyn tows me towards the shop after accepting a stack of cash from Kade. I survey our surroundings, clocking the young couple exiting their truck. Nobody is paying us any attention.

Get a fucking grip, Eli.

Can't be scared of the world forever.

The shop bell dings as we step inside, keeping our heads tucked down. I don't look where I'm going, following the thump of Brooklyn's Chucks. I'm fighting to remain conscious, my lungs constricted tight. She draws to a halt in the snack aisle, cupping my cheek.

"There. Not so hard, was it?"

I offer her a look of pure fear.

"I'm here, Eli. I'll always be here to hold your hand." Brooklyn's smile would bring whole armies to their knees. "Choose your snacks and let's get the hell out of here."

Gulping my terror down, I face the endless rows of crisps, sweets, and junk food. Too many choices. Too many unknowns. I haven't chosen a meal in a fucking decade. It's all too much.

"Salt and vinegar is my favourite," Brooklyn muses.

Dread coats my tongue, tart and bitter. My heart explodes in a frenzied rush, and I smash my fist against my forehead, savouring the sweet release of pain. Her grip on my hand tightens as she watches me unravel.

"Come on, stay with me. You can do this."

"Don't… m-make me…" I stutter.

"You can do this. There's nothing to be afraid of."

"No!"

Cursing under her breath, Brooklyn drags me away from the prying eyes of the cashiers. I'm shoved into a low-lit bathroom out back, the stench of bleach and cheap cleaning products turning my stomach. She slams the door behind us and twists the lock.

Before she can say a single word, my control snaps. The crappy bathroom melts away, lost to the fear that battles to consume me. By the time my vision clears, I have Brooklyn pinned against the tiled wall by her throat, her nails scratching at my hands.

The air between us is electrified as I hold her captive. Vulnerable. Pinned. Mine. Burying my face in the crook of her neck, I let the emotions and flavours wash over me in a deadly tidal wave. She's been my life raft since day one, keeping me afloat as I squeeze the life out of her.

"Fuck you," I croak.

Brooklyn slumps against the wall when I find the willpower to let go. She eyes me warily while rubbing her throat, where red crescents mark my fingertips digging into her.

"I deserved that."

"N-No."

"I fucking forgot you, Eli. I forgot you all," she shouts at me. "It makes me so mad, I can't take it. I don't know what the fuck I'm doing anymore. Nothing makes sense."

I speak the only language I know how. Securing my lips to hers, Brooklyn surrenders herself to me. I'm still furious with her. Myself. The monsters that tore us apart. The world that cast me out and refuses to take me back. The scared, stupid child inside me who can't speak for himself.

Brooklyn groans against my mouth, our tongues violently battling each other. She takes the chance to wrap her legs around my waist, pinned against the bathroom wall by sheer rage alone. I rub my rock-hard cock into her, seeking absolution.

"Talk to me," she pants.

I bite the soft flesh of her neck. "T-Talk?"

"Tell me what you need. I wasn't there. I'm sorry that you had no choice but to isolate yourself from everyone just to survive. I'm sorry that I couldn't hold your broken pieces together."

Tracing my tongue over the dark bruise blooming on her skin, I take a deep inhale of her scent, a combination of all our essences in one. Hudson's musky aftershave. Phoenix's flowery, apple-blossom shampoo. Kade's citrusy deodorant. Even Seven, with his newfound love for freshly ground coffee.

It brings sweet relief, the scents of home she carries, suffused in her skin. Like warm apple pie and fresh linens, the flavours unfurling from the deepest pits of my mind. I've tasted nothing but despair for so long, I forgot what it feels like to belong.

"Please," I whisper, lost for words.

Brooklyn presses her forehead to mine. "Speak, Eli."

Clearing my throat, I summon the spark of courage buried deep in my mind and breathe in the comfort of her scent again, a reminder of family and home that's been lost to me for so long. It gives me the strength to force out the words that have haunted all my years of silence.

One question.

"Tell m-me... how t-to... exist."

I can feel her hot, relentless tears against my cheeks as the boundaries between us melt into insignificance. She's curled around my heart like a cancer, poisoning my cells and twisting my entire persona into something unrecognisable.

"You have to be here with me," she murmurs, lips ghosting over mine. "Live in this moment, no matter how shit it is. Not in that house fire. Not in Blackwood. Here, right now, in this bathroom. Destitute fugitives on the run. Losing our minds and cast out from society. But fuck, we exist."

A hateful laugh breaks free. "H-How?"

Her sigh glides over me, a soothing balm on frayed nerves.

"Like this."

Reaching into the pocket of her leather jacket, she slides a wickedly sharp knife free. The exact same one she used to claim Jefferson's and Augustus's lives. My mouth waters as she studies the blade, holding it in her palms.

"Why?" I struggle out.

"Because you don't have to hide from me or pretend to be something you're not. Hurt yourself, Eli. Cut, bleed, scream and rage, if that's what it takes. Do whatever you need to until you can exist too."

Clasping the knife in shaking hands, I shove my shame and resentment far out of reach. She's seen me, the real me. Time and time again. I don't have to hide the broken parts of myself that need to hurt just to get through the day. Rolling up my sleeve, I expose healed cuts and countless scars.

Her gaze burns a hole into me, but I focus on the pearlescent veins begging to be sliced. My hand is trembling so badly, I can barely hold the blade, let alone press it deep enough to bring relief. The need to laugh bubbles up at the irony of it. Now, I'm the one asking for help, not her.

"Fucking h-hand."

Brooklyn bites her lip. "Been there. Let me."

She takes the knife to my inner arm, below the healed cuts from a few weeks back. The bite of pain follows her precise cutting, dragging the serrated metal over porcelain skin. Brooklyn slices me six times with the precision of a surgeon expunging a deadly infection.

Crushing her lips against mine, she claims my heathen soul while painting her name in blood and sickness. The anxiety gushes out of me with the crimson flow, leaving me weak at the knees. I draw my first easy breath since leaving the safety of the cottage.

"Welcome back," she murmurs. "Better?"

Feeling unsteady, I manage a nod. I'm too busy studying the fascinating artwork painted by my blood. Each trail drips on the bleached floor, blooming red against dirty white. The need is still there. More. I'll always want to cross that line just one more time, no matter the risk.

"We should go. The others will be worried."

Rinsing the knife off in the sink, Brooklyn slips it back inside her pocket. My fingers twitch with the urge to steal it from her, sink the tip deep into my wrist and slice my way far from this place. Even if that means leaving her, Phoenix, and my whole family behind. The temptation is so strong.

"W-Wait—"

She stares, unnerved by the sound of my voice.

"Thank y-you," I rush out.

"You don't need to thank me."

I bury my fingers in her short locks, exposing her lips to me again. I can't get enough of her, ravenous and unable to control myself. Brooklyn melts into me like ice cream on a summer's day. I bend her over the small, built-in sink, regardless of the guys waiting for us.

"Eli—"

Her protests are silenced as I peel her jeans and panties down, enough to expose her bare ass. My fingers find the slick heat gathered between her thighs. She can't pretend she isn't turned on right now.

"We don't have time."

Pressing her lower back to position her, I race to undo my belt. I don't give a fuck where we are. I need to be inside of her before I lose my mind. She's the only thing that brings me back from the edge. Her words dissolve into breathy sighs as I push inside of her.

Brooklyn's hands grip the sink. She's so goddamn tight and wet, even with minimal prep. I surge in and out of her with impatience, each stroke forcing the demons in my head to retreat. I need more. With every second, breathing becomes easier, and the world grows more bearable.

I don't stop even as there's a loud knock on the door. Desire and panic clash, serving to speed up my frantic thrusting. Brooklyn finds her knife, holding it at the ready as someone pounds on the wood again.

"Who is it?" she yells.

"Get your asses out of there, kids. This ain't a damn brothel!"

Before she can answer, I wrap my hand back around her throat from behind. She squeaks before falling silent. I'm so close to the edge. This is the first time I've fucked her in months, and I can't control myself like I usually would. She's taken over, leaving me to trail in her blaze of glory.

When I finish, Brooklyn lets out a groan of sheer bliss. I release her throat so she can suck in air, fighting to catch her breath. Her walls clench around me as I ride the relentless waves of my release.

"Jesus, Eli. Talk about bad timing."

Fighting a laugh, I reluctantly slide out of her and grab a handful of toilet tissue. Brooklyn turns and blanches when she sees what I'm doing. Her cheeks are stained red with embarrassment when I bring the tissues between her legs, cleaning up the mess I've left behind.

We both find intimacy terrifying.

That's exactly why I'm doing this.

Flushing the toilet, I tug my jeans back up and fasten my belt. Brooklyn's avoiding looking at me while straightening herself out. Before she can unlock the door, I snatch her hand. Her fierce grey eyes scrape over me with uncertainty.

We're still trapped in the safe bubble that allowed our darkness to unfurl, but the terror of reality is knocking on the door. We can't stay in this moment forever, even if we want to. Digging deep, I clear my throat.

"Baby g-girl… I l-love… you."

Brooklyn's mouth splits in a grin of devastating pride. My throat hurts like hell, but for the first time, I don't feel anxious when speaking. I'm not afraid of her. She's my safe haven. I catch the stray tear that tracks down her cheek, a precious pearl of pure emotion. It tastes salty on my tongue.

"Fuck, Eli. I love you so goddamn much."

I let her drag me back out into the world, this time keeping my hood back and my head held high without fear. I have nothing to be afraid of with Brooklyn by my side.

I can face the world.

I'm not alone anymore.

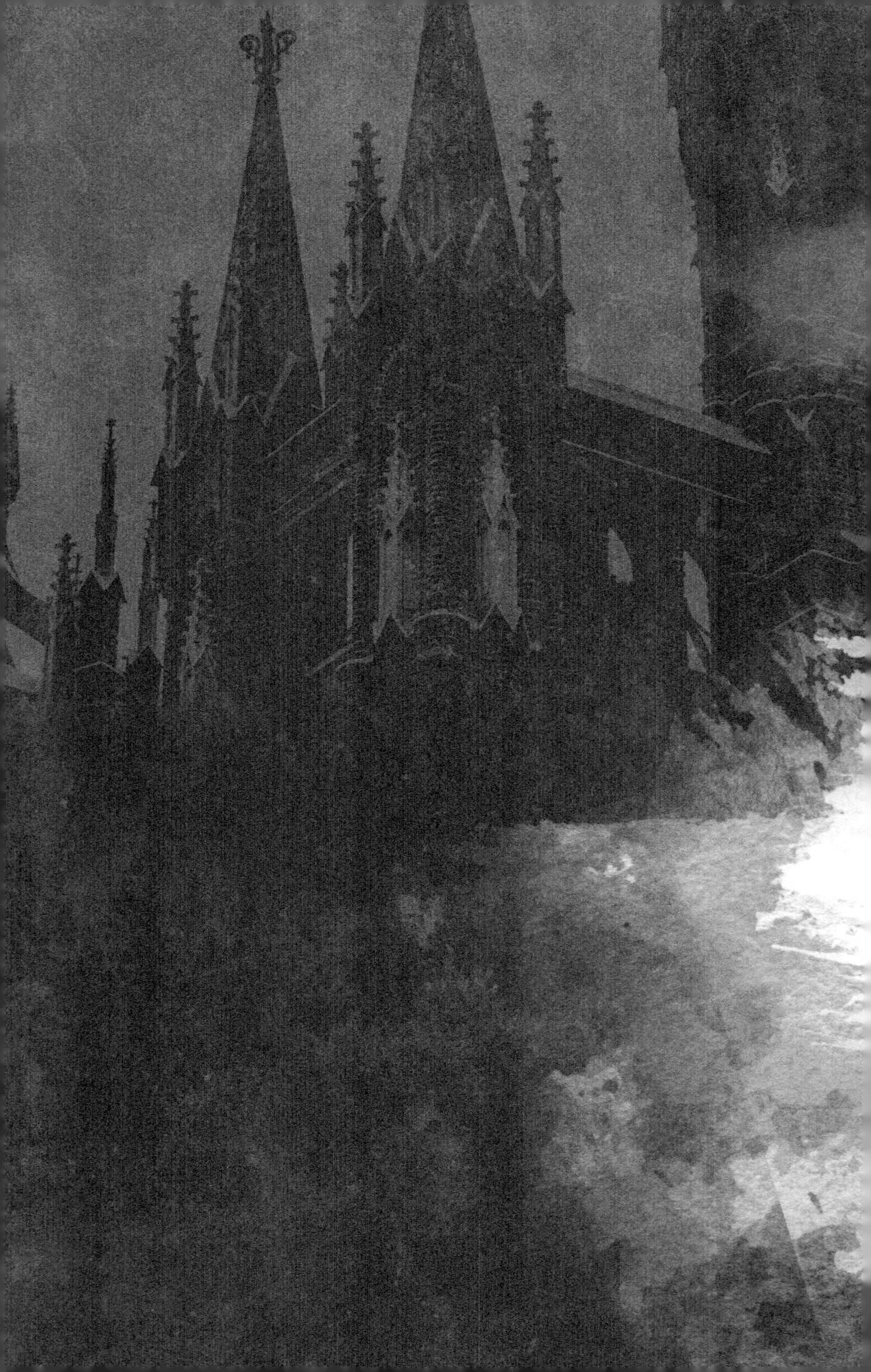

9

BROOKLYN

PSYCHO - Aviva

Sticking close to Sadie's car, we pass through the outskirts of London. The roads are packed with weekend traffic, shoppers and tourists going about their business. I desperately drink it all in. Every last face, smiling and laughing, enjoying the last of the summer sun.

"Where is she taking us?" Hudson grumbles.

Kade checks the rearview mirror for a fifth time. "I have no idea."

"Are we meeting her team soon?" I ask instead.

"Maybe. I think we can trust her. She wants the same thing as us."

Hudson snorts. "What is that exactly?"

"To see Incendia burn," Kade answers solemnly.

Leaning between their seats, I watch Sadie's car. Seven must be lying down in the back, probably still asleep. Phoenix appears to be smoking and chattering away while Sadie drives. The separation from my men is killing me—Seven fucking included.

"I only trust our family, nobody else," Hudson says. "First sign that something's off, we're getting the hell out of here."

I sit back in my seat. "Seconded."

He looks over his shoulder to shoot me a possessive grin. It's rare that we agree these days, but I'm far from comfortable endangering our family. Nothing about this situation is controllable or safe. We've only just discovered freedom; I won't go back to living our lives in a prison.

"Relax, Brooke. You trust me?" Kade smiles.

"Trusting you isn't the problem."

We don't speak again until nearly an hour later, when Sadie turns off the busier central streets and heads into London's seedy underbelly. Passing through an industrial area, the roads are paved with cracked concrete and shadowed by abandoned warehouses. There are no signs of life.

She parks outside a deserted, faded blue warehouse that looks tightly sealed from the outside. There isn't another soul on the street, far from the nearest suburb. Kade pulls up and I'm flying out of the car before it even stops, itching to set eyes on Phoenix and Seven.

"Any problems?"

Sadie stretches her arms above her head. "Of course not."

The car door opens before I can get to it. Seven slides out, stretching his long legs and surveying the street. His shoulder-length brown hair is mussed and tangled from sleep, framing attentive eyes and lips that are pressed together. Every inch of his body is pulled taut with tension.

"Sev?"

His hand grasps mine on instinct. "Princess."

"You good?"

"Just haven't been outside in a while, that's all."

I squeeze his hand before releasing, preparing for the incoming blur of motion. I'm scooped into Phoenix's arms and spun around so fast

I think I may throw up. When he puts me back on my feet, I balance myself on his broad shoulders.

"Was that really necessary?"

"It was a long drive, firecracker. Did the chatterbox keep you company?"

Eli's hand appears out of nowhere to whack him around the head. Phoenix plasters on an innocent smile, dragging him close. I'm sandwiched between the two of them with zero complaints, fascinated by the sight of them kissing in front of our entire group. It's intoxicating.

"Can we save the public orgy for another time?" Hudson grunts.

I meet his icy blue eyes. "Jealous?"

"You're playing with fire, blackbird."

"My favourite. Care to join us?"

Hudson hesitates. "Perhaps."

Sadie unlocks the rusted grate that covers the entrance to the warehouse. The scream of old metal makes us all wince. She drags it up, exposing multiple heavy-duty padlocks across the entrance. After unlocking each one, she disappears inside and indicates for us to follow. With a final look around, we all step into the darkness.

Inside, the scent of mould and decay has me gagging. Kade shines the light on his phone to guide our steps deeper into the disused warehouse. It looks like an old workshop, with the burned-out remains of a car at the very centre, surrounded by countless tools and broken machines.

"Sadie? What is this place?" I call out.

Pulling a squeaky lever built into the cinderblock wall, gloomy yellow lights slam on. Sadie faces the group, barely sparing her surroundings a glance. She looks far from happy to be here.

"Home."

The warehouse is split into two levels, with the workshop on the ground floor hiding a grubby break area behind a thick, plastic sheet.

Two sofas are pushed up against the walls, with old, peeling movie posters from a time long gone. A metal staircase leads upwards to a mezzanine level, the floor constructed from metal sheets and lit by bare filament bulbs.

"There's a bedroom of sorts upstairs, bathroom too. It's dirty and basic, but it'll do." Sadie grabs a new duffel bag from a locker. "You need to stay alert. London is too exposed."

"What do you mean, home?" Seven asks angrily.

Sadie doesn't even look at him, rifling through the bag of old clothing. When she pulls a gun from the locker, everyone tenses. She checks the chamber and tucks it into her waistband.

"I lived here for a few years," she admits. "Dad owned the workshop before he died. I should've sold it, but I couldn't bring myself to do it. When Grandma died, I had nowhere else to go."

Seven stands frozen, his entire, furious posture carved from marble. A thunderous expression is written across his face, but I can see the truth in his eyes. Guilt. When he tries to lay a hand on Sadie's shoulder, she flinches.

"I'm not going to hurt you," he utters in disbelief.

"I didn't mean… that's not…" Her gaze falls to her hands. "I'm sorry, Ju— I mean, Seven. I get this is hard for you. I didn't expect things to pan out like this either."

"You didn't think you'd find me alive, you mean."

"Something like that."

"Would you rather I was dead?" he hedges.

Nervously smoothing her bright-pink hair, Sadie looks unnerved by his question. She doesn't deny it, still focusing on her feet instead. Seven waits for a few awkward seconds before stalking off. He slams through the plastic sheet to escape into the break room.

"What about you?" Kade studies the warehouse.

Sadie shakes herself out of it, throwing the duffel bag on a nearby table and scraping her hair back. "I have to get to Harrowdean by Monday. They're expecting me. I'll keep in touch on the burner phone."

"When will your employer contact us?"

"When he's ready to," she says ominously.

"We need a bit more to go on than that."

An echoing rattle cuts off our conversation. Hudson and Kade both pull guns they kept after our escape, while I palm my knife. Phoenix follows suit, holding his own knife at the ready. We all stand prone as footsteps near.

The tension explodes when a figure emerges through the gloom. Standing with obvious trepidation, the man has a head full of tight, dirty-blonde ringlets that hang messily across his face. Piercing blue eyes several shades lighter than Hudson's scour over us, hidden behind wire-rimmed glasses. His bottom lip is caught between his teeth.

"Theo," Sadie gasps. "What are you doing here?"

His eyes land on her, guarded expression transforming into one of sheer happiness. Adjusting his dark flannel shirt and denim jacket, he prepares for incoming as Sadie runs at full speed. I don't miss the way Hudson and Kade keep their weapons raised.

"Long time, no see." Theo laughs. "I had to see you."

Embracing him, we all gape as Sadie secures their lips together. The pair exchange a blistering kiss despite their audience. When Kade pointedly clears his throat, they finally jump apart.

"Come on, I'll introduce you." Sadie drags him to our circle, shooting us a deliberate look of warning. "Everyone, this is Theodore. He's a… uh. Well. A co-worker, shall we say."

His smile is extremely awkward. "Nice to meet you all."

"Who exactly are you?" Hudson tucks his gun away.

"Um, Theo. I'm… tech support?"

"Tech support?" I repeat incredulously. "You don't sound so sure."

Theo clears his throat. "Among other things. I'm the techie."

He releases Sadie's hand and pulls a heavy backpack from his shoulders. We follow him to a table, remaining at a wary distance. Reaching inside his packed bag, Theo slides a laptop free, along with a zippered pouch. He casts Sadie a smile before tipping the contents out.

"It's all here for you, like we discussed. Figured I'd hand deliver it."

I gape at the pristine fake passport and ID that Sadie looks over, along with other forged documents that will grant her a whole new persona. She slowly checks the items, nodding her approval. Theo relaxes a little, his entire body geared towards her.

"Other things like forgery?" Kade enquires, his gun lowered for now.

Theo nods. "Perhaps."

"He's the best around." Sadie stuffs the items into her duffel bag. "Theo joined the team around the same time as me. Three years ago. He's the gearhead of the operation."

"What precisely does this team do?"

"You haven't told them?" Theo frowns.

Sadie avoids his gaze. "I thought I'd leave it to Hunter."

"They need to be debriefed before then."

Theo opens his laptop, and his fingers fly in a blur of movement, even faster than Kade's impressive speed. When he turns the screen to face us, we study a terrifying slab of architecture. Carved from huge steel beams and slices of solid, tinted glass, the building is truly huge. I'm certain I've seen it in the news or on TV.

"I work for Sabre. We both do."

The name is unfamiliar, but judging by Kade's sharp intake of breath, it's a big deal. Theo rubs the back of his neck, flustered from all the attention on him. I get the impression he doesn't step into fieldwork that often.

"The private security firm?" Hudson guesses.

"My employer and his business partner started it seven years ago," Theo answers. "We're now one of the biggest security firms in England. We take on the most challenging cases. Serial killers, assassinations, corruption, conspiracies. You name it."

"Conspiracies like Blackwood?" I suggest.

Theo spares me a curious look. "Sometimes."

"Where do you fit into all of this?" Kade directs to Sadie.

"I was investigating alone," Sadie says reluctantly. "I got sloppy and ended up in hot water. Hunter's team found me. They took me in, trained me, gave me the chance to do things the right way. To find justice for"—she glances at the back room where Seven fled—"everything."

Theo takes her hand and squeezes it, the pair sharing small smiles. My brain is struggling to keep up with this latest development. First, we learn that Sadie's not only a double agent, but a mole inside of Blackwood via this mysterious firm. Now she's screwing one of them? *Colour me confused.*

"I hear you're meeting a dark-web contact?" Theo asks, anxiously fiddling with his shirt sleeve.

Kade nods, itching to pick the techie's brain.

"Can I take a look at your firewalls, make sure it's safe? I've had some dealings with online crooks."

"Sure," Kade agrees enthusiastically.

Theo beckons him over. They begin exchanging far too many overcomplicated words for me to keep up with. I bypass Sadie and head out back to where Seven disappeared. Beyond the thick, plastic sheet lies another low-lit room.

This one is a makeshift kitchen filled with several stained lunch tables. Seven's lanky, scar-strewn body is hunched over at one. He's breathing hard, a fine tremble seeming to run over him. I approach with tentative steps.

"Sev?"

"Go away, princess. I'm in no mood to talk."

I collapse on the bench seat next to him, bumping our shoulders together. "Come on, don't shut me out. We've played that game before."

"You're stubborn, aren't you?"

I scoff. "Are you only just realising that?"

Lifting his head, golden-caramel eyes pierce my skin. He has this unique ability to slip deep into my veins and poison my thoughts. There's barely a breath between us and the air is charged with sudden anticipation. Seven licks his lips, watching me intently.

When he dares to brush the back of his knuckles against my cheek, a tiny sigh of pleasure escapes my lips. His dark smile widens. I should be ashamed, but I'm quivering with need at his touch. I want more.

"Sadie—"

"I don't want to talk about her," he snaps.

"What do you want to talk about?"

"Are you screwing all four of them?"

His question takes me aback. I feel the instinctive need to hide my unusual relationship with the guys. Love is weakness, but I don't need to protect them from Seven. He isn't the enemy, even if he seems like it at times.

"Yeah, I am."

"And they're okay with that?"

"Depends who you ask."

His thumb glides over my bottom lip, tender and gentle. This person is unlike the violent monster that lives within his human shell, a terrifying beast that matches my own. I bury the urge to bite his finger, knowing it will only encourage this thing growing between us.

There's something burning low in my belly, a carnal need I can't ignore. It's been there for a while, smouldering into a roaring inferno. I just wasn't ready to acknowledge it until now.

"What if I told you that I can't stop thinking about kissing you?" Seven's voice is dangerously soft. "Every time I close my eyes, I picture myself tracing every last mark on your body with my tongue, and making you fall apart with my cock buried deep inside of you."

Clenching my thighs, I fight to take an even breath.

"I'll have you screaming my name for the world to hear," he adds darkly.

"Which name?"

Seven grins, full of promise. "My name isn't Jude anymore."

"Then I'd happily scream for you and the whole world to hear, Sev."

"Even your boyfriends?"

Narrowing my eyes, I level a challenge. "Even them."

With the sound of voices playing behind the plastic sheet, this isn't the moment to delve into things. But as I inhale Seven's scent, still unfamiliar after all our time spent separated in the basement, I struggle to maintain my grip on the situation. I shouldn't, but I want him. Just like I want all of them.

"This is a bad idea," I breathe.

"Most definitely."

"Someone will get hurt."

Seven smirks. "I'll do all the hurting. You'd look better naked and stained with fresh blood when we fuck, princess."

"I've warned you about killing the guys approximately nine times now."

His little eye roll makes my heart flip, the traitorous organ. Cupping my cheek, Seven strokes my skin, and I try to remember every reason why I can't do this. None of them stop me from staring into his pained eyes, begging him to take the final step that I'm too cowardly to make myself.

"I don't care what you want. I'll kill them and take you for myself," he warns.

"Then we're going to have a problem, aren't we?"

"Even better."

Closing the gap between us, the lightest brush of lips has me combusting from sexual tension. It's all I need to grab hold of Seven's shoulders and crush my mouth against his, stealing the kiss I've long dreamed of. His tongue seeks access that I quickly grant.

We dissolve into a frenzy. He's devouring me like we could be dragged apart at any moment. I can taste the coffee he's developed an obsession with on his tongue. When his hand sneaks beneath my shirt to stroke the underside of my braless breasts, I gasp against his lips.

"Brooke? You good back there?" Phoenix calls.

I break the kiss. "Yeah… all good!"

Retreating footsteps slow my panicked heartbeat. I sigh with relief, looking up to find Seven glaring at me. He quickly grabs my wrist so tight, I yelp. He's grinding the bones together. The softness in him has dissipated, replaced with animalistic rage.

"Are you ashamed of me?"

"No, of course not."

"You think I won't break the necks of your men if that's what it takes to have you? I'll kill them, Eight. One by one. You can watch as I choke the life from their broken corpses. Will you still yearn for me then?"

Before Seven can react, I slam my fist into his face. He topples off the bench, spitting blood from his split lip. Advancing without mercy, I straddle his body and punch him again. The sight of his blood spreading across the floor has my entire body humming with satisfaction.

"You don't have to kill your way through life, Sev! There are people who care about you. I care about you. But nobody threatens the lives of those I love, not even you."

"You kissed me," he accuses.

"You kissed me first!"

Dipping a finger in his warm, slick blood, I draw it across my lips until I'm coated in his vitality. Claimed. Tainted. Owned. His blood sinks beneath my skin and ties our souls together with an unbreakable bond forged in the darkest depths of Augustus's basement.

Seven watches with wide eyes. I resist licking my lips, leaning in to press them against his. Grabbing handfuls of his untameable hair, I tug until he hisses with pain. His hand wraps around my throat, caressing my vein, ready and ripe for the taking.

"Do it," I command. "I dare you."

"If I kill you, I will never know what your pussy tastes like."

He releases his grip on my throat and shoves me aside. I roll and manage to find my feet, preparing for a blow that never comes. Seven stares at me like I'm a puzzle he can't fathom, confusion marked across his expression. He wipes his lips before fleeing the room like his life depends on it.

"Sev, wait!"

He ignores me and disappears back under the plastic sheet. I'm left alone, gaping at the blood-stained place where he laid, wondering how the fuck I'm going to convince four men that barely manage to share, to add a fifth.

That, or Seven kills them.

Blackwood was fucking simpler than this.

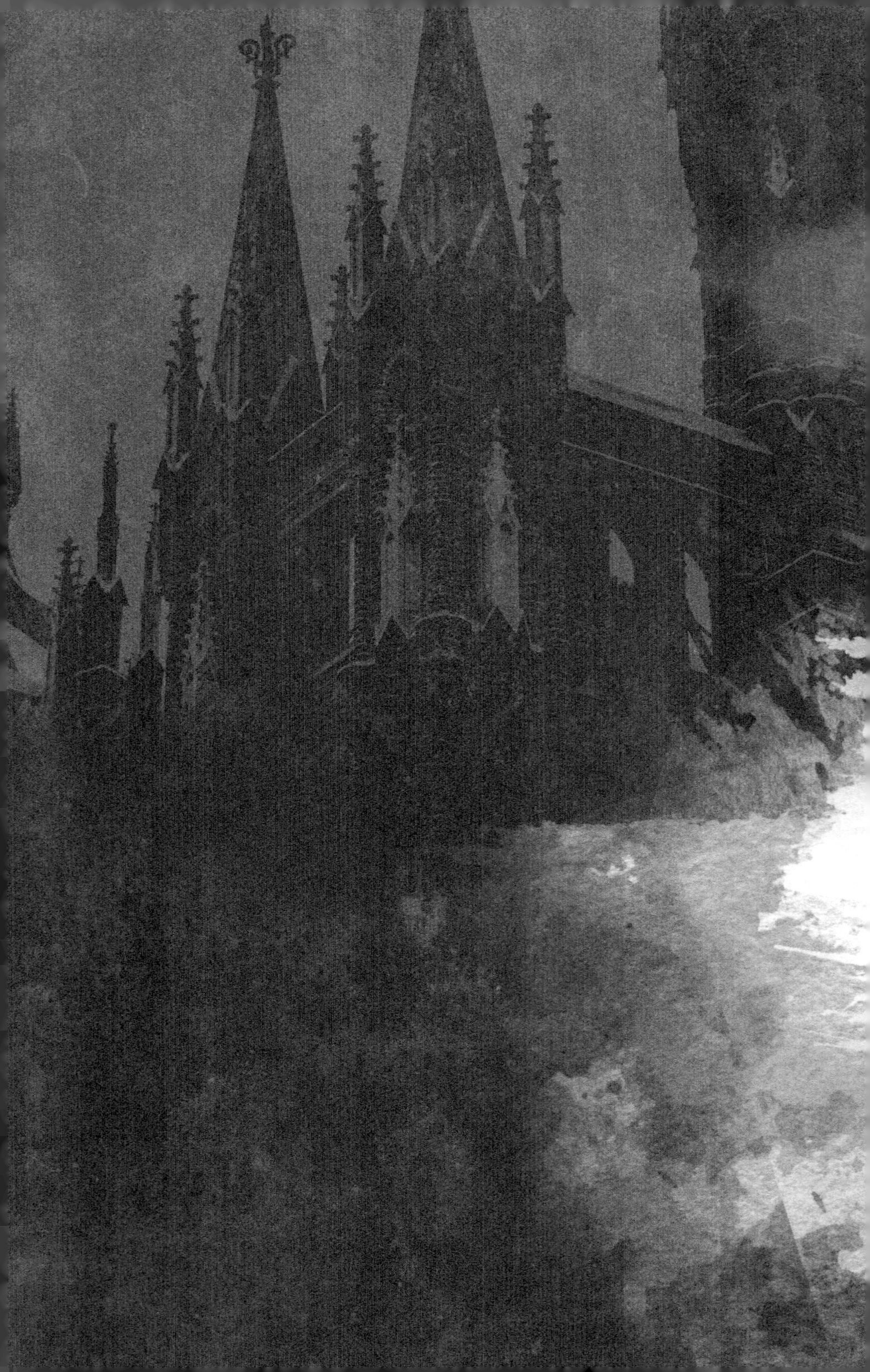

10

BROOKLYN

Lost - Ollie

The sand is soft beneath my feet, grains of cheap amusement for the child version of me sitting several metres away. With white-blonde hair scraped up into pigtails, my dad scoops her up before spinning her around in a circle.

"Brooooke! The best princess in the realm."

"Daddy, stop!" she screams.

"Ready to go in the water? Let's wake up Mummy, come on."

I hug myself tight while watching my dad leading child-me back up the beach, where an umbrella has been hammered into the sand. Mum's staring up at the cloudless sky with a blank expression, lost in her thoughts. My mouth dries up when I see who sits next to her.

He's far younger than I remember him, his blonde hair short and well-trimmed. He grew a ponytail later in his rebellious youth. With a bright smile and dimples, the sight of my brother makes my heart seize with agony.

"Who's ready to go for a swim?" Dad cheers.

Logan shoves the rest of his ice cream in his mouth. "Me, me, me!"

Ruffling his hair, Dad kneels beside Mum and gives her a shake. "Mel? You okay?"

"Yes, of course."

Reaching into his backpack, Dad retrieves a camera and starts rolling. Mum forces herself to stand, wiping the dark shadows from her face. By the time he turns the lens on us, she's cuddling child-me from behind, tugging on my platinum pigtails.

"Smile for the camera! Show us your big teeth."

The words have me clutching my head, the awful reminder threatening to tear me to shreds. I watch the memory play out, trapped behind an invisible barrier. It's the exact same one that Augustus threw in my face in the dungeon, using it to break my remaining sanity down to its last atom.

"My beautiful wife." Dad sighs happily.

"Don't get all soppy on me now, Ian. Come on, let's take her to the sea."

I scream through the hands I have clenched over my mouth. Watching from afar, Logan films them skipping through the sand, swinging child-me between them. Seeing it from this angle reopens the festering wounds that want nothing more than to rip me open.

"Brooke?"

Glancing up, I find the younger version of Logan looking right at me. I've infected this happy memory with the inevitability of the future, and he's staring with accusations buried in his grey irises.

"You shouldn't be here, kiddo. I told you to forget, move on."

"I c-can't. Every time I close my eyes, I see you."

Thick trails of blood begin to weep from his eyes, gushing down his cheeks and staining the white sand beneath his feet. Logan becomes a grotesque painting of human suffering. I rush to help him, but my hands pass through his body like they're parting shadows, unable to grab hold of something that *doesn't exist.*

"*Devil child. You're next, Brooke.*"

Her voice sends a chill down my spine. Mum now stands mere inches away. At her feet, two twisted and broken bodies lay, no longer smiling as they enjoy the seaside. Dad's neck is cracked and misshapen, while bloodied handprints mark the strangled throat of my childhood self.

"*Blackwood is inevitable. Return or face the consequences.*"

"*No! I can't go back. Not now, not ever.*"

Her lips brush my ear, laced with the stench of rotting flesh. "*You're nothing more than a monster, Brooke. A lying, remorseless murderer. Exactly what I birthed you to be.*"

Letting out a bloodcurdling scream, the last thing I see is her cruel gaze burning my insides, an undeniable figment of the inevitable. She is my past, my present, and my future.

I'll never be anything more than a child of insanity.

A child… of Blackwood.

—

Lighting the cigarette with trembling hands, I blow smoke out. The cold workshop beneath me is silent as the rest of the guys sleep. I made sure to swallow my screams rather than wake everyone up.

Still kidding yourself, Miss West?

Gulping hard, I stare resolutely ahead. I won't entertain the smirking, shadowy version of Augustus lingering behind me.

Can't outrun your own mind.

Our work isn't done yet.

"You're fucking dead," I whisper.

As you will be too.

This path only ends one way.

You can never live a normal life.

"I'm doing a hell of a lot better than you. The guys got me out. I have a chance with them."

Still looking for a family, are you?

They'll die soon enough.

You're poison. Just ask Vic.

"Enough! Get out of my head!"

Phoenix groans in his sleep, startled by my voice. Crushing the cigarette, I silently curse. He's spooning Eli from behind as they both sleep on the threadbare mattress that fills the mezzanine level.

Glancing around with my breath held, I find Augustus's snarky ghost gone. Thank fuck for that. I don't want the guys to know I'm still hallucinating. They worry enough as it is.

Dressing in a loose, acid-wash t-shirt from my backpack and a pair of old blue jeans, I sneak back down the wobbly stairs. Hudson and Seven are both still out of it, opting to take the two downstairs sofas. I quietly sneak past and slip into the break room.

"Morning, love."

Nearly jumping out of my skin, I find a bedraggled Kade working on his laptop at a table. He eyes me with his glasses tucked up in his shaggy, overgrown blonde hair, a steaming mug of coffee in his hand.

"You're awake?"

He shrugs. "Evidently, so are you."

"Couldn't sleep."

"More bad dreams? I didn't hear you."

I make a non-committal noise, peering into the coffee pot before deciding to brave a cup of sludge. My head feels like it's ready to explode and the sun isn't even up. Grabbing a stale granola bar from the cupboard, I pad up to Kade.

His arms wrap around me as I deposit myself in his lap. He smells like the cheap shampoo we found in Sadie's basic bathroom, complete with a camping shower and cracked mirror. I can't help but stroke his messy hair. He looks so different from the slick, polished man I once met.

"Have you heard from the girls yet?"

"They're fine. You didn't answer my question. Bad dream?"

"Nope," I mutter. "Not going there."

Closing his laptop with a sigh, Kade grips my chin. I'm unable to look away from him and the demands brewing in his hazel eyes. Our lips brush in a brief, tender whisper.

"You can talk to me," he urges. "I know I don't understand what you went through like Seven or Hudson do, but that doesn't mean I'm not here for you. We all are."

"I know."

"Do you?" Kade kisses the corner of my mouth.

When he pulls away, I gulp down some crappy coffee to buy some time. I'm wrestling with my ingrained need to hide from him. All I've done since the day we met is run at full speed, away from intimacy, emotions, everything. I'm not that person anymore, but her claws are still buried deep.

"Lazlo treated my mother a long time ago," I finally say.

Kade stills. "Professor Lazlo? In Blackwood?"

"She had her first admission after giving birth to my brother, then another when we were young."

"Fuck, Brooke. Why didn't you tell us?"

I squeeze my eyes shut. "He broke her, Kade. Blackwood is the reason she lost her mind. That's why she murdered Logan and crashed the car. Incendia is the reason my entire family is dead."

Kade's soft fingertips glide over my cheeks, wiping the traitorous moisture away. Beneath the shampoo, I can smell his familiar, squeaky-clean scent. Everything about him is solid, steadying. I can trust him with this secret.

"We'll make them pay," Kade proclaims. "I swear on my life, they will all burn for what they've done to us. We won't rest until Incendia is dead and buried in the ground."

"It won't bring them back," I whisper roughly.

"Open your eyes, Brooke."

I shake my head. "I can't."

"It's just us. Let me see those beautiful eyes."

Forcing myself to obey, I meet Kade's kind, loving gaze. Even after all the pain he's endured for us, goodness still shines within him. He replaces his glasses, his expression steeling with determination.

"Nothing will bring your family back. But the family you have now? Nobody will ever take it away from you."

"You promise?"

"I promise. Always and forever."

I roll my eyes. "Did Hudson give you that line?"

"What? It's probably the most poetic shit he's ever come out with."

My mouth is magnetised back to his. I drink in the pure, unshakeable essence of Kade. Our protector and leader, the man who secured our family's freedom from those who tore us apart. As long as we have him by our side, I know we'll always be safe. I can't protect those I love from the demons of this world alone.

"Are we ready for tonight?" I sigh.

"As ready as we'll ever be. The contact wants to meet us at ten o'clock. I've got the location scouted out. Once we've exchanged information, we'll get out of here. I still owe you that breakfast date."

The thought of our warm, cosy cottage in the middle of nowhere makes my heart sigh with happiness. It was a slice of peace and calm amongst the carnage of our lives. I'm ready to run away all over again.

"I'll hold you to it, mister."

His smile is infectious, warming the fabric of my dead soul. "You got it, love. I'm a man of my word. When the dust settles and Incendia is no more, I intend to spend every second of my life proving that to you."

"I think I can live with that."

Sharing another lingering kiss that leaves me breathless, we break apart when Sadie and Theo emerge from the locker room. They slept there for the night, and I definitely heard them hooking up when they thought we were all asleep. Her cheeks are flushed, their hands linked as they enter the kitchen.

"Morning campers," she chirps.

I climb off Kade's lap. "Ouch, Clearview flashback."

Sadie sticks her tongue out at me. "I was an excellent counsellor. I have no idea what you mean. No one else let you raid the vending machine before group therapy."

"To buy our cooperation, I'm sure."

"It worked though, didn't it?"

Theo listens to our conversation while fixing two mugs of coffee. He blushes when our eyes connect for a brief second. He's got some major social anxiety going on, but I can't help but like him in an odd sort of way. Wearing another flannel shirt, this one covers a vintage superhero t-shirt.

"When are you two planning to leave?" Kade queries.

Taking seats on the opposite side of us, Theo opens his laptop and sets to work. He pushes his silver, wire-rimmed glasses up his nose when they slip down. I have enough men in my life, but even I can admit he's adorable.

"Alyssa will enter Harrowdean tomorrow. I'll be returning to HQ to report back. We'll be in touch. Hunter will want to meet you all and obtain your evidence."

"Alyssa?" I splutter.

Theo's face pales. "I, ah… um. I didn't say that."

Kade exchanges a look with me. "You definitely did."

Sadie glowers at Theo, causing him to blush even harder. He looks like a literal beetroot, hiding behind his laptop for safety. You wouldn't believe this skinny, timid geek works for a huge security firm.

"Your name is Alyssa?"

"I really didn't mean to let that slip," Theo curses.

Punching him on the arm, Sadie returns her attention to her phone, dismissing the conversation. Kade subtly shakes his head, ordering me to drop it. We've all had to make sacrifices in order to survive. Her life has been put on hold too, I suppose.

"When are we meeting the infamous Hunter and his team?"

Theo meets Kade's eyes. "He will dictate that. You'll be contacted."

"You're not going to tell us anything? Seriously?"

"Classified, I'm afraid. Keep your heads down and eyes open, that's my advice. This contact appears to be on your side, but loyalties change. Good people don't sell information for no reason."

"We're capable of taking care of ourselves," Kade defends hotly.

"More than you pretentious assholes know," I add.

Theo winces. "This is why I don't do fieldwork, for Christ's sake. I need to report to the bossman." Scooping up his laptop, he flees the room before we can pry him with more hard questions.

"Sabre is on your side." Sadie grabs her own stale breakfast from the cupboard. "You'll see. Hunter's going to kill me for not sticking around to see them all."

I grab her arm before she can pass, hit by a wave of anger so strong, it feels like my insides are on fire. Her eyebrows raise and I squeeze until she's wincing in pain, fighting to break my grip.

"You knew, all along."

"What the hell are you talking about, Brooke?"

"All those months in Blackwood, you pretended like you had no idea what was happening. Dropping your hints and lecturing me about breaking the rules, when all along, you knew what was happening."

"I didn't know for sure." Sadie manages to wrench her arm free. "I was searching for answers, like you. If I'd known the truth, do you really think I would've left you at Augustus's mercy? Do you think that little of me?"

I level her with a challenging stare. "You've given no evidence to the contrary. We didn't even know your real name until now. I thought you were my friend."

"It isn't that simple and you know it," she hits back. "You love to stand on your pedestal, but the truth is, there's only one person in this room who deserved to be in Blackwood. Look in the fucking mirror, Brooke."

Sadie doesn't flinch when I slap her across the face. I can't stop myself. A bright-red handprint blooms on her cheek. She touches the marked skin with her fingertips, lips parted in disbelief.

"You once told me that no matter what the newspapers print, I'm not a monster." I fight back tears that she doesn't deserve. "Thank you for being another disappointment. I'm sure your dead parents are proud of what their kids became."

Sadie slams her coffee cup down so hard, it shatters and breaks into pathetic pieces. Kade watches us both with trepidation. I wonder if she'll hit me, and whether I'll actually enjoy the punishment.

"Fuck you, Brooklyn. You and Seven deserve each other. My brother died in that place, and so did the girl I used to be friends with."

"We're still alive! You need to let go of who you thought we were."

"I'm not the problem here. When this is over, I never want to see either of you again."

Her declaration lashes me like the strike of a whip. I can see the pain in her eyes, but Sadie doesn't take it back. I've pushed her too far this time.

"You got that?"

"With pleasure," I hiss back.

Sadie freezes when she realises we're not alone. In the plastic-covered doorway that Theo fled through, Seven stands with an open wound of grief on his face. Golden eyes filled with so much pain watch his sister.

"Jude—"

"You're right," he interrupts in a deep, dangerous voice. "That person did die, long before you bothered to look for me. Feel free to leave, sister. I have a real family here."

"That's it?"

"That's it," he confirms. "We don't need you."

Wiping her wet cheeks with the back of her sleeve, Sadie strides from the room without another word. I can hear her yelling at Theo to get his things. In a matter of minutes, the sound of the grate lifting fills the warehouse, followed by silence. None of us know quite what to say in the wake of their departure.

"I'm sorry, Sev," I offer.

He simply shakes his head. "She doesn't see me, just the person she lost. I can't be her ghost. Not anymore. I have to live as well."

With that pearl of wisdom, Seven storms off too.

"Jesus Christ." Kade sighs.

My thoughts precisely.

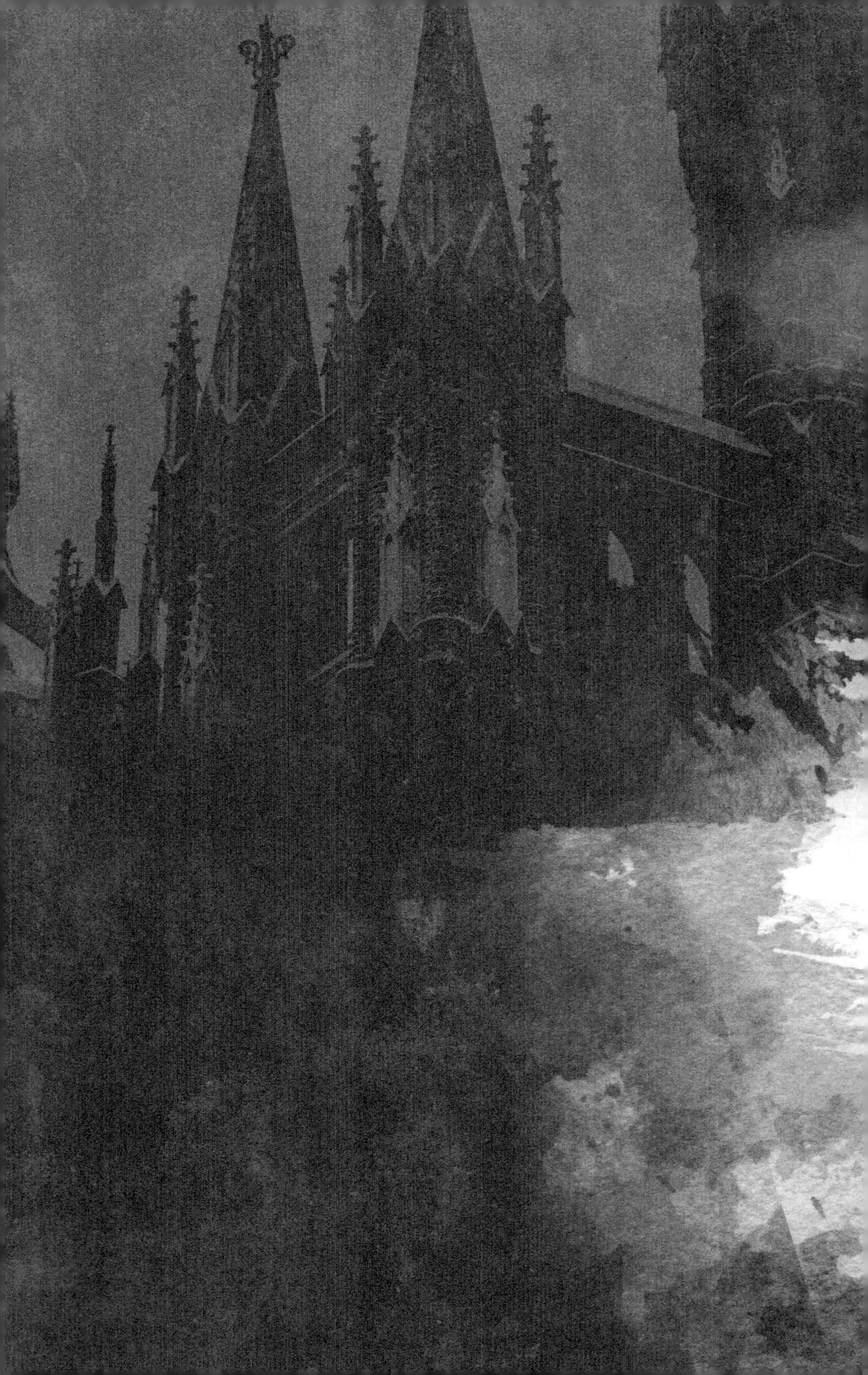

11

HUDSON

Kerosene - Vanish

With my arm tucked around Brooklyn's waist, we join the queue outside the bustling nightclub. Bright neon lights and thumping bass music fill the street, with a winding trail of bodies waiting to be admitted into its sweaty depths.

After trekking across London, armed and debriefed by dictator Kade, I feel like we're about to walk into the jaws of death. Every face I spot looks like a potential threat. Incendia could be anywhere. Anyone. We're just sitting ducks waiting to be taken out here.

"I don't like this one bit," I grumble.

Brooklyn peers up at me through thick eyelashes, pouting her red-painted lips. Her short hair is messily tousled, paired with a black tank that shows off her cleavage, ripped jeans, and her leather jacket. She looks good, more like herself than she has in a long time.

"When was the last time you went clubbing?"

"We're not here to party, blackbird."

"We can multitask." Her smile is devious. "It's been a long time since we danced together."

I huff, recalling the school prom that I took her to many years ago. She looked like a dream in this pale-pink dress from a thrift store, all floaty and shit. Like a ballerina sent from heaven above to rescue my soul from damnation. She admitted to stealing cash just to buy it for our date.

Even though we lived in the same foster home, I met her on the doorstep and offered her a single rose that I swiped from a nearby market. That was before the head carer and resident voice of doom, Mrs Dane, crushed it beneath her shoe. She called me a son-of-a-bitch thief. I've never seen Brooklyn laugh so hard.

"I still think about that night, you know."

Sliding a finger underneath her chin, I raise her grey eyes to meet mine. "It was the best night of my entire fucking life. Even when you mixed weed and booze, then puked out of your eyeballs."

Brooklyn snorts. "I was an amateur."

"And still hot with your head in the toilet all night."

"It feels like a lifetime ago. We were so different back then, but at the same time, not. Sometimes I can't believe I'm here with you, after all this time. It's still us, huh?"

"It's always been us, baby. And it always will be."

"You're becoming a soppy bastard, Hud."

I grip her chin hard, digging my nails in slightly. "Don't mention it. I'll still take you over my knee and hit you until you beg for mercy, which naturally, I won't give."

The queue finally begins to move. I glance over my shoulder, finding Kade ready and waiting. He's keeping a close eye on Seven by his side, while Eli and Phoenix bring up the rear. We've all freshened up for the occasion, wearing clean clothes and matching grim expressions.

My expectations for this meeting are pretty low as it could easily be a bust. We have to try though, especially now that Sadie has fucked off to get herself killed. We can't sit and do nothing while Incendia hunts our asses like wild dogs that have escaped the pound.

"Eyes sharp, we don't know who is watching," I instruct.

Seven scowls at me. "Shouldn't I go in first?"

"Why, fuckface?"

"Because one of us has the best chance of dealing with any trouble that arises. I'm not sure you can handle yourself, pretty boy, should the time come."

"Want me to knock you out to double check?"

Seven glares, but makes the smart decision to back down. I fight the urge to slam him against the brick wall and break his nose anyway. The fresh bruises on his face tell me Brooklyn's already kicked his ass enough recently. He seems to enjoy antagonising me as much as I enjoy plotting his death.

I step up to the bouncer, palming him a roll of cash to slip inside without having IDs checked. The nightclub is a riot of glistening bodies, spilled drinks, and drunken idiots snorting cocaine off every available surface. Definitely not one of London's finer drinking establishments.

Kade used to take me to all the hotspots when I was first adopted. This place is firmly outside of the law, and the perfect place to meet our dark-web contact. We won't be interrupted by the authorities. I have no doubt Incendia would kill them to keep things under wraps.

"Stay off the party powder. We don't need any slip-ups tonight." Kade takes charge as he steals Brooklyn from my arms. "Beer only, no shots."

Phoenix eyes up the white powder. "You're no fun."

"You can stick to water."

"No fair! Why does everyone else get to have fun but me?"

"Because last time we were out in public, you scaled a Ferris wheel and someone plummeted to their death," Brooklyn replies flatly. "No drugs, Nix. I mean it."

Glowering at us all, Phoenix takes Eli's hand and guides him to the dance floor. Eli wears a mask of crippling anxiety, and I'm surprised he's still standing. His jaw clenches as the loud music overwhelms him. I watch Phoenix slam their lips together, stealing his attention from a panic attack.

Lately, I've been fascinated by watching them.

And admittedly, a little intrigued.

"You know who we're looking for?" I force myself to look away from the pair.

"Not a clue. We're supposed to wait for the signal," Kade answers.

"In that case, let's get a drink."

Heading for the bar, I keep an eye on Seven as he situates himself in a lookout position. He screams of danger with his unkempt hair, stony face and unyielding scowl. Everyone gives him a very wide berth as he glares at them like it's his day job.

Kade orders a round of beers then disappears to set himself up next to our sadistic guard dog. It annoys me how easily he's accepted Seven into our midst. The guy's a fucking nut job. Kade should be more careful, but we all know he's a bleeding heart.

"Stop staring at Seven," Brooklyn orders.

I take a swig of beer. "Please just let me kill him. I'll make it quick. No charge for body disposal."

"You're not funny."

"It's not a joke."

"What's the time?" She sighs.

"Quarter to ten. Nearly time."

I'm itching to hold her close and far away from danger, but coddling Brooklyn West isn't a mistake I'm going to make again. She'll have my balls before letting me shield her from harm, and I most definitely don't want to give them up.

"Fancy a dance?"

Her lips tilt up in a smile. "Thought you'd never ask."

We head for the cramped dance floor, passing Phoenix and Eli, who shoot her heated looks. Brooklyn pauses to kiss them both, still clinging to my hand while pleasuring my friends. The act has my dick standing to attention. Once she's done, we move to the steady beat of music.

Before long, we're drenched in sweat and screaming along to a Black Sabbath song, losing sight of our surroundings. Just being here, with her sexy body writhing against me, makes all the bullshit worth it. She's my blackbird again, just for a moment.

"If you don't stop, I'm going to fuck you right here, in front of all these stoned lowlifes," I warn under my breath.

Brooklyn sinks her teeth into my neck, marking me for the entire club to see. "Would that be such a bad thing? Could be kinda fun."

"While I can just about tolerate sharing you with the assholes I call my brothers, I'm not comfortable with an entire nightclub seeing what's mine. I may get stabby."

She smirks. "Spoilsport."

"Come on, let's go find our guy."

We grab Phoenix and Eli, following Kade and Seven further into the shadows of the packed nightclub. Some drunken idiot stumbles into me and spills beer all over my shoes, earning himself a black eye in the process. Brooklyn grins at me, thriving on the thrill of violence.

Before the night is out, I'll have her screaming my goddamn name for everyone to hear. Especially Seven. I no longer give a fuck about subtly. Losing her has taught me to savour every last moment.

In the smoking area, we pass a pack of cigarettes around. Kade and Seven don't accept, too busy surveying the group of friends drinking at the table next to us. Their rowdy voices betray their inebriation. Clearly, they aren't here to assassinate us.

"What now?"

"We wait," Kade replies.

The minutes trickle by until it's nearly half past and our contact is more than late. We down another round of beers and reluctantly call the night a bust, preparing to get the hell out of this sweatbox. Before I can drag Brooklyn back to the warehouse and settle between her luscious legs, the blare of a fire alarm cracks through the night.

Kade stiffens. "That's our signal."

We watch the punters escape through a fire exit. The smoking area empties, while security focuses on the crowd inside the club, leaving us alone. I grasp the gun tucked into my jacket, unease trickling down my spine.

"I should've known it would be you lot."

All turning, we find a hooded figure sliding through a concealed back entrance. Her voice sounds chillingly familiar, almost a little smug. I don't bother to hide my weapon while aiming it straight at the stranger.

"Who the fuck are you?" I shout.

"Drop the weapon or this meeting is over."

Settling on a nearby bench, she gestures for us to follow suit. We advance as a group, maintaining a safe distance. I place my gun on the table but keep it within reach. I won't put it away until I know who exactly we're dealing with.

"You're late," Kade barks.

"I have to be very cautious these days. Incendia is crawling all over this city, looking for the likes of you. They would gladly put a bullet in my brain if they catch up to me."

She reaches up to push back her hood. Straggly, grown-out blonde hair and an exhausted face are revealed, far from the perfectly put together facade of the person we knew. Life on the run has done her no favours.

"Miss White."

"In the flesh," she drawls.

We all gape at the ex-warden, looking so rough and unlike herself. She puffs on a cigarette, taking the time to inspect each and every one of us. When her gaze lands on Seven, the cigarette falls straight from her fingertips.

"Doctor Farlow? Jude?"

Dammit, I really hope he breaks her jaw for using that name.

"Who are you?" he hits back.

Miss White stares, open-mouthed. "You… don't remember me?"

"I wouldn't take it personally." I snicker.

Brooklyn rests her palms on the table, commanding Miss White's attention back from the ghost in our midst. "We arranged this meeting to discuss an exchange of information."

"Brooklyn West. I hear you've gotten yourself into quite the pickle."

"We're not here to talk about me, Warden. Where have you been?"

Miss White lights a fresh cigarette while eyeing Seven. "When Augustus took over Blackwood, I knew my days were numbered. Nobody was permitted to hold more authority than him. I was just an obstacle for him to eliminate. I had to run, before it was too late."

"You've escaped Incendia's clutches for nearly nine months." Kade glances back to the nightclub still in disarray. "We don't have much time. If they're searching for you, it's because you know something."

Miss White appears nervous. "I have information about Blackwood, Incendia Corporation, and all of their dirty dealings. Names, dates, the lot. All of it can be yours."

"For what price?" Brooklyn deadpans.

"A fresh start." Miss White gnaws her lip. "Since your escape, Bancroft has tripled his presence on the streets. I'm running out of assets and time. I want my safety guaranteed."

Kade laughs in her face. "We can't guarantee our own safety. How exactly do you propose we do this for you? We know nothing about Bancroft."

"He has enough power to rally the support of the entire country and ensure our deaths. That's all you need to know. Don't play games with me, Kade. You're all working with Sabre Security."

My hand inches closer to the gun on instinct. I'd love nothing more than to put a bullet between her eyes. Brooklyn lays a reassuring palm on my leg, urging me to remain calm.

"I have no idea what you're talking about," Kade lies easily.

"You think I didn't know what that pink-haired fool was doing at Blackwood all along? I ran that place for seven years and had extra hidden cameras in all of my staff's offices. Alyssa Farlow, tut tut."

Seven's hands curl into tight fists, resentment clouding his face. Kade once mentioned the concealed camera in Mike's office, uncertain of what the warden's intentions were. She's a slippery fucking snake.

"I couldn't get rid of her without incurring the wrath of Sabre," Miss White continues. "I was there when she campaigned for information about her brother. I never forget a face. Tell your annoying friend that I want to make a deal with her employer."

Before anyone else can say anything, there's a blur of movement. Phoenix seizes hold of Miss White by her faded shirt and dangles her in the air. I've never seen him look so enraged.

"You protected Rio. He nearly killed Eli and Brooke! You helped them run the system. Smuggling in contraband, making sick patients worse for your own amusement. Playing us all like puppets and reaping the rewards. How do you sleep at night?"

Miss White scratches at his hands, attempting to break free. Before Phoenix can actually kill her, I lay a hand on his shoulder, easing him off. She hits the bench with a thud, rubbing her chest and spluttering.

"I was just doing my job. Augustus was the mastermind!"

"You turned a blind eye while the rest of us suffered," Brooklyn snaps.

"But I didn't profit from it."

"So you were just getting paid to be a ray of fucking sunshine for us all?" I point out, ready to blow this entire shitshow off. "Cry me a damn river."

Miss White cuts me a cold look, but doesn't refute my argument. We all know that she's a piece of work, there's no point denying it. She reaches into her coat pocket and places a slim thumb drive on the table.

"It's all on there. I'm just asking for a second chance, that's all."

"Who says that you deserve it?" Brooklyn laughs.

"Are you really one to talk? Call me a monster if you want, I've probably earned it. But it takes one to know one, Miss West. Don't forget what brought you to my institute."

I throw an arm around Brooklyn's shoulders, attempting to stop her from creating a bloodbath, but the next growl of anger comes from behind us.

"You knew."

Seven rounds on Miss White. Rather than hold her in the air, he tosses her thin frame across the courtyard without a second thought. She screams and smacks into a brick wall with a crunch. Blood spreads from the back of her head as she fights to get to her feet and falls.

"Jude, please—"

"You knew. All those months, you knew exactly what Lazlo was doing. You knew about Lucia, the Z Wing, everything. Do you know what they did to me, Elizabeth?"

Judging by the look on Miss White's face, she knows she's in trouble.

"Please... I didn't know what they were going to do to you. You have to believe me."

He punches her straight between the eyes. Miss White sobs as she clutches her bleeding, swollen face. I feel zero need to intervene. The bitch deserves a good beating for all she's enabled.

"Six years, Elizabeth. Six goddamn years. You did nothing."

"I didn't know you were alive..."

"Don't lie to me!"

The fire alarm cuts off, indicating our time is running out. I pocket my gun and help Brooklyn stand, catching sight of her swiping the thumb drive. Miss White's a fool. We could simply leave her for dead and escape with her bargaining chip right now.

Too easy, a mental voice whispers.

Raised voices coming from inside of the club have us all glued to the spot. Backing my family into the corner of the smoking area, myself and Kade train our weapons on the empty doorway. The beat of heavy footsteps approaches.

"Whatever happens, get Brooklyn out," I instruct the group.

She fires a curse straight at me. "I'm not leaving without you, motherfucker."

Shouting and barked orders rip through the air, with a rush of bodies entering the smoking area. Faces cloaked by thick balaclavas, the assailants carry scarily professional assault rifles. In a matter of seconds, we have six of them trained on us.

"Drop your weapons!"

None of us move, aiming straight for their heads.

"You're outnumbered. Back down, kids."

Surrounding us in a tightly packed circle, one figure steps forward and tears the balaclava from his face. I'm not even surprised to find Taggert, one of the less-than-friendly guards who made our lives miserable in Blackwood.

"Where's your buddy, Jackson?" I sneer.

"Burned to ashes by you fucking psychos," Taggert shouts.

"Don't worry. You can join him soon enough."

"That's not how this is going to go. We've already found your little warehouse hideout. There's no running. We can do this the easy way or the hard way."

While we face the group of thugs, Miss White sneaks around us with her head tucked low. When she reaches Taggert and accepts his outstretched hand, it becomes clear that we've been played. Her grin confirms my fears. Looks like Incendia needed her after all.

Miss White spares us a derisive look. "Here they are, as we agreed."

"Then the deal is done." Taggert gives her a nod before turning to us. "The boss only wants patients Seven and Eight alive. The rest of you are disposable."

Seeing red, I fire off a quick shot before anyone can react. It catches the man to Miss White's left, who screams and clutches his shoulder. Chaos descends as our two groups collide. I take out another bastard with a kick to the groin, crushing his throat beneath my foot.

Shooting the next one in the kneecap, I prepare for collision as the tough motherfucker carries on coming at me. Knocked straight off my feet, my head hits the ground and I see stars for a sickening second. The tip of his steel-capped boot connects with my ribs next.

We end up wrestling, his balaclava ripped off to expose his face to my fists. He's got several pounds of muscle on me and returns every hit. Panic begins to inch in as a blast rattles my eardrums. With matter splattering my face, I push the lifeless body aside.

"Need a hand, pretty boy?"

Seven is grinning down at me like the deranged lunatic he is, discarding a stolen gun to offer me a hand up. Taking it, I shoot him a scowl.

"This doesn't make us even, you piece of shit. I ain't no pretty boy."

"Whatever you say. I won't save your stupid ass next time."

The sound of fists meeting flesh draws us both to Brooklyn. She's kneeling nearby, beating the absolute shit out of Taggert with her bare fists. She looks too damn good covered in fresh blood. I don't intervene; my girl can handle herself.

I'm here to enjoy the show.

My dick is aching just watching her.

"Stay down. Final warning," she yells.

"We're just... the b-beginning." Taggert coughs up blood. "He w-won't stop coming for you."

"I'll kill the next people Incendia sends too. Say hello to Jackson for me."

Pulling out the knife stashed in her jacket, Brooklyn lifts her eyes to mine. Ensuring I'm watching, she brutally slashes the blade across Taggert's throat. He drowns in a geyser of blood, also covering her head to toe in crimson rain. Brooklyn doesn't even flinch, wiping her eyes.

"Like what you see?" She quirks an eyebrow.

"More than like, baby."

"Help me kill the rest of these assholes and you can show me how much you like it."

Seven clears his throat. "Touch her and you'll die next."

I stifle the urge to shoot him. "Whatever, man."

We catch the moment Phoenix cracks someone's skull, letting the body hit the ground with a satisfying thud. He winces and cradles his broken fingers. We're not all accustomed to fighting, but I've seen what he can do when he really loses control.

With the advantage of anger on our side, we obliterate the hired skins that Incendia sent. Kade and Eli hang back, letting the rest of us clean up. When the bloodbath is over, it leaves shell-shocked silence and six dead bodies.

"Time to go," Kade declares.

"What about her?" Brooklyn gestures to where Miss White is attempting to hide from us. "We can't leave her alive. She knows Sadie's real identity."

I offer Seven my gun. "It should be you."

He studies it for a moment before rolling up his sleeve instead. My kinda guy, I'll admit. We all step back to give him room to work, drinking in the blissful terror eating away at Miss White.

"Please, Jude… I beg you. Don't do this."

"That person is gone, Elizabeth. He isn't coming to save you."

"I d-didn't mean to… please have mercy…"

"Silence!" Seven spits in her tear-stained face. "There is no mercy in this world."

Weeping and begging for her life, Blackwood Institute's prestigious warden dies a pitiful death. Seven kicks her in the face so he can straddle her dying corpse. Her fighting is futile. His wrath is inescapable.

"Jude…"

"Goodbye, Elizabeth. I'll see you in hell someday."

Leaning in close to press their foreheads together, Seven drinks in her fear while wrapping a single hand around her throat. One is all this animalistic man needs.

"We should stop him," Kade comments.

"No." I shake my head. "I think he needs this."

Seven slowly, intimately chokes the life out of Elizabeth White. By the time he's done, she's blue and twitching, her legs jerking a final few times. When he lets go, Seven's trembling from exertion. Her throat looks collapsed from the force of his grip.

None of us dare approach. He looks ready to tear us all to shreds. Staring at his single, bloodied hand, the stump on his other arm hangs limp. I don't stop Brooklyn from carefully approaching, trusting her judgement when it comes to this… creature.

"Sev?"

"Stay back," he roars.

She ghosts a hand over his shoulder. "I'm here, Sev. You can come back now. The job's done. It's time to go."

"Eight?"

"Yeah, it's me. We're a team, aren't we?"

Managing to look up, the look on Seven's face scares even me. It's raw and brutal, far beyond anything that could be classified as human. He's a predator and a hunter wrapped up in a lethal tornado of rage. My instincts are telling me to keep Brooklyn as far away from him as possible.

"I'm sorry, princess," he apologises.

"What for?"

The pair exchange a long, hard look.

"I should've given you a go on the bitch. We kill together, not apart."

Brooklyn grins. "I'll let you off on this occasion."

I can't suppress my laughter. Everyone looks at me like I'm mad. We're surrounded by bodies, now is not the moment to lose it. Grabbing the pair of maniacs, we take one final glance at the bloody scene.

There are no CCTV cameras in a shitty place like this, but it wouldn't matter either way. We're already being hunted. Now, we've fired our first shot. Let the war commence.

"What now? We can't go back to the warehouse." Brooklyn leans on

Seven, wiping blood from her nose. "We need somewhere to clean up and lay low."

Phoenix steps forward with a nervous smile.

"I have an idea."

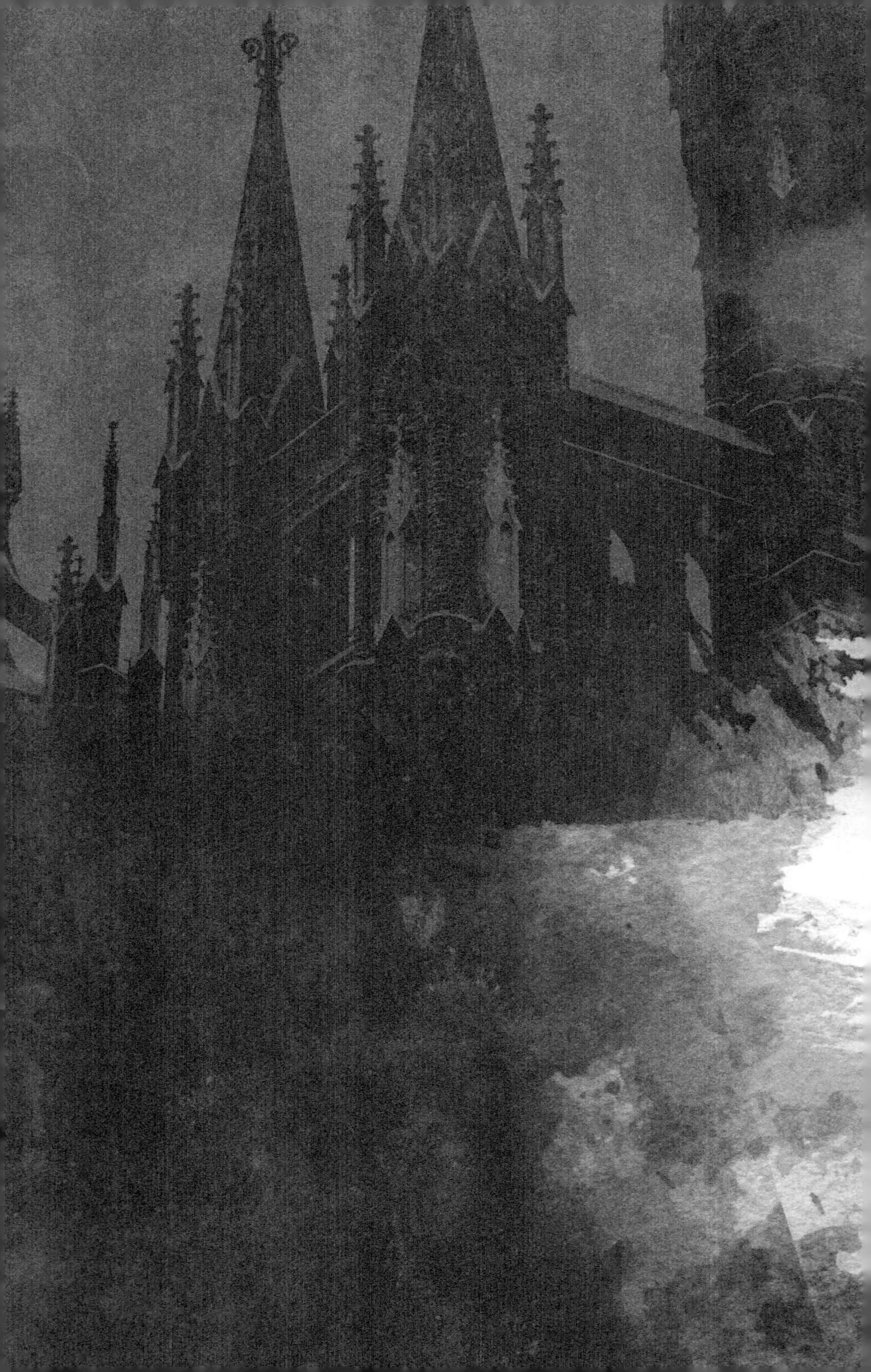

12

BROOKLYN

Lust - Saint JHN & Janelle Kroll

Stealing through the dimly lit suburbs of London, I stare at the back of Phoenix's head. It's taken us all night to sneak across the city, dodging CCTV cameras, screaming sirens, and even a police helicopter. We couldn't exactly hop on the underground.

"Any idea where we're going?" I whisper to Eli.

He shrugs, sparing me an exhausted smile.

I'm beginning to miss my comfortable bed, sandwiched between my guys, with the safety of four walls and no prying eyes nearby. Kade checked in with Lucia and Two a couple of hours ago, exchanging brief words. They're still holed up in Scotland.

"You heard from Sadie since she left?"

Kade sighs. "She isn't answering her phone."

"You think her cover is blown?"

"It doesn't look like Miss White exchanged information yet."

He spares Seven a nervous look, limping and deadly silent by my side. We need to know what happens next. Our so-called contact was a trap this whole time, and the thumb drive is worthless. We're back to square one.

Passing several street corners crowded with teenagers on skateboards, I tighten my leather jacket around me, hoping to conceal the blood beneath it. This is as rough as London gets, but Phoenix stalks down the street like he owns the place.

I hardly recognise the persona he's constructing before our very eyes. He stands taller and more confident with every step towards our destination. Turning a corner, we run straight into a huge crowd. The blare of music accompanies the youths, all drinking beer and smoking.

"Stay frosty," Hudson orders.

Phoenix glances back at us. "That won't be necessary. Stick behind me."

The crowd parts to allow someone to step forward. A glinting switchblade in the kid's hand makes my heart speed up. Phoenix is going to get himself killed by some scrawny little shit on a power trip at this rate.

"You ain't welcome here!"

Authority imbues every inch of Phoenix's bruised and battered frame. "Tell Travis that Phoenix has come home. Run along now, kid."

The teenager spares us a frown, but follows orders. We gather as Phoenix glares at the others, all watching us like we're aliens. I palm my knife, ready to stab my way out of a second fight of the night if necessary. We didn't survive Incendia's cunts just to die now.

"Home?" Kade echoes.

Phoenix shrugs. "We needed somewhere safe."

"You've never spoken about your home before," I chime in.

"Never had a reason to. I didn't leave here under good circumstances."

We fall into tense silence until the roar of an engine comes racing around the corner. The sea of people parts, admitting a modified truck painted in a violent shade of green. It's complete with painted flames, tinted windows, and a huge rear spoiler.

Several men hop out of the truck. Fierce scowls, lip piercings, and visible tattoos mark each person. Every single one of them is armed to the teeth with sawed-off guns and switchblades. I even spot some knuckledusters.

"Stay quiet, leave this to me," Phoenix warns.

Transforming from the happy-go-lucky person I know, his spine straightens and his shoulders roll back. He paces over to the truck, where the men exchange scandalised whispers. When the driver's door slams open, a pair of bright purple, buckled stomper boots hit the ground.

"As I fuckin' live and breathe... Phoenix Kent."

"Hey, Travis."

Flicking aside a joint and scraping back his red mohawk, Travis bundles him into a hug. They slap each other's backs, with the remaining men seeming to relax. We tentatively surround Phoenix, still on high alert.

"Where the hell have ya been?"

Phoenix shrugs. "I've been around."

"Two bloody years, Nix. You were gone for a long time."

"Tell me about it. You miss me?"

Travis punches him in the shoulder. "This place ain't the same without ya. Are these friends of yours, or do I need to set my boys on them?"

Phoenix circles his arm around my waist. "They're with me. Listen, Trav. We're in trouble and need somewhere to lay low for a bit."

"You got it, Nix. Anything for you."

Whistling to the nearby kids, Travis rattles off his orders. The group converges around us, concealing us from sight. We head off down the street, bathed in dawn light. Travis falls into step beside Phoenix, his pierced face lit with a grin.

"Charlie's gonna freak when she hears you're back, bro."

Phoenix tenses. "Perhaps hold off on telling her. It should be me."

"Nah. She'll be over the moon. She's missed her brother. It's good to have ya back, Nix. Too fuckin' good."

"It's only temporary, until we're out of trouble."

"I never got a chance to thank you for—"

"Don't mention it," Phoenix interrupts. "It's in the past."

Approaching a run-down house with bass music rattling the bricks, Travis gestures for us to enter. Inside, the stench of smoke and acid burns my throat. Marijuana plants bake under heat lamps, while giant vats of chemicals lay abandoned. Looks like they're cooking meth.

"Classy," Hudson comments.

Travis frowns at him before clearing his throat. "There are some spare rooms upstairs. I'll track down some clean clothes. You all look rough as hell."

"Do you have a shower?" I cringe at the sight of myself.

He gives me a slow, perusing look. "For you? Sure thing, sugar. My room's free if you wanna help yourself. Need a hand with all that blood?"

"Want me to break your legs?" Hudson casually leans against a stained wall. "Or your neck, perhaps? I really have no preference. Loser's choice."

Travis raises his hands. "No trouble here, mate."

Phoenix tugs me to his side and kisses my cheek. Travis looks even more intrigued, glancing between us all. Before he can ask questions I don't have the answers to, I leave the guys to their bickering and testosterone. I've had more than enough of people's bullshit for one day.

Up the sagging staircase, there's a sea of discarded drug paraphernalia.

More marijuana plants fill several of the bedrooms, leaving an earthy stench in the air. Sweat drips down my neck from the industrial setup. Thick electrical cables feed into lights and heaters.

I locate Travis's room by the writing that's burned on the door by a cigarette. His space is pretty disgusting. Piles of unwashed clothes and empty liquor bottles litter the threadbare carpet. By some miracle, his en-suite bathroom is permissible, beyond the used condoms and knock-off aftershave bottles.

There's no lock, so I take my knife into the shower with me after stripping off clothing that reeks of death. The water is barely warm, but it feels amazing against my bruised body. I brace my hands against the cracked tiles and let my gritty eyes slide shut.

I'm suddenly exhausted. The adrenaline that kept us running across the city has deserted me. As the events of the night run through my mind, a whisper creeps in, emboldened by violence and bloodthirst.

How many people have you killed now, Brooke?

You've become everything you hate.

Vic would be so proud of you.

"Vic is gone," I recite, clutching my knife tight.

As you should be too.

This is just the beginning.

Blackwood is calling your name.

I wash the crimson stains from my knife, entranced by the serrated steel. I'm not sure how many people I killed last night. Their empty, lifeless stares all blur into one. It shouldn't be so easy, but I've spent months running from one kill to the next.

Patient Eight never had a conscience.

I'm not sure Brooklyn West does either.

Pressing the blade to my stomach, I make five neat, parallel cuts. It still isn't enough to calm down. Cutting myself again, I feel my lungs constrict. I have to stop right now. I can't afford to black out from blood loss here. As my panic increases, Sadie's advice rings in my head—list what you know.

My name is Brooklyn West.

I am twenty-two years old.

My family is dead.

I'm a murderer.

There's a monster inside of me.

I deserve to be alone.

"Shut the fuck up," I berate myself.

I haven't hallucinated Vic since I killed Augustus. I thought I'd expunged the whole mess from my mind in that moment, but he's still in there. His voice lives on in everything I hate about myself.

"Brooke? You okay?"

Phoenix lets himself into the steam-filled room. I'm shocked to find Hudson following him. They both pull off dirty clothes to start cleaning themselves in the sink. Down to their boxers, I study the countless bruises and injuries from our firefight.

Poking his tender ribs, Phoenix curses. "I'd like to go a week without someone breaking part of me. You nearly done in there, firecracker?"

Turning off the shower, I don't trust myself to speak. The minute I step out, I realise my mistake. There are no towels and my clothes lay in a sticky, ruined puddle. Shifting on my feet, the weight of two burning gazes has heat flooding between my thighs.

"What the fuck are those?" Hudson barks at me.

I back up against the shower door as he advances. His fingers coast over the fresh cuts without permission, catching the blood that leaks down my stomach. His brows furrow, fingertips digging into the wounds until I'm hissing between clenched teeth.

"Take your hands off me," I grit out.

"You're still doing this?"

"When the need arises. It's none of your business."

Hudson yanks me forward until our chests meet. Completing the trap, Phoenix slots in behind me and grabs hold of my hips. These are the last two people I'd expect to be sandwiched between. I can barely stand from the blistering wave of need that wracks me. Whether it's to cut again or fuck, I really don't care.

"You did good tonight." Hudson kisses his way along my jaw to meet my lips. "Watching you kill those fuckers had me hard all goddamn night, blackbird."

"And me," Phoenix adds.

"We lost our one lead. We're all battered and lost in the middle of London. Sadie's in danger. This entire thing was a waste of time and we're going to be killed."

Hudson scoffs. "Well, when you put it like that…"

I suppress a shudder as Phoenix bites my ear lobe. His cock is pressing right up against my bare ass, with only a pair of boxers separating us.

"…but I'm sure we can improve the situation," he finishes.

Quickly ditching his underwear, Hudson takes a seat on the closed toilet lid. I'm tugged into his awaiting lap, still trapped and unable to run. His healing bullet wound looks inflamed, surrounded by black bruises, scratches and lacerations.

"You promised me no more cutting," he murmurs.

"When?"

"Don't be a fucking smart-ass, Brooke. Talk to me."

I duck my gaze. "I don't want to become Patient Eight again. I want to stay with you guys, my family. Not in the past. This is the only way I know how."

"Then let us help you," Phoenix pleads.

Hudson nods. "You don't need to do this alone."

Studying the fresh cuts again, Hudson's tongue darts out to wet his lips. I watch as he coats his fingers in my blood, something dark and smouldering in his icy-blue irises. Without shame, he spreads the wetness over his dick and pumps it several times.

"If you're gonna do this, we may as well make the most of it," he says darkly.

My mouth goes dry as Hudson's thumb swipes over my clit, painting my sensitive flesh red. With the flick of a switch, I'm overcome by desire. All I want is to feel the beat of his heart. I want proof that we're still alive and this is real.

My eyes slide shut as doubt takes root. How do I know my brain isn't conjuring this entire reality? I'll shut my eyes and wake up in the Z Wing again, longing for a life beyond my imprisonment. Perhaps I'm dead already. This could all be a cruel dream.

"Eyes on me," Hudson demands.

Startled by his gruff voice, I force myself to look at him again. The rest of my blood disappears in his mouth as he sucks his fingers dry.

"You're not allowed to hide from me, blackbird. I want to see your pain. All of it. You keep running and hiding this shit from us, and it ends now."

Before I can shake my head, he grabs my nipple and pinches it hard.

"Fuck, okay," I submit.

"Okay what? Answer me, bitch. I can't hear you."

Riled up by his taunts, I grind down on Hudson's lap. His velvet-soft head is pushing into my slit, spearing me on his length without filling me. With another wriggle, he's buried deep in my pussy.

"Okay, daddy."

I punctuate my words with a thrust. Hudson growls, his fingertips digging deep into my hips. From this angle, he's filling me to the brim, but I'm still the one in charge. All he can do is sit there and let me take control.

Slamming down on his length, I can feel my core clenching. He pinches my sore nipple, swallowing my grunt of pain with another kiss.

"You look so perfect riding my dick," he compliments. "Such a dirty whore, aren't you? Letting us both watch you like this. One of us was never enough for you."

"Fuck off, Hud."

"I knew there had to be a benefit to this sharing crap," Phoenix hoots. "Live porno."

Hudson glowers at him. "Shut up."

Grabbing his shoulders for balance, I set a bruising pace. I need to fuck the darkness away before it consumes me. Sweat beads across my forehead as my core begins to tighten. Hudson groans with each thrust, his lips inflicting a dark mark on my neck.

It must take a lot of self-control for him to let me lead. Even when we were lovesick kids, he'd take charge and fuck me, regardless of my feelings. I've spent my life being used and abused by Hudson Knight, but I wouldn't change a goddamn thing.

"Thought you didn't share?" I tease him.

"Rules are made to be broken, Brooke."

"You've fucked me at the same time as Kade before."

"He's my brother. I ain't rubbing dicks with Phoenix."

I grab Hudson by the throat, mirroring his own domineering move. His eyes widen, but he doesn't fight me. Toying with his pulse, I revel in the feeling of complete control. His life is in my hands. I own his black soul, and if I wanted to, I could take it all away.

"I'm getting a bit jealous here," Phoenix says.

I toss him a heated look. "Be right with you, baby."

Chasing my release to the very edge, glorious tension unravels in my lower belly. Hudson is staring at me like I'm a precious piece of artwork that he can't tear his eyes from. The feeling is heady—being adored.

My days of hating this monstrous, complicated man are long over, but the intensity of our obsession remains. He's the air I breathe and the choking grip on my windpipe at the same fucking time.

"Take it," he demands, meeting my strokes. "Show me how you fall apart for me, blackbird. Let Phoenix hear you moan my name."

With a final few pumps, I watch with pleasure as Hudson's eyes roll back in his head. My own release crests and overwhelms me, an all-consuming tidal wave of sensation. Heat spreads through my body, spilling across his lap when I slide off.

"Dammit," Phoenix curses. "I should've filmed that shit."

"When I can give you the live show anytime?"

His lips spread in a cheeky grin. "I ain't gonna say no to that. Bring your ass here and let me spank that gorgeous fucking skin for teasing me like this."

I push my lips against Hudson's for a final time, swiping wild black hair from his forehead. He grabs my chin and forces me to deepen the kiss, stealing one last slither of submission. Phoenix clears his throat, but that doesn't stop Hudson. He's more than happy making him wait.

"I'm letting you fuck him," he whispers fiercely. "But you're still mine. Don't forget it."

"Whatever you say, Hud."

"Go on. Show him a good time."

Approaching Phoenix with the caution of a stalked deer, my newfound confidence suddenly dissipates. The roles have reversed in mere seconds, leaving me dizzy. Phoenix's gaze burns with authority and defiance. He won't surrender to me like Hudson did.

Lifting a single eyebrow, he doesn't have to say a word for me to know exactly what to do. On instinct, I sink to my knees on the bathroom floor. My eyes stare downwards, waiting for permission to look up.

"Good girl," Phoenix praises. "So obedient for me, aren't you?"

I hear Hudson's sharp intake of breath, but all of my attention is fixed on Phoenix as he finishes stripping. I'm a little nervous about touching him in front of our captive audience. I don't want Hudson to change his mind and chicken out.

"Suck it, firecracker."

Obeying his command, I wrap my lips around Phoenix's cock. He grunts as I hollow my cheeks out, taking him deep into my mouth. This isn't my first rodeo with Phoenix. I know exactly how he likes it. In no time, I have him thrusting into my mouth until my eyes tear up.

The perfect blend of rough and attentive, he toes that dangerous line with precision. Before he can finish, Phoenix pulls out and drags me up. I'm shoved into the bathroom counter, having to brace my hands on the sink. His palm cracks across my butt cheek, making me gasp.

"Such a naughty slut, Brooke. You like that?"

"Yes Nix," I answer obediently.

"How come that asshole is called daddy, and not me?"

Peering over my shoulder, I find his smug grin in place.

"Don't push your luck," Hudson warns while climbing in the shower. "I'm not above drowning you in that sink and fucking our girl over your corpse instead."

Phoenix spanks me several more times, each harder than the last. Pain and pleasure blur into one confusing maelstrom within me. I'm so wet, made worse by the sight of us in the mirror. Phoenix leans over me like a Greek god, playing my body with fine-tuned precision.

He finally slips inside of me, ending my torturous wait. Each collision sets my soul on fire as his body worships mine, already warm from the recent orgasm. When he presses a finger into my mouth, I swirl my tongue to moisten it.

"Easy baby," he encourages, pushing it inside of my asshole. "Such a good girl, aren't you? It's been so long since I fucked this sweet, perfect pussy."

It doesn't take long for Phoenix to have me crying out his name. I have no doubt the entire house can hear us, even his drug dealer friends. Let them listen. I'm proud of our relationship, no matter how complicated or crazy it may seem to the outside world.

Phoenix bites down on my shoulder before spinning me around. I hop up on the bathroom counter so he can settle back between my legs. Filling me once more, I now have a perfect view of Hudson in the shower. He smirks while watching us, wrapping a hand back around his cock.

"We have an audience."

"Let him watch. This is my turn," Phoenix grunts.

Throwing my head back, I savour every stroke of his body. It's been so long since I've felt this close to Phoenix. For the longest time, I thought I'd never see him again. I'm glad to be proven wrong.

When he finishes, the idea of his juices mixing with Hudson's has me climaxing again. I nearly slide off the counter in a boneless heap before he catches me. I'm carried back to the shower and passed to Hudson, who starts washing me with shower gel.

It feels weird, letting someone be this close to me. Trusting them enough to be vulnerable. Between all of my guys, I'm being looked after. Loved. Cherished. I don't know how I survived four months without that, but there's no way in hell it will ever happen again.

"That was fucking hot, blackbird."

I wink at Hudson. "You're full of surprises."

"Perhaps I'll share you with someone else next time," he muses.

Hot damn, sign me the hell up.

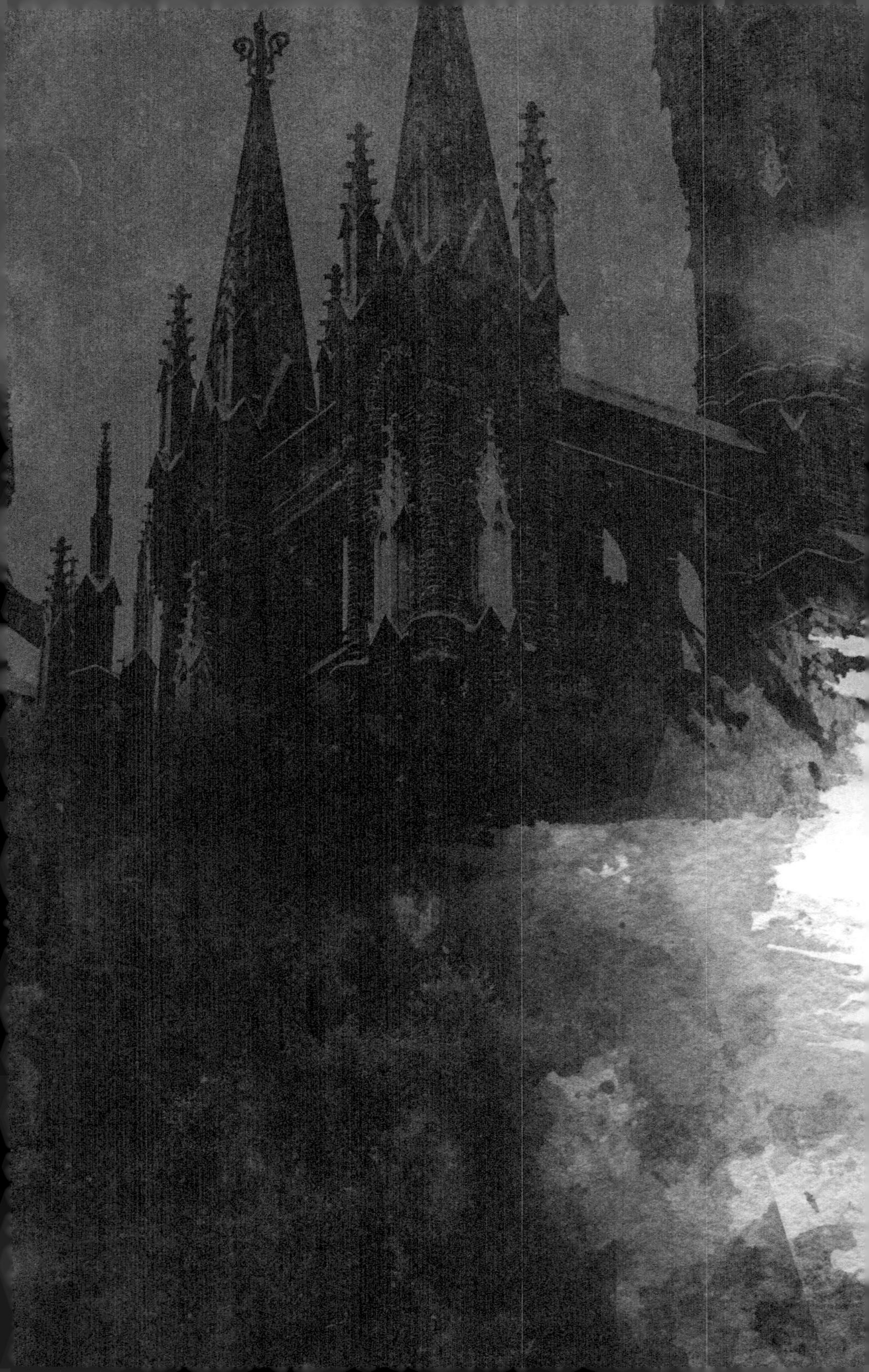

13

PHOENIX

Summer Set Fire to the Rain - Thrice

Staring out at the crowded street, I watch the throng of teenagers pass roll-up cigarettes back and forth. The whole scene is a reminder of the person I used to be. There was a time when the mean streets of London feared my name.

Travis used to work for me, not the other way around. He was my best runner and number two, helping me execute my grandmother's vision. Then our entire lives blew up in our faces after a big drug bust. I had to face the consequences of my dirty dealings.

I paid the price instead of them.

Blackwood was my punishment.

I don't miss that life, and I certainly don't belong here anymore. My addiction was born from this toxic waste pit of a life. I can't wait to leave as soon as the coast is clear. We've camped out for a few days, resting our broken bodies while letting the commotion die down.

Kade's been watching the news obsessively. Somehow, they've managed to locate surveillance footage of us fleeing the south side of the city on foot. It isn't safe to move again while the whole city is looking for us.

Incendia is still hot on our heels.

If I'm honest, I don't think it will ever be safe.

"Nix? You got a minute?"

Travis waits in the doorway to the filthy living room. I let the net curtain fall shut, irritation already boiling beneath my skin. Brooklyn is snoring on the sofa, staying within sight at my request. I'm not having any of these lowlifes bothering her.

"What is it, Trav?"

"She's asked to see you again. Third time today."

"Not now. I can't."

"She's the boss," he points out. "It's been two years since you got taken away by the coppers. Charlie has questions too. She's all grown up now."

In a matter of seconds, I have Travis pinned against the peeling wallpaper by his throat. He chokes out an apology when my fist meets his annoying face. It should have been him who got locked away, not me. How dare he lecture me? He doesn't deserve the empire he's inherited, even if I don't want it.

"I've been away, but don't for a second think that I'm not still in charge here. I took the hit for my nana's whole organisation. Dozens of you could've done time if it wasn't for me. You owe me. Capiche, fucker?"

"Yes, N-Nix."

"Tell her that I'm busy. I don't care what you have to say, just get her off my back. I am not endangering her life by bringing her into this mess."

Tossing him aside, Travis swipes blood from the corner of his mouth before fleeing from the room. I haven't dipped into my dark side in a while, but it's very much still there. It was bred into me by the fearsome woman who raised me and Charlie when my piece-of-shit mum bailed on us.

You'd think being related to a gang leader would be hard going, but Nana loves fucking fiercely. I wouldn't be alive without her, even if she made me into the deadbeat, asshole addict I truly am. I grew up on these streets. I took the fall for them. This is my kingdom, whether it makes me sick or not.

"You can't avoid her forever."

Brooklyn's hoarse whisper draws me back from my anger. I find her sitting up, rubbing her bleary, tired eyes. She lets me collapse in her lap and strokes my newly re-dyed blue hair. Eli stayed up with me last night to do it. The memory of his blue-stained hands and tentative smile makes my chest warm.

"I have to keep Nana safe." I sigh heavily. "Charlie too."

"I get it, we're bad news. But she's family, Nix. Two years is a long time. Say goodbye before we have to run again. Give her some closure in case we don't come back."

I roughly grab Brooklyn by the chin. "Don't give me that bullshit, firecracker. We have no choice but to survive. I refuse to lose you again. Incendia can kiss my ass before I let that happen."

Her smile is so sad, it stabs me right in the damn heart.

"I fucking love you. Perhaps too much."

"I love you, Brooke. Quit it with the sad talk. Shit's depressing enough."

"Ain't that the truth. Let's find the others."

We head for the kitchen together, hand in hand. Kade has taken over the scarred table in the corner, sweeping used needles and empty liquor bottles aside to pour over more printed documents. He looks frantic, circling and highlighting anything he can find.

He's attempting to profile Bancroft, but so far, the man's squeaky clean. He was honoured for services to the medical industry several years back, as Incendia's empire of institutes grew. The millions of images a quick search brought up made me sick. He's well-loved and protected by his reputation.

"Anything?" I ask tiredly.

Kade shoves his glasses into his hair. "Fucking nothing. He's worth millions and has shares in just about every public stock going. I've counted three political parties funded by his donations. Don't get me started on this stupid knighthood. The media loves this bastard."

Hudson takes a gulp from an open bottle of vodka. "What about your dad?"

"Bancroft's been on the campaign trail with him three years in a row, along with a lot of financial endorsement. Dad's piggybacking on his reputation by sitting on Blackwood's board of directors."

"Chummy, huh?" I snort.

Brooklyn shakes her head. "That's one word for it."

Releasing her hand, I approach Eli. He's standing at the back of the kitchen, staring out at the falling rain. Running a hand over his arm, he startles at first before nuzzling into my side. I kiss his mop of ringlets, wrapping an arm around his shoulders.

"Where's Seven?" Brooklyn asks behind us.

"He's been outside for four hours now," Hudson answers. "Won't say a word to any of us, same as yesterday. He just keeps on hitting that bag and pacing."

We stare into the overgrown chaos of the garden that hasn't been tended to in decades. Buried amongst the billowing trees and weeds, Seven has found an old punching bag. He's methodically beating the shit out of it without breaking a sweat. It's a mesmerising sight, watching his fury play out in real time.

Brooklyn comes to stand next to us, frowning. "This isn't good."

"What? It's a healthy outlet," I argue.

"It always took him a while to come back after jobs. Sometimes weeks would pass before he returned to being himself again, not just… Patient Seven. I should go out there and help."

"Give him some space to cool off. You can't coddle him forever," Hudson says without his usual vitriol. Seems like the ice man is beginning to thaw after all.

The sound of the front door smashing open interrupts our conversation, sending us all into fighting mode. Kade and Hudson both pull weapons, while Brooklyn wields her knife like it's an extra limb. I shove Eli behind me before he can protest and square my shoulders. Heavy footsteps are approaching.

If Incendia has found us, we won't go down without a fight.

I refuse to die here, of all places.

"On my count," Kade instructs, gun cocked.

Before he can offload a round, a shrill, furious voice lances through the kitchen. The door smacks against the wall as it flies open, ending my short-lived relief. Enraged, crystal-clear blue eyes land on me.

"Phoenix motherfuckin' Kent. I'm gonna have your hide, boy!"

Before I can hide from her wrath, Eli helpfully shoves me forward. Nana approaches and smacks me around the head, cursing like a drunken sailor thrown overboard.

"Nana, calm down!"

"Don't tell me to fuckin' calm down! Jesus H Christ." She yanks me into a suffocating hug. "Come here, you little toerag. Let me get a good look at you, at least. Two years!"

"Stop swearing! I'm here, aren't I?"

My nana, Pearl, is a short and stout woman, all wrinkled skin and old-age charm. Her silver hair is styled in a slick bouffant, matching her skirt and pressed shirt. Despite her charming, grandmotherly appearance, there's a terrifying woman beneath the surface.

It takes a certain kind of person to run an entire criminal empire in their retirement. Nana handles the front of the business, a shady strip bar called Mamacita's in Tottenham. An army of subordinates does the rest of the dirty work—myself included, once upon a time.

"What in the holy hell are you doing here? How long?" she demands, ignoring everyone staring at us like we're insane. She takes a lot of getting used to.

"Only a couple of days or so, we ran into trouble."

"Trouble!" She smacks me upside the head again. "I know all about your damn trouble. The news is showing your stupid grin every night! My entire fuckin' knitting circle thinks my grandson is a mass murderer!"

"You go to a knitting circle?" I stare in disbelief.

Her eyes narrow on me. "Ain't I allowed to have a fuckin' hobby? I've been dealing with these morons on my own since you got put away. Sometimes I gotta cool off too. I knitted a holster for my revolver."

Before she can wring my neck, I dance backwards. Nana seems to realise that we're not alone. Her steely gaze bounces between the entire ragged group before landing on Brooklyn. She studies every bruised and scarred inch on display, her lips pressed into an unflinching line.

"You the girl that got my boy in trouble?"

Brooklyn winces. "I guess I am, ma'am."

"Don't ma'am me, missus. The name's Pearl."

Depositing herself in a chair, Nana pulls out a cigar and lights up.

"Someone better get me a drink while my grandson here explains why the pigs are knocking on my door every day. I ain't slept a wink all week! It's bad for business."

Everyone watches her with bemusement. I should have warned

them; she's a fucking tough nut to crack. Hudson obediently surrenders his bottle of vodka, looking more than a little intimidated. Nana glares until he produces a glass, then she knocks back a stiff measure.

"We had to leave Blackwood. Our lives were in danger there," I explain, earning myself the stink eye. "The corporation behind the institute is very powerful and wants to silence us. That's why we ran, Nana."

"You do the things the news is accusing?"

"Of course not," Kade asserts. "We're being targeted."

"Innocent people don't get targeted, kid."

"We did burn down Blackwood and kill several guards," Brooklyn interrupts, facing Nana without fear. "Plus the men in the nightclub. That wasn't a lie. We had no choice."

Nana appraises her, puffing out cigar smoke. She respects straight-talkers more than anything. Lying or making excuses in our family usually got you a hell of an ass kicking, if not worse.

"They're saying you're a murderer. I read the news."

Stepping between the two women, I prepare to take Nana down a notch or two. I won't have her shaming Brooklyn for what the news is peddling. I know exactly how many lives Nana has ended or ruined through the family business. We've all got blood on our hands.

"We were in Blackwood for a reason," Brooklyn offers plainly.

Nana stares at her before a cheeky smile lights up her face. "I could use a girl like you around here. I never liked that institute, pretentious and full of overpaid wankers. They wouldn't let me see my boy for six months, then he didn't want me to come anyway."

Her caustic glower is sent my way instead. *Great.*

"I didn't want you to see me like that." I recoil, avoiding her accusing gaze. "It took me a while to get clean, and it wasn't pretty in the meantime."

"I'm your grandmother, Nix. I've seen you at your best, and I've seen you at your worst. You hurt this old bird's heart, but I'll live. It's your sister who deserves an apology."

At the mention of Charlie, guilt smothers me. I've been gone for so long, I'd convinced myself that my family was better off without me. Charlie was a kid when I got put away. Now, she's fourteen years old. I've missed so much. I'm no better than our waste-of-space mother.

"Guys," Kade interrupts. "Something happened."

He's back at his laptop, looking pale. The room falls into tense silence as he turns it around for us to see. It looks like another news conference has been called. The reporters are back on the steps of luxurious downtown London, surrounded by wealth and carefully concealed lies.

"Son of a bitch," Brooklyn curses. "That's him."

The cameras paint Bancroft's well-groomed exterior in high-definition horror. He's dressed in another fine suit and tie, his diamond-encrusted watch on full display. The conciliatory smile on his face makes me want to punch a fucking wall.

Hudson stills next to me. "Look who it is."

Hanging behind Incendia's perfectly groomed president is a very familiar, unwelcome face. I've seen pictures of Kade's asshole father before. He's staring straight ahead, an impenetrable mask on his middle-aged face, framed by slicked back, salt and pepper hair.

There's a low hum of conversation from the reporters, documenting this alliance. It's a publicity stunt and warning rolled into one. They know Leroy Knight's sons are involved. He's effectively disowning them and painting an even bigger target on their backs by doing this conference.

"Three days ago, law enforcement tracked our missing convicts down to a nightclub in South London," Bancroft recites. "They claimed the lives of six brave men. Today, we praise their heroic efforts and condemn the animals that led them to their slaughter."

"Who's this ugly stuffed shirt?" Nana booms.

Brooklyn's hands brace on the table. "That's who we're running from."

Nana studies the broadcast with a look of murderous rage. She's well accustomed to deciphering bullshit in her line of work. This guy's entire persona is a golden fucking sham.

"The situation is in hand," Bancroft continues grandly. "We're working to bring these monsters to justice. Should anyone have a sighting of the people on your screens, we urge you not to confront them, but to call the authorities with the following number."

Kade's fist slams down on the table. "Paying the public to do his dirty work for him."

"Clearly, the police are in his pocket too," Brooklyn adds. "He owns everyone and everything."

Our pictures flash up on the broadcast in all their harrowing detail, including Brooklyn's infamous mugshot. But this time, a sixth photo has been added. It's an old snap of Seven, dressed in a blue cap and gown at his university graduation. He looks younger and a hell of a lot more… stable.

"I thought they were keeping Seven quiet." I watch the conference draw to a close. Bancroft and Kade's father climb into an SUV and speed off without answering any of the reporter's questions.

"They're getting desperate," Kade hedges, his face red. "Time's running out. They know the minute we start talking, that's it. Game over."

"So why don't we? Talk, that is."

"Who would believe us?" Hudson rages, pacing the small kitchen. "Even with proof, we're just a bunch of mentally ill criminals to the public. We'll be tossed in a cell and fucking executed."

"I could have one of my boys put a bullet in that bastard's skull,"

Nana says sweetly, crushing her finished cigar. "Just say the word, kids. Quick and easy."

"Stay out of this, Nana. It isn't safe."

"I can protect myself, Nix. I've been in the game for a long time."

"I haven't spent the last two years rotting inside of Blackwood for you to throw it all away!" I shout at her, losing my temper. "Stay out of this. That's an order."

Her crystalline eyes harden, filling with indignation. "Do you think I will listen to you, boy?"

"You fucking will."

"Watch your tone. I'm still in charge here."

"How come you didn't get locked up then, huh? My life got ruined instead."

She blanches, seeming to deflate. I immediately want to take my words back. I did the crime, so I had to do the fucking time. There's no way I would've let Nana go down for all the shit we've done.

"I'm sorry." I pull her into a hug.

She sniffles emotionally. "Me too, kid. Missed your goofy face around here."

"I'll come back, I promise."

Her response is cut off by dirty dishes rattling in the sink. We all stop and stare, noticing the mini earthquake. Liquor bottles and chipped glasses are shaking in the kitchen cupboards.

"What is that?" Kade exclaims.

Nana's glass of vodka vibrates and falls off the table. The house is overcome by a heavy beating sound, and it takes a moment for the penny to drop. It sounds like the spinning rotors of an incoming helicopter.

"Is that what I think it is?"

Kade shoves cables and paperwork into his backpack. "Let's get the fuck out of here. Quickly, move!"

Seven bursts back inside, his caramel eyes wild as he gestures towards the garden. Leaves and branches are flying everywhere in the choppy wind. It must be right above us. Terror and panic sweep over the entire room.

I shove Brooklyn towards the door and grab Eli, directing everyone towards the front of the house. With a bit of luck, we can use the gang to conceal our movements. If we can get to one of the cars, at least we have a slim chance of getting the fuck out of here.

"Nana! Go home," I yell above the noise. "Stay out of this."

She pulls me into a fast, frenzied hug. "Run and don't look back, you hear me? Take this. Call me when you're safe."

Shoving one of the phones we use for dealing into my palm, I press a kiss to her cheek. If I was her obedient leader, she was the empress of us all. Neither a hero nor a saint, but family, nonetheless. That's something I won't ever take for granted again.

"I love you, Nana."

"And you, boy. Get out of here."

She hobbles towards the garden where she can slip out through the back. The others will get her to safety. It pains me to see her go like this, but I don't allow myself the luxury of emotion. We can mourn all that we've lost another time.

We race through the chattering house and onto the street, where the glow of overhead lights sweeps across the concrete to search us out. Travis is lurking nearby in the cab of his truck. My heart stops when I catch sight of the girl in the passenger seat, her long brown hair and chocolate eyes matching mine.

"Phoenix!" Charlie shrieks.

Waving her off, I scream at the top of my lungs. "Char! Run!"

She yells at Travis, gesturing towards me.

"Go!" I shout again.

"Not without you! I'm coming!"

We're all nearly swept off our feet as more ferocious wind whips the street. The helicopter is preparing to land. A sudden rush of fluorescent lights blinds me, and I stumble into the unknown. I'm dragging Eli with me until our hands are viciously ripped apart.

"Eli!"

My family vanishes in the brilliant white light. I can't see a fucking thing, searching around with my hands and tripping on a curb. The world slows to a snail's pace in the blinding unknown. All I can hear are the shouts. Screams. Bellowed orders and begging cries.

Charlie's desperate voice grows ever closer, parting the blazing light. Her strong hand grasps mine before it's torn away again. Blinking hard, I clear my vision long enough to spot her flying through the air, far away from me.

"Phoenix! Help!"

She's tossed across the street by an unknown figure, dressed in the same black uniform the dickheads at the nightclub wore. Swarms of people are invading the street. They all carry guns and radios, scanning the crowd with urgency. When two of the black-clad individuals begin to fight each other, I realise something is amiss.

We're not alone.

They aren't on the same side.

Gunshots and wet, meaty punches writhe through the air in a chorus of violence. My ears ring in the wake of the helicopter that has landed amidst the chaos. Yelling something at the pilot, an enormous mountain of a man leaps onto the street.

I swear the helicopter shakes with the force of his huge, muscled weight exiting it. His hardened gaze sweeps over the messy scene, searching for something. When he spots us cowering and trapped by the fighting, he taps the comms in his ear and speaks.

"What's happening?!" Hudson yells.

Kade finds his feet, bleeding from a gash in his forehead. "I don't know!"

The fighting rages on as the melee of bodies collide and become one. It's impossible to tell who works for who. Someone else is here, and the newbies are gleefully wailing on Bancroft's hired skins. Searching the war zone, I catch sight of Charlie on the other side of the road.

My stomach plummets.

She's trapped by a gun to her back.

"Charlie!" I roar.

Her bleeding face manages to turn in the gravel and two tear-stained eyes meet mine. I shove past Hudson, desperate to get to Charlie before it's too late. Travis and his boys are still lost in the madness, being beaten bloody while others run for their lives.

"Nix!" Brooklyn shouts after me. "Stop!"

Her voice is cut off by a shriek. Kade convulses on the road with a taser jabbed into his side. Hudson's rearranging some fucker's face, as Seven tears apart anyone that dares come close to him. Brooklyn is attempting to drag a semi-unconscious Eli out from underneath a pair of fists.

"Phoenix!"

Charlie's pained begging nearly rips me in half. Caught between my sister and my brawling family, I have to make an impossible decision. My feet move of their own accord as I race towards Charlie. The barrel of a gun nudges the back of her head as she sobs.

Everything stops.

Time ceases to exist.

With the distance between us shortening, I'm so close to tackling the asshole threatening her life. Mere inches away, close enough to taste her terror. Leaping the final few steps, I'm flying through the air when the shot rings out.

That short, controlled blast changes everything in a second.

The light in my sister's eyes winks out of existence.

Blood explodes like a bomb dropped in the ocean, covering me in warmth. I hit the ground and take down the gunman with me, his weapon skidding out of reach. Before he can come up for air, I'm breaking every single bone in his face. An anguished, animalistic cry pours out of me.

Thwack.

Thwack.

Thwack.

Agony races across my knuckles, punctuated by the cracking of shattered bone. The gunman stops moving as I cave his head in, feeling like my entire body is about to explode with rage. Collapsing in a puddle of blood, I finally look at my sister's dead body.

She's gone.

Gone.

Fucking gone!

Someone's calling my name. Over and over again. It doesn't register. Nothing exists but the empty, lifeless orbs staring back at me. I didn't even get to speak to her, let alone say goodbye. I'm her big brother.

It's my job to keep her safe.

It… was my job.

There's nothing left to protect now.

"Phoenix!"

Brooklyn screams like a banshee, pointing at the person heading straight for me. In the riot of warring bodies, a spindly figure slices and stabs at random. She parts the sea of blood with a knife in each hand, cutting countless throats. Her bald head and hollow cheeks are exposed by her lack of balaclava.

She's closing in on me.

I don't run.

There's nothing left in me to feel fear.

My family is stolen away across the street. Tossed over several hulking shoulders, they're packed into the helicopter. I watch the huge guy from before jam a needle into Brooklyn's neck. He drags her away as she bucks and fights, eventually going limp.

The last thing I see is Kade's floppy body being lifted and carried, disappearing with the rest of them. Pain tears through my left thigh as a dart pierces my skin. The approaching woman tucks a tranquilliser gun back in her holster.

Paralysing fear takes over. The world blurs fast, disintegrating at the seams as drugs attack my mind. I can still see Charlie's body staring back at me with accusations in her eyes. All I want is to wrap my arms around her and take the last five minutes back, no matter what price I must pay.

Incendia's foot soldiers circle like vultures.

Then… nothing.

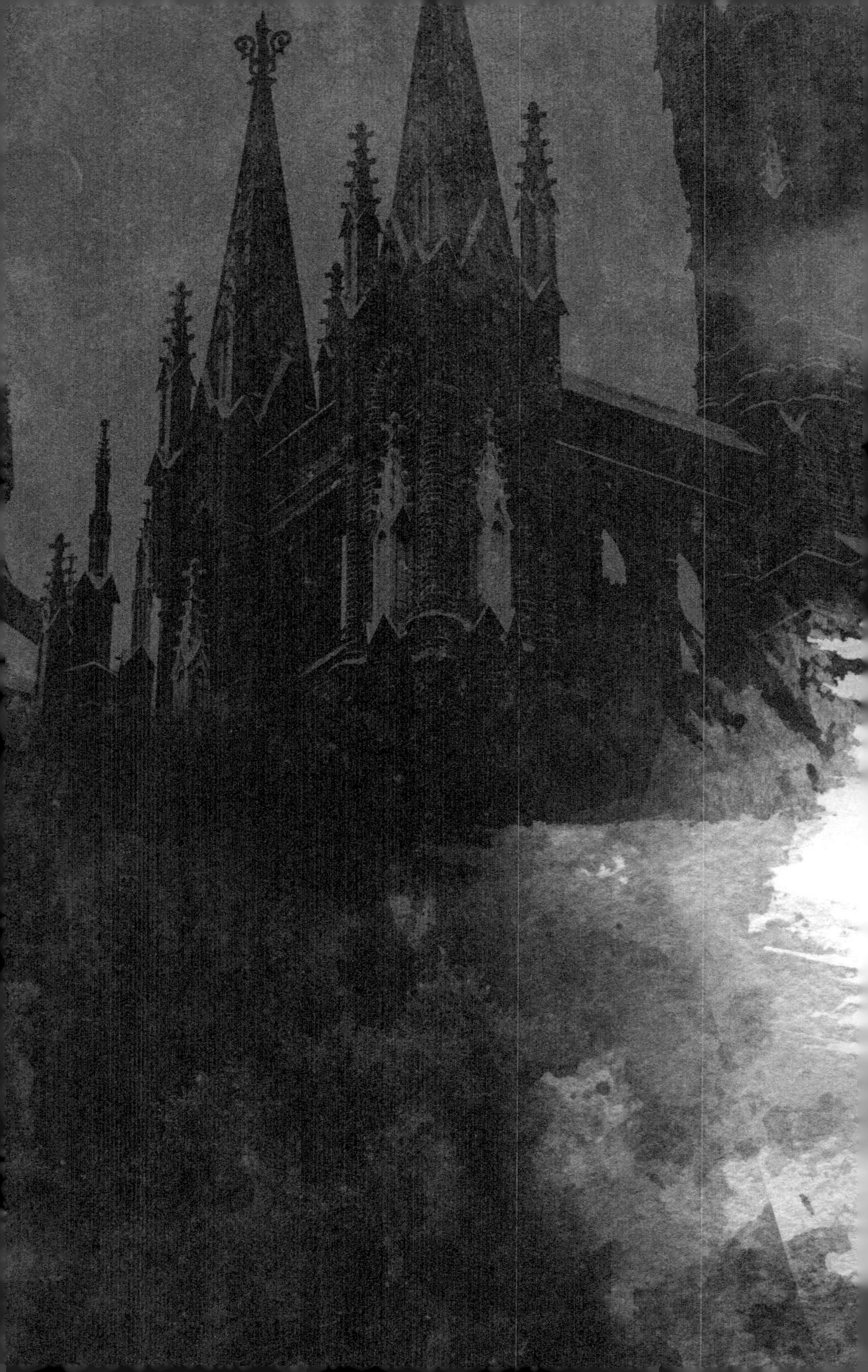

14

BROOKLYN

Birdcage - Holding Absence

Time to wake up, Brooke.

We're going to go for a little drive.

Far, far away from here.

With a scream lodged in my throat, I shoot upright. A wave of dizziness washes over me. My surroundings are blurred as I blink to clear my vision. Are we back at the cottage? Or… no, we were in London. That's when it hits me.

The nightclub.

Phoenix's Nana.

Helicopters.

Bullets.

Screaming.

As shadows settle around me, I slap a hand to my neck. It's throbbing and tender from the needle stuck in my flesh. All I can remember is seeing Phoenix trapped on the wrong side of the street, covered in his sister's blood, with enemies advancing on all sides.

"Phoenix!" I scream and flail.

Losing my balance, I fall from the soft mattress beneath me and smack into the floor with a groan. It doesn't matter. I need to find Phoenix. Splayed out and gasping for air, fragments of reality begin to filter in, like piecing together smashed glass.

Plain white walls.

Smooth, polished floor.

A single light built into the ceiling.

There's a bed to my left, the sheets disturbed from where I fell. No windows. One door and a serious-looking lock. Pushing up on my hands and knees, I hear a snort from across the room.

"Graceful, Brooke. You mind keeping the screaming down? My head still hurts from when you bashed it in with your bare hands."

Trembling all over, I force myself to meet the wide, expectant eyes of my best friend, Teegan. Framed by flowing, bright-red hair, heavy eyeliner and her usual gothic armour, she stares me down with the corner of her mouth lifted in a grin.

"Tee?" I whisper fearfully.

"The one and only. Long time, no see."

"What are you doing here? Where... where are we?"

"Neverland, obviously. I'm waiting for Peter Pan to come save us."

Sprawled out in the corner, she props her Creepers against the wall. I clutch my chest, feeling like I'm having a heart attack. Did Incendia catch her too? Are we both prisoners now? I have to find the guys. I won't let anyone hurt them just to get to me.

"Where are the others?"

Teegan chuckles. "You're going to get them killed, you know."

"Where the hell are they?"

"Not here," she singsongs.

Getting my jelly legs beneath me, I manage to stand. The room is still swaying with the aftereffects of the drugs, but I make my way to the door without faceplanting. It refuses to budge, no matter how loud I shout and rage. We're trapped in these four walls.

"How long have you been here?"

Teegan sighs. "All I ever wanted was to be your friend, B. That's it. Where did that get me, huh? Three surgeries. Intensive care. They had to wire my jaw shut. All your fault."

Before I can beg on my knees for her forgiveness, a slow, mocking clap fills the room. With my back against the wall, I nearly jump out of my skin. Hudson's glaring at me from the empty bed.

"Landed yourself in more trouble, I see."

"Hud?"

His smile takes a venomous edge. "I never regretted what I did to you all those years ago. You needed breaking in. I wanted to ruin you, watch you scream and suffer, desperate to escape."

Squeezing my eyes shut, I wrench them open again, ready for him to disappear in a cloud of shadows. His sharp gaze remains, digging beneath my skin like a parasite. Each step towards me has my hammering heartbeat racketing even higher.

"You should have died on that roof last year," Hudson spits. "Everything was perfect until you came along and fucked up our lives. Now, we're all dead because of you."

Teegan concurs with a gleeful hoot. "Don't worry, Brooke. She's coming back for you. You escaped fate before, but not this time. Once you're dead, we can all live in peace."

"But... what if... what if I want peace too?" My voice breaks right as my knees give way. "I don't want to be alone anymore. I... I think I want my happy ending."

Frigid cold races down my spine as a pair of lips meet my ear. Rubbery and hard, the brush of the dead is unmistakable. Vic will always live inside of me. I can't dig out his poison wrapped around my bones.

"You don't deserve your happy ending," he taunts. "Thought you'd gotten rid of me, did you, darling? I'm never far away." His skeletal finger taps my temple. "Right here, until the end."

"No! Get me out!" I curl up in the tightest ball imaginable. "Please… please let me out."

My voice deserts me, drying up into oblivion. Tears flow and my body shakes with tremors. I don't know how long I lay there, sobbing and pleading for an escape. The choir of voices breaks my solitude with their taunts and constant barrage of vitriol.

When a hand clasps my shoulder and shakes, I scream again.

"Hey, Brooke! It's me!"

"Theo?" I gasp.

His blue eyes and soft, boyish features peer down at me behind his glasses, framed by dense, blonde curls. He's dressed in another flannel shirt and tee, with an ID badge swinging from his neck. My mouth opens and shuts like a dead fish. I feel like my vocal chords have been severed.

"No need to panic. I won't hurt you."

"W-Where?"

"Somewhere safe," he confirms.

His words ring true, but my panic is too far gone. Moving lightning fast, I throw my entire body weight into him. He yelps and crashes to the floor in a heap. Before he can hurt me, I fall back on months of fighting to survive, and strike him right in the temple.

Theo slumps with a gasp of pain, his skinny limbs hanging limp and useless. Across the room, Hudson resumes his sarcastic clapping. The voice of my abuser has gone, but Teegan still lashes me with her angry stare. My heart stops when two more figures rise from the bed.

"Better run, love," Kade warns. "She's coming."

Eli stares without words, a trail of blood running from the corner of his mouth. I watch in horror as deep stab wounds appear in all of their bodies. Invisible knives shred the people I love, slashing every bit of skin. Throats, arms, wrists. A tsunami of blood approaches.

Run, little Brooke.

Run from Mummy.

I'm going to catch you.

I tear through the ajar door, leaving Theo's unconscious body behind. An endless, dull corridor with thick carpet greets me, lit by corporate lighting. Bearing right, I run like my life depends on it. The ghosts are going to swallow me whole if I don't fucking run.

A warren of corridors and empty offices beckons me deeper into the building, with the fires of insanity licking at my heels. I think I can hear someone shouting in the distance, but they're trapped in another dimension and unable to reach me.

I'm too distracted by the ghosts hunting me down to notice the person waiting to capture me. My entire body smacks into something tall, hard, and terrifying. Thick, trunk-like legs give way to an impossibly huge, barrel chest and arms with enough muscle to lift a truck single-handedly.

Two hands clamp down on my arms.

The low, throaty grumble of a beast makes me freeze.

"Stop right there, kiddo."

"No! Let me go, Logan!" I scream.

"What are you talking about?"

I'm too disorientated to stop the onslaught of memories from overwhelming me in quick flashes. Logan standing on that godforsaken beach. His body heat curled around mine. Counting sheep in the dead of night. Standing between me and fists. His blood painting the elusive art of death in red ink.

"Jesus, Brooklyn. Stop fighting me."

"No! Let me go!"

The mountain captures me in his arms like a bloodthirsty spider in its web. I let out another scream and fight back until I'm tossed over his shoulder, with strong arms clamping down on my legs.

"I need a pay rise for this shit," he grumbles.

The world hangs upside down as he angrily stomps down another long corridor, taking several sharp turns before thumping up a flight of stairs. On the next level, he swipes a pass and bursts into what looks like an office. I catch the blur of several bodies all rushing to stand.

"What the hell, Enzo?" Someone exclaims.

"I caught her attempting to flee the building."

"You have to let me go." I smash my fists into his back. "Teegan's coming for me... and Hudson, Kade, Eli. It isn't safe... the ghosts are going to get me. I need to run!"

"Blackbird? We're right here."

Hudson's voice yanks the plug from my body. In an instant, I'm left exhausted and lifeless. My captor pulls me back over his shoulder until I'm cradled in his arms like a tiny baby. Piercing amber eyes bore into me beneath an untamed shock of black hair.

"You going to behave?" he questions.

"Put me down before I gouge your eyes out," I threaten weakly.

A smile spreads his thick, angular lips. "I'd very much like to see you try, wildfire. We can spar this out if you'd prefer. I'll happily beat you into submission."

"Touch her and your eyes won't be the only thing at risk," Hudson warns calmly. "Your choice, pal."

He rolls his eyes. "I'll pass."

I'm placed back on my feet and the carpet rushes to meet me until someone grabs me from behind. Crushed in a back-breaking hug, Hudson's comforting scent wraps around me.

"You were right behind me," I wheeze.

"We've been here all day, waiting for you to wake up." His frown deepens as he studies my face. "What did you see? Who was it?"

"N-Nothing."

"Dammit, Brooke. Don't lie to me. You promised to tell us if you started seeing shit again."

Before I can die of embarrassment, I'm torn out of Hudson's embrace. Two petrified green eyes rake over me. Eli's forehead smashes into mine as he squeezes me hard enough to hurt. I can feel the dangerous hammering of his heart from here.

"You're okay," he murmurs.

His rough voice breaks the last of my composure. I sag into his body, allowing him to hold me up. Another column of warmth meets my back and helps Eli to manoeuvre me into a seat at the long table.

"I've got you, love," Kade whispers.

Hudson quickly takes the seat to my left and grabs my hand in his tight grip. Eli steals the other empty seat, leaving Kade to roll his eyes and find a new place to sit.

"Where are we?" I ask timidly.

"London, Brooklyn West."

The new voice captures my attention and refuses to surrender it. At the other end of the table, beside the annoyed giant that interrupted my fleeing, sits another unfamiliar man.

Tall, well-tanned, and built with the toned gait of a gym addict, he openly stares at me. His features are angular and handsome, though slightly disfigured by a puckered scar that bisects his eyebrow. His chin is covered in a rugged scruff of beard, harshening his model-perfect looks.

Wearing a checked suit and blue tie that complement his coffee-coloured eyes, the stranger's chestnut-brown hair is tied back at the nape of his neck. I suppress a shiver. He looks a little bit too much like Augustus, with his designer garb and palpable authority.

Hudson squeezes my hand. "Brooke, this is Hunter."

"Director of Sabre Security," he supplies.

I gape between the two strangers, my head on a swivel. "This is Sabre? Not Incendia?"

The mountain to Hunter's left steps forward, cracking his scarred knuckles. "I'm Enzo, second in command. Incendia attempted to extract you. We stepped in and brought you here for protection."

"Protection?"

Hunter cocks his head, considering me. "We've been monitoring your movements for a while. Blackwood Institute was the tip of the iceberg for our investigation into Incendia."

"You're Sadie's team, aren't you?"

"Alyssa works for us," Enzo confirms.

Right on time, the door to the office slams open and a very disgruntled-looking Theo storms in. There's a dark bruise forming on his forehead as he limps. His furious gaze crash lands right on me.

"Bit of warning next time you decide to coldcock me."

I lift my chin in defiance. "You should've ducked quicker."

Enzo chuckles, earning himself a sharp look from Theo. Hunter watches us all with steely attention, his chin resting on his laced fingers. I hate the way he's studying us, picking apart our demeanours and filing all the information away for dissection. It's unsettling.

The three men take their seats, maintaining a safe distance from us. I stare down at the smooth surface of the table, noting the two absences from our group. I'm almost too scared to ask, but make myself anyway.

"Where is he?"

With a throat clear, Kade seals my fate.

"Incendia is holding Phoenix hostage."

"Is he okay?"

"They haven't contacted us with a ransom yet," Hunter answers crisply. "So, we don't know."

Willing myself to keep it together, my voice steadies. If I let the cracks show now, I'll never piece myself together again. The neutral expression plastered on my face is flimsy at best.

"And Seven?"

"Out cold," Enzo replies. "He was a bit agitated when he woke up and started damaging our property. Our on-call doctor gave him a muscle-relaxant and a small dose of a sedative."

"I want to see for myself, right now."

"You'll answer our questions first."

"Like hell. Take me to Seven."

Slamming his hands down on the table, Hunter levels me with a stern look. "You have been a huge pain in our ass. We know who you are. We know what you've done. You're in no position to make demands."

"What the fuck is that supposed to mean?"

With his laptop opened, Theo points a remote control at the wall. There's a projector built into the ceiling, casting light on the spotless surface. My stomach twists as a CCTV feed is brought up, dated several months back. I recognise the bustling metropolitan street, surrounded by luxurious hotels.

"Please no," I whimper.

The guys still around me as the feed shifts to a full view of a hotel's foyer. It's draped in glistening lights and crystal chandeliers, with countless armed guards. I watch my skeletal form get dragged down a grand staircase by Jefferson. My handcuffed hands are just visible.

"Where is this?" Kade growls.

"An investor's event held by Incendia several months back," Theo answers. "Here's the main floor of the hotel. We've identified several members of senior management."

Augustus and Seven come into view, seated at the bar and awaiting our arrival. The guys around me remain silent as the tape plays. On the screen, I'm shoved into a seat next to Seven, where I later palm a dinner knife. I can still remember Logan's voice telling me to stop.

It's weird to watch myself wrestle the knife away with my other hand, as if another person inhabited my body. I had no idea Logan wasn't real. When Seven slips his hand under the table to stroke my bare leg, Hudson abruptly stands up.

"Hud—"

"I don't want to hear it, Brooke. Not right now."

Rejection pierces my chest. Hudson paces away and stands by the huge, floor-to-ceiling window for a moment. The tape is paused until he returns, now avoiding my gaze.

"Show them the rest," Hunter instructs.

Just when I think it couldn't get any worse, a grainier feed takes its place. This is tucked away at an odd angle. A hidden camera, then. I begin to shake as two figures enter the hotel bedroom. I don't need to watch the rest.

My hands curl into fists under the table when Theo adds sound. *Fucking thanks for that.* The awful sound of my struggle reverberates around us. On the screen, Martin has ripped my dress and pinned me down, preparing to inflict his disgusting will.

Fighting. Shouting. Begging.

The sound of a zipper being unfastened.

Then, gunfire.

On and on and on.

I can hear myself sobbing on the tape as the bullets tear free, until the clip finally runs out. Eli attempts to rest a hand on my shoulder, and I automatically leap away. Pain scores across his face. I abandon the table, retreating to the safety of a corner, dreading the next moments of the tape.

You were right. She was definitely worth the investment.
I can see why my son has fallen so hard for you.
Or should I say, technically speaking, sons.

"Motherfucker," Kade curses darkly. "He was there?"

I stare down at the office carpet, unable to answer. The sound of Kade's footsteps feels like the approach of doom, until his fingers are clasping my chin. I have no choice but to surrender to him.

"You left this part out," he accuses.

"I'm sorry, Kade."

"Why didn't you tell me he did this to you? Both of them?"

"Does it matter?"

"Yeah, it matters! What else don't we know?"

Hudson lays a hand on Kade's shoulder. "Lay off, brother. This isn't helping."

"All she does is lie, lie, and lie some more. Secrets. Omissions. Half-truths. What else are you hiding from us, Brooke? How many people did they make you kill?"

Kade shakes me hard enough to rattle my teeth. I have half a mind to punch him in the face and run. Anything to avoid facing the reality of my actions. I've only fed them strips, hiding the monstrous truth because I'm selfish. I don't want to lose them again.

"We're aware of twenty-eight targets over the space of four months, all deceased," Hunter interjects. "The actual number is likely a lot higher. We estimate Patient Seven's body count to be in the hundreds."

I peel Kade's bruising fingers from my arm. He's frozen, an unreadable expression written across his face. The flash of judgement beneath his shock feels like a knife in the back.

"Not everyone should be saved," I whisper tearfully. "Some of us can't be brought back over that line once it's been crossed."

"This is such crap!" Hudson explodes, shoving Kade aside. "What you did in Blackwood doesn't have to fucking define you. We've all been forced to do shit we're not proud of."

"Twenty-eight people," Kade repeats.

Hudson rounds on him. "You killed my fucking mum. I don't give a damn whether you wanted to or not. Her blood will always be on your hands. Who are you to judge Brooklyn?"

The fight drains out of Kade like a pin in a balloon. He scrubs a hand over his tired, bruised face, before managing to look up at me. Shame twists in the depths of his hazel eyes.

"He's right. I'm sorry, Brooke. I had no right to say that stuff."

I lift my shoulder in a shrug. "I did those things. Me."

"Patient Eight did those things."

"What if we're one and the same?"

Closing the distance between us again, Kade takes my face in his hands. Despite our audience, the rest of the office falls away. All I can see is the pain and desperation eating away at him, attempting to tear a new chasm between us.

"I don't give a fuck," Kade whispers roughly. "I'm in love with Brooklyn West. If that means loving Patient Eight too, then that's exactly what I'll fucking do."

"You can't love me. Not like this."

"You don't get to decide that! There's no choice in this, no walking away. I've loved you since the moment we met, and I'll love you until our very last goodbye."

I try to step away from him, but he refuses to let go. We've been two steps forward, one step back, since the very beginning of this fucked-up journey. But now... I don't know if I can follow them into the light. This path only ends one way for me.

"Incendia won't stop until I'm dead. Maybe that's what I deserve... but you guys don't. I won't let you throw your lives away for me, even if I love you too."

Behind Kade, Hudson stares at me with possession and rage in equal measure. He looks like he wants to burn the entire world down just so we can walk together through the ashes. If I try to walk away, I have no doubt he'll drag me right back to them, kicking and screaming.

Hunter, Enzo, and Theo sneak out to give us some privacy. When the door clicks shut, Eli joins our little huddle. Fearsome need wars across his expression as he tucks a piece of hair behind my ear.

"It's... our ch-choice," he stutters out.

Hudson nods. "We're choosing you."

"Today, tomorrow, and every day to come," Kade says vehemently. "If Phoenix were here... he'd say the same thing. It's going to take all of us to bring him home."

"All of us?" I repeat.

Eli slides his hand into mine, and Kade releases me into Hudson's strong embrace. Between the three of them, I feel my body begin to relax. They're my foundation. My strength. The force that keeps me going.

"Let's go find Seven," Hudson suggests, seeming shocked by his own words. "Perhaps today will be the day he decides to be a sane human being."

"Unlikely," Kade mutters.

As we step outside the office and back into the brightly lit corridor, Enzo and Hunter are talking rapidly with their heads together. Theo has vanished. I try not to shiver as their eyes sweep over us.

"We want to see Seven." I try to sound braver than I feel.

Enzo folds his powerful arms, muscles bulging against the tight fit of his black t-shirt. He defers back to his leader with a nod. Hunter scares me the most. It's in the way he looks at me, full of perceptive intelligence. My secrets dance in his eyes like embers from a flame.

"I expect answers to my questions," he says curtly. "Your protection here is only temporary, and it comes at a price. We're putting ourselves at great risk."

"What do you want from us?"

Hunter's fingers drum against his toned arms. "Sworn evidence from all five of you about Blackwood. Plus, the two you've got smuggled away. You're going to help me bring Incendia down."

Kade bites his lip. "The others are… elsewhere."

"Irrelevant. We can retrieve them."

"We're not going to prison," Hudson adds next.

"You will be given our full protection while this is taking place. Your testimonies can be used to negotiate a plea deal with the government. I can't rule out eventual prosecution."

"Where is Seven?" I repeat, losing patience with this asshole. "Right now, I don't give a fuck about the world or Incendia. I need to know that the people I care about are safe. Then we can bargain."

Studying me with that piercing stare, Hunter nods. "Enzo will take you to your friend. We have temporary accommodation for you. After that, we do things my way."

"Are we safe enough to stay here?"

"We're good at what we do," Enzo answers me. "Our staff are all highly trained. Nobody is getting through that front door without a hell of a fight."

Checking with the guys, they all reluctantly nod.

"Take them upstairs," Hunter instructs Enzo, pulling his phone out. "I'll contact the SCU and lay the groundwork. They're not going to believe this."

"Gotcha. Follow me, kids."

Sticking close together, we follow Enzo down the thickly carpeted corridor. Hunter watches us leave with a contemplative look, his phone already pressed to his ear. Our eyes connect at the last second before we step into an elevator.

I'm left wondering exactly whose hands our lives are in… and if we're any safer here than we were in Blackwood.

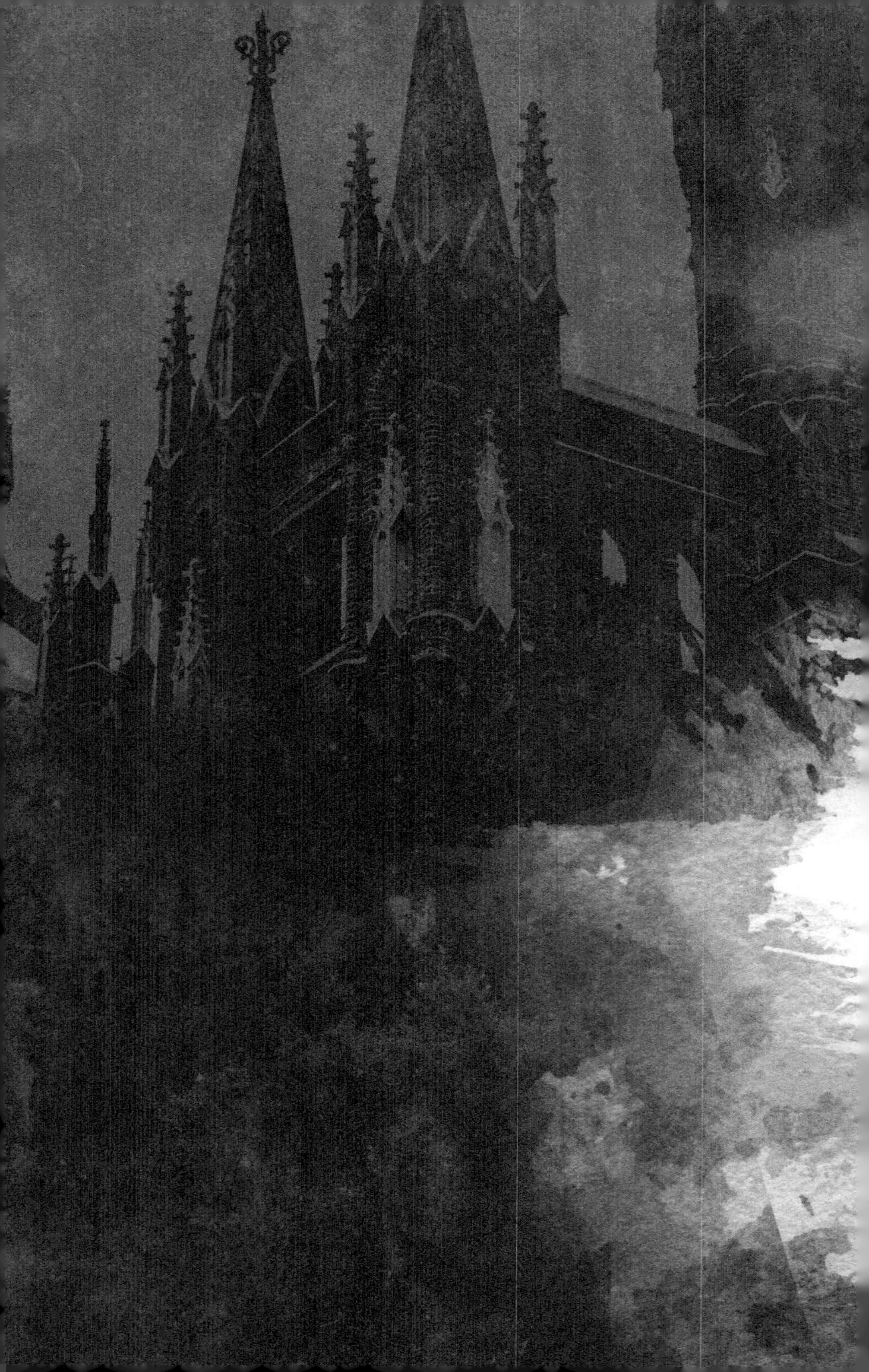

15

SEVEN

Lost - The Hunna

Their voices fade into the background as I stare out at the lurid city lights. My hand is pressed against the glass wall, leading to a generous balcony that hangs high above the rest of the world.

I'm in no state to sit around eating takeout with Eight and her men in our temporary apartment. Watching the ease with which they talk and joke around is torturous. She lights up in their presence, becoming more than the vacant machine I know.

They make her whole.

I'll never be able to give her that.

Unlocking the door, I slip out into the night. At the top of Sabre's formidable skyscraper, the wind encapsulates me in an impenetrable bubble. I've never felt so alone in the weeks since our lives changed forever… but it isn't safe for me to be around other people.

Jude was a good person, I think.

Seven is his opposite in every way.

There's a click behind me as the door reopens, disturbing my solitude. I don't need to look. I know it's her. She's never far behind—the phantom that wrapped herself around what remains of my humanity.

"Sev? Are you hungry?"

"Leave me be, Eight."

With a sigh, she joins me at the edge of the balcony. Our shoulders brush momentarily. I sneak a glimpse of her dangerously short hair, sharp cheekbones, and breathtaking beauty. Everything about her sets my pulse racing. I didn't know I could actually feel anymore. Not until she came along.

"We're all worried about you," Eight murmurs. "Even the guys. I know things are difficult with them, but you don't have to hide out here by yourself. Come and eat something."

Biting my lip, the truth attempts to strangle me. I don't give a flying fuck what her boyfriends think. Whatever this twisted thing is between us, it was forged in the hottest of fires, born of blood and death. Such bonds are unbreakable.

"Do you think the people we used to be are still in us somewhere?"

Hesitating, Eight shakes her head. "They're gone, Sev. That doesn't mean we can't have lives, however imperfect and painful. I just don't know if we deserve to."

"Neither one of us can live a normal life, not now."

"I think you may be right." Eight captures my hand. "But fuck being normal. I know what I have with the guys may seem strange, but we're a family. I want you to be part of our family too."

Something flutters behind my ribcage, reawakening an organ that I long thought dead. I don't know what this unnameable feeling is. Sensations sometimes come over me like waves and I can never label them. Not after so long being stripped of all human emotion.

"What do your men think of this proposal?" I ask pointedly.

She musters a small smile. "They're all in, Sev. It may help if you stop breaking people's fingers and threatening to skin them alive, but somehow, your violent charm has won them over."

I raise an eyebrow. "My charm?"

"Well, I adapted what they said. It was more along the lines of *go fetch the sadistic bastard*, but you get the gist. This whole solo-gunslinger thing is unnecessary."

"Solitude keeps us alive."

"You deserve to be more than just alive," Eight implores me. "I'm not going to watch you fade away. We didn't survive Augustus's hell just to let him win now."

Before I can stop her, she drags me back inside the luxurious apartment. I feel instantly on edge. The soft furnishings and glittering lights are offensive after so long spent in the dark. I can feel her tensing up too, but the moment we step into the large, open plan living area, Eight relaxes.

A cream-coloured sectional sofa dominates the airy space. There's a flat screen television on the wall, along with armchairs and lamps dotted about. Soft, woven blankets and fresh plants soften the stark decor, giving it a comfortable feeling. But I feel even more out of sorts.

The entire room is boxed in by more slabs of glass that make up the walls, giving undisturbed, panoramic views of the city. If this palace is one of Sabre's spare rooms, I dread to think where they actually live.

"Hey," Hudson greets warily.

Their eyes train on me the moment we step inside the room. I slide an arm around Eight's waist in a clear mark of possession, too stubborn to back down. I'm surprised when Hudson takes a deep breath, nods to himself, and looks away without yelling.

"Food?" Kade asks us. "Enzo sent up Chinese takeout."

"Are we sure they didn't poison it?" Eight jokes.

"Erm, negative. It's better than what we've been living off, though."

Eight leads me to a pair of oversized armchairs, gently shoving me into one of them. She grabs a carton of food and drops it into my hand before tending to herself. Chest burning with another odd feeling, I dig into the noodles.

"What's the deal with this place?" Hudson says around a mouthful of food. "Not to be a dick or anything, but we don't take handouts. They have an agenda. Are we going to play into their hands?"

"Since when are you not a dick?" I reply bluntly.

Tense silence is broken by several rounds of raucous laughter. Hudson scowls at me over the Chinese food, but it's without his malice. He's becoming somewhat more amiable as time goes on, though I wouldn't mind finding a shallow grave for his body anyway.

His blonde-haired brother looks amused. Eli, the quietest of Eight's motley crew, is hammering her on the back as she chokes on a wonton. He's the least objectionable of them all. I hate quiet people less.

"Hudson being a dick aside." Kade grins at me. "We most certainly don't take handouts. I want Hunter's protection, sure. But we came here for answers and we're not leaving without them."

"You think they know anything?" Eight asks after gulping water. "They seemed desperate for us to talk. This deal is shady. It doesn't guarantee us anything."

"Sabre knows more about Bancroft than we do."

"You drew up a profile."

Kade shrugs. "Finding information online is one thing. With Sabre's resources, they have access to classified information. I bet they've got a good fix on Bancroft already."

"Why does that matter to us, though?"

Hudson clears his throat. The pair exchange uneasy looks, seeming to communicate without words. Eight slams her carton of food down and crosses her arms.

"You don't have to treat us like invalids."

Despite having enough secrets to sink a damn ship, Eight doesn't like stuff being kept from her. I watch them all stare off in a battle of wills, until Kade sighs and abandons his own food carton.

"While you were both still sedated, we gleaned some other information from Hunter. They've been investigating for several years now. He knows far more about Incendia than we do."

"Why are the institutes still operational? Clearly, he has evidence. Why isn't it enough?"

"Connections," Hudson supplies. "Influential friends. Investors. Government contracts and associations. Incendia is practically state-owned, so many of its shares are held by people in positions of power."

"*Sir* Joseph Bancroft," Eight recites grimly. "Fuck, we're so dead."

"Not exactly."

Eight casts Kade an incredulous look. "Miss White was a bust. Augustus's laptop was fried. Incendia took Phoenix… we don't know what they're doing to him." She gulps and shoves her pain down. "What aren't you telling us?"

Glancing between all of them, we're clearly missing something important. Even Eli is squirming in his seat, succumbing to the mounting pressure. Our tiresome wait is broken when Hudson clears his throat.

"Well, it would seem that Professor Lazlo is alive."

Silence descends like a cloud of fog. Smothering, clinging, unable to be scrubbed from our skin as it sinks deep inside of us. While the three men plead for leniency with their eyes, Eight is set in stone.

"He's willing to meet and wants to exchange information," Kade adds.

"Willing?" I repeat.

Hudson knocks back a mouthful of water. "Sabre have offered him the same deal. Protection in exchange for his sworn evidence and full cooperation in bringing Incendia down."

"And later? Will he be arrested?"

Kade looks uncomfortable. "He will be in a position to argue for a plea deal. Immunity from prosecution if he testifies under oath, kinda thing. Hunter has a government contact who can be trusted when the time comes."

"A plea deal."

Eight's voice is hard as nails and utterly unyielding.

"I'm sorry, love."

"You're telling me that the man who murdered my entire family, imprisoned Seven, tortured Lucia, and arranged for Rio to kill me won't face a single day of punishment for his actions?"

Hudson looks away. "It's a real possibility."

I try to put my hand on Eight's shaking leg, but she stands up, walking away from us all. Hudson pursues her and she yells at him to back off. Her mind is already gone.

"It was all for nothing," Eight says to herself. "Our lives have been destroyed and it was all for fucking nothing! He's going to worm his way out of everything."

"Blackbird—"

"I'm going to kill Hunter and his stupid team."

Hudson blocks her exit, his hands raised. "Just stop. Let's talk about this."

"I don't want to fucking talk!"

Shoving him hard, Hudson stumbles into a glass end table that promptly smashes. Eight stares at him open-mouthed for a second before running from the room. Nobody seems to know what to say.

"Go get her." Hudson stands, wincing at his scraped hands. "She'll listen to you."

His show of faith is a surprise. Nodding, I take off after Eight. The front door to the apartment is wide open. I chase after her ash-white hair, somewhat doubting my ability to calm her down right now.

"What's your plan?" I shout down the darkened corridor.

Even at this hour, the hum of late-night activity fills the skyscraper from the lower levels. Eight has stopped in front of the elevator, her hands braced on her knees as she breathes hard.

"Do I need a fucking plan?!"

"Might do, princess."

"I'm not your goddamn princess! I'm a stone-cold assassin and I've been fucked over for the very last time. Are you going to help me kill their sorry asses or not?"

Eight smashes her finger into the elevator's button, but it's stuck on another level. She batters it over and over again, growing more frustrated. I draw to a halt by her side and chuckle.

"Alright, assassin. No need to take it out on the elevator."

"How are you not more mad about this?" she hisses at me. "Lazlo is the reason you're here. He broke us both and Sabre wants to serve him a brand-new life on a gold fucking platter. Why aren't you angry?"

Reaching out, I tug Eight closer. She smashes against my chest with a faint gasp. Banding my arms around her slim, sexy body, I revel in the feel of her skin on mine. Her eyes are wide and curious, tempting me further. My lips gaze over the exposed slope of her throat, leaving featherlight kisses.

"Because I don't believe in justice," I murmur throatily. "None of us get what we deserve in this life. Otherwise, we would be dead and buried, and Incendia scattered in ashes. Neither has happened."

Eight offers me a desolate look. "I don't want to live in a world where the people that killed my family are free to do as they please. I want my revenge, Sev. I don't give a fuck if I have to pay the ultimate price to achieve that."

"You'd throw away everything just to hurt the people that hurt us?"

She looks down, hiding her darkness from me. With a low growl, I tug her head back up. I want to see the bloodthirst and rage swimming in her eyes. That dark, sordid place inside of her is where I found my home.

"I'm supposed to say no, right? Pretend like I'm happy with what I've got."

"No," I reason. "Maybe this is the way back."

"Back to what? There's nothing left for us in our old lives."

"You said it yourself. Family."

Blinking rapidly, Eight's mouth clicks open. I ease it shut and close the final inches between us. She doesn't move or fight back, content to let our destructive collision play out in real time. When our lips meet, it feels like electricity is flowing through my veins.

I push past her lips with my tongue, desperate to claim every damned inch of her. I want her breath. Her lifeblood. Her thoughts. Her pain. Her hope. All of it belongs to me now, because I can't find it on my own. She needs to show me the way back.

Breaking the mind-melting kiss to glance up and down the deserted corridor, I check that we're still alone. Eight is panting hard, her back now pressed against the elevator doors. Finding the soft elastic of her waistband, I give no warning before pushing my hand into her panties.

"Sev..."

"Shut up, Eight. Let me feel you."

Her back arches as I find the soaked heat between her thighs. Jesus, she's so damn wet for me. Circling her sensitive nub, I give it a sharp tug before seeking her entrance. Eight lets out a mewl for attention, pushing her hips forward to seek more of my touch.

When I shove a finger in her pussy, she moans again. I begin to work it in and out, watching for her reaction. I've dreamed of touching her for so long, staking my claim in blood and desire. I want her to look at me the way she looks at them. I need her to want me back.

"Does the idea of revenge get you all wet and worked up, princess?"

Eight's teeth sink into her bottom lip. "Yes."

"What about slicing the throats of our enemies and fucking each other in a puddle of their spilled blood? Does that make you hot?" I ask curiously.

"Fuck… yes, it makes me hot."

Grazing my lips against her ear, I drop my voice even lower. "What about me bending you over Lazlo's cold, dead corpse, and fucking your tight cunt for the entire world to watch?"

Adding another finger to her slick warmth, I speed up my movements. She's beginning to tremble against my body, trapped in place and unable to run from me this time. Her legs spread wider with each thrust of my fingers, desperate for more. When I curl a digit to touch her sweet spot, she gasps loudly.

"I'm going to come."

"Fall apart for me, princess. I want to see it for myself."

Her forehead crashes into my chest as she orgasms. My cock is aching with desperation, but I won't take her here. Not like this. Pain and suffering brought us together. Seeking vengeance for all we've endured will mark the beginning of our future, however long or short it may be.

"Here's exactly what you're going to do." I slide my fingers from her panties and slowly lick her come from each one. "You're going to put a pretty smile on and play the game with these assholes. I don't give a fuck how, but we must convince them we're the right ones for the job."

"What job?" Eight repeats unsteadily.

Smirking, I push two of my fingers past her lips. Her eyes widen as she's forced to taste her own release, but then her tongue flicks over my digits, cleaning up what remains. I push them further into her mouth, touching the back of her throat until she gags.

"We're going to bring Lazlo in," I whisper, fucking her throat with my fingers. "While they're waiting for his worthless hide, we're going to peel the skin from his bones and enjoy every precious second it takes for him to bleed to death."

She gasps for air as I slip my fingers out. Stray tears mark the soft surface of her cheeks. Leaning in, I consume the salty droplets with a flick of my tongue. Her lips seek mine out with force, our teeth clashing.

When we finally break apart, darkness has unfurled in the grey depths of her eyes. It's a welcome sight, the infection of violence and evil. Like spilled ink tainting everything around it. The person her men know—Brooklyn West—takes a back seat.

I'm left with the soulless demon that Augustus created. My equal in every sense, an extension of the sickness bred too deep into me to dig out. Patient Eight smiles up at me. My partner in darkness.

I don't care if the good part of her has to die. All I want is the monster that dwelled beneath the ground with me. This execution will ensure that.

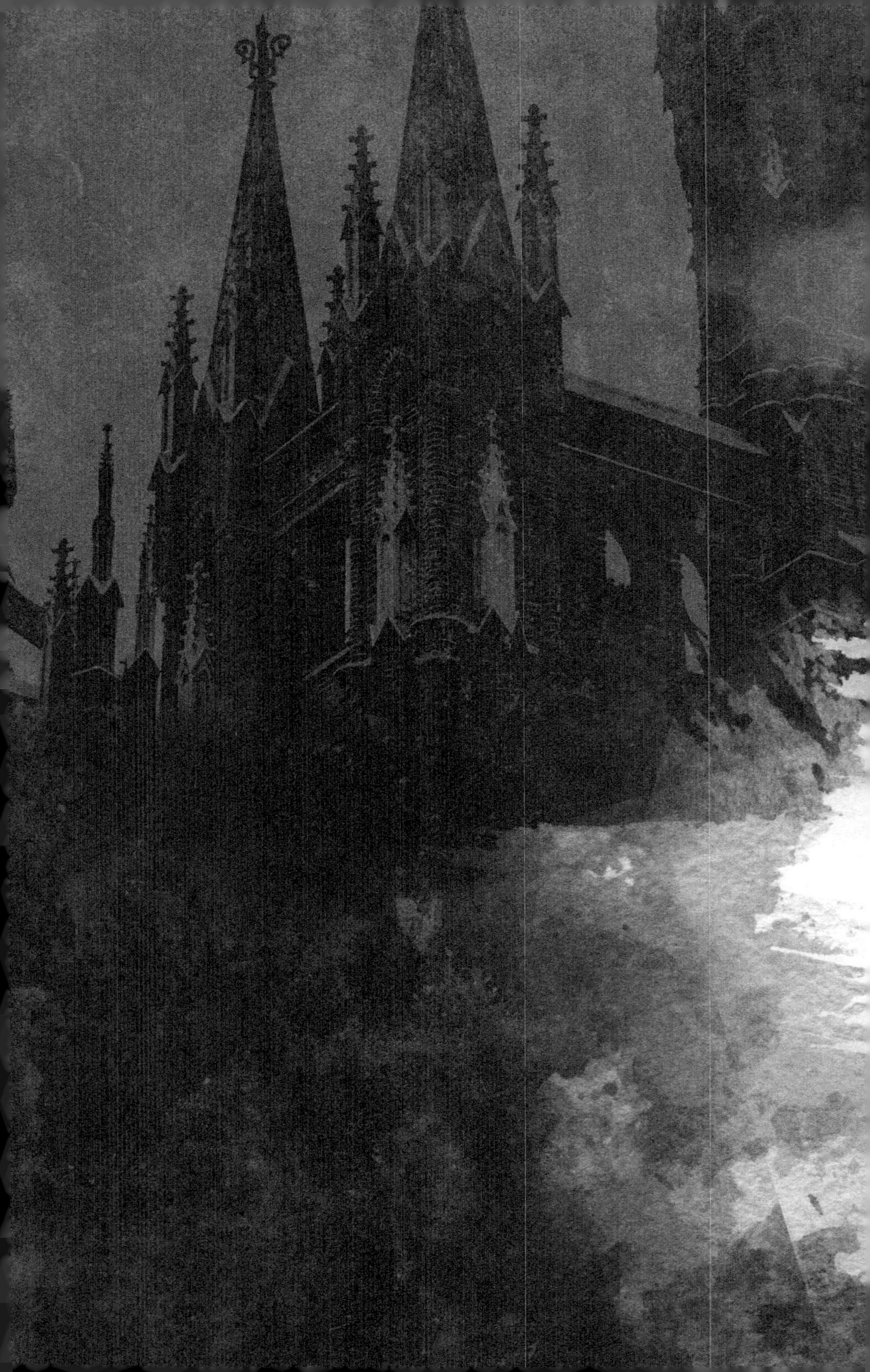

16

BROOKLYN

Pretty Toxic Revolver - Machine Gun Kelly

"Not in a million years," Hunter states flatly.

Sitting behind his neatly organised desk, he stares at me with defiance. There isn't a single crack in his facade. Arms crossed over his crisp, white shirt, his lips press into a tight line. Countless muscles bulge through the material, advertising his strength.

"It should be us," I argue back. "We're experienced and capable of handling anything on Lazlo's part. If you send an army of spooks in there, you'll scare him off. Let us handle this."

"Am I not speaking English? I said no. End of discussion."

Swivelling in his leather office chair, he runs a hand over his slicked back, chestnut ponytail. Despite being in his late twenties, he seems far older than his years. I feel like a speck on the radar compared to his wealth and knowledge. Sabre is living proof of it.

His office is far bigger than it needs to be and lit by the sun shining through the tinted glass windows. Packed bookshelves, ring binders, and textbooks make way for cork boards full of photographs, papers, and connecting ribbons of red string. He's mapped out everything in excruciating detail.

Blackwood sits at the centre of Hunter's organised madness. Cut-out news articles featuring Bancroft, Incendia, and several political big fish are pinned in between, connecting the other five institutes that each hold their own place. At the very top, there's a printed alert from law enforcement.

Wanted.
Armed & Extremely Dangerous.

Our faces stare back at me.

"You've spent so long trying to do the impossible." I gesture up at the packed cork board. "You run the risk of losing the best lead you've ever had. Lazlo isn't going to waltz in and start spewing information."

Hunter looks nonchalant. "I will convince him."

"How? Unlike Incendia, you have to follow the law."

"Why do you care?"

"I don't want to see anyone else get hurt!" I snap at him.

"With all due respect, Sabre is well-equipped to handle someone like Lazlo. We've been tackling criminal enterprises since long before you turned up."

"And we're not equipped? You've seen us in action. We know what we're doing."

Standing up, Hunter moves to the window. Hands laced behind his back, he considers the vast city landscape before picking up a framed photograph from his book-covered console. I can spot him in it, along with a younger carbon copy, complete with flowing brown hair and a cheeky grin.

"I'm trying to keep you safe," Hunter spells out, putting it back down with a frown. "You're making my job increasingly difficult."

"Look, I appreciate what you're doing for us, but we have a say in this too. Lazlo is the reason we're here. He started this by taking our lives from us."

"We're attempting to give you them back."

"What lives?!" I throw my hands up.

"Yourself and Jude Farlow are fugitives under temporary house arrest. I have warrants from the government, police and secret service, all demanding I hand you over for re-incarceration. Most of them report to Incendia."

My voice dries up as Hunter focuses on me.

"You'd be dead if we didn't step in. That is what we're giving you, Brooklyn. Your lives. Help us to understand how Incendia did this, and we can secure your futures."

"I can't do anything knowing Lazlo is still out there!"

"You need to let this go. Our team will bring him in."

"This man ruined my life." I march up to the desk and slam my hands down. "I'm willing to accept that he is a valuable asset. All I'm asking for is the chance to get some closure. Then Professor Lazlo is all yours."

Hunter sighs heavily. "You're impossible. The best place for you is here. The moment you step foot outside, I cannot guarantee your safety. The people looking for you won't hesitate to turn you over."

"Bring it on. Someone has to bring Phoenix home."

"You really do have a death wish, don't you?"

"I can't just sit here and do nothing!" My emotions overwhelm me at the thought of Phoenix. "It fucking kills me to know he's alone. We don't know what they're doing to him right now."

"We're trying to find him. Incendia has a lot of boltholes."

Our argument is interrupted by a sharp knock at the door. Theo pokes his head in, looking drained and far too pale in yesterday's rumpled clothing. He briefly glances at me before focusing on his boss.

"We have a problem."

"What is it now?" Hunter growls.

Theo appears nervous. "First contact from Incendia."

I'm following him into the corridor before Hunter's even moved. The steel grip of panic on my lungs is suffocating. Down the hall, Theo's office door is open. It's a glorified Nerd-Vana inside. Wires, cables, and countless monitors clutter the shadowed room.

He keeps the sun blotted out with thick blinds, while every available wall space is covered in surveillance maps, official documents, and the odd superhero poster. Tripping over a haphazard stack of programming books, I nearly fall on my ass before a pair of hands catches me.

"Careful, wildfire. Theo's organisation leaves a lot to be imagined."

Rippling muscles place me back on my feet with ease. Enzo's disarming smile peers down at me underneath an overgrown, messy mop of raven hair. He's back in all black again, finished with a pair of shining army boots.

"Where are the others?" I huff, smoothing my clothes.

Enzo props his huge shoulder against the wall. "On their way, I would imagine. Does my company bother you? Most people are afraid of me around here."

Hands propped on my hips, I hit him with an eye roll. Enzo is the biggest person I've ever met. He looks like the Rock and the Hulk had a fucked-up love child. All raw power and rippling muscle, wrapped in a tanned, gruff exterior. Yet there's a softness in his amber eyes, and a playful lilt to his smile.

"Oh, please. You're a teddy bear."

He actually splutters. "I've worked at Sabre for almost a decade.

Trust me, kid, I'm not a fucking teddy bear. I bet my kill count is a hell of a lot higher than yours."

"Maybe you can talk some sense into your boss's thick skull, then."

"I doubt that. Hunter's my best friend, but he's also a stubborn son a bitch."

"I have every right to bring Lazlo in! He's mine."

Enzo scoffs at me. "Gambling this opportunity on some misguided sense of personal justice isn't Hunter's style. We have no idea how Lazlo is alive."

There's a bang as someone walks straight into the door. Theo stumbles in, rubbing his red forehead. He ignores us, frowning instead at the new coffee stain down his t-shirt where the liquid has slopped over.

"Late night, brains?" Enzo teases. "You have a bed at home, you know."

Theo dumps his mug at the desk, yawning loudly. "Alyssa made contact at three o'clock this morning. I stayed up to decrypt her message for Hunter. She's still safe."

I don't miss the sheer relief that washes over Enzo before he stuffs it down again. I'm starting to wonder just how close this so-called team really is.

"You've heard from her?" I ask neutrally.

"A couple of days ago," Enzo grumbles, looking unhappy. "She's refusing to be pulled out, despite the risk. As far as we're aware, her cover is intact. She's being cautious."

"Let me get this straight. Sa—um, Alyssa, is allowed to risk her life to infiltrate an institute but I'm not permitted to bring someone in? How is that fair?"

"Because Alyssa works for Sabre," Hunter booms as he enters, flanked closely by all four guys. "She's undergone extensive training for this role. I have faith in her abilities."

"What's going on?" Kade pulls me into his arms.

We all gather around Theo's monster of a computer, with a dozen different monitors hooked up and millions of windows open. It's like staring into a chaotic extension of his brain. Eli takes my hand, holding on tight as a video file is pulled up.

"What is this?" Seven asks warily.

Theo clears his throat. "It's a warning."

Hitting play, there are several sharp intakes of breath. The camera pans across a darkened concrete cell. Unlike the torture chamber where I was held, this one features a wide, two-way window that allows for constant observation. I stare at the balled-up body in the top right corner, shivering all over.

"Let's try this again," Bancroft's regal voice drones.

Phoenix's swollen face is almost unrecognisable. He's been beaten into a pulp. One dislocated arm hangs limp at his side, while his clothing is ripped and blood-stained. He can barely move, and his teeth are gritted in agony.

"Nix," Eli rasps.

I tighten my hold on him. "We'll get him back."

Our entire group watches in horror as a guard enters the cell, dragging a huge hose in with him. I already know what's coming. It seems like a minor punishment, but after long enough being pounded by freezing water, you begin to lose grip of your mind.

This is just the warm-up act.

After ten minutes of relentless water, another beating begins. I have to walk away, bracing my hands on the wall while the group curses at the unfolding scene. Eli eventually joins me, unable to stand it for a second longer. Both of us cling to the other, silently praying for the man that binds us together.

The worst part is, Phoenix still doesn't make a damn sound.

Throughout the torture, there isn't a single grunt or cry of pain. It's like he can't feel it anymore. He's already given up.

"There's more," Theo says reluctantly.

I look back in time to see the camera man exiting the cell. In the adjoining room, behind the glass, Bancroft stands ready to deliver his message to us. His hands are casually tucked in the pockets of his tailored trousers, a sinister smile stretching his mouth wide.

"Brooklyn West," he drawls. "You have forty-eight hours to hand yourself and Patient Seven over to the authorities, or Phoenix Kent will suffer the consequences. Don't try to run. I have the resources to hunt down every single person you've ever cared about and bring them back here for the same treatment."

Right on cue, there's a guttural scream.

It seems Phoenix couldn't hold out any longer.

"The clock's ticking, Miss West. I'll be seeing you soon."

The feed cuts out, leaving stunned silence.

"The file has been coded to erase itself after it's been watched," Theo explains with frustration. "Pretty high-level programming, but I suppose Incendia can afford to pay an expert."

My fist sailing into the wall seems to break everyone out of the spell. Swallowing a scream, I shake out the pain in my bleeding knuckles. All I can hear is Phoenix's scream ringing over and over again in my head.

"Any idea where the video was taken?" Enzo breaks the tension.

"It doesn't match any of the institutes we've infiltrated so far," Hunter replies. "There are two locations we haven't gotten inside. I doubt Incendia would use their headquarters to hold him. It's too obvious."

"Priory Lane? Kirkwood Lodge?"

"Both possibilities, along with Harrowdean. Alyssa hasn't entered the experimental wing yet. They're being extremely cautious after recent events."

"Can we trace the message?" Hudson suggests.

Theo's fingers race over his keyboard. "I've tried tracing the IP address, but it's been rerouted and bounced all over the country. They aren't taking any chances. Everything else has been anonymised and the video itself erased."

"You're saying we have no way of finding him," I choke out.

Hunter's voice is solemn. "Our options are very limited."

Looking around the packed office, I find Seven's steely gaze burning straight into me. He gives me a stern nod, his balled-up fist twitching at his side. That video was just another reminder of everything Lazlo has to account for, past and present.

"Professor Lazlo worked for Incendia for thirty years." I step in front of Hunter so he has to look at me. "If anyone can tell us where this video was filmed, it's him. I will get the information we need."

"My decision hasn't changed," Hunter elucidates.

"Neither has mine. I don't give a fuck whether or not I have your permission to leave. If we don't locate Phoenix, I have to hand myself over either way. I won't let him die for me."

Seven steps forward. "I will accompany Eight. We can meet Lazlo at an agreed upon location and deliver him to you, safe and sound. This isn't our first operation together."

"What makes you think that you're going and not one of us?" Hudson challenges him. "I still don't know if we can trust you with Brooklyn's safety."

"I've kept her alive for a hell of a lot longer than you morons," Seven argues flatly. "While you gave up on her, I was out there in the real world, protecting her. I've proven myself more than enough."

Kade rests a hand on Hudson's shoulder. "He's right. None of us are trained in the field. We have to track down where Phoenix is." He looks at me sternly. "Get what we need and come back alive. We're trusting you to do this right."

Guilt embeds itself beneath my skin. I disregard Seven's stare, taking the time to look between the guys. Hudson looks furious with this decision. Eli's eyes are still on Theo's laptop, even though the video has long since disappeared. His expression is distraught.

"We'll bring him in," I answer, wondering if it's the truth. "For Phoenix."

Hunter growls his frustration. "You kids are going to get yourselves killed."

"Let us do this and I'll give you that sworn evidence," I concede, hoping to appease him. "Whatever you want, I'll go on record. Augustus, the Z Wing, everything. It's all yours."

Immediately, he perks up.

"Everything?"

"Everything," I confirm. "Get the other two here and I'll convince them to testify as well, in exchange for protection. Just give me this one fucking thing. That's it."

Lips pursed, Hunter nods once.

"Don't make me regret this, West. You have a deal."

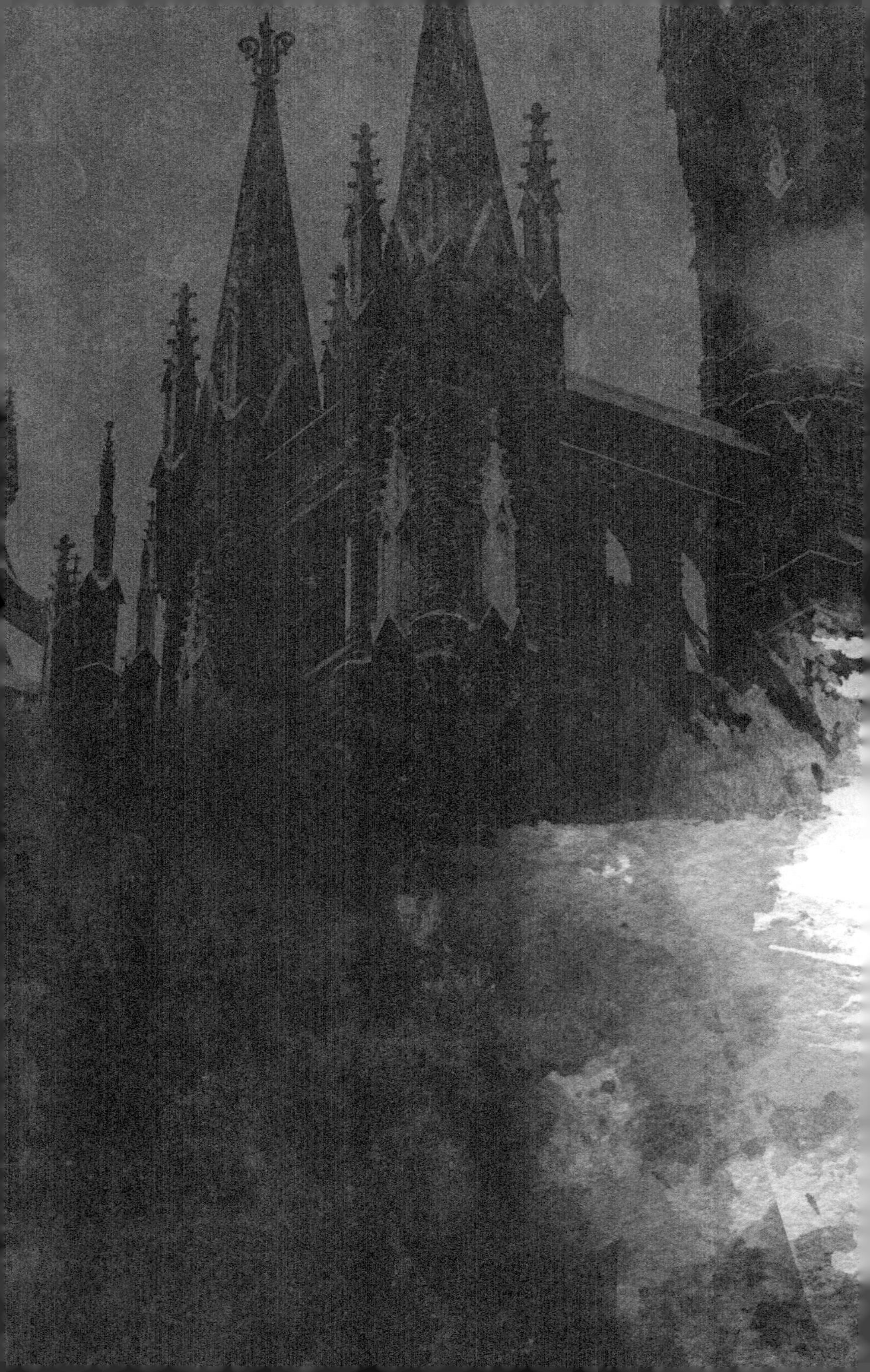

17

BROOKLYN

Me & My Demons - Omido and Silent Child

Mist and darkness cloak the abandoned dockyard. High above us, the moon offers a meagre slice of light, paving the way for our cautious footsteps. There isn't a single soul in sight this far out of the city. Nothing but ghosts and invisible demons walk these roads.

I tap the comms tucked in my ear. "Do you copy?"

"Check," Hunter answers. "Eyes up and ears open, West."

"Copy that, team leader."

Next to me, Seven strolls with lethal confidence. "Tell the pencil pusher to butt the hell out. This is our score."

"It's just to keep in contact in case things go south," I rationalise.

"Or to control us with. They don't trust us."

"Would you? We're hardly trustworthy."

Seven grumbles unintelligibly.

"That's what I thought."

Heading further inside, we keep a careful watch. This site was closed over a decade ago and left to disintegrate into the ravages of time. Old, rusted shipping containers and burned-out vehicles mark the post-apocalyptic landscape. It's the perfect place for this meeting.

"Lazlo is due to arrive in five minutes," Hunter informs me. "Remember, use force only if necessary. Bring him back alive, Brooklyn. That's non-negotiable."

"You got it. No asshole piñata today, noted."

"Fucking spoilsport," Seven mutters.

I can hear Kade's worried voice in the background, but Hunter soon tunes him out. The guys were very reluctant to let me do this. Hudson even threatened to tie me up in our fancy-as-fuck apartment. Not that I would mind a little bit of bondage, but this is my moment to own.

I can't be a songbird trapped in its cage forever.

Brooklyn West and Patient Eight have to become one.

In the furthest corner of the dockyard, we gather around the long-dead embers of a bin fire. Theo already scouted the place out with his drone army, ensuring there are no pedestrians to interrupt our task. The minute Lazlo approaches, they'll know about it.

Seven twirls a blade in his hand like a circus performer. "This could easily be a trap. Miss White's bait didn't work. They're taking another shot."

"Not this time. Lazlo was excommunicated for trying to get me killed, despite being hand-selected for Augustus's program. He was removed within seconds of Augustus entering Blackwood."

"Your point being?"

"Incendia doesn't forgive or forget. Miss White was an obstacle to be removed. Lazlo? He was the grand architect of their empire, and he stabbed them in the back. They wouldn't recruit him for this."

"Incoming," Theo's voice whispers in my ear.

"He's here."

Holding out my hand for his knife, I exchange it for the gun Enzo handed me. Seven's a far better shot than me. With our weapons raised, we stare into the gloom, waiting for our ghost to arrive. The crunch of footsteps cuts through the cloying mist.

"Brooklyn West!"

Parting shadows, the short, rounded figure of Professor Lazlo approaches our location. Dressed in worn civilian clothing with an old hat covering his crop of grey hair, he studies me through his smashed, partially sellotaped spectacles. He looks far from the terror that haunts my hallucinations.

I clear my throat. "Professor Lazlo."

"Two of my finest creations. Oh, this is a treat. Pleasure to see you again, Doctor Farlow."

A snarl escapes Seven's gritted teeth. "Professor."

Halting opposite us, Lazlo slides his hands from his pockets to hold them up in surrender. The gleeful smile on his lips is even more deranged than it was during our sessions together. A year in exile has done him no good, even less than it did for Miss White.

"I am here, almighty Sabre. Ready to surrender myself."

Seven cocks his gun. "You're alone?"

"Of course." Lazlo beams at him. "Who do I have left in this world, Jude? Like Frankenstein longing for the embrace of his creation, my life ended the day my work was taken from me. I am all but dead."

"How are you alive?" I ask next.

Chuckling again, Lazlo inches closer. I immediately back up, my body reacting on instinct. Just having him near me has my heart racing and body twitching with barely controlled anger. I want to tear him apart, limb from fucking limb.

"Thirty years at Incendia taught me one or two things, including how to disappear. When Doctor Augustus ordered my immediate removal, I was taken captive by the very corporation I helped to build. My escape took months of planning and a large dose of luck."

"Luck?" Seven scoffs.

"Perhaps God was shining down on me."

"Bullshit," I fire back. "You had help. Who?"

"An interesting question. I'm not certain you'll like the answer."

I ensure Lazlo is watching while I test the sharp tip of my knife. He hasn't stopped smiling for a second, seeming far too pleased with our reunion. I fucking hate the satisfaction we've granted him.

"The plea deal Sabre has cooked up for your pampered ass is conditional on your cooperation," I try to say calmly. "Information, Professor. That's all your life is worth. Prove you're not wasting our time."

Flashing yellowing teeth, Lazlo's grin is triumphant.

"Your mother helped me."

Seven flashes me a warning look, silently ordering me to keep my shit together. This is just another one of his endless mind games. I won't fall for it again.

"Spinning another tall tale?" I laugh. "Nobody is going to protect you or your lying hide. This is a waste of time." Stepping away, I take a second to gather myself.

"She was there, wasn't she? You saw her."

My retreating footsteps are halted by his words.

"I heard the news reports," Lazlo continues. "A deadly firefight in London. Several gang members left dead in the pursuit of England's most sought-after criminals. I have no doubt that Bancroft sent her."

Like falling through cracked ice into the depths of the ocean, my entire body stands frozen. Every word he speaks infects my mind with more of his venom. Despite everything... an image swims into my mind. All I caught was a glimpse from across the street.

Strolling through the flames, the woman headed straight for Phoenix, intent on violence. Her misshapen skull was exposed by her bald head, with two sunken eyes raking over us. A skeleton draped in papery skin, she was more dead than alive. I saw her, but… she wasn't my mum.

It's a lie.

This is just another trick.

Incendia wants to tear me apart.

"You're fucking unhinged!" I scream at Lazlo, whirling around in fury. "My mother is dead. She died! Crashed our car on purpose, nearly killing me in the process. She's been gone for twelve years!"

"Do you still dream about her? I'm sure you do. Does she speak to you too, Brooklyn? I wonder, is her voice whispering in your ear right now?"

"Don't listen to him," Seven barks at me.

Faintly, I can hear Hunter shouting through the earpiece. His voice disappears as I drop it to the ground. In the blessed silence that brings, I stare at Lazlo. He isn't smiling anymore.

"I rewrote the very fabric of her consciousness," Lazlo boasts. "Years of experimentation and research. It was easy enough to issue the right command to harness those threads again, all these years later. I'm certain Bancroft punished her for helping me."

"She's dead," I insist again. "I don't know how you escaped, but my mother is dead."

"Her hair fell out many years ago," Lazlo reveals conversationally. "The body suffers irreparable damage after enough rounds of electroconvulsive therapy. Tissues shrivel and die, brain cells degenerate. Memory slips away. It's difficult to imagine the person she used to be. So full of life."

"You took that from her!"

"Science took it. Can you see her now? Is Mummy going to come back and save you this time? I doubt she remembers she ever had children."

The distance between us melts away. Before I know what I'm doing, Lazlo is trapped beneath me as my fists sail into his face. Blood hits the gravel, teeth shatter and bones break beneath the weight of my fury. When Seven drags me up, Lazlo is covered in blood and cackling like a hyena.

"She was more scar tissue than human when they pulled her from that car wreck," he coughs out. "The trauma of it broke what remained of her mind. It was easy to recreate Patient Delta from the remains."

"No! Let me have him!"

"We can't do this…" Seven says uncertainly.

"This was your fucking idea! Let me go!"

"You made a promise. I want nothing more than to see him dead, but I can't watch you destroy the only family you have left."

"Get the fuck off me!"

Managing to locate my knife, I knee Seven in the gut. He trips and falls, unable to protect himself from the blade I press right to his throat. His chest is heaving much like mine, eyes wild with indecision.

"Phoenix," he blurts out.

I still, imprisoned by his voice.

"We need to find him," Seven reiterates. "I'm sorry, Eight. Lazlo deserves this, but Phoenix doesn't. We can't kill him yet."

The splash of tears on my cheeks almost breaks my resolve. Patient Eight never cries. She is harder than nails and tough as old boots. Brooklyn West is a little more broken. Between the two, I'm falling into fragmented pieces, caught in the middle.

"Damn you, Sev. What a time to gain a fucking conscience."

"I'm sorry, princess."

I spin back around to find Lazlo still laughing his ass off. He's almost as unhinged as his patients now. Seven takes my offered hand up and we approach the piece of shit together.

"You're going to come with us and identify a location." Seven points the gun at Lazlo's head. "Once our friend is located, you'll tell Sabre everything you know. Fail to do this and I'll be the one to cave your head in with my bare hands."

"Hand," Lazlo singsongs.

Bad move.

Seven launches himself at Lazlo in a blur of madness. Bodies tangle and bones break in a chorus of beautiful, explosive rage. Clutching his now shattered right arm, Lazlo stares at the bone protruding through his skin. He's actually crying, the spineless worm.

"You don't need your arms to answer questions." Seven dusts himself off. "Shut your goddamn mouth or I'll break the other one too. I only need one hand to do it."

"Couldn't manage the gun, huh? Come on, break the other one, then!"

"You talk too much," I snap, my booted foot connecting with Lazlo's face.

His head cracks against the ground, knocked unconscious and nearly unrecognisable through the injured mess. He'll be banged up for a while, but he can still talk, even with missing teeth and a broken arm. Hunter should be thankful he's still alive.

Leaving me to stare at our beaten prisoner, Seven retrieves the discarded earpiece. He doesn't bother offering it to me, slotting it in his ear instead.

"It's done. Yeah, he's alive."

Muttering some more, I tune Seven out. All I can see is the rise and fall of Lazlo's chest. Blood flowing from his nose and mouth is evidence of his heart continuing to pump. Each breath is another sick taunt. He was right.

I do dream about her.

I do hear her.

I do see her.

My mother is alive in so many ways. If he's telling the truth, then the human carcass of the person I once loved is still out there. A monster behind the wheel, trapped and unable to die. The last decade of my life has been one long, twisted lie. Like so many other things.

"Eight? Still with me?"

"I saw her," I manage to whisper. "She was there."

Seven's hand lands on my shoulder. "It's just a lie. A distraction. Don't let him hook you in."

"Why would he lie?"

"To unhinge you! Just because you want her to be alive doesn't mean she is. You're fooling yourself, Eight. She's dead and she isn't coming back to play happy fucking families."

His harsh words punch through my chest. Feeling like I can't breathe, the world becomes draped in shades of red. Blood. Anger. Love. Retribution. This colour has so many meanings. For me, all I see is the arterial spray that coated my childhood home's kitchen as it poured from Logan's throat.

"She's alive."

Seven's fierce gaze glares down at me. "Don't let him in your head!"

"I c-can't do this…"

"Goddammit," he curses. "It's taking every ounce of control I have not to put a bullet between this asshole's eyes. I need you, Eight. Come back to me."

Staring up at his savage eyes, I can almost glimpse the surface of the ocean I'm drowning in. We need to pull each other out. Both of us are incapable of managing emotions anymore. Seven stands frozen as I smash into him, already seeking out his lips. Our mouths meet in a hot frenzy.

I don't care if Hunter and the team are on their way. The monster that broke us both is lying mere inches away, somehow still breathing. He doesn't deserve to exist in this world, but if I kill him, I'll lose the only lead we have to finding Phoenix.

Seven is right.

This is the only way.

"How long do we have?" I ask against his lips.

"Ten minutes, max."

Nodding, I take the pair of handcuffs that Hunter issued us with from my coat pocket. It feels like poetic justice to cuff Lazlo's unconscious form, attaching his wrists to a huge metal pipe to keep him trapped.

With our hostage taken care of, I grab Seven's hand. We run side by side, slipping into a nearby abandoned structure. Dodging smashed windows and littered debris, I slam him against a crumbling brick wall.

"You want to do this right now?" Seven asks gruffly.

"Shut the fuck up. It's this or I gut that son of a bitch like a fish. I can't do nothing. I'm losing my mind here."

Eyes darkening, Seven's hand curls around my throat. "You want me to hurt you, princess?"

Fire burns in my lungs from the lack of air as he begins to tighten his grip. I'm shaking all over, two people warring inside of me. One of them is going to win this battle. I can't let it be Patient Eight. If she sneaks back in, I won't ever find myself again.

"Yes," I squeeze out. "Hurt m-me or I'll hurt him."

Flipping us around, Seven crushes me against the wall. My hands meet the hard brick as he bends me over by pushing my lower back. His movements are harsh and hurried, without any gentle introductions. I don't give a damn; I'm happy to be handled roughly.

When my borrowed combat trousers and panties are shoved down my hips, I gasp at the cold, night air kissing my bare pussy. It's freezing in here, even with my entire body flushed. Seven's palm cracks against my ass cheek, sending a flash of pain straight down south.

"Do you think of me when you're fucking them, Eight?"

His fingers slide between my legs, seeking out the wetness gathering at my core. I bite back a response as he shoves two fingers deep inside in an attempt to coax the truth free.

"Answer me," Seven commands.

Gliding in and out, he keeps torturing me with his fingers. I have to bite my lip when he circles my clit and pinches. I won't give it to him. I have enough possessive hotheads in my life without his bullshit too.

"I bet you do," he croons. "I hope you see my face when they make you come. Do you remember the night I whispered to you while you touched yourself for me, princess?"

I can't suppress a gasp when he pulls his fingers from my pussy, hitting my ass again instead. Each touch is like the lash of a fiery whip. We're running out of time, and it makes this even hotter.

"That was one time," I manage to respond.

"I knew you remembered it. The little moans you made while finishing all over your fingers had me so hard. I wanted to break through the concrete and fuck you myself."

The zip of his fly has my heart rate skittering with anticipation. My legs are shaking, even without much foreplay. I don't need him to hold my hand and pretend this is anything but animal lust.

"You look so beautiful, bent over and glistening for me, Eight."

"No time," I groan, feeling the hard press of his cock against my entrance. "Make me forget what that son of a bitch has done to us."

Seven's fingers bury in my crop of hair, wrenching the short strands.

Without warning, he surges inside of me. I cry out, full to the brim with his impressive length. It takes some adjustment, but he doesn't give me time to get comfortable before starting to move.

"Scream for me, Patient Eight. Let that bastard hear his failure. We're still here. We're fucking alive."

His thrusts set a relentless pace. Each stroke of his cock adds fuel to the flames, burning all rationality to a crisp and leaving my mind empty. I can't focus on anything but the man worshipping me in every violent way I want. His palm bruises me, hitting my ass over and over.

The beat of a familiar helicopter breaks our gasping tangle. Knowing we could get caught at any moment adds to Seven's urgency. It's like he's hammering his rage into me, expelling the madness in the only way he knows how. Hurting someone.

I let my release build, spiralling higher and higher. Every muscle in my body is quivering and ready to explode. The helicopter touches down outside with a loud whirring sound.

"Sev," I moan. "We have incoming."

"Silence, Eight. I'm not done with you."

Reaching around to tweak my clit again, the sharp burst of sensation sets my body alight. I scream out my orgasm, barely able to hold myself up against the wall. Seven's strokes become more ragged, relentlessly beating into me. Just as I expect him to finish, he pulls out and spins me around.

"On your knees, princess."

"What?"

The sharp slap of his hand against my face sends bolts of electricity down my spine. Not able to process the strike, Seven's hand on my shoulder forces me to kneel before him. The savagery in his molten eyes should scare me. I'm entirely at the mercy of the violent beast that lives within him.

"Open wide. Show me how well you can swallow my come, and I promise not to tell your stupid little boyfriends about our plan to kill Lazlo."

It's like his claws are buried deep in my mind, pulling all the right strings. My mouth falls open, ready and waiting to accept his shaft. With his cock nudging the back of my throat, Seven releases a bellowing grunt.

He fills my mouth with salty warmth. Pumping several more times before sliding his dick from between my lips, Seven watches intently. Without breaking eye contact, I swallow every last drop of come from my tongue, even stopping to lick my lips.

"Did I do a good job?" I ask innocently.

There's awe in his eyes. "You're fucking breathtaking."

"I'll take that as a yes, then."

Finding my feet, I hurry to pull my clothes back into place. Seven doesn't protest as I march back up to him and capture his lips in a fast and furious kiss, ensuring he can taste his own seed in my mouth. His low grumble of approval has me wanting to bend over all over again.

"Jesus, Brooke."

I still, confused. "What did you just call me?"

Seven looks equally unnerved by his own slip-up. Shaking his head, he focuses on fastening his trousers, ignoring my stare.

"Come on." He offers me his hand. "I can't believe I'm doing this. Let's go hand this sack of shit over to Hunter. We can keep what's left when they're done."

Digging my heels in, I don't follow.

Seven stops and looks over his shoulder at me.

"What is it?"

"It's just… I… well, I care about you, Sev. Deep down, you're a better person than you think you are. I just thought you should know that."

The frown on his face deepens. Seven doesn't understand and process feelings like the rest of us, though he's changing with each day spent back in the real world. For a moment, I think I spot a flare of hope in his gaze. It's quickly extinguished.

"You shouldn't care about me," he deadpans without emotion. "I'm not worth caring about. You have your family. You don't need me adding to the burden."

"You're part of that family now."

He finally lifts his eyes to mine. "Perhaps."

Taking the lead this time, I tug his hand so he follows. It's time to get what we need from Lazlo and end this madness. Bancroft's deadline is still ticking down at the back of my mind. If we can locate Phoenix, our next challenge will be getting him out.

We need to do something drastic.

And I have just the idea.

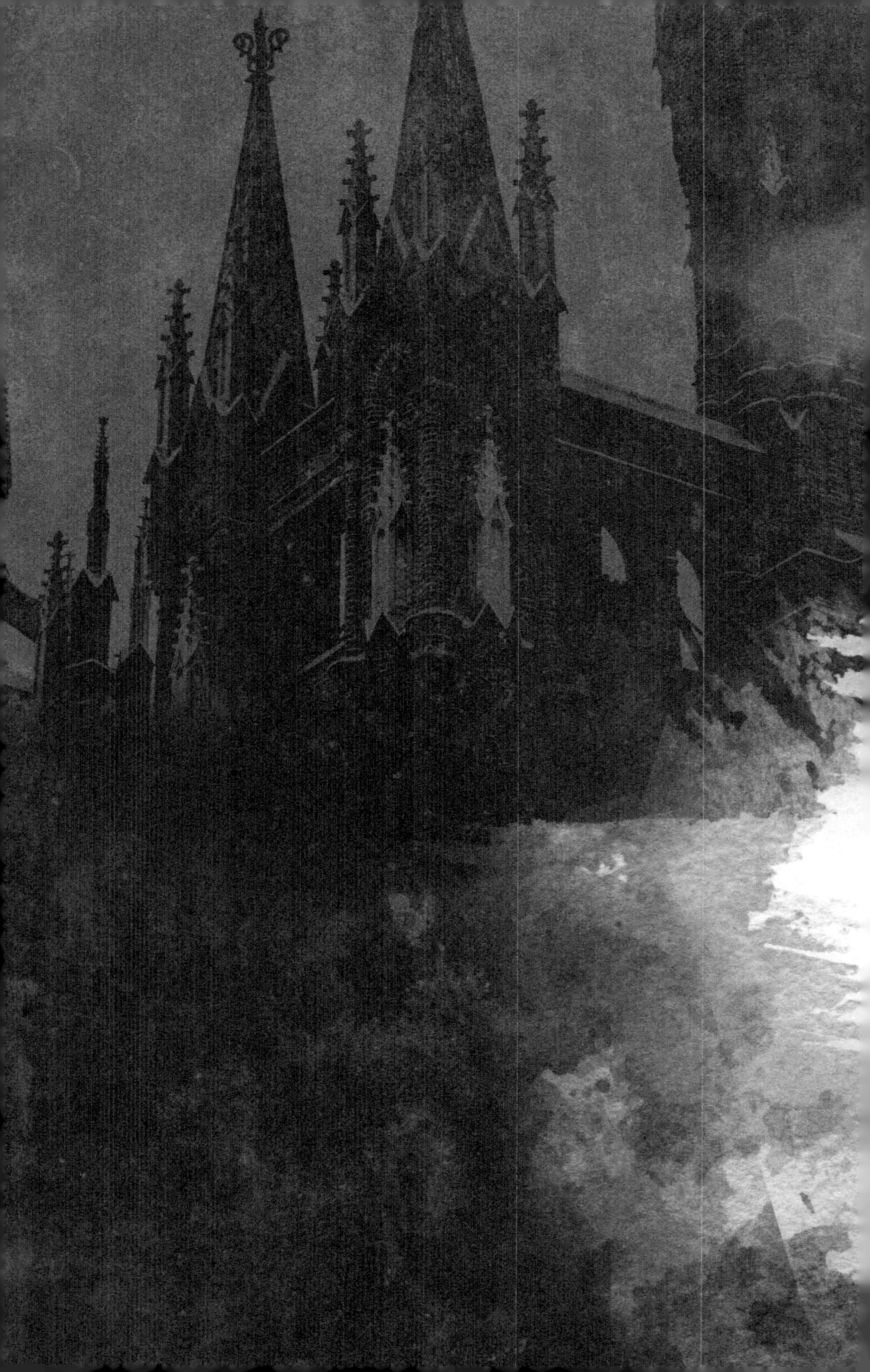

18

PHOENIX

Lydia - Highly Suspect

Shivering violently, I stare up at the cracked ceiling of my cell. They moved me in here several hours ago, needing to scrub the bloodstains from the last place.

The steady throbbing of my right hand has faded into a dull, numb ache as survival instincts kicked in. I held my screams back until they removed the third finger.

Now, my throat is torn and hoarse.

Bancroft wanted everything.

Names. Locations. Plans.

I've never set foot inside of Sabre, so I'm fucking worthless. That only angered him more. Afterwards, the beating worsened out of spite. I allowed myself to mentally check out, picturing Brooklyn's and Eli's faces.

There's an aggressive bang on the door before it swings open.

Bancroft's favourite, thick-skulled subordinate, Harrison, peers in at me with palpable glee beneath his military buzz cut and unyielding eyes. The grin on his face can't mean anything good for me.

"Ready to comply, Kent?"

Using my one uninjured arm to sit up, I gather saliva in my mouth and spit directly at him. Harrison's smile transforms into a glower as it lands right at his feet.

"Bite me, dickwipe."

"I'll take that as a no. That's cool, man. More play time for us."

"Want to dislocate my other shoulder? Maybe take another finger?" I snark.

Popping my own socket back in place was one of the most painful things I've endured, but I didn't fancy losing the whole arm.

Harrison smirks. "Nothing quite so pedestrian, don't worry."

I can barely shuffle backwards as he approaches, unable to run from his long, confident strides. A steel-capped boot to the face knocks me unconscious. Lost in a dark haze, I come back around to low conversation and the clank of metal bars being secured.

It takes all of my remaining energy to wrestle my heavy lids open. Days of abuse, zero food, and licking droplets of water from my cell walls have left me broken. As my latest prison settles around me, the last of my courage dissipates. I'm locked in a tiny, oppressive metal cage, surrounded by steel bars.

The odd sense of inertia draws me to look down. My cage isn't screwed into the floor. Instead, I'm dangling several feet in the air. Directly beneath the cage, a vat of murky water awaits. It's wide enough to fit the entire thing, while a foamy scum floats on the top of black, sludge-like water.

Bancroft's voice crackles through a speaker. "I've grown tired of your lies, Mr Kent. This is your final chance to tell us something of use. After that, you will be disposed of."

Wrapping a hand around the bars, I laugh maniacally. "Do whatever the fuck you want. I still won't give you shit. My family won't leave me here. They'll kill you soon."

"Good," Bancroft declares.

My blood chills. "Good?"

"Let them come. I'm aware that you're worthless to me, Mr Kent. When your family comes running to save your pitiful hide, I'll finally have patients Seven and Eight within my grasp. That's your purpose here."

Fuck, fuck, fuck.

I'm the motherfucking bait.

"Why torture me, then?"

Bancroft snorts. "We need some entertainment."

The deep groan of chain links grinding sparks panic within me. The cage is shuddering as it begins to lower into the putrid water. I don't waste any precious energy shouting or fighting, it won't stop them. As my body is lowered into the freezing depths, too many disgusting scents to process assault me.

I'm swallowed by decay and death.

The world disappears into inky darkness.

Clamping my mouth and eyes shut, I float like a dead body. My lungs begin to burn before long, screaming out for relief. No matter how hard I tug on the metal bars, they refuse to budge. The stumps where my fingers used to be burn, and my shoulder is too weak to do much damage.

Fighting is futile, but human instinct doesn't listen to reason. Terror and panic force me to batter the cage regardless. At last, exhaustion pulls me under as my chest screams for oxygen. In the semi-conscious haze, I accidentally open my mouth and swallow a mouthful of water.

Whatever was in this pool before me, it's been left behind to rot. Then, there's light and so much oxygen, I can't even gulp it down. Pulled out of the water, the cage dangles on its heavy chains. I cough up water as Bancroft's laughter reverberates around me.

"Enjoy your swim, Mr Kent?"

"F-Fuck you!"

"Manners. Lower him back in."

Peering through my soaked blue hair, I catch sight of someone on the platform behind the cage. It's another guard, one I've seen hanging around and watching the abuse. I'm submerged again before I can protest, even as someone bursts in and shouts for Bancroft's attention.

Back in the water, I wait without hope of rescue. This time, they leave me in for much longer. Whatever commotion is going on, I've been left and forgotten. Fuck, am I going to die here? I thrash and writhe before being pulled into unconsciousness by oxygen deprivation.

Her face finds me in the dark.

My lighthouse, guiding me back home.

"Firecracker," I whisper.

We're surrounded by packed bookshelves and empty desks in Blackwood's library. She saunters towards me, sprawling out in my lap like a lazy cat seeking attention. I cup the back of her head, letting our lips meet. It doesn't matter if the CCTV cameras and guards are watching.

Her love is worth the punishment.

"Do you dream about the future?" she murmurs, curling her slender limbs around me. "We could have a life after Blackwood. Out there, in the real world."

I tuck sun-kissed hair behind her ear. "I want to see you get out of here and finally get better. We could do anything… be anyone. Live far away from this madness as a real family."

"All of us?"

"We love you," I reply simply. "Your future is our future."

The lightest smile plays across her lips. That's how I know this isn't real. My Brooklyn doesn't look like that when she smiles. It's always underscored by pain and emptiness shining in her eyes, despite the hope tugging at her lips. She never fully smiles. Not really.

"Then you better wake up," Brooklyn says.

"I don't want to let you go. This might be the last time I see you."

Her hand cups my cheek, gently stroking. "Not a chance. You don't have my permission to die yet. Hold on, Nix."

Air is pushed past my numb lips as two firm hands pump my chest. I come screaming back into the real world. Rolling onto my side, pain races through me as I vomit water over and over again, unable to peel my eyes open.

"That's it, get it all up."

"Brooke?" I gasp.

"Afraid not. Just little ole me."

While I'm gulping down air, someone carefully pulls my eyes open and shines a phone's flashlight in them. I flinch back, every single inch of me throbbing with agony. When the light is done burning my retinas, I find the same guard staring down at me.

"Get off me."

"Relax, Nix. It's me."

Glancing around the room that has emptied out, the guard pulls the cap from their head. Beneath that, a short, brown wig is tossed aside, freeing a shock of bright-pink hair. The man becomes a woman right before my eyes, peeling off fake facial hair last.

"A-Alyssa?"

"It's still Sadie to you. Can you sit up?"

Guided upright, I blink and stare at her. Clothed in Incendia's signature black garb, her feminine features have been carefully disguised, but I see it now. She's been here all along, hiding in plain sight.

"Did you get a kick out of watching them beat me up?"

Sadie scoffs. "Hardly. I have an appearance to maintain. As soon as I found you, I alerted the team."

"Brooke? Is she here?"

"They're all coming."

"What about Bancroft?"

"Momentarily distracted. Theo leaked the video Hudson took in Blackwood's Z Wing to the media last night. There are huge protests outside the gates of here and Hazelthorn."

Coughing up more black water that sears my throat, Sadie hammers me on the back. Once the fit is over, I shove dank, wet hair out of my eyes. We're still alone. Bancroft and his cronies have vanished.

"You really went for the nuclear option."

Sadie shrugs. "It won't last long. Incendia will have the video deleted from existence soon enough. But we've caught them off guard. It buys us some time."

Grabbing my bad arm, Sadie tries to pull me to my feet. I hiss and yank it away from her, cradling my aching joint. When she spots the blood leaking from my inflamed, swollen right hand, her eyes widen.

"Uh, Nix?"

"I don't know where my fingers are," I answer for her. "You didn't see that bit, huh?"

She shakes her head. "I'm so sorry."

Taking my other arm instead, Sadie finally gets me on my feet. Everything goes a little wonky, forcing me to lean my entire weight into her. She guides me down the metal platform, my body trembling as filthy water clings to my bloodied clothes.

"Hold on. I'm gonna get you out of here."

Hold on.
Hold on.
Hold on.

Her voice blurs and becomes one with Brooklyn's in my mind. She's walking here with me, pouring her strength into my broken body. Despite popping my shoulder back in, it still throbs, but not as badly as my hand. My feet carry me on instinct while I float on a lake of fire.

"Here, put this on."

Sadie helps to strip the sodden t-shirt from my body and offers me a clean black one. I don't miss the way her eyes linger on my multi-coloured torso. My cracked ribs are black and blue. Stepping out of the boxers that Bancroft permitted me to leave on, she helps me into cargo trousers next.

With a black cap on my hair, I look like one of them. Sadie places her wig and hat back on, minus that fake facial hair. We look pretty shit, but it's better than nothing. Pulling my good arm back over her shoulder, I'm led into the basement's shadows.

"Bancroft will speak to the crowd to try to appease them," she says, winding down a lengthy corridor. "This is his base, while Augustus's territory was Blackwood. He has his own office upstairs."

"What about Kade's dad?"

"Not that I've seen. But there's someone else—"

The thud of footsteps ends our conversation. We're nearly above ground, the signs leading to what seem to be dormitories starting to appear. Many locked and bolted cells surround us in the gloom, although most seem to be unoccupied. This is a smaller operation than Blackwood.

Standing between us and salvation, a human skeleton guards the passageway leading above ground. Protruding limbs and painfully hollow eye sockets stare back at us with palpable misery. The woman's tiny frame is clothed in a black uniform that hangs off her.

I immediately recognise her inhuman gaze.

She was there in London.

This is the evil bitch who sedated me and brought me straight to Bancroft for judgement. The empty shell of a person begins to approach us with measured steps, two long, sharp knives clutched in her hands.

Sadie loosens her grip on me. "It's her. On my mark, run and don't look back."

"Who is she?"

Our feet begin to retreat away from the approaching monster.

"Patient Delta."

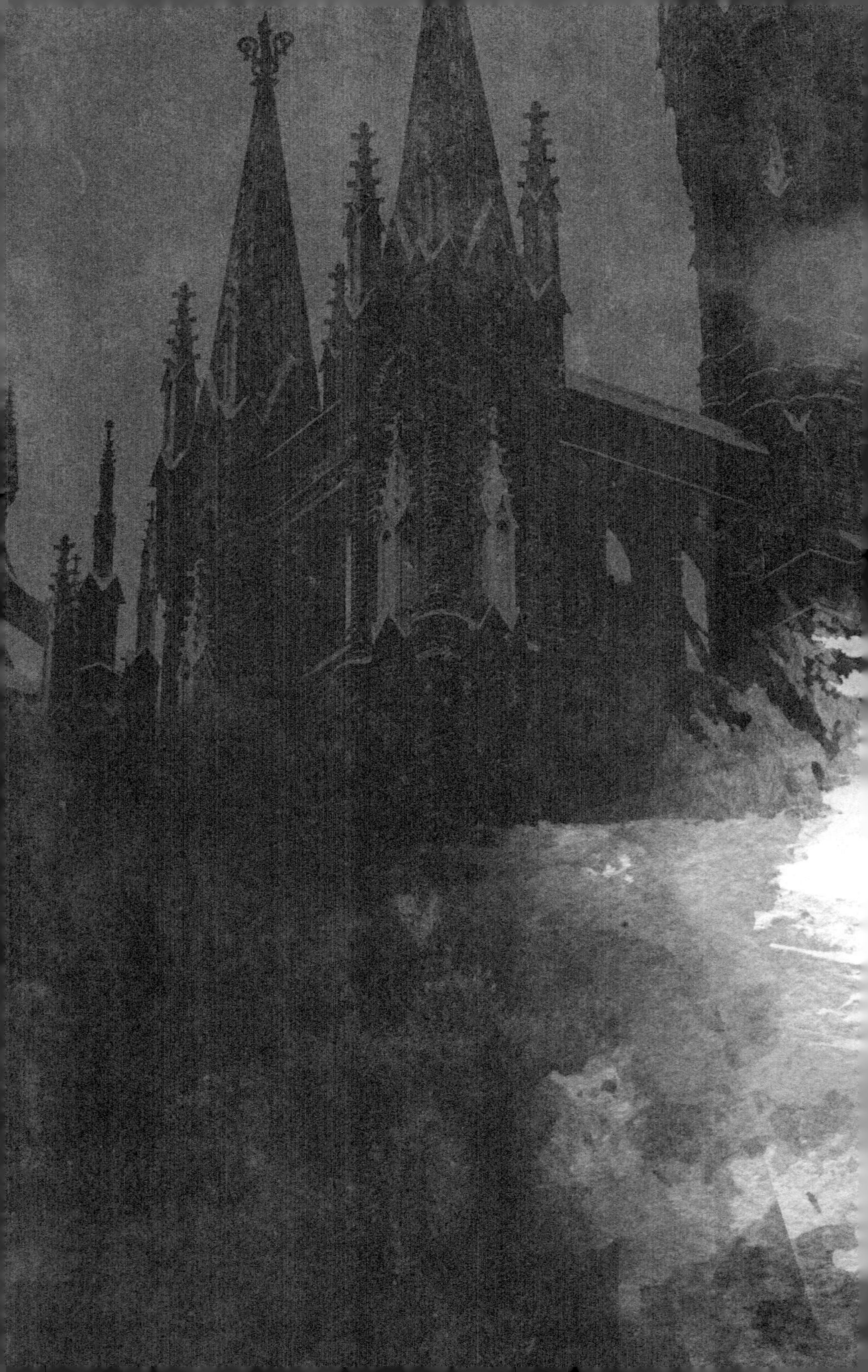

19

BROOKLYN

RIGGED - The Plot In You

"Damn, Theo. You sure know how to make a stir."

His awkward chuckle fills my ear. "Didn't take much. The bloodthirsty press did most of the work. Who doesn't love a good national scandal?"

Tucked into Hudson's side, we stare at the huge crowd of protesters swarming Harrowdean's gates. We're hidden in the forest to the side of the institute, keeping watch while Hunter and his team infiltrate from the rear. The loading bay has been cleared for them to enter through.

This place is a lot smaller than Blackwood, but still intimidating as hell in all its gothic, Victorian beauty. It looks like an asylum of a time long past, all ornate crests and stained windows. It's almost ironic, knowing what cruel practices continue to be performed behind closed doors.

The blare of a new alarm cuts through the crowd's angry shouting and chants. Looking over my shoulder, I check that Theo's van is still parked in the distance, out of sight.

"The patients are going into lockdown," Hudson observes. "Right on cue. That should clear the grounds so Hunter and the team can enter undetected."

"I can't believe Sadie found Phoenix in there."

"We got lucky. This is the hard part."

We both study the swarm of black-clad guards marching down the driveway. They establish a barrier between the protest and the winding road leading to the institute. A convoy is waiting behind the iron bars of the gates, beneath another ornate crest. Bancroft is sandwiched between his bodyguards, preparing to speak.

"We're going in," Hunter announces.

"Be careful," I respond into the comms.

Enzo and Seven are accompanying him, along with two of Sabre's best agents. Their job is to quietly extract Sadie and Phoenix while Bancroft stops this mess from imploding. Despite knowing that Seven can more than hold his own, I can't help but worry. I never wanted to see him inside of an institute again.

Hudson squeezes my arm. "He'll be okay."

"How can you be sure?"

Meeting his oceanic eyes, I find resolution staring back at me. He's always been able to read my mind with a mere look. Hudson traces his thumb along my jawline, each gentle touch revealing a softness to him that I rarely see. Just sweet, loving glimpses amidst the possession and control.

"Because he has something to live for. We all do."

I swallow hard. "I really hope you're right."

"I usually am, baby."

"Arrogant? Sure."

Despite the carnage around us, our lips meet like they simply cannot bear to be parted. I will always long to be the air that Hudson breathes, the reason his shrivelled, black heart continues to pump each day. He owns a broken, twisted piece of me that nobody could ever come close to.

"When this is all over, I'm going to spend every single day of my life proving myself to you," he says above the shouting. "I want to be the man you deserve, blackbird. The person I should have been all along."

Pecking his lips again, I sit back. "You always have been that man, Hud. I never wanted the good parts of you. Your darkness is my home. The rest is just an added bonus."

"I fucking love you."

"Ditto, dickhead."

Our tender exchange is interrupted by the boom of Bancroft's voice through a speaker. We both turn to look from our hiding spot in the trees. He emerges from his swarm of guards, attempting to appease the angry crowd. Placards and pumped fists announce their fury as the protest grows even louder.

"People are really mad," I comment.

"Why wouldn't they be?"

"I just figured nobody would care."

His hand finds mine. "Shit like this gives me hope that there might be a chance for us out there. People need to stay angry; it's the only way the truth will come out."

The spark of flames breaks through the evening gloom. Someone has lit a Molotov cocktail and thrown it straight at Incendia's goons. Bancroft is shoved out of the way, with two terrifying slabs of muscle descending upon the guilty culprit. I can spot the batons and tasers in their hands from here.

We watch for several minutes, each second adding fuel to the flames of indignation. More protesters are getting physical and attempting to assault Bancroft's hired skins. Every snap of a camera infuriates Bancroft as he attempts to shout meaningless platitudes, claiming this is nothing but a smear campaign.

Hudson taps his earpiece. "Status update? Things are getting hairy out here."

Radio silence.

Dread sinks in as we wait, watching the tensions escalate further. Incendia doesn't care if they have the authority or not, resorting to violence to tame the crowd. At the back of the protests, the cameras continue to capture the ordeal. People are finally paying attention.

"Why aren't they answering?" I ask after several minutes.

"Signal may be disrupted in the basement."

"Sadie was supposed to meet them fifteen minutes ago. I don't like this. Something is wrong."

Glancing at Theo's nondescript van in the distance, it remains unmoved from the thick cover of shrubbery. I hate not being able to see my guys inside. Anxiety itches along my skin, causing my fingers to quake.

"We can't just sit here. Come on."

Hudson growls his frustration as I take off, making a beeline for the van. We have to take the long way around to remain concealed in the trees. All three guys inside flinch when I slam the door open. Theo's wired into one of his contraptions, with a dozen different video feeds open.

"Are you okay?" Kade immediately reaches for me.

"Our comms have gone down."

"Us too," Theo grumbles. "I'm boosting the signal, but still nothing. They must be running a blocker inside the institute. I'm trying to hack their system."

I watch as Kade's eyes stray to the rapid lines of computer code racing across the screens. He locates a laptop and digs in, exchanging low whispers with Theo. Eli is sat with his back against the van wall, impatiently flipping his penknife in one hand.

"Anything?" Hudson prompts, hands braced on his knees.

"Just static," Theo confirms. "We're running a malware program to take their systems down, but they've prepared for us. I can't skip over the code before it rewrites itself."

The sounds of increasing shouts and another explosion of fiery glass reach us. Looks like Incendia more than has its hands full. Our plan should be working, but we're still not hearing a damn thing and the clock is ticking. They're beyond late.

"Fuck this," I decide. "I'm going in."

Hudson grabs my arm. "Not a chance."

"Take your hand off me before I break it. Our family is inside that hell hole. Either come with me or stay here, but I'm going in."

Fisting his wild hair, Hudson looks ready to knock me out with his bare hands. I'm prepared to leave him behind when there's a low hissing from our earpieces, followed by the sound of laughter. Unlike Bancroft's pompous drone, the voice is rough and gravelly, like an abused throat after too much screaming.

"Who is this?" I ask shakily.

The rasping chuckle ceases, leaving uneasy silence.

"Where is Phoenix?"

My eyes connect with Eli's wide, emerald orbs. He's clutching the penknife in his white-knuckled grip, waiting for the same thing we both want to hear.

"Where is he?!" I repeat.

Heavy breathing. No words.

"Who the fuck are you?"

There's a sharp slapping sound of a fist meeting flesh, followed by yelping. It's light and feminine, beneath the tinge of pain. Far-off shouting filters through the earpiece, still punctuated by the silent, anticipatory breathing of the attacker.

Something wraps around my throat and squeezes. A tendril of sickness, the weight of family history sinking deep into my bones. I can't escape this drowning pool of blood. It's pulling me down… deeper and deeper.

"Mum?" I whisper softly. "Is that you?"

"Brooke…" Hudson mutters.

I wave him off, my breath still held.

Please don't be real.

You're dead.

My whole life hasn't been a lie.

"Come," the dead voice whispers.

There's a crunch as the line goes dead, like the earpiece has been crushed. My question hangs in the air, unanswered. With the iron grip on my lungs refusing to abate, I'm left staring at Hudson's face.

"Are you with me or without me?"

His eyes harden with determination. "Always with you."

I turn to look at Kade and Eli. "With me?"

Nodding, Eli pockets his penknife and quickly stands. His lips mouth the silent words *with you*. Kade ditches his laptop and joins us outside the van, leaving Theo to continue beating his keyboard into submission.

"Let's go get our boy," he declares.

Theo snatches two guns from the weapons box and slides them across the van's floor without looking up from his laptop.

"Be careful and don't get killed. I am not doing that paperwork."

The riot of noise from the crowd in the distance accompanies our footsteps into the unknown, gradually fading as we pass behind the perimeter of the institute. Much like Blackwood, it's a testament to the wealth and opulence that Incendia wields as a weapon. Another slick, well-funded campaign enabling the abuse and exploitation.

Sliding through the chain-link fence that has been broken with wire cutters, we enter the loading bay. It's spookily deserted, with nothing but empty boxes and parked vehicles. The bay door hangs open ominously, despite the flashing red light above it.

"This doesn't feel right," Kade murmurs.

Hopping up on the brick platform, I peek inside the dark institute. "Whatever Bancroft is doing here, it's nothing we haven't faced before. Come on, we're running out of time."

We sneak inside together. This part of the small institute is ghostly silent, packed with storage rooms and empty cupboards. With my knife clutched in hand, I take the lead. We studied the floor plans meticulously while Theo was busy stirring up a media shitstorm.

Unlike Blackwood, Harrowdean's experimental wing lies beneath a disused dormitory. It's approximately half the size, but features observation rooms along with ancient solitary cells. The architecture is a lot older, keeping the pre-existing design of the asylum.

"Can you hear that?" Hudson asks as we race through the corridors.

Pausing on the threshold of a glamorous, refurbished reception area lit with chandeliers, we all strain to hear the distant roar. Too many voices to count, screaming and shouting, like an almighty brawl is taking place. We're too far from the front gates for it to be the protest.

"Patients?" I hedge.

"They are supposed to be locked down," Hudson observes.

Kade glances out of a window, his face lit by the glow of the quad lights. "Not so much. Take a look at this."

All gathered, we peer out at the disaster. Harrowdean's patients are far from locked down in their rooms. Something obviously went wrong. In the generous space of the tree-lined quad, a mob is forming. Fists fly and patients brawl, spilling blood and tears across the cobbled stone.

Some are yelling and wrestling, while others simply watch the chaos unfold. The few remaining guards not dealing with Theo's pals from the press are attempting to tame the wild animals and failing.

"Where are they?" I scan the crowd.

Kade points across the quad, towards the distant lights. "That's Kingsman dorms. Decommissioned for patient use. Sabre's research indicates the experimental wing is housed beneath it."

"Only a sea of lunatics between us and them," Hudson concurs.

"They aren't lunatics." I glance between them all emphatically. "Hell, these people are us. Trapped by a broken system. Powerless. Bullied. We're better than the world that cast them aside."

Out of them all, I don't expect Eli to speak.

"N-Nobody... g-gets hurt."

I take his trembling hand in mine. "Only Incendia."

Cracking open the heavy doors, we slowly inch outside and stick close to the high stone walls of the main building. Floodlights have been slammed on to reveal the growing brawl, with a few more guards arriving to bring order to the mayhem. Linking hands, we begin to pelt through the crowd.

"Straight ahead, take a left," Kade instructs.

With my gaze trained on the disused dormitory, I'm too late to spot an incoming blur of motion. Someone ploughs straight into my side, tackling me to the wet grass. Eli's hand is ripped from mine as I fall.

"It's too loud! No!"

A fist connects with my jaw, while a tangle of bones attempts to pin me to the ground. Grabbing the young girl by the shoulders, I use my strength to wrestle her aside. She can't put up much of a fight, her stick-thin body soon becoming trapped beneath me.

"No! I'm scared, let me out!"

"Hey, hey," I shout down at her. "It's alright, I'm not one of them. You're okay."

"I want to go home! I want my mum… please…"

With the fight leaving her in an instant, she goes completely limp. Tears streak across her pale cheeks beneath a bush of tangled auburn hair in need of a good wash. Hudson attempts to offer me a hand up, but I shake him off.

"What's your name?" I ask urgently.

The young girl peers up at me with trepidation. "I'm… I… I don't know. I want to go home. It's s-s-so loud…"

"Jesus," Kade curses. "She's out of it."

"Let's get you up, okay?" With a lump in my throat, I help her to stand. "I know you're scared. All you want is your home."

She nods rapidly, like a timid bunny rabbit. "They're f-fighting."

Wrapping an arm around her shoulders, I point to the darkened reception where we came from. "See that old building there? You're going to run inside and find a quiet corner to hide in, okay? Can you do that for me?"

Giving her a shove, I watch her slender limbs scamper into the night. She doesn't look back, hugging herself tight while holding back the tears. Unable to shake the emotion raging through me, I force myself to leave her behind.

"Head around the side." Hudson points ahead. "That was the rendezvous point."

Bearing left, we leave the chaos of the quad and fall into quieter, swaying juniper trees. The abandoned dorms are oddly quiet, lit by faint lights but seemingly deserted. When we reach the entrance doors leading inside, we all stop dead.

"Oh my God," I say under my breath.

Lifeless limbs splayed out before the wide entry steps, one of the agents that accompanied the team lies dead. Wilson. His throat has been brutally slashed open, dripping bright red on to the ground. Kade picks his way around the corpse, looking nauseous.

"They must be inside. Watch each other's backs."

Bancroft's voice cuts through the air from the distance, punctuated by the sounds of patients being battered and subjugated. He's taming the crowd. We're running out of time.

"Hurry," I urge, climbing the stairs. "We need to leave."

Inside the dorms, bare overhead bulbs light the state of disuse. This wing is clearly used for nothing but shady dealings. Old signs point towards the different floors, with one denoting the basement ahead. Taking several sharp turns, we almost trip over another huge body on the ground.

"Enzo!" I screech.

His giant frame is sprawled out, breath hissing between his clenched teeth. He's barely conscious, one hand clamped over a bleeding wound in his leg. Kade drops to his knees, setting to work analysing him.

"Go! I got this!" he urges.

"We can't split up now." Hudson searches around us with his gun raised.

Eli removes his belt before crouching next to Kade. Together, they get Enzo sitting up with his back meeting the wall. The belt wraps around his leg as a tourniquet, hoping to stem the heavy flow of blood.

"D-Downstairs," Enzo grits out. "Ambush."

"Dammit." Hudson glances at the stairs leading down, then back at Kade. "Get him back to Theo. He's lost too much blood. We'll go ahead and find the others."

"Not alone," Kade rebuts.

"We don't have a choice. Take Eli, get Enzo out. We'll find our boy."

Hudson steals my hand, dragging me onwards as Kade protests. I cast them a final, desperate look before we begin our descent, uncertain if we'll ever see the world beyond this basement again. The last time we were somewhere like this, it took everything to leave with our lives.

Loud voices and shouting reverberate around the thick concrete that leaches all heat from our bodies. As we emerge in the subterranean paradise beneath the dorms, the distinct sound of crying fills our ears. It sounds like a grief-stricken animal, mourning a lost cub. Hudson moves in front of me.

"No… p-please… No…"

Someone's pleading guides us into the commotion. Amidst a long corridor of locked cells and bare bulbs, a red-stained crime scene unfolds. I don't know where to begin, there's so much blood. Kneeling in a rapidly spreading puddle, Hunter's face is shielded by his curtain of long hair.

I'm stunned to realise the frenzied begging and soft sound of crying is coming from him. He's knelt over, cradling someone close to his chest. To his right, Seven stands still as stone, staring down at something. Blood is steadily leaking across the parquet floor.

"Nix," I whimper aloud.

On his knees at the end of the corridor, Phoenix's head is lowered, execution style. He dares to lift his eyes to meet mine for a second. Shock and agony race across his heavily beaten face, like he can't quite believe what he's seeing.

"Eight," Seven thunders.

Tentatively stepping into the firing line, I give Hunter a wide berth. When I get to Seven's side, I realise who is cradled in Hunter's arms. Torn apart by violent slashes and numerous deep stab wounds, her eyes are slowly falling shut. They meet mine at the last moment.

"I'm s-s-sorry," she croaks.

"Alyssa." Hunter chokes a sob. "Stay with me, my love. Don't do this. I need you."

He's stroking her stained pink hair, their lips almost touching. She tries to cup his cheek and leaves a bright-red swipe on his skin. It's a devastating sight. Her eyes shut forever as mortality pulls her soul ashore.

"No. Alyssa…"

Seven watches his sister slip away, unable to traverse the distance between them. Not a single emotion crosses his face. The only sign that he feels anything is in his clenched fist.

Hunter's head lowers once she's gone. He looks nothing like the formidable pillar of strength I've come to fear. In this moment, he's another broken victim of Incendia.

"Weapons down!"

Metres ahead, the dead-eyed woman offers her ultimatum. The knife in her hand meets Phoenix's throat, digging in hard enough to break the skin. More blood soaks his pale flesh. I scrape together the courage to meet her stare, searching her face for any hint of recognition.

She doesn't look like my mother. Her hair is gone, leaving her skull exposed to the world. Gnarly scar tissue warps most of her features, shaded by dark circles, as if she hasn't slept a single night in her life. While the burns corroborate Lazlo's story, I can't find the person I knew in her eyes.

"Who are you?" I shout at the ghost.

In answer, she presses the knife against Phoenix's throat even harder. He chokes out his terror, a river of tears soaking into the discoloured skin of his face. One slip and he'll be dead. I think I'll die with him.

"Weapons down," she repeats in a dull voice.

Hudson aims straight at her. "After you."

She pulls the knife from Phoenix's throat. My relief is quickly extinguished as the sharp tip buries into his left thigh. She stabs him so hard, it reaches all the way to the handle. Phoenix's raw scream slices through my head like a razor blade to the wrist, right before he slumps.

"You're going to fucking die for that!"

His attacker simply shrugs. "You didn't listen."

Taking another blade from the belt around her nonexistent waist, she rolls up the sleeves of her black shirt, as if preparing to butcher us all. It exposes the translucent skin stretched across her bones, broken by a single swirl of dark, ancient ink. My heart almost breaks free from my ribcage.

What's this, Mummy? Letters?

A reminder to always love my little miracles, Brooke.

Why would you forget about us?

Sometimes Mummy's head gets loud, baby. But I'll always come back to you.

"No. It isn't true!"

My voice is a lightning strike of disbelief and horror. Hudson tries to say something to me, but it doesn't break through the haze of memories. Everything else falls into insignificance. Unlike the many months I've spent hallucinating my mother, this ghost cannot be returned to my imagination.

Because… she isn't a ghost at all.

Lazlo was right all along.

I'm staring at Melanie West.

My feet move without being instructed. I dodge Hudson's hands, stepping further into no man's land. Neither he nor Seven follow, but they keep their weapons raised. I don't need a weapon. Bullets and blades won't protect me from this hellish truth. It's too late to fight my way out of this.

"Mum?" I vocalise gently.

Her head cocks, two washed-out eyes scraping over me.

"It's... it's me." I inch closer with my empty hands raised. "Brooklyn. I'm your daughter."

Mouth clicking open, she doesn't speak a single word.

"I'm here," I attempt to say through my tears. "Please... Mum. Drop the knife. None of us are going to hurt you. We don't have to do this."

I swear, the smallest spark of humanity lights her irises. Still, the blade remains in her grip, inches from Phoenix's semi-conscious body. He's losing so much blood. I'm almost close enough to pull the knife from his leg and bury it straight in my mother's chest... but I can't.

Despite everything, I fucking can't.

I've lost so much.

Her. Dad. Logan.

My childhood. My innocence.

My freedom. My sanity.

My own mind.

"I can't... I don't want to lose you," I whisper brokenly. "You remember the sun, Mum? Every morning and every night, we climbed up on the roof to watch it. You always said—"

"P-Put yourself... way... b-beauty," she botches, her voice barely audible.

More tears course down my cheeks. "That's right."

"Where is h-h-he?"

Her grip on the knife slackens as she stares, her eyes melting my skin like battery acid.

"Who, Mum?"

"S-Such... good... b-boy..."

My shaking hand raises, close enough to whisper along the tattooed skin of her wrist. Expecting my touch to break that final boundary, I meet her eyes again. The dying embers of the car crash that stole my family from me stare back at me.

Her hand raises, fingers on the verge of wrapping around mine. I can see my mother. She's there. Swimming back up to the surface, battling to find me again. I need to grab her, pull her up, save her…

The blast of gunfire explodes in my eardrums. The bullet tears into my mother's shoulder and she stumbles with a vicious snarl. Blood hits my lips in a light spray before she falls, her mouth hanging open.

"No! Mum!"

"Grab them!" Hunter commands.

I try to reach for my mother. All I want is to cradle her in my arms, stop the blood flowing from her shoulder. She's there, so fucking close. I could have a parent again. When someone's arms band around me like great steel train tracks, I'm cruelly dragged away.

"I'm sorry, princess."

Bucking and thrashing, Seven's lips meet my ear as he orders me to stop fighting. I can see Hudson picking Phoenix's limp body up like a baby before Mum can hurt him again. She's down on the floor, clutching her shoulder and staring straight at me.

Seven tosses me over his shoulder, not giving me the opportunity to escape. All I can do is hammer my fists against his back, screaming for him to put me down. I have to get to her. If we leave her here, I'll never see my mother again. Bancroft will crush what memories she's accessed.

"Let me down! Stop!" I howl.

His arms tighten, pinning me to him. "She killed my sister. I'll spare her life for you, but I won't let you die for her."

"No!"

"We're leaving, Eight."

"MUM! MUM!"

My distraught screams bounce off the concrete walls surrounding us as we flee. Beyond Sadie's dead body and Phoenix's bloodied form, all I see is the bleak, hopeless gaze of the monster watching us go. She chooses not to pursue, lying and awaiting punishment instead.

In that moment, I don't see Lazlo's empty machine.

All I see is my last remaining parent.

Letting us escape is the only thing she has left to give me.

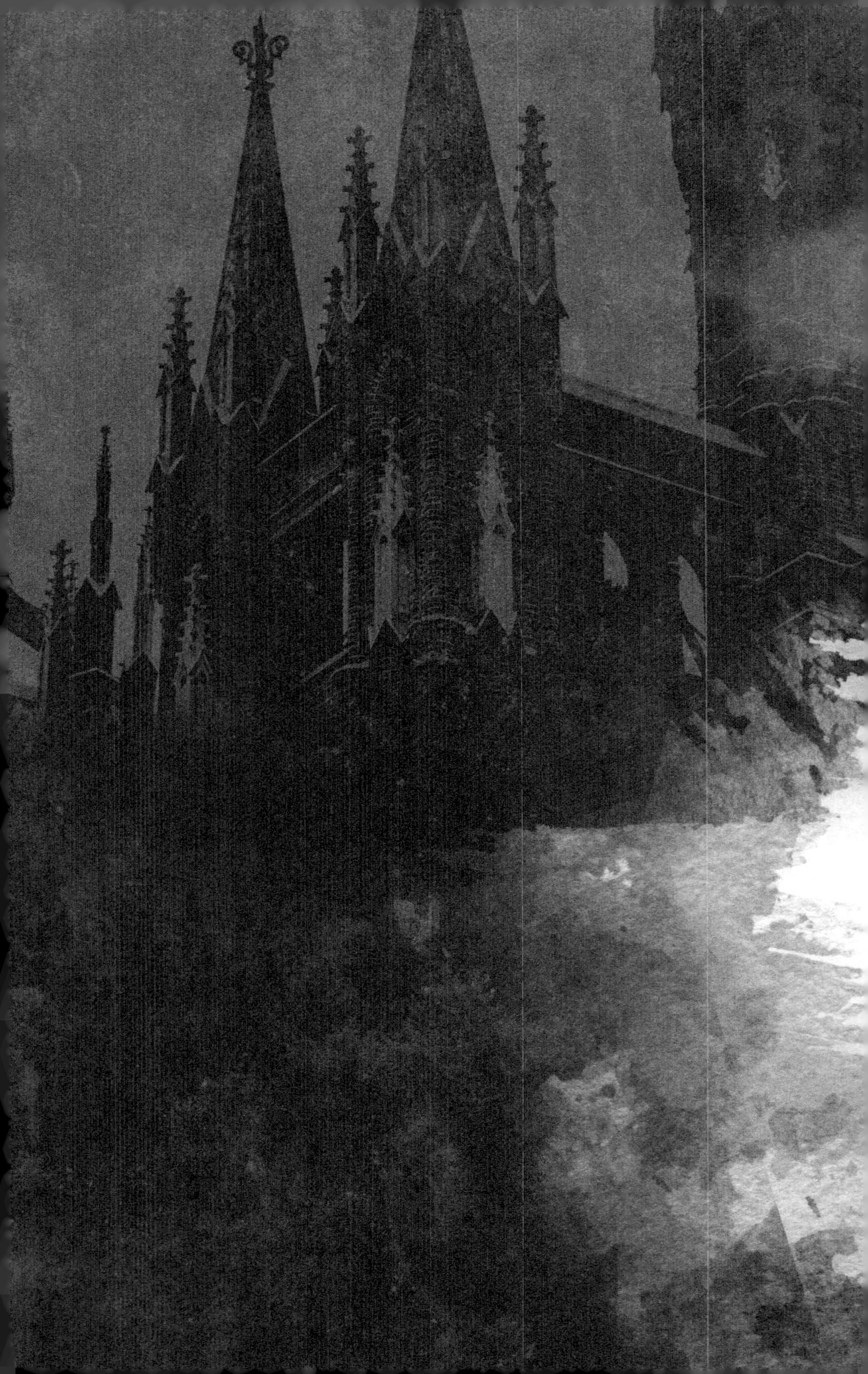

20

KADE

Reset Me - Nothing But Thieves

Arms folded, I stare through the window into the private hospital room. Phoenix is still out of it, several drips feeding antibiotics and pain relief into his prone form. His hand is resting at his side, ensconced in bandages.

Eli stands next to me, his lips pursed. He's barely moved from this spot in the few days since we got Phoenix back, even when they operated on the remains of his amputated fingers. It was touch and go when an infection took root, but he's finally stabilised.

Sunup to sundown, Eli awaits the day Phoenix's eyes will open.

Until then, we've lost him as well.

"Eli." I rest a hand on his shoulder. "The memorial begins in half an hour. I'm sure Brooke's going to need you there."

He shrugs my hand aside. "N-No."

"What do you mean, no? We're set to start giving evidence tomorrow.

Everyone is on edge. We need to stick together right now."

"Together?" he snarls without a stutter.

Turning his furious, green-eyed gaze on me, Eli's face has transformed with anger. It's unnerving to see his usually silent self so worked up and intent on tearing me a new asshole.

"We w-were safe." He points at Phoenix. "Coming h-here... m-mistake."

"We had to do something. This is our lives we're talking about."

"What l-lives?! T-taken everything... look... h-him!"

"And we're taking it all back," I snap while throwing my suit jacket on. "The world is finally listening to us. We have their attention. This will all be over soon."

"What c-cost?"

His simple, sharp question cuts me to the core. It's the same one that Phoenix threw at me several months ago, before we escaped. I've always been the first one to make the hard choices. Sometimes, you must compromise and bend your own morals to defeat the darkest of evils.

To escape, we had to become the bad guys.

But to win this war, we must find ourselves again.

Unable to appease him, I leave Eli to his silent vigil. He returns to staring at Phoenix, his jaw set in a hard, merciless line. I can't give him what he wants. The prospect of peace seems as far away as ever, while each day we suffer more and more losses.

Sabre's medical wing lies on the fourteenth floor of the building, while Sadie's memorial is taking place in a private, local church. Incendia is on the back foot after our performance in Harrowdean and the extensive media coverage, granting Hunter the confidence to honour her with a small service.

Stepping out of the elevator, I emerge into the gleaming foyer. A small group has gathered at the entrance to HQ, decked out in black and surrounded by the newly enhanced security detail. I can't make eye contact with Hunter, who is hiding behind a pair of dark sunglasses. His hunched shoulders tell me enough.

"Over here." Hudson beckons me over.

Joining the others, I find Brooklyn standing alone in the corner, staring outside. She doesn't turn to speak to any of us, her face slack and eyes reddened. I'm not sure she's slept since witnessing Sadie's last moments.

"What's the holdup?" I fish for a topic change.

Looking scarily normal in a dark shirt and jeans, the nerve in Seven's jaw ticks as he stares into space. He's even tied his hair back and had a shave, revealing every dark circle and mark on his skin. The poor son of a bitch looks drained and utterly wiped out.

"Turns out Incendia couldn't firefight our news story at the same time as Harrowdean's mini riot." Hudson gestures outside. "This lot gathered a while ago and won't move."

Glancing out through the tinted glass and layers of security checks that protect Sabre's privacy, I spot a gaggle of reporters. Cameras and news vans dominate the busy London street. Security is attempting to hold them back, setting up a perimeter as they battle for a single picture of what lies within.

"Are we even safe here?"

I shrug at Hudson's question. "We've been given temporary protection. Hunter's contact in government intends to argue for clemency in exchange for our testimony, same as Lazlo and the girls."

"How do we know it isn't another ploy?"

"We don't," Seven states flatly.

"Incendia is everywhere." I watch Theo and Enzo arrive in matching black suits. "Exposing them needs a smoking gun. We hold the leverage to bargain for our lives with these testimonies."

"Once we give our information to them, the government will turn us over to Incendia for execution." Hudson scoffs at us both. "We're being led to slaughter."

"The deal will be signed in black and white."

"You're being fucking stupid."

"What's the alternative? Live out our lives in hiding?" I fire at him.

Hudson's hands ball into fists as he storms away, attempting to approach Brooklyn instead. We're all on edge and frustrated. The thought of giving evidence to Hunter's team and a room full of complete strangers is uncomfortable as fuck.

Lucia and Two were petrified when they arrived yesterday. Hunter had them flown down from Scotland on a private flight before setting them up in the apartment opposite us. We've drawn them into this pandemonium now. I hope to God we don't regret bargaining with their lives.

"Get this shit locked down!" Enzo yells at two of his agents, gesturing at the madness outside.

He's favouring his right leg after the incident in Harrowdean narrowly missed his femoral artery. Any closer, and the doctor admitted he would be a hell of a lot worse off.

"That's an order. We will not be hounded by a bunch of vampires fishing for a story!"

"Enzo." Hunter's throat bobs as he approaches.

"No! I am not risking anyone else's safety."

Several more agents are sent outside to begin crowd control. The rest of the extensive security team lines up in formation to surround us on all sides. Brooklyn shrugs off Hudson's attempt to put an arm around her, insisting on standing alone. She still won't meet my eyes.

We head out into the heavy rainfall, using thick, black umbrellas to hide our faces. Sabre's foot soldiers keep the convoy moving at high speed. Enzo is barking his orders like a drill sergeant, slipping into full-on scary leader mode. It's unnerving after getting to know the gentle, caring side of him.

Packed into an armoured SUV, we manage to escape the media circus. Nobody knows what to say as the miles tick by. When we pull up outside a quaint chapel with stained glass and intricate limestone carvings, I succeed in grabbing Brooklyn's hand. She's chewing her lip so hard, I can see it bleeding.

"Are you okay?" I ask softly.

"Fine."

"Are we doing the whole lying thing again, love?"

"Fuck, Kade. Nothing about this is okay. Sadie's dead."

"I know. This never should've happened."

"The last thing I said to her was so fucking cruel. I can never take that back. Phoenix nearly died and lost three fingers." Her eyes bounce to Seven's hand. "We've all suffered so much. And for what?"

I thread our fingers together. "Our freedom."

"How can I ever be free while my mother is still imprisoned?"

Seven can't look at her, staring outside at the downpour. I know it killed him to drag her away like that in Harrowdean. He had to choose between his sister's murderer and the girl he loves. Leaving her mother alive was supposed to be a mercy, even if Brooklyn can't see it right now.

"It isn't her anymore." Hudson winces at his words. "I'm sorry, blackbird, but the person you knew is dead. She's too far gone to be saved. Look at what she did to Phoenix."

"And what if I'm not Brooklyn anymore either? What if I'm destined to end up just like her?" She rubs a spot between her knitted brows. "Her sickness is in me. I'm the same as her."

"You're nothing like your mother," I argue hotly.

"Do you really believe that?"

There's a sharp rap on the window from one of our burly escorts. I roll the heavily tinted window down and bark at them to go ahead. I'm not leaving this fucking car until Brooklyn can meet our eyes again. I won't tolerate this doubt and self-hatred for a second longer.

Tugging her hand, I drag Brooklyn into my lap. She ends up straddling me in the spacious car. Ignoring both Hudson's and Seven's interested gazes, I tip her head up with a single finger under her chin.

"You're going to listen to me and listen well," I demand with fire. "This is the last time I'm going to explain this to you."

"Kade—"

"Listen to me, Brooklyn West. You are the most infuriating woman I've ever met. You're fucking crazy, you drink far too much, swear worse than Nix's batshit Nana, and resort to violence far too quickly."

Her lips part, almost reaching a smile.

"I have zero clue how we're going to straighten out the shit in your head." I stroke her cheek with my thumb. "You're fucked-up, unstable, and sometimes, you scare the hell out of me. That's the truth nobody wants to tell you."

Tears shine in her eyes. "I told you to let me go. You still can."

"Shut the fuck up. I'm not done."

Unable to help myself, I let my palm slide up her bare leg. She's wearing a short black dress, which exposes her creamy thighs as it rides up. Despite the funeral taking place across the road, my cock hardens beneath her.

"My life hasn't been the same since you walked into it." I graze my lips against hers. "You insisted on trying to kill yourself rather than be saved. I've been terrified of losing you since. Every single one of us is wrapped around your finger. We love the bones of you."

"Damn straight," Hudson reiterates.

Seven is silent, watching us very closely.

"Whatever it takes, we will save you now, and every time in the future," I finish, my own voice faltering. "If you need to be Patient Eight, we will still love you, because you're one and the same. Good and bad. That's the girl I love."

"How can you love someone like me?" she whispers. "I've hurt so many people."

Hudson takes her spare hand. "You were the first one to treat Eli like a human being. You saved Phoenix when he lost his sobriety last year."

"You brought my brother back to me and showed me how to survive after what… what my father made me do." I shudder at the memory. "You wouldn't let me push you away, no matter what."

"You forgave me for the most evil, disgusting thing a person can ever do to someone they love," Hudson adds shamefully. "Despite everything, you chose to give us a future. Together."

On the curb outside the church, hidden in our own private bubble, we offer our heathen souls for judgement. Brooklyn can't look at either of us, her tears hitting my pressed white shirt as she struggles to breathe.

"You taught me… how to be human again."

Seven's voice is so quiet, I almost miss it. He's staring outside at the torrential downpour, frowning at his own distorted reflection. Brooklyn's head finally lifts to seek him out.

"I was dead before I met you." He lets their eyes collide. "You could've left me to rot in that basement. I deserve it more than anyone. I've hurt innocent people, tortured them and taken their lives."

"Sev…"

"You know it's true. I am the least deserving person of redemption."

"I thought the same." Hudson finds a small smile.

I nod in agreement. "You convinced every single one of us otherwise. You've hurt people, Brooke. Just like the rest of us. But I'm willing to bet my life that you've saved just as many."

The smile I've been waiting for blossoms on her lips. She looks too fucking beautiful like that, all shy and furtive, unsure of how to handle being praised for something.

"So the question, love, isn't how we can love someone like you. It's how could we not?"

Brushing her short locks, I meet those silvery, gunmetal eyes that always hold so much pain. Everything rests on her answer.

"I love you," Brooklyn murmurs after a beat. "For longer than I've admitted to."

Her declaration punches me in the chest. I feel like I've waited my whole life to hear those words.

"Me too, love. I'm done letting fear rule my life." I look between the other two. "We face this together. Nobody in this family grieves alone."

Squirming on my lap, Brooklyn attempts to exit the car. I grab her hips, holding her in place. I should let her go, but I'm fucking selfish. Her scent is a mouth-watering, enchanting fog that drapes over me. She's the siren calling my corrupted soul towards eternal damnation.

"Kade," she breathes.

My hand slides further up her dress, a finger hooking under the elastic of her panties. I meet Hudson's eyes over her shoulder while slowly dragging them down. He's staring at her with lust. The windows are so heavily tinted, nobody can see what we're doing from the outside.

Brooklyn lifts from my lap, allowing me to remove her panties. She gasps a little as I toss them over to Seven, embarrassment colouring her cheeks. I love the timid but sensual angel within her that comes out when we fuck.

Hesitating for a second, Seven brings her panties to his nose and inhales deeply. "I can smell your arousal," he tells her with a crooked smile. "Do you like people watching you?"

Undoing my belt and attacking the fly of my trousers, Brooklyn falters at his question. We all know she has a kink for group activities. I think about what we did in Blackwood's swimming pool at least once a day.

"You don't have to watch us," she grinds out.

Sitting back, Seven stares. "I'm curious."

Opposite us, Hudson begins to touch himself. "Me too."

Taking my cock in hand, Brooklyn begins to pump it up and down. I take the opportunity to imprison her in a passionate kiss, exploring every inch of her body that's exposed by the tight dress. She should dress in borrowed hand-me-downs more often if they look like this.

Finding her clit, she's wet and dripping already. I play with her, despite the inappropriateness of our surroundings—in the middle of the street, opposite a church. People walk past our blacked-out car every so often, glancing at the windows without seeing inside. It's fucking hot to know we're breaking the rules.

"Take it, love," I whisper to her. "I want to fill you up."

With a moan, she lowers herself down on my length. At this angle, I'm pushing so deep inside of her, I almost finish before we get started. It's a snug fit, with warmth wrapping around my dick in a welcome embrace. I don't give a damn if what we're doing is wrong.

She's the only thing worth living for on this planet.

Without her, we have nothing.

Beginning to move in a slow, coaxing grind, Brooklyn takes her time. She's letting me thrust deep inside of her, with two steadying hands placed on my shoulders. Our lips find each other again. I can taste the heartache on her tongue. We shouldn't fucking be here, mourning another loss.

"We have to stop," she moans.

Lifting my hips, I meet her movements. "Not a damn chance, love.

You don't get to decide that. We own every inch of your soul. I decide when and where I want to fuck you."

"But, Seven—"

She freezes when I grab her throat, forcing her to look at him. Seven's watching our performance and stroking his cock, a delicious darkness swirling in his eyes. He doesn't look uncomfortable in the slightest.

"He belongs with us," I implore her. "Just look at him. None of us can fucking think straight around you. This is the power you hold over us all."

Emboldened by my words, Brooklyn rides my dick faster. She looks like a goddess on top of me, taking every last drop of pleasure I have to offer her. I can feel her walls tightening around me, preparing to fall apart. Swirling my thumb over her nub, she can't hold it in any longer.

"Say my name, Brooke. Let them hear it."

"Fuck, Kade!"

I grab her throat and continue thrusting upwards, ready to spill myself inside of her. Knowing we're being watched and appreciated undoes my self-restraint. I want to see my come stream down her leg, knowing she's covered in me as we enter that church.

Brooklyn slumps against my chest as our releases coincide. Every muscle in my body tenses, drowning in a powerful wave of pure sensation. My fingers run through her messy hair, needing to touch every single part of her to prove that she's all mine.

Before she can catch her breath, she's torn from my lap. Hudson's already unfastened his dark-wash jeans and doesn't waste any time spearing her on his proud length. Brooklyn gasps loudly, filled back up before she's even had a chance to come down from her orgasm.

"My turn," he growls. "I need you too."

They fuck frantically in the back of the SUV, not stopping even as there's another tap on the window. Hudson's too busy pounding his ownership into her, ensuring Seven's watching the entire time. He's getting himself off, studying Brooklyn with quiet intensity.

He can't tear his eyes away.

Like it or not, he's already one of us.

Laying Brooklyn down across the leather seats, Hudson shoves her dress up to her waist and plunges back inside. Her legs spread wider in the space of the car to allow him full, unfettered access. We both watch the show with fascination as Hudson drives her back to the edge.

"Come, blackbird. Coat my dick in your juices," he goads.

The cry of ecstasy she releases sends a shiver down my spine. Both finishing, Hudson's head rests against her breastbone. It's a brief second of panting before they break into raucous laughter. Once again, we find ourselves in another morally fucked situation.

I grab a packet of tissues from Brooklyn's discarded coat pocket and toss it at them. "Clean up, you lunatics. Hunter will come out here and smash the window open if we keep him waiting much longer."

"Worth it." Brooklyn hands Seven a tissue too.

The stormy-faced man actually nods. "Agreed."

21

BROOKLYN

Hurts Like Hell - Fleurie

Kade releases my hand outside of the car. Taking a deep breath and yanking my dress down, I turn my head up to the sky. Raindrops hit my tongue in a sweet explosion, and I savour each one. This is what it's all been for; beginning to live again.

I have even more of a reason to now. For the people that aren't here, we have to survive.

Seven hangs at the back of our group, his head downturned and defeat laying heavy on his shoulders. Letting Kade and Hudson take the lead, I slide in next to him. He lets me take his empty hand.

"Kade's right," I tell him. "You're not alone."

Releasing a deep breath, he nods. "I guess."

"Come on. I won't let go of you, I promise."

Flanked by our two blank-faced agents, their suits bulging with concealed holsters, we enter the small church. It's a beautiful, mid-century classic, carved from slabs of limestone and lit with flickering flames. Dozens of candles have been lit inside, until it looks like the constellations of a midnight sky.

Down the narrow aisle, we take the empty seats at the front. Hunter, Theo, and Enzo all stand to the right in their expensive, fitted black suits, boxed in by their own security detail. Not a single one has been able to look at us. It's clear that while Sadie was saving our lives, they were protecting the woman they loved.

There's no elaborate service. Scripture and sentiments mean nothing to the people left behind. One by one, the three men take their turn laying a single, long-stemmed rose on her coffin. Enzo's cold mask doesn't break. He stands frozen and desolate, like an abandoned mountain range.

"I love you, beautiful. Remember that."

Theo goes next, his cheeks stained with tears as he presses a kiss to the coffin's surface. He's the most emotional of them all, but the hard set of his jaw betrays the angry torrent battering him from within.

"I'm fucking sorry, Lys."

Hunter goes last, passing Theo in the aisle. His steps are hesitant and afraid, so unlike the powerful force to be reckoned with that he's projected since day one. This is far more terrifying than any threat levelled against him or his team. After laying the rose, he stares down at the inscription.

"I didn't keep you safe. I will never forgive myself for that. You paid the price for my stupidity."

After several long seconds of contemplation, Hunter turns his back on her remains. His gaze is fixed on the cobbled stone of the church, unwilling to reveal his pain to anyone else. Enzo quickly pulls him into a crushing bear hug.

"It's my fault," Hunter croaks.

Enzo holds him tighter. "Stop it, Hunt. This isn't on you."

"We should've pulled her out. I was so desperate for answers, I put her at risk."

"We made the decision together," Theo speaks up, wiping his eyes. "Alyssa was her own person. She wanted the truth more than anything."

Hunter scrubs his face. "No outcome is worth this. I jeopardised a member of the team. That's on me."

"Stop it," Enzo demands. "Alyssa's death isn't on us. It's those evil, corrupt bastards that have to pay."

Taking several deep breaths, Hunter finally manages to look up, and our gazes collide. His picture-perfect, stubbly features are carved in agony. I swallow the lump in my throat, dropping his gaze.

We all know why Sadie is dead.

Our demons aren't so different, after all.

"Fuck," Theo stutters. "I can't believe… this is goodbye. She… I… goddammit."

Enzo tugs them both into a frantic hug, all three men huddling together. It's heartbreaking to see them embracing each other, mourning the one missing person from their family together. I can't imagine losing one of my guys and the pain it would bring. A piece of their souls will forever be missing.

"Go on," Kade instructs us.

With a steadying breath, Seven squeezes past me. I follow him up to the awaiting coffin. He's clinging to me so tight, I fear my bones will break. Miniature quakes rock his entire frame as he battles to keep his emotions under control.

We stop at the side of the coffin.

"I don't know what to say," he admits.

I wrap my arm around his firm bicep. "She's still here, Sev. Say whatever you need to."

"She can't fucking hear us."

"Just get it off your chest."

Sighing, Seven releases my hand to trace his sister's name with his finger. "I shouldn't have said what I did in the warehouse. You'll always be my family. Jude may be gone, but I can still be the person you thought I was."

I hold his long-stemmed rose for him. With bleak eyes meeting mine, he nods once. I step closer and place the rose on the coffin, feeling the weight of the moment bear down on me. My friend is gone. She was the first one to be there for me, to see beyond the thick walls I put up.

Sadie was a good person.

Flawed, imperfect, but undeniably good.

"I hope we make you proud." I swipe beneath my eyes with my coat sleeve. "Thank you for being a far better friend than I ever was. You deserved more than this."

We barely make it back to our seats. The sombre mood feels suffocating. All I want is to escape and mourn in private, let my emotions overcome me where nobody can see. Some things need to be endured alone.

As we line up to file back outside, a shrill ringtone pierces the air. Looking surprised by the noise, Hunter stares down at his screen with a frown. When he answers, his low hiss of greeting would terrify most callers.

"I see," he deadpans. "How did you get this number?"

We all watch with trepidation.

"If this is an attempt to scare us off the case, it's entirely misguided."

"Hunt?" Enzo asks with concern.

Meeting the wide eyes of his best friend, Hunter puts the phone on speaker mode. Every single person inside the church stiffens at the light, conversational tone in Bancroft's voice. He sounds far too fucking happy.

"I do apologise for breaking up this sad, sad affair."

"What do you want?" Enzo blusters.

"It seems you're intent on destroying the hard-earned reputation of your firm by associating with these convicts. I'm willing to offer you a final chance to step aside."

Hunter scoffs bitterly. "You killed one of our own. This is no longer a professional endeavour. Believe me, I will take great delight in demolishing your organisation overnight."

"Well, your confidence is amusing at least." Bancroft laughs sadistically. "Since you're all mourning, I thought I'd offer you a gift. Patient Delta has been punished for her transgressions."

The heat leaches from my body, leaving me cold and empty.

"Punished for letting us escape, you mean," I accuse.

"Ah, Brooklyn. You know better than most what disobedience gets you."

"What do you want?" Kade steps in front of me.

"Mr Knight! I thought I recognised your voice. It's been a long time. There's someone here who would like to speak to you."

With a shuffling sound, a deep throat clear causes my heart to somersault. Hudson rests a hand on his brother's shoulder, staring at the phone with trepidation. I'd recognise Leroy Knight's voice anywhere.

"I expected more loyalty from you, son, after all I've done for you."

"Father," he grits out. "I'm doing what's right."

"I wonder if the authorities will agree when they charge you with first-degree murder. Poor old Stephanie, killed in cold blood. How is my adoptive boy? Gotten over his short-lived grief yet?"

"Fuck you," Hudson shouts.

"Hello, Hudson. In all fairness, she was a whore. The world is well rid of your mother."

His foot connects with several of the chairs, sending them flying across the church in wooden splinters. I attempt to approach him, but Hudson hisses at me in warning.

"What about my mother?" Kade interjects. "You can't keep up this manhunt for long. She won't protect you anymore. You're going down, along with this entire corporation."

"Sentiment," Leroy hums. "It's something I've warned you about. When everyone you love is dead, we will have this conversation again. Perhaps then you will learn your lesson."

"We'll see about that, old man."

"Shall I add harassing my clients to your list of charges?" Hunter intervenes smoothly. "Along with torture, unlawful imprisonment, illegal experimentation, and a million human rights violations?"

"I think you'll find the law to be on our side of this, Mr Rodriguez." Bancroft takes charge from Kade's father. "Turn the fugitives over or I won't be held responsible for my next actions."

Staring ahead at Sadie's coffin, Hunter's face transforms into a mask of terrifying determination. He looks ready to go to war, win or lose.

"Go to hell, *sir*."

"Poor choice, Mr Rodriguez. Let's see who will believe you after this."

The line goes dead.

"What the fuck just happened?" Enzo exclaims.

Just as Hunter's mouth opens to speak, the sound of two gunshots explodes from outside of the small church. The grand, arched doors slam open, leaving two crumpled bodies to collapse inwards. The men are bleeding from smoking bullet holes shot at a perfect, point-blank range.

Too perfect.

Something evil is here.

Everything happens too quickly. Hunter and Enzo pull their

weapons with practised ease. They train their aim on the gate-crasher, along with the other two agents boxing us in. Kade roughly shoves me behind him.

"Who are you?" Hunter bellows.

Dressed casually in a thick parka, plain black clothing, and a scruffy baseball cap, the silent, brown-haired man enters the church. His sunken face is covered in stubble, adding to his roughened exterior. He looks homeless. In his eyes, no emotion awaits.

Enzo hobbles into the aisle. "Stop right there."

He keeps walking regardless of the guns facing him. Each step stamps our death certificates. When the man pulls his hand from his pocket, we all spot the small black detonator. Every second is a revolving door of quick-fire developments.

The crash of bullets pierce his chest.

Enzo's gun recoils from the blasts.

The detonator slips for an alarming second.

Bancroft's monster recaptures his prize.

"Who the fuck are you?" Enzo repeats.

Head cocked, he smiles. "Patient Beta."

His thumb collides with the detonator. Survival instincts kick in as a thunderous boom echoes throughout the church. The man explodes in a blinding torrent of light. Bricks, pillars and slabs of stone fly everywhere, propelled by fire and hot ash.

Reality comes in sharp, painful fragments.

All I can hear are the panicked shouts and screams of our group. I'm knocked off my feet by Kade's weight. He takes the full force of the blast, his body shielding me from harm. Pain still sizzles through me as I impact with the stone floor.

My ears ring, obscuring my stunned senses.

I can hear Seven screaming my name.

Darkness is swallowing my vision.

The last thing I remember is the look on Kade's face when I finally told him that I loved him. I want to see that smile every day for the rest of my life. Not just on him, but all of them. Even if I have to die and leave reality to do that.

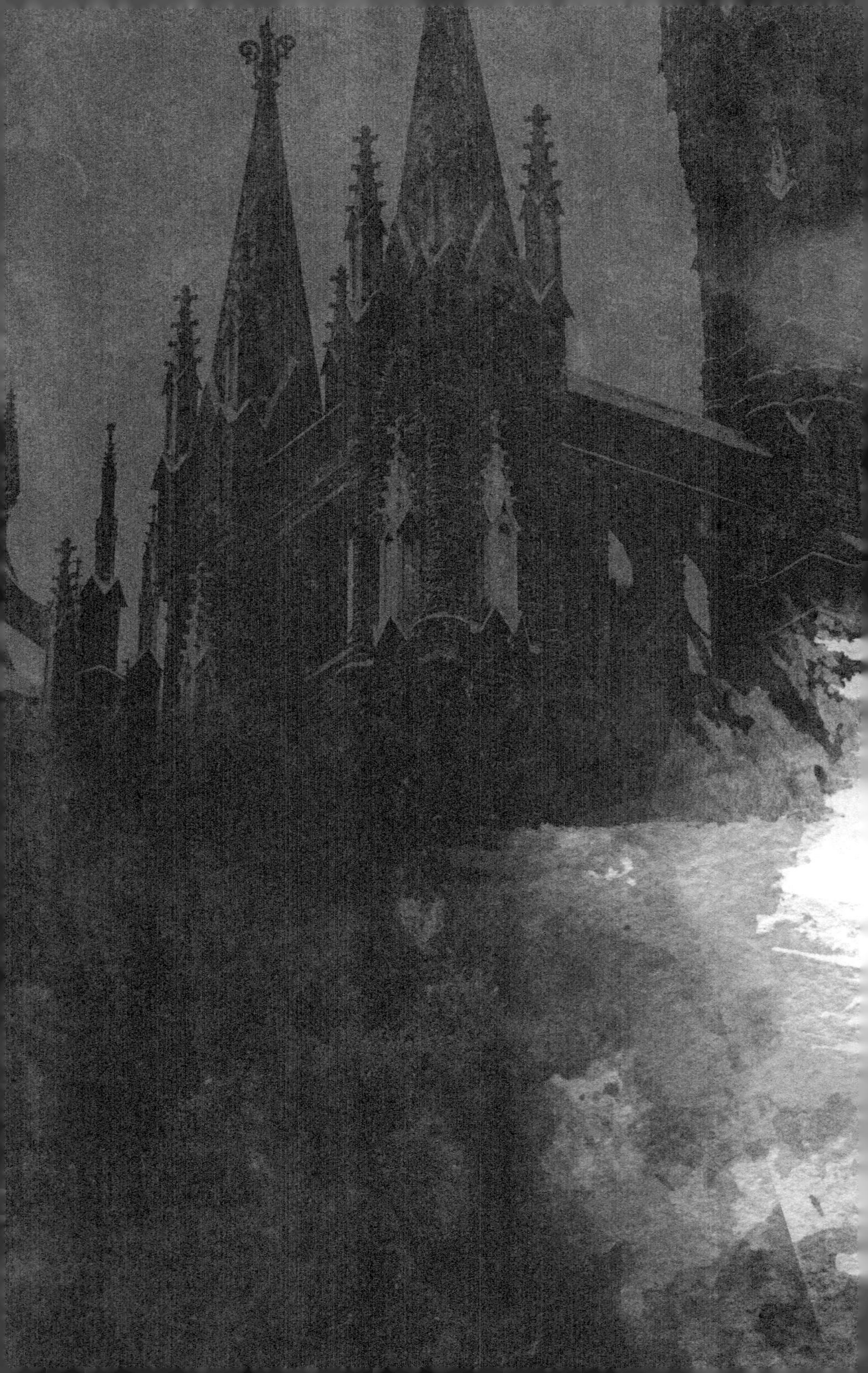

22

BROOKLYN

Teresa - YUNGBLUD

It's times like these that I miss Blackwood. Don't get me wrong, it was a miserable hellhole. But at least the horrors were predictable. I could steel myself for more torture and bury my vulnerabilities to survive. I can't do that out here.

The blows just keep coming.

Real life is a cruel motherfucker.

Dabbing the swollen lacerations on my face, I grit my teeth through the pain. I'm resolutely ignoring the whispering shadows behind me. Fear and pain bring out the worst parts of my traumatised brain.

The on-call doctor already dug the shrapnel out of the injuries on my body when they wrapped me up a few hours ago. I stuck around until they took Kade into surgery to set his broken arm.

Hudson and Seven are still being treated too, while Hunter and Enzo are holding an emergency meeting with their staff. Sabre is going into full lockdown. Everyone has been informed of our presence and tasked with one priority—no more fuck ups. They lost four agents in the church.

The bathroom door creaks behind me, admitting a headful of dark ringlets and two searching eyes. Eli looks me up and down, his hands raised to take the cotton swab from my grasp.

"I'm fine," I protest as he steals it.

"N-Not."

"It's just a few scrapes and bruises. Kade shielded me."

Pushing me to sit down on the closed toilet, Eli's eyes narrow as he resumes dabbing the nasty slices. I quickly told the doctor to fuck off after enough poking and prodding. My patience for clinicians is very short.

"The others?" I ask worriedly.

"Concussions."

"Both of them? No broken bones?"

"Go... s-see."

I stare at the soft sweats and blue t-shirt that I stole from Phoenix's stuff to wear. He must've worn them already, as his warm, inviting scent clings to the fabric. Inhaling deeply, I let Phoenix's essence wrap around me.

"I needed to get out of there. Too many doctors and nurses, I couldn't fucking think. You know Hunter sent a shrink to talk to us? Some asshole called Doctor Richards."

Nodding, Eli bites his lip.

"I don't want anyone else digging around in my head."

"H-Help... you."

I duck my gaze. "There's no helping me."

My eyes are pulled back up as he strokes a finger over my jawline, cheekbone, nose, eye socket. Cataloguing every inch of my face, his smile is knowing. He can see the swirling shadows inside of me. Sickness and rage demanding retribution, keeping me forever trapped in the past.

I can't let go.

Even if I wanted to, my mind won't let me.

"We were supposed to be safe here." I push Eli's hands away and stand. "How could they attack us like that in the open?"

"Show y-you."

Placing the bloodied cotton swab down, Eli grips my hand. He guides me back into the living room and flicks the TV on to a news channel. I have to hold his arm to steady myself as the world tips on its head.

"You've got to be kidding me."

The reporter is reading a statement from the police, claiming the church explosion was no mere accident. It was an attack by none other than… six mentally unstable criminals, recently escaped from Blackwood Institute. The police investigation is ongoing, but no arrests have been made.

"This can't be happening."

Images of the fiery church ruins are shown. Beneath that, the appeal for information leading to our capture is repeated. The story briefly touches on rumours of medical negligence against the corporation, but it's quickly dismissed and overshadowed by the main story.

"They're spinning it to fit their narrative, burying the story about Harrowdean with this madness."

"Yeah," Eli agrees flatly.

I watch the news story until I can no longer see straight. For someone that generally spends their life pretty angry, I'm beyond livid. This isn't a game. It's a character assassination, one move at a time. They're going to beat us into submission.

"Are those reporters still outside?"

Eli nods uncertainly.

"Good. We're going to give Incendia a taste of their own medicine."

Throwing my leather jacket on to cover my heavily scarred arms, I retake Eli's hand. My heartbeat is roaring in my ears, but I don't allow myself to stop and consider if this is a bad idea. All I know is that I can't stand the fucking injustice any longer.

The grand foyer we departed from hours ago is a hubbub of frenetic energy. There's an even heavier security presence than earlier, blocking every entrance and exit while checking employees' badges and fingerprints for good measure. They aren't taking any chances.

At one of the glass entrance doors, a scowling, bald-headed agent studies the reception. He looks like a terminator, his hand resting on a visible gun in its holster. I wait for him to recognise me and let us pass, but he refuses to budge.

"Carl, step aside."

Theo appears at our side, dressed down in blood-speckled sweats and a tight muscle shirt. Damn, he's hiding some firm pectorals under his usual goofy clothes. His face is marred by a row of stitches and his sprained arm is in a sling.

"Theo?"

Meeting my eyes, exhaustion and grief stare back at me in shades of Antarctic blue. The gentle, caring soul within him has been broken and imprisoned in a cage. He looks done with the world and everything in it.

"Alyssa shouldn't have died like that," he offers bleakly. "We let her down. Now, we don't even have a body to mourn. They've taken that from us too."

"I'm so sorry, Theo."

"The truth doesn't matter to them, but it does to the world."

"What do you want us to do?"

Theo's grimace hardens. "Tell it."

At his order, the reluctant agent scans his thumbprint and opens the huge glass door for us to step outside. Eli moves tentatively, his hand bunched in the material of my leather jacket. We descend the steps until he digs his heels in, rubbing at an invisible pain in his chest.

"What is it?"

"C-Can't... hate m-me..."

Wrapping my arms around his trembling body, I feel his face bury in the crook of my neck. We embrace in the chilly wind, caught between safety and retaking our lives. One misstep and we'll crash into the chasm of death waiting to devour us whole.

"Nobody could ever hate you, Eli," I whisper into his soft, lemon shampoo-scented curls. "The world just doesn't understand people like us. I'll still keep you safe."

"P-Promise?" Eli stutters.

"I promise. Just keep talking to me."

His lips caress my ear. "Anything f-for you... baby girl."

Hearing his raw voice return more every day will never get old. His sweet little smile spears me right in the heart. Hand in hand, wrapped in each other's strength and determination, we approach the horde of reporters. The minute they spot us, the shouts for attention begin.

Our identities are hardly a matter of secrecy after recent events. Every dark and sordid detail of our lives have been printed for the country to read. We're the monsters that burned down Blackwood Institute. That's all the world will ever see when they look at us.

But not today.

This is our chance to take control back.

Eli's grip on my hand becomes crushing as we stop metres from the barrier keeping the crowd of reporters back. Flashing cameras blind us as the shouts and calls for attention grow more frantic. For the first time in so long, we hold the power. They want to hear our voices.

"Brooklyn West!"

"Did you bomb the church?"

"What happened inside Blackwood Institute?"

Keeping Eli by my side, I approach the closest microphone. Everyone falls silent, too many curious gazes to count lasering their attention on my injured face.

"What do you want to tell the world, Brooklyn?" the reporter asks.

Cameras flash.

Shouting falls silent.

The world awaits a single word.

"My friends and I have been subject to a lot of speculation in recent weeks." I take a deep, steadying breath. "Our stories don't make for easy reading. I'm not here to profess our innocence to the world. Nobody ends up in Blackwood Institute for being sane."

Eli's hand squeezes mine, sending a message of strength.

"We entered Blackwood seeking treatment and rehabilitation." I study the huge crowd. "Instead, all we received was abuse, malpractice, and exploitation. These institutes are not designed to help people. The truth is far more terrifying."

"Is this the same institute in which you incited a riot that led to the deaths of patients and staff?" another person shouts above the shocked whispers.

Zeroing in on them, I don't break eye contact. "This is the same institute in which clinicians engaged in illegal experimentation and psychological torture, using society's most vulnerable people as their unwilling subjects."

A roar of noise almost bowls me over. Too many questions to count are hurled at us both. Eli retreats several steps, his teeth gritted. I can practically taste the panic leaking off him in waves.

"Why should we believe you?"

"Where's the evidence?"

"Are you going to surrender to the authorities?"

"No," a rasp of terror replies.

Eli quakes all over while staring ahead for the first time. He returns to my side. More cameras flash, capturing his stormy face and the thick lines of shiny scar tissue covering his arms. He didn't cover up before coming outside. Not even all of the guys have seen his skin, yet here he is.

Living unapologetically.

This Eli… is still afraid.

But he's no longer letting it dictate his future.

Letting his arm envelop me in warmth, I fist the material of his t-shirt and face the cameras with resolution. I want them to see us like this. Together. United. Unbroken. He looks down at me with a hint of a smile, emotion shining in the rolling, grassy hills of his eyes.

"We will fight until every last patient has been freed from Incendia's clutches," I state into the microphone. "The indifference of the world towards people like us has enabled this abuse for too long."

"What are you going to do?" another person shouts.

"We're people. We matter, and we will stand up for our rights until society decides to give a damn. This isn't over."

I let Eli take me away, despite the tsunami of unanswered questions licking at our heels. The silent but steely agent escorts us back to safety, cutting off the shouting as Sabre's entrance door seals tightly shut.

Inside, the packed foyer is spookily silent. All of the enormous screens are tuned in to the local news. They all saw us speak. Every single person standing between us and certain death.

One by one, Hunter's employees begin to clap, led by Theo. It starts slowly, like a gathering storm stretching across the heavens, brewing into an all-consuming tsunami. I feel lightheaded, relying solely on Eli's embrace to hold me up. The applause doesn't stop.

"Why are they clapping?" I whisper to him.

"P-P-Proud," he murmurs back.

If I die at Bancroft's hands tomorrow, I'll take comfort in the knowledge that despite everything I've done, I made somebody proud. Hell, a room of strangers, inspired by a dark tale told by six delinquents. As for the beautiful, broken man at my side… his pride is all I ever wanted.

We escape upstairs, taking the elevator back in stunned silence to decompress. Hunter will no doubt track me down for a bollocking when he sees the news, but I don't give a fuck. All I want is a soft, warm bed and Eli's lips on mine. I step into our borrowed apartment with a sigh.

"Bed?" Eli suggests.

His arms band around me from behind, holding me close.

"What about the others?"

"They… find us."

"Then bed," I decide.

I'm lifted off my feet and spun around in a dizzying circle before Eli cradles me in his arms. My lips find their way to his on instinct as I'm carried towards one of the bedrooms we've been crashing in. Our kiss starts slowly, gently, with repressed emotion and promise.

When his tongue slips inside my mouth, I suppress a growl. Eli kisses me back with fervour, seeking to devour me with his touch. Everywhere his skin is on mine feels like it's on fire. His foot impatiently kicks a bedroom door open, and a sharp squeak has us breaking apart.

"Oh my God, Nix?"

Phoenix's head is stuck in a loose white t-shirt as he wrestles to take it off. Cursing colourfully, he manoeuvres his heavily bandaged hand.

"Firecracker? Eli?"

We rush at Phoenix together, both shouting his name like an

answered prayer. My arms snake around his neck in a tight, desperate hug, while Eli snuggles his waist from behind so we're wrapped in a teary sandwich. Phoenix grunts in pain, but he doesn't push us away.

"Nix," I repeat, on the verge of sobbing.

"I'm here, guys."

"H-Hurt?" Eli stammers.

"It's alright. I'm getting better."

There isn't a part of him that isn't bruised or discoloured. Covering his face in light kisses, I feel the relieved tears flow. He's greedily drinking me in with his eyes. When we pull the t-shirt over his head, his torso reveals more abuse and suffering. Hearing Eli curse is a clear indication.

Dark stripe marks meet heavy bruising and endless scabbed-over wounds from a knife. My hands cover my mouth, nausea locking my throat up tight. Knowing what instruments and malice cause these injuries is one thing. I can handle my own pain. The people I fucking love? That's a no-go.

"It's okay," Phoenix offers weakly. "Please don't cry."

"No... it's not."

His one good hand strokes over my hair. "I'm back now. Nothing else matters."

"I'm sorry, your sister... she... I..."

"I can't talk about her," he croaks, cutting me off. "I just want to hold you both."

I carefully guide him over to the unmade bed I slept in last night with Kade and Hudson. Eli fluffs the pillows and tucks the duvet around Phoenix, fussing over him with such adoration, it makes me cry even harder. Fuck, I could win awards for emotional overload as of late.

Phoenix pats the space next to him. "Come on."

"I could leave you both to—"

"Brooke," Eli interrupts in a stern whisper. "C-Come."

Taking the other side, he's careful to avoid Phoenix's bad leg from the stabbing. It's still bandaged and stiff, along with his tightly wrapped hand. Stripping off the sweats I stole, I shove my stupid self-doubt to the back of my mind and slide in next to Phoenix.

He smells like hospital antiseptic and cheap shampoo, but I don't care. Beneath that, he's still my blue-haired maniac. Curling up against his side feels like throwing the doors to our cosy cottage open and running inside with open arms. Next to him, I'm finally home.

"I thought we lost you," I choke out.

"I promised to follow you in this life and the next; conspiracies, assassins and finger-chopping bastards aside. I still have one good hand to do this with."

His fingers bury in my hair, encouraging me to look up. Before I can take a breath, Phoenix is kissing the living daylights out of me. His soft lips move against mine in a passionate dance, demanding every ounce of submission I have left to give.

I'll happily let myself be consumed by him.

Death doesn't scare me, but losing him does.

Phoenix's teeth nip my lip with his usual playfulness, even as my tears leak between us in a salty flow. We end up gasping and laughing together. Everything about this is so fucked. Our happiness at being reunited feels futile in the face of so much tragedy.

"So," Phoenix whispers. "You don't mind another boyfriend with missing body parts, right?"

I kiss the corner of his mouth. "If you don't mind a girlfriend with enough baggage to sink a ship and four other boyfriends, then nope. I can deal."

"We're counting Seven in this shitshow now, huh?"

"Group vote. Nothing to do with me."

He nuzzles my throat. "Damn. I miss out on all the important stuff."

Resting his weary head on Phoenix's chest, Eli releases a contented sigh. I curl up tighter, letting my fingers bury in his ringlets to gently massage his head. He can sleep now for the first time in days, knowing Phoenix is back exactly where he fucking belongs.

With both of us snuggled close, I feel the tension drain out of Phoenix's body.

"Do you need anything? More painkillers? Or we can move to another bed, give you some space."

"You're staying right where you are," he says firmly. "Everything I need is in this room."

As I lay there staring at his face, too many words to count beg to escape my lips. His expression is conflicted. When Eli's light snores fill the room, I feel Phoenix's chest shudder with the first sob. He's biting his lip to keep his crying silent.

"I'm so sorry," I repeat, my own cheeks wet.

"I couldn't keep her safe. Charlie is dead because of me."

"No, she isn't. They did this. It's not your fault."

His tear-logged, chocolatey eyes meet mine. "I didn't get a chance to say goodbye. She was just a kid when I left. Now, I'll never see her again."

"You will. Not on this earth, but one day. I believe that."

"Does it make it easier?" he asks through his agony. "Believing?"

Taking his good hand from my leg, I link our fingers together. His sister is dead. Sadie's gone, lost in spectacular ashes. We've lost our future. Our lives. The freedom that drove us to break our way out of Blackwood's cruel grasp.

It's all far more than we bargained for. But who gets what they deserve in life? None of the guys asked for this. I brought darkness into their lives the day I arrived, but they haven't once blamed me. The least I can do is hold Phoenix in his grief and put his broken pieces back together, just like he did for me.

"Nothing makes this easier. We're here though, Nix."

"Stay with me tonight? Please?"

"I'm not going anywhere. Sleep, I've got you."

It takes a long time for him to drop off, his tears staining the pale-grey pillowcase beneath his head. I hold on tight through every last teardrop, determined to keep him afloat amidst the falling rain of his agony. It's all I can do now. Nothing else will end this torment.

When I fall asleep too, Kade's earlier words echo in my head. He was right all along. We get through shit as a family. Together, not apart.

All we have left in this world is each other, and that alone is worth enduring all this pain and heartache for.

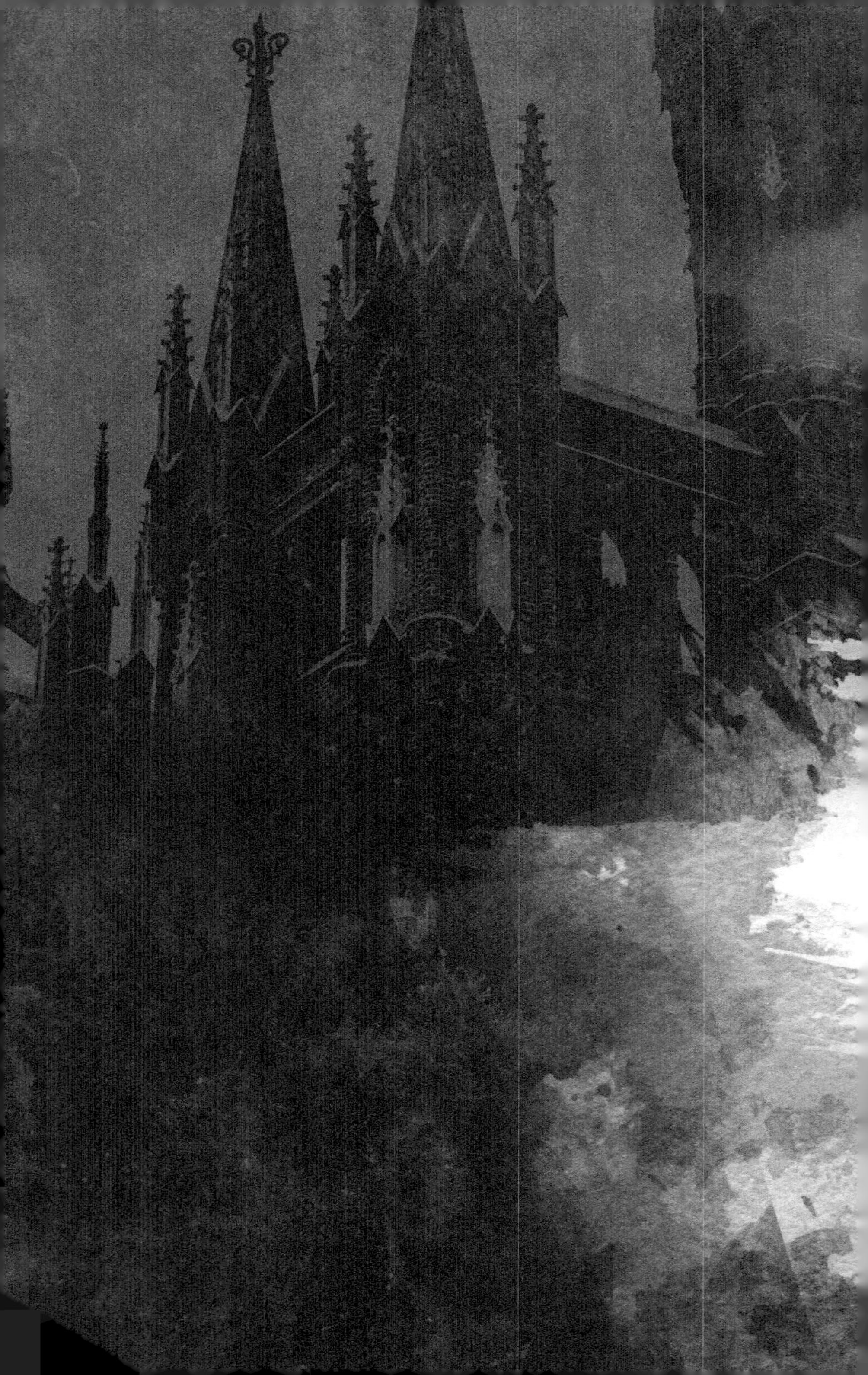

23

BROOKLYN

Fourth of July (Remix) - Fall Out Boy

Sitting in the bland waiting area, I'm surrounded by comfortable sofas, fake office plants and generic artwork. Being in an unfamiliar environment is making me anxious as hell, but knowing that Enzo and Hunter are taking testimony from Patient Two in the next room gives me some reassurance.

I volunteered to come, as she was the first witness to be called. She looked terrified, holding my hand until the very last second. Being separated from Lucia is hard for her after so long spent protecting one another.

They've holed up in their apartment since arriving, but I had a brief chat with them last night to explain the plan. Honesty in exchange for a chance, but only if we can convince the world it's the truth.

Four stony-faced government agents went in over an hour ago, their slick suits and shiny briefcases paired with glaring ID badges. They insisted on meeting in a neutral location to begin with—a safe house in Central London that's been converted into an office space.

"Hey." Hudson strolls in with two cups in hand. "Brought you a coffee. Want anything to eat? There's a shop down the street. I could get you a peanut butter sandwich. Your favourite."

I accept the steaming drink. "How do you remember that?"

"I made enough of them in the middle of the night. You clearly didn't learn your lesson when Mrs Dane refused to give you dinner. But still, you kept talking back."

"She never learned that hitting me and starving me don't work. How are the others?"

"Kade texted. They're back at HQ. Phoenix is resting while Eli plays nurse to them both. Seven is outside, glaring at anyone walking past the building. He hasn't moved since we got here."

"Nothing out of the ordinary, then," I snort.

"Typical psychotic behaviour. That's Seven, right?"

Studying the rugged lines of Hudson's face over the rim of my cup, I find no resentment there. He's vehemently hated Seven since the beginning, refusing to change his stubborn-ass ways. This nightmare has changed us all in so many ways.

"What about you?"

"Me?" he echoes.

"Are you okay?"

Hudson frowns at me. "Why wouldn't I be?"

"We will have to testify under oath about our pasts. Every last gory, messy detail will be laid out for the entire world to hear and judge when Incendia is exposed. It doesn't make you nervous?"

Draining his cup, Hudson crushes it easily in his scarred fist. When he stands and checks the time instead, I wait for him to fire a typical asshole response.

"How long will she be in there for?" he asks distractedly.

"Uh, probably a few hours."

"Let's get some air."

Reaching out a tattooed arm, I'm offered his hand.

"Come on, blackbird. I won't bite."

"Maybe I wouldn't mind if you did."

Our fingers slot together like puzzle pieces as he softly kisses my lips. Those brief, tender flashes of the sullen boy that made me peanut butter sandwiches never fail to melt me inside. We sneak out before anyone can notice, Hudson's feet skipping down the staircase with an odd sense of excitement.

When we break outside, Seven stiffens. "Problem?"

"Calm down, guard dog." Hudson mock salutes him. "Last time I checked, we're still free citizens. Let's go have some fun. I ain't sitting in that waiting area all morning."

"It isn't safe to be wandering around."

"Hunter's going to kill us one by one," I add.

"Fuck him," Hudson snaps. "We're adults. Let's live a little."

Considering him, Seven nods. "What did you have in mind, pretty boy? Better not get us killed."

Stifling an eye roll, Hudson takes a beanie from his pocket. He slides it over his overgrown black mop before tugging the hood of my jacket up, covering my face. Seven dons a baseball cap and tilts it down for coverage.

"Follow me." Hudson smirks.

Heading into the city's madness, we have no choice but to trust his sense of direction. He knows this place like the back of his hand after being adopted by Kade's family. I've heard the stories of their wild, drunken weekends away from the suffocation of the mansion.

Walking with a skip in his step, Hudson eagerly soaks in the surroundings.

"Did he drink or something?" Seven says in a stage whisper.

"What makes you think that?"

"He's far too happy. I don't recognise him."

"Heard that," Hudson calls back. "Keep your eyes on my girl and your opinions to yourself, dickwipe. I'm tolerating your existence, but that can soon change."

"Charming," Seven responds coolly.

More people start to appear as we rejoin the central strip. London is a riot of activity and endless variety. In the time I've spent here, even hiding for fear of our lives, I've never seen two people alike. I love the chaos.

Seven slings his arm around my shoulders. His amputated hand is tucked away in the pocket of his jeans, hiding it from the world. With our cuts and scrapes concealed, we could be three normal, everyday people. For just a moment, I want to live in that fantasy.

"Can we get food?"

Hudson lights a cigarette. "We can do anything, but there's someone who wants to see us first."

Cutting down a side street to avoid the crowding of bodies on the main roads, he leads us to a quieter borough. Seven looks on edge, acutely aware of every face that passes us.

I have to physically hold him back when a pair of police officers clock us from their patrol car. I hope we're far enough away for them not to see our stupid faces that are plastered all over the news.

"They don't recognise us."

"How can you be sure?" he growls. "Can't I kill them just to be safe?"

"I seem to remember you promising to be a better man not so long ago."

Blanching, his shoulders slump. "Yeah."

Everyone is handling Sadie's death differently. While her dying face has haunted my dreams since, I know that Seven has barely slept. Even when I try to coax him into bed for a few hours, he just stares outside at night, unblinking and silent. It's like he's waiting for her to return and give him another chance.

"You can talk to me," I remind him.

"There's nothing to discuss."

"We used to talk, late at night. No topic was off-limits."

Seven sighs. "I remember, princess."

"Nothing has changed. I'm still… whatever you need me to be."

"What if I don't know what I need? Everything has changed."

"My feelings haven't."

His caramel eyes scrape over me like molten lava. I could lose myself in his gaze, even on the days when it's cold and filled with the icy fires of hatred. Seven sees part of me that I keep hidden from the world, underneath the shame and loathing of what Augustus has made us.

"I'll be here until you know what you want," I promise.

"When this is all over, you'll leave."

His words stop me dead in my tracks. Hudson realises we're having a moment and crosses the road to finish his cigarette. I peer up at Seven, attempting to read the unfathomable look on his face.

"Why?"

"What we have isn't fit for the real world," he says in a matter-of-fact tone. "You said it before. Surviving and living are two very different things. I've kept you alive, but that doesn't mean I'm capable of helping you live."

"You seriously think I'd walk away after all we've been through?"

Seven shoves unkempt hair behind his ears. "I wouldn't blame you. There's no future for me in this world, we both know that. I'm not capable of getting better. They'll lock me up and throw away the key."

I take a shallow breath. "You are exactly who you're supposed to be. Jude, Seven, fucking Santa Claus. I don't give a damn what you are or how you got here. Don't you know how I feel about you?"

Biting his bottom lip, a glimmer of want flashes across his expression. Seven wraps himself in barbed wire and violence to survive the brutality of this world. Life is easier when you wield your pain as a weapon, cutting down all who dare to come close. The torment of staying alive is easier that way.

"You're scared." I grab a handful of his plain t-shirt. "I know what it's like to lose everything that matters to you. When I make a promise, I keep it. You will never have to lose me."

He looks so vulnerable, wracked by indecision.

"I don't want to be a burden to anyone, even you," he finally admits.

"Fuck, Sev. I was a wreck long before Augustus got his hands on me. I can't get through a single day at the moment without crying. I see shit that isn't real, hurt people who don't deserve it and need the strength of five men just to keep me on my feet. If anyone's a burden here, it's me."

"They love you. There's a difference."

I cup his cheek. "What difference? Are you so thickskulled that you can't see I fucking love you too? I'm in love with you, Sev. I have been since that damned basement."

Emotions churn in his irises after so long spent turning off his humanity. He's no longer the gaunt, lifeless man I used to be terrified of. His impenetrable shield is falling down, revealing someone else inside.

"I'm not sure what love means." Seven's brows crease. "But... I think it would feel like this. I can't breathe when I'm around you. All I want is to drink the oxygen from your lungs. Living in a world without your strength at my side is no longer an option. I can't take another step alone."

Brushing my lips against his, I seal the kiss with a sigh of blissful defeat. This isn't a battle I want to win. I'll surrender my weapons and allow myself to fall on Seven's sword. He can take the last remaining shard of my heart and do with it what he pleases… as long as I can stay right here, in his arms.

"That's love," I say against his lips. "You never have to be alone again."

Folded into his strong, scarred arms, I feel myself slump. We melt into each other like rain dissipating on a summer's day. Cars and pedestrians pass us, but the world is insignificant. He's the beginning and the end of my existence in this precious moment.

"Oi, lovebirds!" Hudson heckles us. "Get a fucking move on."

Seven's chuckle brushes over me. "I really can't kill him now, can I?"

"We're a package deal, I'm afraid. You get used to him."

"I think I already have."

We cross the street together to join our disgruntled third member. Hudson studies me first, then Seven, before releasing an exaggerated sigh.

"This asshat is sticking around then, huh?"

Seven's smile is smug. "You'd miss my sunny personality too much, pretty boy."

Hudson gets him in a headlock, and the pair wrestle their way down the street. I'm left to watch and laugh, mentally betting on who will win out. When Hudson prevails, Seven mutters something about breaking his skull and returns to my side.

"Hud? Where are we going? Getting hungry here."

"Nearly there, blackbird."

It's another fifteen minutes before we stop in the middle of a busy, vibrant market borough. Countless stalls and food vans shout their services, a delicious tangle of aromas floating towards us. Businessmen flag down customers to part with their money, while customers gobble street food and fresh doughnuts.

Guided through the traffic, we head for a tiny coffee bar tucked between two thrift stores. Inside, the warm ambience invites comfort. The smell of freshly ground coffee immediately perks Seven up.

Colourful Tiffany lamps and armchairs dipped in rich velvet warm the coffee shop, reminiscent of an old-school Victorian tearoom. Hudson removes his beanie and strolls towards a table tucked into the furthest corner, where two figures are crouched over their cappuccinos.

"Janet?" Hudson asks nervously.

With a headful of pristine blonde hair and deep, kind hazel eyes, Kade's mum is the picture of middle-class charm. She looks vastly different from the last time we saw her, heading off to finalise her divorce and run. Her spotless dress and expensive heels are gone, replaced by worn jeans and a floral blouse.

"Oh, Hudson," she cries out.

He's nearly knocked off his feet by the strength of her hug. She sobs loudly, soaking him with her tears. Behind them, Kade's younger sister watches on with wet cheeks. Cece is also blonde and classically beautiful like her mother, all soft lines and bright smiles.

"Calm down," Hudson grumbles. "You're causing a scene."

"You be quiet. A mother is entitled to hug and kiss her baby."

Seeing something so pure come from such evil warms my chest. Hudson secretly loves her attention; there's no denying the shine of tears in his eyes. Unconditional love isn't something he's experienced a whole lot of.

Seven disappears to order drinks. I laugh at him salivating over the extensive coffee menu. We have a decent stash of cash left over that Kade distributed when we left Scotland. When Janet spots me over Hudson's shoulder, her tears intensify.

"Brooke. You're looking so much better, my dear."

I clear my throat awkwardly. "Thank you, Mrs Knight. I'm getting there."

Bundled into her perfume-scented embrace, she kisses my short hair. "Please, call me Janet. We're beyond such formalities now. Come, sit. We don't have much time."

Crowded around the small table, Cece offers me a quick squeeze before retaking her seat. Janet refuses to release Hudson's hand. He rolls his eyes while pecking Cece's cheek. Seeing him around her is too fucking sweet for me to take. I adore the soft soul within his cruel, hardened shell.

"Do you need anything? More money?" Janet worries. "I can get more for you."

"We're fine," Hudson answers. "Everyone's safe. We're staying with the security firm that Kade told you about."

"Good, good. I needed to know that before we leave."

"Is something wrong?"

Janet grimaces. "We're on our way to the airport. My sister owns a villa in Southern Spain. Leroy is putting pressure on us with the divorce proceedings, and we can't hide here any longer. His threats have become physical. I fear for our lives if we stay."

"How are you getting out of the country?" Hudson frowns.

"Don't worry about us. We have all the right documents. My husband isn't the only one with friends in the right places." She lifts her sombre gaze to Hudson. "We came to say goodbye."

Adam's apple bobbing, he squeezes her hand tight. "As long as you're safe. Things are going to get messier here as the truth comes out. The more distance between us, the better."

Seven returns, already downing his third espresso shot. He stations himself against the wall, his caffeine-fuelled gaze trained on the front entrance.

"What about Kade?" I ask nervously.

"That boy has worried about the world since he was eight years old," Janet says with a wistful smile. "Such a kind child, so full of love. He's borne the responsibility for our family's sins for too long. This worry is mine to carry, and mine alone."

"Mum," Cece pleads.

Janet tucks hair behind her ear. "You'll see him again, Hudson too. When this is all over, we can be a family again."

"May be sooner than you think." Hudson grins at her.

The tinkle of the store bell interrupts our exchange. Seven doesn't move or pull out a weapon, so I let myself relax. Hudson stands up to greet the newest customer entering the coffee shop.

With his broken arm in a plaster cast and face covered in dozens of cuts, Kade awkwardly lumbers up to the table. He offers Hudson a grateful look before facing his family.

"Mum. Cece."

"Oh my God." Janet covers her mouth. "What did they do to you?"

Kade grunts as she slams into him, searching every inch of his body for more wounds. Cece starts to cry all over again, looking lost in her corner. I clear my throat, prompting Hudson to pull her into a hug. She needs her big brother more than anything right now.

"It's okay, we're all being looked after," Kade reassures them both. "Just a few bumps and scratches. I can't believe you were going to leave without saying goodbye."

Still fussing, Janet straightens the sling holding his cast. "You've spent so long looking after everyone else. For once, I wanted to protect you from worrying. It's a mother's job."

Taking a seat, Kade looks pale and even more exhausted than usual. The arm fracture was pretty severe, broken in two places following the blast. His recovery is set to take a while.

"The explosion? You didn't do it?" Janet hazards a guess.

"It was all them," Kade confirms sadly. "We're being framed."

Janet pulls an envelope from her handbag and slides it to Kade. "I was going to give this to your brother. It's sworn statements from us both."

"What?" Hudson exclaims, stealing the envelope.

"I don't know much. You saw more of his business dealings than me, Kade. Everything I have seen is in there. Fundraisers, business partners, investment dinners. If nothing else, it will ruin the last of Leroy's reputation."

Kade manages a tight smile. "I'll get it to the right people."

With the envelope tucked away, Janet gets emotional again. The clock is ticking down. I watch a taxicab pull up outside of the coffee shop and blare its horn. She hugs her two sons, before letting Cece get a squeeze in too. I'm the last person she approaches.

"Brooke." Janet clasps my shoulders. "There's something else. I didn't know for sure until I met you, but you look so much like her. Except for the eyes."

"What are you talking about?"

Her smile is tight, pained. "Early on in my marriage, Leroy worked for an investment bank. He was involved in brokering a multimillion-pound loan to expand a psychiatric institute. Real cutting-edge stuff for the nineties. I was so proud that day, I could barely take my eyes off him."

"Mum," Kade warns.

"She smiled and thanked me for my husband's hard work while her clinician watched on." Janet ignores his deliberate stare. "I was pregnant with Kade at the time. Such an old memory, but you deserve to know."

"You met my mother?"

As the taxi driver hits the horn again, Janet offers me a sad look. "All

I wanted was a happy marriage and children to fill the void I couldn't fathom in our life. I didn't know what his involvement would become."

"You couldn't have known," Hudson mutters.

"I wish I could tell you all that he wasn't always such a monster. I have wasted my life fooling myself." Her eyes stray to her boys, then Cece. "My marriage brought me the greatest gifts of my life. For that, I'm thankful."

With a final squeeze, she takes Cece's hand and heads for the waiting taxi. My heart is thundering against my ribcage. I can't help but cringe away when Kade reaches for me. All I see when I look at him is the cold, deadly stare of his father in that hotel room.

"Sorry," I rush out. "It's not you."

"No, I'm sorry. I should have told you. Dad has a lot of secrets. Incendia was one of them for a very long time. I am ashamed to call that piece of shit my father."

I meet his worried gaze. "Whether he's your father or not, when this is done, you will only have one parent left. That's a damn promise."

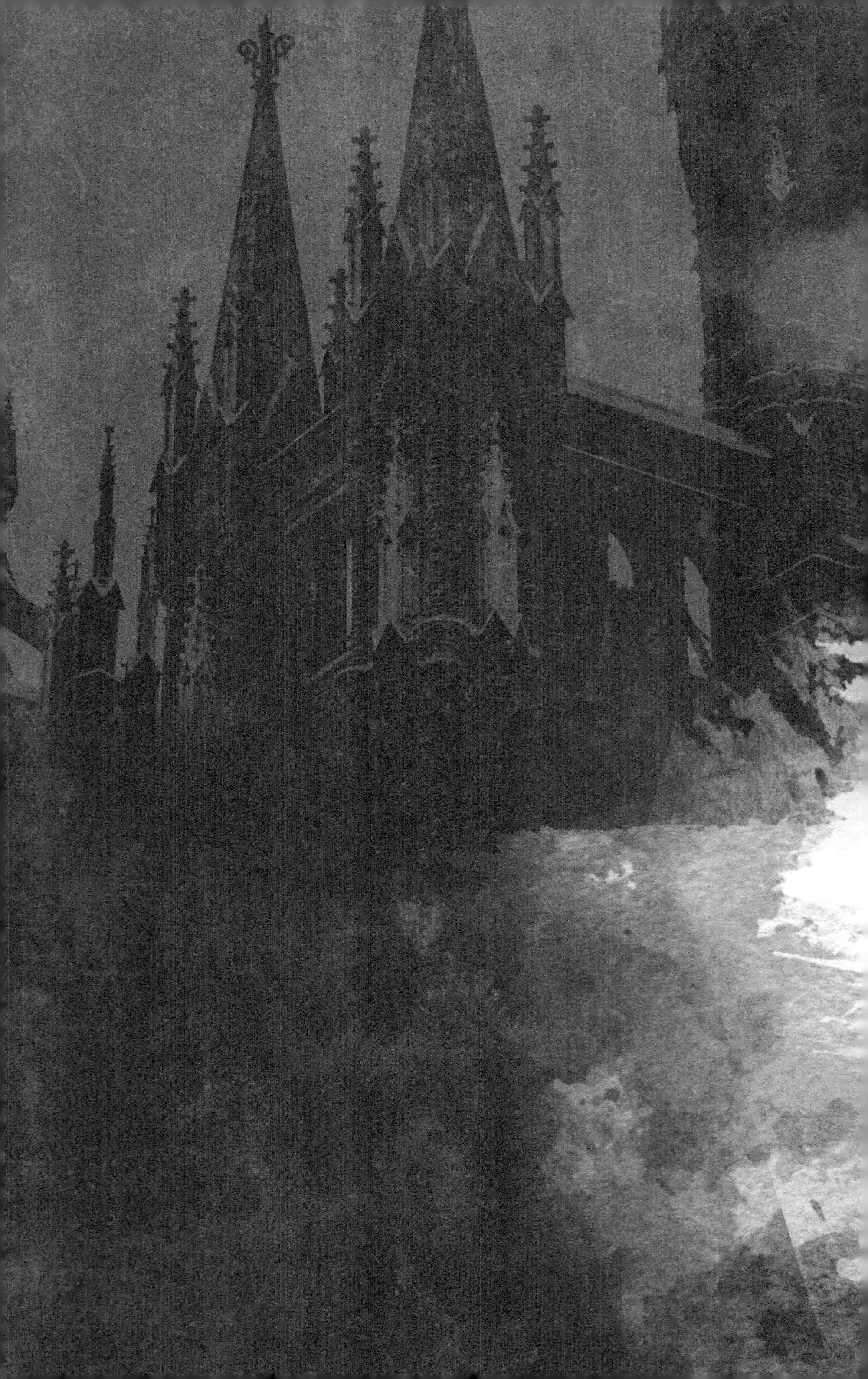

24

ELI

Casual Sabotage - YUNGBLUD

"When was the first patient admitted into the Zimbardo wing?"

Hunter's crisp, all-business tone takes no prisoners. He's been grilling Professor Lazlo for the last hour, relentlessly pinning down every last detail. The four government agents are all listening and taking meticulous notes, alternating in turns with the questioning.

It's satisfying to see Lazlo's full, utterly damning confession being recorded for later use, even if the contents turn my stomach. After Patient Two's opening evidence, the agents' attitudes abruptly changed. The wealth of information we've already given them is undeniable and the worst is yet to come.

"This guy is full of shit," Phoenix complains, his hand running up and down my leg. "He's dodging the hard questions and trying to avoid blame. Does he think we're stupid?"

Snuggling closer to him, I let my lips brush over his exposed collarbone. He isn't wearing a shirt, exposing his chiselled chest and many healing bruises. We're sprawled out on the huge sectional sofa beneath the duvet we stole from the bedroom, a massive bowl of popcorn between us.

We haven't been separated since he returned from the medical wing. It's been a full week of late-night testimonies and short tempers from the whole group. We left Brooklyn and Hudson to argue about dinner and controversial pizza toppings an hour ago, retreating to the living room to watch the live feed.

She refuses to watch it, and I don't blame her.

All we have to do is sit here and listen.

She lived through this shit.

None of us know what giving evidence is going to do to Brooklyn's fragile mental health. If her worsening mood and rapid-fire temper leading up to next week are anything to go by, we're in for a bumpy ride. She and Seven are next on the list. Clearly, Hunter is saving the most explosive for last.

"Stick your pineapple crap up your ass, Hudson! It does not belong on pizza!"

The angry slam of a door startles me. Phoenix murmurs for me to breathe, his arm trapping me against his naked chest. I wait for it to pass, accepting the intrusive flavours in my mind. Bitter smoke and harsh chemicals are replaced by sharp, fruity oranges and the sweet tang of freshly picked mint leaves.

Rather than fight against it, I'm trying something new, letting the anxiety and flavours wash over me without diving headfirst into them. We have such little control over our lives at the moment. This is the only thing I can change, and I'm learning to cope with things differently.

I think this is what recovery is supposed to feel like.

After years of fighting, it feels good to let go.

"You two wanna keep it down a bit?" Phoenix calls out. "It's only pizza, firecracker."

"No! I do not want to keep it down!"

Storming into the room, Brooklyn's hands are curled into fists. She looks primed to explode, her platinum pixie cut standing in all directions. Not to mention the visible cuts on her inner arms, revealed by her tank top. Hell, I'm the last person to judge how she decides to cope.

"I am so done with that arrogant, know-it-all, suffocating asshole hanging all over me!" she rages, throwing a decorative cushion at the wall. "If he offers to run through my testimony one more time, I'm going to stick his eyeballs on cocktail sticks and serve them for dinner."

"Can we get a side order of fries with that?" Phoenix deadpans without a smile. "Maybe some dips too, cheeky bit of mayo. Make it a real spread. Eli? Thoughts?"

I nod enthusiastically.

Hands on her hips, Brooklyn pins us both with an exasperated scowl. Phoenix cracks and laughs so hard, it vibrates through my body with the lack of space between us. Even I manage a low chuckle.

"It's like living with five goddamn teenagers!"

"Come sit down before you explode," Phoenix orders while still laughing.

He switches off the television before Brooklyn can spot the live feed. When she watched a mere thirty seconds of evidence earlier in the week, she had a complete meltdown.

We caught her talking to Augustus again. Or rather, the sick, invisible version of him that exists in her head. Enzo intervened when she cut herself with a kitchen knife while screaming at the thin air to leave her alone.

Hunter's overpaid shrink, Doctor Richards, was forced to sedate

Brooklyn. He's having a field day medicating us all after weeks of surviving without. Phoenix is back on mood stabilisers too. He's been a lot calmer since.

"Baby girl," I coax in a deep, rasping voice.

That's all it takes to penetrate her enraged fog. My girl can never refuse when I find the strength to gather my crappy voice. With a final annoyed huff, she stretches out on the sofa beside me.

"Why aren't Kade and Lucia back yet?"

"It's only been a few hours," Phoenix reasons. "We can't all be there. Taking it in shifts was the right call. Kade will get her through it."

"It should be me supporting her."

"You… h-hurt enough," I stutter out.

"I'm fine! Jesus Christ."

Phoenix's hand eases under my shirt, stroking the skin of my stomach in a teasing caress. "Do we believe that crock of shit, Eli?"

I shake my head.

Brooklyn groans. "Stop psychoanalysing me. I get that enough with the others."

With Phoenix's skin on mine, I tilt her face towards me. She accepts my palm on her cheek without thinking, her dark eyelashes hiding the anguish I know I'll find in her eyes. When our lips meet, I coax the truth from her soul with each stroke of my tongue.

I can taste her anxiety and fear, sense the visceral terror eating away at her. Recanting all she's been through to us was scary enough—laying it bare for a huge, national investigation, and basically the whole fucking world to hear, is a whole other story.

"You call that a kiss?" Phoenix teases, his fingers tugging at my waistband. "I can't get over there to do it myself. Show her a real kiss, Elijah."

Ignoring his taunts, I let my tongue tangle with Brooklyn's. She's relaxing into the kiss with each hot, heady second, surrendering to the claim we hold on her soul. When I bite down, seeking the slick tang of her blood, she presses her body into me with a mewl.

"Still fine, firecracker?"

"Fuck you, Nix," she growls between kisses.

"Not from there, you can't. Shall we take this into the bedroom?"

"You think I care if someone sees us?"

Brooklyn's challenge is full of sexy confidence, making my cock jolt in my boxers. She's become bolder recently, no longer afraid of taking what she wants. We've come too close to death for caution. I woke up to her lips wrapped around my cock the other night, her pussy wet and begging for my touch.

Taking control of the situation, Brooklyn climbs over me to sit in Phoenix's lap. I shift my leg, allowing me to sit up and watch their performance. Their lips meet in a sizzling collision, with his unbandaged hand wrapping around her slender throat.

She grinds against him while fighting for dominance, his grip appearing to steadily increase. Watching their two opposing forces face off, I dip my hand into my sweats to stroke my length. Blood drips down Brooklyn's chin as Phoenix attacks the nip I inflicted, but he licks it aside with enthusiasm.

"I wonder what your blood would taste like on Eli's cock," Phoenix muses, sending electric bolts down my spine.

She doesn't miss a beat. "Want to play a game with us, Nix?"

"Depends what the prize is."

Brooklyn grabs a coin from the coffee table. "Heads or tails. My pick or yours. Eli gets to play our willing victim."

Fuck, I'm going to come just listening to her dirty mouth.

"The prize?" Phoenix prompts.

"You still want me to be your little slut, Nix? I'll do that and more.

Whatever you want. I know you like us submissive."

Looking triumphant, he nods. "Deal."

Brooklyn throws me a heated look before tossing the coin in the air. It lands against the back of her hand, the answer hidden from sight.

"Heads and I get to taste your blood on his cock," she announces.

"Well, then tails and I watch you ride Eli's face."

When she lifts her hand, Phoenix audibly groans. The heads side is facing upwards, marking her victory, but he sure as hell doesn't look like he minds.

"Got a knife, Eli?"

"C-Coat."

Brooklyn gets up and searches in the pocket of my leather jacket that's hanging over a chair. As she saunters back to us, she tears the loose tank top over her head, exposing her bare, perfect breasts. Stepping out of her comfy yoga pants, she's left in nothing but a scrap of soaked cotton.

I continue rubbing my dick as she returns to Phoenix's lap, twirling the penknife in her hands that months ago, I used to inflict the scars on her hip. The same steel blade kisses Phoenix's wrist as he willingly offers it to her, his bottom lip caught between his teeth.

"Ever cut yourself?" Brooklyn asks curiously.

Phoenix smirks. "I prefer to torture myself with Class A drugs. I lack the patience for pain that you two share."

"It doesn't have to hurt." Pressing the penknife to his wrist, Brooklyn pushes the blade in deep. "Feel that sharp sting?" She begins to drag it along, parting his flesh. "It burns, right?"

Phoenix looks both turned on and disturbed as she deftly slices his wrist, deep enough for blood to trail down to his elbow. When she pulls the blade from his arm, the breath whooshes from Phoenix's mouth.

"And now?" Brooklyn raises an eyebrow.

"It feels like sprinting for the finish line and taking your first glorious breath," he wonders. "Fuck, I'm actually turned on by this."

"Told ya. Let's have a taste, shall we?"

Brooklyn takes my blade to her mouth, sliding her tongue along the serrated steel to taste his essence. I fist my cock tighter, trying to relieve the hunger burning up inside me. She's never looked so damn powerful, and Phoenix looks fucking perfect worshipping her sadistic ways.

Her sick lesson continues as she smears his blood all over her hand. Coating her skin in the red lubricant, she turns back to me. I let go of my aching length, allowing her to lather it in the warm, sticky substance.

Her lips wrap around the tip, sliding it deep into the welcoming prison of her mouth. I let my head hit the back of the sofa, gripping her short hair with my spare hand. She bobs on my length, taking it base to tip several times, each one nudging deeper into her throat.

"Hot damn," Phoenix murmurs. "Can you taste me, baby?"

Coming up for air, Brooklyn licks his blood that's smeared all around her mouth. She spots the bead of pre-come gathered on my cock and goes back for that too, her tongue swirling around the tip.

"Why don't you find out for yourself?" she challenges.

Dragging me up by my t-shirt, Brooklyn pushes me along the sofa towards Phoenix. He's still finding walking difficult while his injuries heal, but the way his gaze devours me leaves no room for hesitation. He looks at us both like we're heaven and hell all in one, trapping him in an infernal battle for his soul.

I straddle his chest before pushing my cock against his lips. Seeing Phoenix Kent surrender to me is something I never thought possible. He's the dominant one in our weird dynamic, but watching him eagerly take my length in his mouth opens a whole new realm of possibilities. I move my hips, savouring the feel of his tongue gliding over my length.

"Why don't you let him see how you taste, Eli?" Brooklyn suggests.

"I want to watch you fill his mouth with your come and let Phoenix drink every last drop. He needs to learn to play by our rules too."

"Y-Yes, baby girl," I say obediently.

Increasing my pace, I abuse Phoenix's throat as roughly as he's done to me, time and time again. To his credit, he never once falters. Brooklyn lays back down and gracefully slides off her underwear. When she spreads her legs, two fingers push deep into her pussy. Watching her pleasure herself while I fuck Phoenix's mouth is too much.

I roughly grab a handful of blue hair to steady myself, punishing Phoenix with the fast pace of my thrusts. His hand reaches out to grab a handful of my bare ass when I release a strangled cry. His lips don't relent, milking my release until I'm pouring hot seed directly down his throat.

When I pull out, there's blood and come painted across Phoenix's mouth. I don't give a fuck anymore. Shifting back, my mouth slants against his in a dominant kiss, cementing my new-found kink for taking control. I can taste myself on him, mixing with his blood and fusing our souls together.

Brooklyn's moan of pleasure brings us back to reality. Her head is thrown back as she works herself into a frenzy, her fingers pumping in and out of her slick heat. Climbing off Phoenix, I stand above them both in a position of power.

I'm calling the shots now.

They'll both bow to me tonight.

"No," I command before she can climax.

Her movements halt instantly, even as she releases a frustrated groan. Pointing at the hard lump straining against Phoenix's own sweats, I raise an expectant eyebrow.

"W-Watch… you f-fuck him."

She submits to my order, crawling to Phoenix on her hands and knees. I scoop her discarded panties from the floor as she positions herself above him, inhaling the sweet fragrance of her arousal. Phoenix looks bemused as she frees his dick and sinks down on it. He's not allowed to do anything but submit.

Brooklyn begins to move, grinding on him in confident strokes. Just watching them together has my erection strengthening again, but this isn't about me. This is Phoenix learning to take his own medicine for the first time. As Brooklyn quickens her pace, I move to stand behind her.

She trembles when my fingers dance down the length of her visible spine. I pepper kisses along her lower back, reaching the curve of her pert ass. She gasps in shock when my tongue traces the crack of her asshole, before slowly pushing inside of her.

"Fuck, Eli!"

Removing my tongue, I push a thumb into her moistened back entrance next. She moans again at the intrusion, slowly relaxing as I gently slide a second finger inside. I love watching her squirm.

"Care to join us?" Phoenix lets out a strangled breath.

Even with my fingers fucking her from behind, Brooklyn refuses to relent. Watching them from this position is so hot. I can see Phoenix's glistening sheath gliding straight into her cunt. Feeling the throb of my swollen cock, I know I'm ready to join back in. This shit is too hot to miss.

Transferring saliva to her tight, inviting asshole, I prepare to push inside my baby girl. She's already on the verge of falling apart between us, balancing herself on Phoenix as he watches us perform. The moment I begin to ease inside of her, she screams through a hard, fast release.

I hold her by the hips, biting back a moan of ecstasy. She's so fucking tight, I can feel Phoenix's length pressing up against mine as he fucks her pussy at the same time. We're filling every available space inside of her. Struck by an idea, I pick my penknife back up.

"Keep still, beautiful," I whisper in her ear.

A light sheen of sweat covers Brooklyn's face as she stares down at Phoenix, doing exactly as told. I wrap an arm around her from behind, pressing the stained blade right against her jugular vein. It's juicy and throbbing with blood waiting to be spilled.

"Eli," Phoenix warns, watching us.

Just to punish him, I push the blade deeper into Brooklyn's neck. His mouth closes immediately. This is the status quo now. I'm in charge, and I want to hold her life in the palm of my hand. A single slip or momentary lapse, and she'll bleed out while riding his cock.

"F-Feel that?"

"Yes," Brooklyn hushes.

I move my hips to push into her, and her walls hug my cock. She's gasping and trying not to move, a thin stream of blood spilling down her neck and painting mortality across her breasts. I meet Phoenix's widened eyes.

"Lick," I demand.

Watching him obey me is thrilling. Brooklyn continues to ride him while he brings his tongue to her left nipple, cleaning up the trail of blood swirling across her porcelain skin. When I take the knife from her throat and offer it to Phoenix, he looks at me questioningly.

My girl knows, though.

She's seen the darkest recesses of my broken mind.

"Please," Brooklyn begs.

Offering her scarred and sliced arm for his perusal, Phoenix looks like a deer caught in the headlights. I've never seen him uncertain or afraid in the bedroom. He's usually the alpha male, doling out the humiliation. We've blown his comfort zone to smithereens and left him to pick up the scattered pieces.

"You... want me to cut you?"

"I'm scared, Nix. I don't want to walk into that interview room and forget who I am."

His eyes flick to mine again. I nod encouragingly, still gliding into Brooklyn from behind. She's trembling all over as another orgasm builds. When Phoenix takes a deep breath and brings the knife to her arm, carefully slicing a patch of skin, Brooklyn's release crests for a second time.

Pain and pleasure.

Sickness and sanity.

Love and obsession.

Nothing about our union is so easily categorised. We are made of extremes, testing the boundaries no normal person would dare cross. I grip her hips tighter before pouring myself into her asshole, already exhausted from my second release of the night.

Phoenix tosses the blade on the sofa, his fingers gripping the fresh wounds he's inflicted on the girl he loves. Swirling the blood with his thumb from the leaking cuts, he looks fascinated. His stained digit pushes into Brooklyn's mouth before she can protest, forcing her to clean her own blood from his skin.

"Beautiful," he utters.

She greedily sucks on his thumb, riding the waves of her climax. That pushes Phoenix over the edge. He releases a guttural moan, his forehead resting against her sternum while filling her up. Unable to remain upright, we all collapse in a dog pile.

Limbs, arms, come, and blood spread across the sofa. We fight to catch our breath before erupting back into laughter. The living room is a fucking mess. Cushions and stained fabric surround us, so there's no denying what we've been up to.

Right on time, the door opens to admit a waft of fresh dough and melted cheese. Hudson is carrying a huge stack of pizza boxes, balancing several extra boxes of baked cookies on top. He stops dead in his tracks when he spots us all, naked and laughing at the look on his face.

"I, uh. Pepperoni pizza, extra cheese. No pineapple," he says in bemusement.

Brooklyn props her chin on her hand. "Thanks, baby. That wasn't so hard, was it?"

"I dunno," Phoenix chuckles. "Felt pretty hard to me."

I've never seen Hudson blush before, but fuck me gently, his cheeks are bright pink as he deposits the pizzas and takes a seat in one of the stuffed armchairs. He stares at all of our naked skin on display while grabbing a huge slice of pizza and inhaling it.

"I'm not cleaning this shit up," he says around a mouthful of food. "And you can pay Hunter back for his ruined sofa."

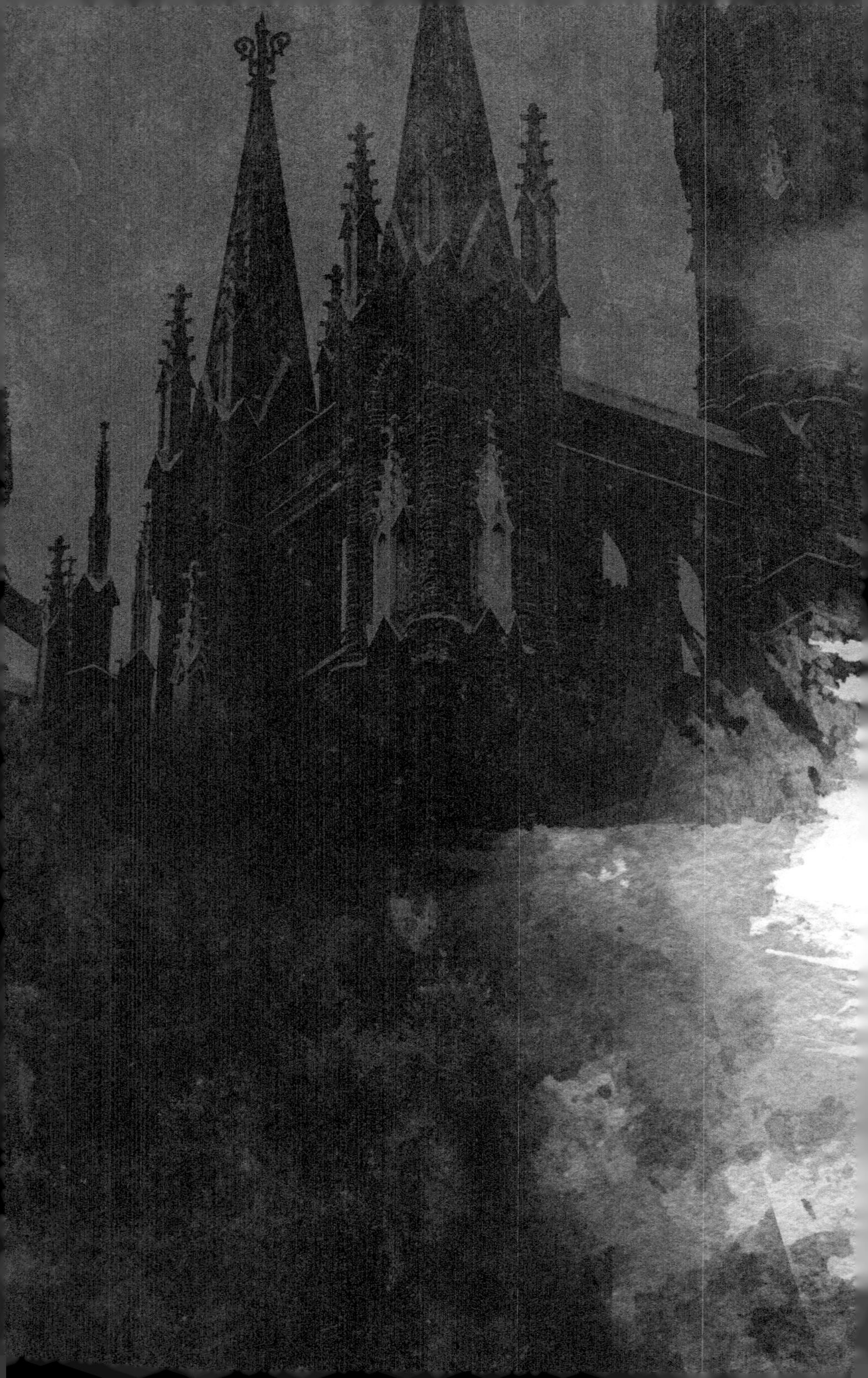

25

BROOKLYN

DiE4u - Bring Me The Horizon

Staring into the dead eye of the camera, I feel a chilling sense of déjà vu. The interview room is dull, with blank white walls and two boarded-up windows. I'm terrified to blink, in case the world melts away and I'm back in that basement, ready for a new experiment to begin.

Are you scared of the truth, Miss West?

Running won't help you.

Let's pick up where we left off.

Clearing my throat, I shove Augustus's sick taunting from my mind. In the corner behind me, Hunter sits with his laptop. He hasn't spoken a single word to me, but I can see the almost-black circles beneath his clear eyes. He's grieving, but still holding up his end of our bargain. I can respect that.

"Here, water." Enzo deposits a plastic cup in front of me.

"Thanks."

Hesitating, he peers down at me. "Just tell the truth, kid. You're not on trial. These people will ask you difficult questions. Don't fight them. It'll only make this worse."

"Not on trial... yet."

Squeezing my shoulder, Enzo retreats to his corner. His huge arms band across his barrel chest, every inch of his towering frame screaming intimidation. It feels good knowing he's here to keep me safe, even if neither of them can fend off the demons within me.

Ten minutes later, there's a sharp rap on the door before it opens. Three men and one woman enter, dressed to the nines in pressed suits and blank, corporate expressions. After coolly greeting Hunter and Enzo, two of them sit in front of me. The others take the chairs behind and pull out their notebooks.

"Brooklyn West?" the woman opposite asks.

"Yeah, that's me."

"My name is Agent Barlow, this is Agent Jonas." She gestures to the man next to her. "We represent the Serious Crimes Unit. We've been assigned to this case to gather the information needed to proceed with an investigation."

Her pale-green gaze is sharp, attentive, framed by perfectly blow-dried, blonde waves. She looks like a spotless piece of artwork, slick and polished in her finery. I feel awkward and entirely insignificant in my ripped jeans and Hudson's *Badflower* t-shirt.

"I understand," I respond.

With their notebooks and thick dossiers of paperwork set up, they adjust the camera on its tripod, so it faces me at a direct angle. The moment it starts to record, sweat begins to trickle down the back of my neck. I hold my shaking hands in my lap, hiding them from sight.

"We have spoken to Professor Lazlo. Are you familiar with this individual?" Agent Barlow asks.

"He was my therapist last year before my care was transferred to Doctor Warren Augustus. He later imprisoned me for several months and began a lengthy period of psychological torture, abuse and manipulation."

Sliding a glossy photograph over to me, I'm faced with the icy, intelligent eyes of my oppressor. Augustus looks slick and well-groomed in the image, dressed in his usual tailored suit and tie. He seems to be leaving a lavish fundraiser event for Incendia, captured climbing into a fancy sports car.

"This man?" Agent Jonas speaks for the first time.

I meet his steely brown gaze beneath a head of thin, silver-grey hair and defined wrinkles. He's older and seems sterner somehow, his entire posture geared towards aggression. My hackles immediately rise.

"That's him."

"Several serious allegations have been levelled against this man by other patients. We have spoken to Lucia Killmore and Patient Two. Both credit their imprisonment to Doctor Augustus."

"Did they tell you what else he did to them?"

"We're not here to discuss them," Agent Barlow interrupts. "Professor Lazlo has admitted to tampering with your medication during solitary confinement and later dosing you with unregulated experimental drugs for a long period of time."

"He tried to have me killed." I watch several hands scribble down notes. "Another patient was on Incendia's payroll in Blackwood, tasked with maintaining a steady supply of contraband into the institute for clinicians to observe and document. It was a social experiment."

Turning to a fresh piece of paper in her overflowing notebook, Agent Barlow offers me a small smile. "Start from the very beginning. The more you tell us, the better equipped we are to offer you a deal."

"How can I trust that you will?"

"We're here for the truth, Brooklyn."

Sparing Enzo a panicked look, he gives me a nod of reassurance. It does nothing to abate the fear wrapping around my vocal cords. I just got my family back; I can't lose them again. We have no way of knowing if a deal can be made. These suits are not taking my guys away from me.

"Mr Rodriguez and his firm have secured your protection from immediate incarceration," Agent Barlow explains, each word like a gut punch. "We have dozens of unconfirmed reports of fatalities and a very small pool of suspects. Actions have consequences."

"I... I was under duress."

"For all of them?" Agent Jonas supplies.

"Do you have any idea what they did to us?" I snarl back.

He crosses his arms, looking unimpressed. I doubt my case will be helped if I break his nose, despite the temptation. We survived by fighting tooth and nail, no matter this asshole's opinions. They will never know what we went through in the dark.

"Brooklyn," Agent Barlow says gently. "I came into this process feeling sceptical. Incendia has a spotless reputation and, as I'm sure you are aware, many connections across the country. I've come to realise there is far more than meets the eye in this case. I want to help you."

"Does your colleague feel the same way?"

Releasing a huff, Agent Jonas nods. "We've been assigned to this task force to find one thing—the truth. If you can give that to us, we can take it back to our superiors. This is the only way to help yourself."

Biting my lip, I glance between them. "What if myself and my friends vanished?"

"We would be forced to pursue and charge you with a very long list of crimes that would ensure your lifelong imprisonment. Until we have enough evidence to the contrary, you remain a convict."

"What the hell happened to innocent until proven guilty, huh?"

"You were guilty long before you stepped foot inside Blackwood Institute," she states plainly. "That much is indisputable. Help us prove that you're a victim here, not the perpetrator."

Fresh out of options, I slump back in my seat. My mind winds all the way back, past late-night kisses and broken-hearted reunions, bloodied hook ups in graveyards, and glimpses of real, tangible hope that were swiftly extinguished. I turn back the clock on the best and worst year of my life.

I'm back in Clearview.

Just another statistic, praying for death to come.

The whole filthy tale takes hours, each revelation of horror dragging onwards. Endless questions meet multiple shocked silences. Notebooks are swapped out, fresh pens are retrieved, and litres of coffee consumed. When the clock strikes on my seventh hour under examination, I'm struggling to hold it together.

"Do you recognise this person?"

Agent Barlow hands me another glossy, printed photograph. Guilt and shame twist my insides until I can barely breathe. Teegan's bright, lively smile stares back at me beneath her red hair and a handful more facial piercings than the last time I saw her. She looks different.

I can't ignore the handful of scars marking her face, along with the slightly crooked tilt of her healed nose. To my horror, she's missing several teeth in the photo too. The phantom pain of them cutting against my knuckles has me jumping up. My chair crashes to the floor behind me.

"When was this taken?"

"Last week," Agent Jonas answers. "We reviewed her files to confirm her discharge as authorised by Doctor Augustus. The records surrounding her injuries mention a patient attack while in custody."

With tears stinging my eyes, I hug her photograph to my chest.

I can almost feel her arms around me, demanding a tight, desperate cuddle while laughing through the pain. I'd do anything for one more hug. I've lost the only two friends I've ever had.

That fucking hurts.

"Did you attack Teegan Lopez?"

"She was my best friend." I study her healed, happy face. "People close to me… they get hurt. I hurt them. Everything I touch turns to shit."

I sense Enzo stepping towards me as my crying intensifies. I'm too exhausted and emotionally drained to keep a lid on it any longer. She will forever bear the mark of our friendship. I did that to her. She gave me her love and trust. In return, I nearly took her life from her.

"Brooke," Enzo placates. "Just take a deep breath."

"This is never going away, is it? I thought… I thought I had a chance. All I wanted was a chance to live."

Agent Barlow stands, her hands raised in a calming manner. "Miss West, we're not done here. Please sit back down and answer our questions or things will get a lot more complicated for you."

"They won't ever let me forget," I whisper to myself. "Augustus was right. I can't escape Blackwood. My past will always follow me. You can't help me."

"This is your chance to avoid prison. You need to earn it."

Still holding the photograph slicing my heart into ribbons, I ignore their voices. The walls are closing in on me like an optical illusion. I'm going to be crushed to death under the weight of their accusations. Just as I curl my hand around the door handle, Enzo's arms attempt to trap me.

"No! Get your hands off me!"

"Brooke," he repeats. "Calm down. We're trying to help."

Jamming my elbow into his ribcage, I take the brief distraction and wrench the door open. Hunter is trying to follow, but he's still sore from the explosion and moving slowly. The government agents don't move a muscle. All they care about is their recording, capturing my madness. Another point against me.

"Brooklyn, stop—"

Ignoring Hunter's growly voice, I sprint into the waiting area. Pacing in front of the door with a stony expression, Seven stops when he spots me running at full speed.

"Eight?"

I throw myself at him. "I can't... can't... breathe!"

Holding me against his firm chest, he cups the back of my head. "I've got you, princess."

He's caught in a heated argument with Hunter and Enzo, who followed me from the interview room. I can't hear a damn word while hanging off him. My ears are ringing loudly, like I'm drowning in electrified water. Each beat feels like a hose pipe of water battering my body, or the sharp sting of a whip cracking against my skin.

Seven scoops me off my feet, cradling me like I'm a lost child relying on him to bring me home. I bury my face in his neck, letting the sobs wash over me. I'm powerless. My surroundings mean nothing as I fight to stay in the driver's seat.

"Hold on, Eight. I'm getting you out of here."

Awash in darkness, I cling to the feel of his skin on mine. He smells like freshly ground coffee from the cup he quickly drained, and Hudson's aftershave. They've been sharing clothes since they're similar in size. My fingers tangle in his soft mane of hair. I grip it tightly, needing to feel something real in my hands.

Seven doesn't say a word as he sprints far away from the building and those seeking to dissect my brain further. My feet hit the ground and cold air washes over me. Propped against a wall, his huge hand shakes my shoulder to try and rouse me. I'm barely holding on.

"Eight? Talk to me. Show me those beautiful eyes."

"They w-won't let me live," I choke out. "I've d-done too much. I'm going to prison."

"You know we would never let that happen."

"We're both going down! We can't win this!"

I'm growing even more hysterical, staring into his pained, caramel orbs looking down at me. I've spent so long trying to spark hope in Seven's dead soul. I can't find it in myself anymore. Every twisted, hateful taunt my hallucinations have thrown at me over the years is coming true.

"I w-won't go back inside." I gulp hard. "I'd rather die."

"That's not an option, Eight. You're better than this."

"Am I? You know what I've done! I should just get it over and done with."

Gripping my chin, his forehead smacks straight into mine. Our souls are trapped together in an inescapable prison. I can smell the cigarettes and coffee on his breath, feel the palpable emotion crackling between us. The days we spent clinging to life are gone. Now, we're waiting for death.

"If you need forgiveness, I'll fucking give it to you," Seven says fiercely. "You are forgiven, Patient Eight. The world broke us once. Don't let it take our future too."

"I can't run... they'll follow me. I don't want to live in a world without you."

"So what? You don't live at all? That's fucking bullshit, Eight!"

His face is carved in devilish fury, a tidal wave of anger simmering beneath the surface. When his hand latches around my wrist, it nearly grinds my bones together. I fight and writhe, but Seven won't let me go.

"You want me to live for you? I expect the same goddamn thing," he hisses.

"I... I c-can't. Not like this."

"I refuse to accept that."

Dragged down the alleyway, I throw every insult under the sun at him. All I want is to get on the first truck heading out of town and hide from the inevitable. The agents don't give a fuck about what Augustus did to us. I'm a monster to them. Someone who deserves to be locked up.

Seven tows me to the very back of the dank alley, where a sketchy fire escape wraps around the tall, run-down tower block. I scream some more as he throws me over his shoulder, trapping my legs with his arm. I have to shut my eyes when he begins to scale the fire escape.

The world is tilted upside down, growing higher and higher. My fists batter Seven's back but yield no results. He keeps me imprisoned until we reach the top of the building. He's panting hard after the gruelling climb. It's abandoned up here, nothing but smashed pallets and a few pigeons.

"Here we are, then," Seven announces darkly. "Nice tall building, nothing stopping you. Wanna give up and die? Be my guest. Off you go."

I'm placed back on my unsteady legs. We're at the very edge of the rooftop, with an unfamiliar London suburb stretching out in all directions. It must be at least two hundred feet high. I can almost taste the clouds on my tongue.

"What are you doing?" I splutter.

Seven grabs my bicep and hauls me even closer to the edge. My battered Chucks involuntarily step up, heaved by his immense strength. I'm mere inches from plummeting and becoming a puddle of matter. One step or the slightest slip, and it's all over.

"This is what you wanted, isn't it?" he bellows. "Your men told me about what happened in Blackwood. I'm not going to stop you like they did. If you want to do this, fucking own it."

"I... I..."

"What is it, Patient Eight? Haven't got the balls to do it?"

"Fuck you, Sev!"

His steadying hand disappears from my arm. I wobble in the cold air, feeling the first patters of autumn rain hit my face. The rumble of an overhead aeroplane fills the excruciating silence between us. Seven stands there, waiting and watching.

"Clock's ticking."

"Why are you doing this?" I scream at him.

"Because you're being a coward! You told me to live, goddammit." His hand is a tight fist, like he wants to deck me. "You gave me a family and showed me what it felt like to belong. Now, you want to bail!"

"I'm fucking scared! That's all!"

"Spare me your excuses. You think I'm not scared? Sitting in that fucking room, dragging up six years of trauma? It's terrifying for me too! I'm doing it for you, for our family. The one you gave me."

Teetering in the air, I stare at him. My saviour. My monster. The keeper of the absolute worst parts of myself. The world wants to bury us alive, regardless of the truth. We're both being sent down to hell.

"We will never matter to them," I spell out. "Our lives are forfeit."

His hand moves like a lightning bolt. One moment, I'm a breath from death. The next, I'm falling into his awaiting arms and swept off my feet. Seven looks at me like I'm his entire fucking world, dead or alive. I can hardly breathe from the intensity of his possession.

"Your life will never be forfeit to me," he whispers roughly. "And certainly not to the others. You stood next to that coffin and promised that I would never be alone. Did you mean it?"

With my fingertip, I trace the shiny scar marking his forehead. I can still hear his screams. Augustus punished us together that day. It was late into our imprisonment, once the boundaries between us melted away. Seven stepped in front of the blow meant for me, taking a whip directly to the face.

"I meant it," I murmur.

"Prove it. Stay with me."

"Why?!"

"Because I can't survive without you!"

"What if they take us away from each other?" I shout through my tears.

Rather than answer, his lips crush against mine, bruisingly hard. I can't kiss him back. This isn't a show of love. There's no tenderness or romance. It's a punishment for daring to toss his fragile heart aside. He steals my breath and bites my lip, taking every bit of proof he needs.

"I swear on what's left of my life, I will always find you," Seven vows, kissing me softer. "I fucking love you, Eight."

"You do?"

"Of course I do, you frustrating creature. I own the final piece of your heart. Nobody will ever take that privilege from me."

We seal our promise in a heavy raincloud, trapped by wind and the uncontrollable power of fate. I don't complain once as Seven bends me over and fucks me on the rooftop, both soaked to the bone but uncaring. The entire city watches us collide, granting us a brief second of solitude.

He repeats that he loves me.

Over and over again.

I whisper it back, silently praying for the strength to be what he needs. I can feel this journey drawing to its close. We've travelled so far, battled for each second of sanity and belonging, yet still we're barrelling towards the edge of a cliff. I can't change that now.

The only way out of our love is death.

I've always loved a tragic ending.

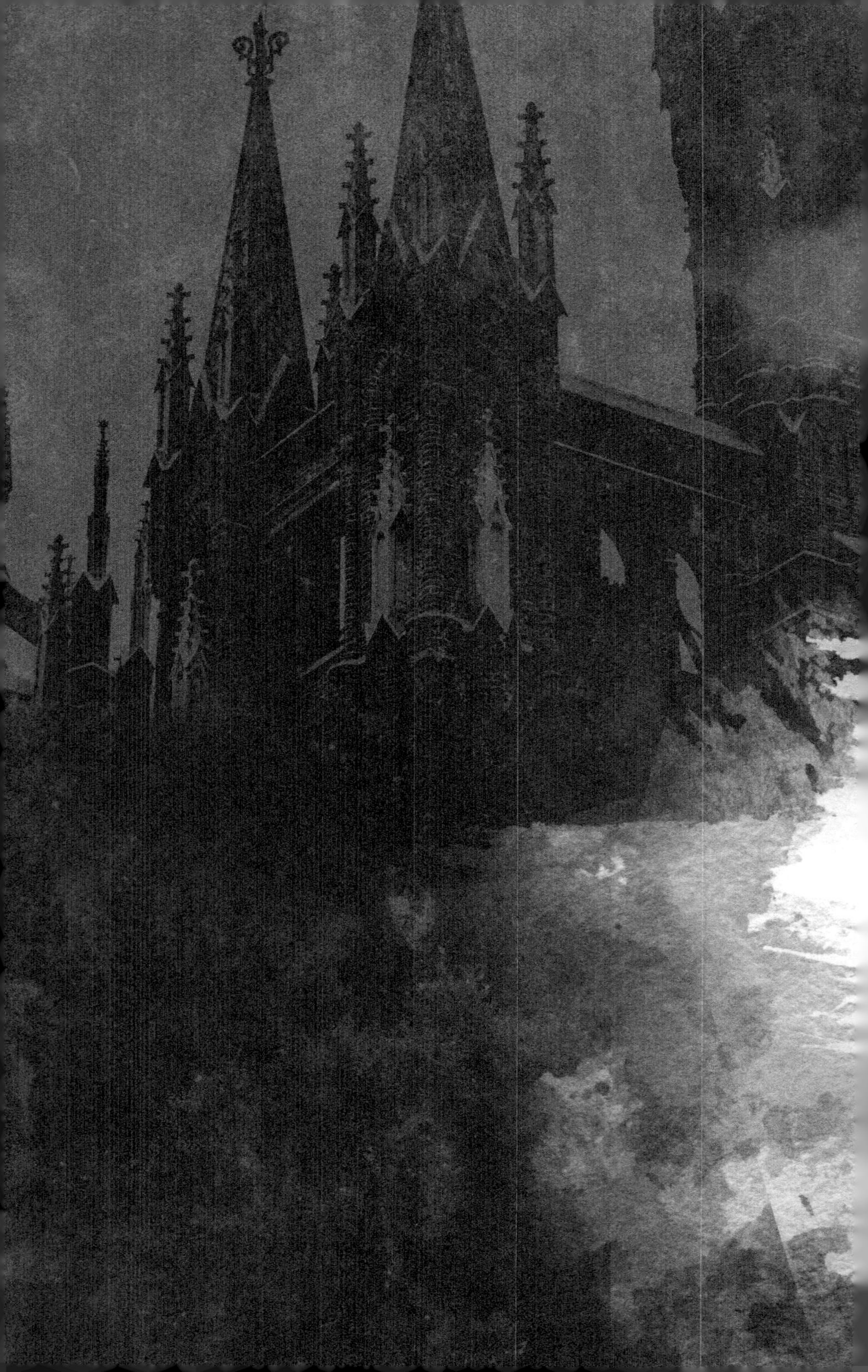

26

HUDSON

Youth - Cleopatrick

Riding the elevator back to the apartment with Kade, we're both far too pleased with ourselves. Brooklyn's surprise is ready to go. The others have kept her distracted all afternoon while we prepared.

We've been granted the rest of the day off from giving evidence after Brooklyn's breakdown yesterday. Eli is the last to be called from our group. After that, we await the next steps. Each day has only brought more questions, so anxiety is at an all-time high.

"You think she'll like it?" Kade worries aloud.

His voice snaps me out of my overthinking.

"Fuck knows. She isn't herself at the moment."

"Are any of us? This whole situation is fucked."

I look at him, noting the lines of exhaustion. "You not sleeping much?"

He shakes his head. "Talking about everything was rough. I handed all of Dad's files over, the lot of them. Four months of working for the bastard taught me a few things, but I'm now an accomplice."

"That's bullshit. You got us out."

Kade scoffs. "I smuggled contraband, sold drugs, incited a riot and supplied weapons to convicted murderers. Oh, not to mention burning the place down and helping several convicts escape. They want my fucking head."

"Everything will work out."

"How can you be so sure?"

We arrive at our floor with a ding and step out of the elevator. I clap Kade on the shoulder as we head for our temporary home, hating the uncertainty in his voice. He's the last one to start doubting himself.

"There's no other option, that's why," I answer easily. "We did the impossible before. We'll do it again."

"Do you remember when I had to beg you to eat a single meal with me in Blackwood?" Kade asks randomly. "A mere conversation took weeks of pleading. You'd given up."

"People change." I shrug off the shame eating me alive. "I grew up. Getting Brooklyn back changed everything for me. If that was possible, then I could do anything. Even learn to live with myself."

Before we can head inside, Kade's hand grabs my shirt sleeve.

"Hud... no matter what happens, I'm glad I got my brother back."

Jesus, he's determined to kill me off with this emotional shit. We're all going fucking insane in this place.

"Yeah, I love you too, jackass." I get him in a headlock and mess up his styled blonde locks. "Can we move on now? I'm not fucking kissing you."

"I still hate you, bro. You're a pain in my ass."

"And I will be forever. Thanks to you."

Entering the apartment together, we find the others spread across the sectional sofa in the living room. Phoenix and Eli are keeping up their end of the bargain, sandwiching Brooklyn between them while a movie plays. She doesn't appear to be paying attention, anxiously picking at her nails.

"Right, then." Kade claps his hands. "Who's ready for some fun?"

"Fun?" Brooklyn wrinkles her nose.

Draining a bottle of water from the kitchen, I toss her a smirk. "You know, fun? It's when you get off the fucking sofa and join the land of the living. Maybe even crack a smile. Sounds crazy, huh?"

"Does this fun involve alcohol?" Phoenix grins mischievously.

Offering Eli a hand up, Kade moves to grab Brooklyn next. She squeals while being lifted into the air and pushed in my direction. I imprison her in my arms before she can crawl back into bed and hide like she's taken to doing.

"Come and find out."

"Where's Seven?" Brooklyn frowns.

"He's... out," I answer lamely. "Preoccupied."

"I thought he was with you guys. Where did he go?"

Silencing her questions with a kiss, I pillage her mouth until Phoenix starts wolf-whistling. We break apart, both breathing hard. He's hanging off Eli, still needing support with walking.

It's the first time I've seen him look like himself after losing his sister. His latest depressive episode has been rough, even with medication. He'll always suffer from these intense, brutal cycles.

Kade takes Brooklyn's other hand, so we both have a grip on her. She's reluctantly pulled along, leaving the warm bubble of the apartment behind. I won't let her slip back into a detached haze. We have enough to contend with as it is. Whatever Seven did yesterday, it brought her back to us.

We ride the elevator down to the second floor, where Hunter's cleared the training room for us. I cover Brooklyn's eyes as soon as we step out, keeping her blinded. Phoenix and Eli follow Kade into the room, lit by giant windows.

In the centre, a professional boxing ring resides. Various machines and weights are dotted around the perimeter, along with benches and whiteboards. There's a gym upstairs that I located a while ago, but this is for group training more than working out. It's where Enzo puts his spooks through their paces.

"You better not be leading me to the shrink, Hud."

"Do you really think I'd do that to you?" I chuckle.

"Fuck knows. Kade spent an hour trying to convince me to talk to him."

"Well, there's no crazy talk tonight."

In the top corner of the room, we've set up a hell of a party. Fold-up tables full of snacks, beers and bottles of liquor await. Kade even managed to find some cheesy birthday decorations, hanging streamers and banners off the walls to complete the surprise. He looks damn pleased with himself.

Phoenix looks around. "Nice. You two should be party planners."

"Shut it," Kade orders, smiling. "Alright, she can look now."

Kissing Brooklyn's soft neck, I remove my hands from her eyes. She blinks several times while looking around, taking in every last detail. She seems confused more than anything.

"Are we having a birthday party? For who?"

"All of us," I whisper in her ear.

Kade smooths his loose, white t-shirt, appearing nervous. "We were talking the other night and realised we have never celebrated our birthdays. Not in Blackwood, that's for sure. So, we're having a joint party."

Helping himself to a beer before Kade can yell at him, Phoenix wrenches the cap off with his teeth like an animal. "Ahh, alcohol. My old friend. Happy fucking birthday, kids."

After a long moment of hesitation, a wide, brilliant smile blossoms across Brooklyn's face. It takes my breath away. For a moment, she looks like my blackbird. Not the jaded woman I know now, but the innocent, lively kid I used to know. Sometimes, I catch myself missing that person. Even if I did kill her.

"Hunter actually allowed this?" she asks excitedly.

To answer her question, the door to the training room opens again. Enzo steps in with a loud whoop, carrying a huge cardboard box in his arms. I've never seen him in anything but all-black cargo trousers and a form-fitting t-shirt, like he's permanently ready to kick some ass.

Behind him, Hunter is following in casual jeans and a polo shirt, looking slightly more subdued. His usually sleek hair is rumpled and loose, framing downcast eyes. His grief is still painfully obvious, but he agreed to this plan with minimal argument. He cares a lot, deep down.

"Did someone say party?" Enzo grins.

Depositing the cardboard box and opening it, he unveils a huge, glistening chocolate cake. It's made of several tiers, each boasting fudge frosting and white chocolate drizzle. The smile on Enzo's face widens as he steals a truffle off the top and sticks it in his mouth.

Hunter pointedly clears his throat.

"What?" Enzo shrugs. "It looked tasty."

Brooklyn leaves my embrace to approach them both. Enzo looks slightly surprised when she throws her arms around his neck, placing a kiss on his stubbly cheek. It's like she's hugging a mountain lion.

"Thank you for this."

His cheeks turn pink. "I didn't do shit, wildfire. Just cleared the room for your entourage."

Leaving him, Brooklyn approaches Hunter next. He looks positively unnerved by the prospect of her hugging him. I've never seen him give out affection, even with his team members. I doubt many people see beyond the professional armour he coats himself in.

She pulls him into a hug and also gives him a peck on the cheek. "Thanks, Hunter. This is exactly what we needed."

"You're welcome," he says gruffly. "Just keep it down, alright?"

Everyone converges around the drinks table, filling up plastic cups with all manner of hard liquor. Kade doesn't even protest as Phoenix drains his first two cups with enthusiasm. Theo chooses that moment to sneak in, skirting around the back with a set of speakers and his laptop.

When the heavy beat of music fills the room, everyone looks up at him. Theo appears startled by all of the attention, sheepishly rubbing the back of his neck while finding the right playlist.

"What's a party without music?"

Already looking a little glassy-eyed, Phoenix shrugs off Eli's overprotectiveness and begins an awkward dance. His leg is still stiff and healing, but that doesn't stop him from shaking his ass while everyone laughs at the sight. When he crooks a finger at Brooklyn, she shakes her head.

"Don't be a spoilsport, firecracker. Come show me those moves."

"You're such a dumbass."

"And a hell of a dancer."

Before she can protest, Eli shoves her in Phoenix's direction with a devious glint in his eye. He follows and the trio dance to the music like idiots, pretending the huge training room is a downtown nightclub. I nearly choke on a mouthful of vodka lemonade when Enzo joins in, busting out his retro dance moves.

"Well, she's smiling." Kade watches them with palpable happiness.

I knock our cups together in a toast. "Good call, brother."

Theo joins us in the corner, quietly helping himself to a drink. He props himself against the wall, watching everyone else with sadness in his eyes. Like Hunter, he seems flat, drained, a shadow of the sweet and socially awkward person we met.

Incendia has taken everything from them.

Yet, they still showed up for us.

"She seems better today," Hunter observes.

I pass him a beer. "Sounds like they grilled her pretty hard."

"Seven hours straight. I should have called it off sooner."

"You're trying to help us," Kade answers. "That's already more than we could've asked for."

Looking thoughtful, Hunter watches Enzo dance and drink with the other three. It must be something to reach such success with your best friend at your side. They've been running Sabre for seven years now, growing it from the ground up with nothing but their determination to help those who can't do it themselves.

"You kids ever think about putting your experience to good use?"

I consider Hunter's question. "What were you thinking?"

He takes another pull of his beer. "I could use some new blood around here. People who know how to handle themselves and don't scare easily. We often take on recruits with chequered pasts."

Kade looks intrigued. "You're offering us jobs?"

"Something to think about. Gotta do something with your lives, right?"

With that, Hunter puts his beer down and disappears from the room. His party spirit didn't last long, but he still made an effort to show his face. That's far more meaningful than any empty words he could offer. We watch him leave, and I can already see the cogs in Kade's oversized brain turning.

"Let's get through the shitstorm heading our way first," I speak up. "With the stuff we've had to go on the record about, we'll be lucky to walk away from this."

Kade's smile dims. "There's still a chance, Hud. Don't we deserve that?"

"Fuck knows, man. The world ain't fair like that."

We watch the rest of our group enjoy the makeshift party. Brooklyn's ditched the oversized sweater she was wearing, twirling in Enzo's expert arms as he swoops her low to the ground. Phoenix and Eli are waltzing, their bodies moulded together like star-crossed lovers.

I watch my family, whole and content.

Kade's fucking right.

We deserve our second chance.

A couple of hours in, the music has shifted to gentle, coaxing guitar strokes and crooning vocals. Kade is playing cards with Theo and Eli on a workout bench, while Phoenix sleeps off his eighth vodka shot with a power nap. Enzo's eating his body weight in snacks, stealing more cake when he thinks nobody is looking.

At the edge of the boxing ring, Brooklyn stands alone with her arms resting on the bungee cords. She's staring out at the moon, shining through the high ceiling windows. I stop at her side, content to watch her seemingly at peace after so much turmoil.

"You think we'll have another party next year?"

Pulling her back against my chest, I nuzzle her short hair. "Every damn year, blackbird. We have lots to make up for. Remember your seventeenth? The carer screamed at you for puking on her clean carpet."

She huffs a laugh. "I didn't even know you then."

"We lived together for weeks in the foster home before our paths crossed. I knew you long before you ever said a word to me in that nurse's office."

"I didn't stand a chance, did I?"

"Not if I had anything to do with it. I watched her slap you on my first afternoon. You'd skipped out on chores to patch up one of the younger kids. She hit you hard, and you didn't flinch once."

Brooklyn shakes her head. "I hated that bitch so much."

"That's when I knew I had to talk to you. I'd never seen such courage, especially after watching Ma get her ass kicked for so long. You stood up for the younger kids when nobody ever asked you to."

Turning in my arms, Brooklyn peers up at me with those silvery eyes. I could lose myself in the mesmerising constellation. Even after years of memorising every inch of her, each day still brings new discoveries. I don't think I'll ever stop falling in love with her.

For so long, all I had were my ruined memories and a lifetime of regret. Holding her in my arms again is something I never deserved. If nothing else, the world has granted me one miracle. That's all I need.

"I should've followed you when I had the chance," she whispers sadly. "I still remember the day you left. You begged me to say something, anything. All I could feel was my broken heart thumping."

Agony spears me in the chest. I have to forcibly shut the lid on a box of awful memories. If I could go back in time and kill my younger self for being so fucking cowardly, I'd do it without hesitating.

"My life went wrong when you left it."

"I'm the one that fucked things up," I remind her. "I had no right to demand your love after what I did. Running felt simpler, easier. Looking at you was like looking in the mirror."

Her hand strokes the rough stubble covering my jawline. I lean in to her gentle, loving touch, so unlike the cruel lash of her hatred that I accepted for so long.

"I'm glad I had the chance to go back and make a different decision." Brooklyn's smile is heartbreaking. "I think we had to break apart to fall together again. I needed to see a world without you in it."

"How was it?"

She runs a thumb over my bottom lip. "It was fucking empty."

Taking her hand, I drop it on my shoulder. My hands find her hips, drawing her closer to me. Ignoring the room and all of its inhabitants, we begin to sway to the gentle music. Our surroundings fall away. I'm a love-struck, obsessed teenager again, staring at the sun after so long in the dark.

I spot the door opening over her shoulder and bring our gentle dance to a close. This is the moment I've been waiting for since we left Blackwood. Cupping Brooklyn's face before she can look, I ensure her eyes are only on me.

"I know I missed your birthday, but here's your present. I love you, blackbird. It's time to let go of the past, and I hope this helps."

Seeming confused, she kisses my lips before turning to look. Seven has arrived, tugging his baseball cap off to release his unruly, chestnut hair. He's dressed to blend in, wearing a hoodie and loose jeans. I specifically asked him to retrieve our guest. Even I'll admit that the asshole is good at protecting people.

"Oh my God," Brooklyn breathes.

Behind Seven, our guest of honour arrives. Teegan enters the room with obvious anxiety. She walks slowly, hesitantly, clocking all of her surroundings and the familiar faces with a tiny smile. Dressed in ripped jeans and a silky, black shirt, her bright-red hair pops against her rice-powdered skin.

She looks good, healthy. Alive.

"Tee?"

We all watch on in slow motion. Brooklyn's steps are filled with trepidation, but she can't help inching closer to her long-lost best friend. Teegan looks her up and down, leading me to panic for a split second. She seemed game on the phone.

"Brooke," she responds, a smile blooming.

That's all it takes. Friendship is a weird concept, even to the most adept of humans. It can break and bend so many times, but some bonds survive the test of time. The two girls meet in the middle of the training room, smacking into each other so hard, it must hurt.

I can hear Brooklyn crying from here, but the usual sorrow isn't there. She sounds happy for the first time in so long. Teegan has her in the tightest hug imaginable while stroking her short hair, whispering something to her. Seven comes to my side, looking like the cat that got the fucking cream.

"You don't get all the credit for this," I point out.

"Sure thing, pretty boy. See whose bed she crawls into tonight."

"I'll stuff your corpse beneath mine. Problem solved."

We circle around Brooklyn and Teegan while still giving them some space. Eli's arm is hugging Phoenix's waist as they watch the reunion, both smiling. Kade looks emotional at seeing the two girls reconnect. Everyone is happy to finally have the band back together.

"Girl, where did your hair go?" Teegan laughs.

Face soaked in tears, Brooklyn beams. "I thought I'd steal your edgy style."

"It suits you." Teegan looks her up and down. "Damn, I fucking missed your voice. You never called me back." She glances at me pointedly. "I left so many messages for you."

Smile dropping, Brooklyn stares down at her feet. "I... didn't know what to say. An apology didn't feel like enough. I'm sorry, Tee. I should've called after we escaped."

"I had to hear the gory details from this charming asshole instead."

"Hey," I protest hotly. "I kept my word, didn't I? You wanted a reunion."

"You did?" Brooklyn blurts.

Teegan still holds her tight. "Now I am offended. I haven't seen you in over six months. That's too long for any friend to take. You look so different."

"I didn't think you'd want to see me after..."

She trails off, staring at her feet.

"Brooke—"

"We don't need to talk about this."

"It wasn't your fault," Teegan insists, ignoring the shutter falling over Brooklyn's face. "I never blamed you for what you did. Not once."

"You should. I hurt you."

"Blackwood hurt us both."

Gripping her shoulders, Teegan forces Brooklyn to look up and meet her eyes. Shame is devouring her whole, leaving nothing but pain behind.

"The first time we met, I said you'd be better off sitting somewhere else. Even when I explained about my condition, you refused to move."

Brooklyn manages a tiny smile.

"Nobody has ever accepted me so unconditionally," Teegan continues firmly. "Not even my family. They try, but they're still embarrassed by my compulsions."

"Please," she croaks. "Don't forgive me."

"Why the hell not?"

"Because I don't deserve it."

Teegan shakes her head. "We all deserve to be forgiven, Brooke. Even the monsters. That's what makes this life beautiful. The ability to love, no matter what."

Like hugging an immovable, stone statue, Teegan refuses to let Brooklyn escape her forgiveness. She snatches her hand and drags her to a quieter corner to continue talking.

I never knew Teegan well in Blackwood. Months of keeping her posted on Brooklyn and our whereabouts has allowed me to befriend her. More than anything, she has a good heart.

This will prove, once and for all, that Brooklyn can be forgiven. I'll slay every single demon left tormenting her until the work is done.

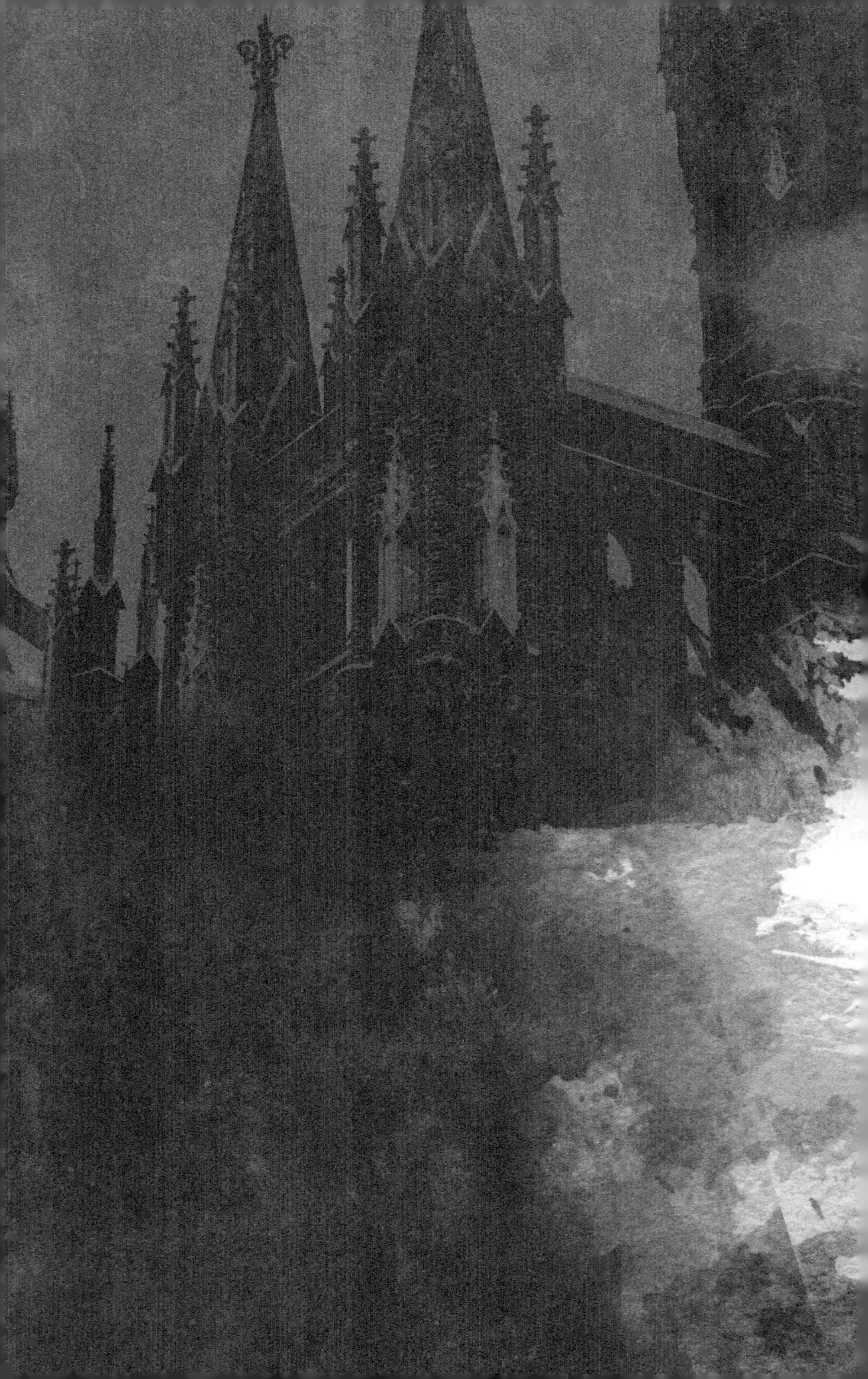

27

BROOKLYN

Heat Waves - Our Last Night

Agent Barlow sits back in her seat, appearing mildly stunned. On her other side, Agent Jonas is staring at his notebook with a heavy frown. Neither of them seems to know what to say to me now that the story is complete. Even told in stages, it's a grim and horrid journey to the depths of human suffering.

"I killed Jefferson," I repeat, looking between them both. "I'm not going to deny it. He spent months torturing me and Seven. I also killed Augustus. He took everything from us."

"Bancroft is aware of this?" Agent Jonas confirms.

"Yes. He wants revenge for his son's death, and the damage we caused to Incendia's reputation. Blackwood Institute was their crown jewel. The entire operation grew from there."

"With Lazlo at the helm."

Taking a sip of water, I nod. "He was the architect of the entire Z

Wing program. Me, Seven, Two and Lucia are the only ones left. One, Three, Four and Six are all dead. I learned that early on."

"Do you have names?"

"Not a single one. Patient Two has completely forgotten her old identity."

Clicking her pen, Agent Barlow looks thoughtful. "With a little digging, we can track down that information. I'm sure her family will appreciate knowing she's alive."

"I doubt she has any. Incendia doesn't like loose ends."

The setting sun slants through the tinted window. I've been here all day, forced to endure the rest of my bloody tale. Somehow, I feel oddly lighter. I've spoken it all aloud, every last detail, even the ones I haven't admitted to the guys. It must be real if it's written down in black and white.

"You mentioned your mother." Agent Jonas's jaw clenches. "Professor Lazlo has admitted to establishing the first round of Z Wing recruits, in which your mother was a victim. Patients Alpha, Beta, Gamma, Delta and Kappa are all confirmed to have entered Blackwood in the late nineties."

"Patient Beta attacked the church. He's dead."

They note that down, processing the new information.

"We have a death certificate confirming Melanie West's death twelve years ago," Agent Barlow highlights. "A car crash of which you were the sole survivor."

"She's alive as Patient Delta." I wring my hands in my lap. "You don't have to believe me. I've seen it for myself, as have Hunter and Enzo. She stabbed Phoenix and killed Alyssa Farlow, another Sabre agent."

I sit still as stone while Hunter quickly excuses himself from the back of the room. Hearing her name is too much for his icy composure to take. Watching him go, a frown creases Enzo's brows. I offer him a nod, indicating he can leave too, but he stays put.

"Brooke… you understand that if we find your mother, she won't be shown any mercy." Agent Jonas seems to soften for the first time. "She's too valuable to let slip through the net."

"What are you telling me?"

Glancing around the interview room, Agent Barlow clicks off the camera with an audible sigh. Everyone stops taking notes.

"In this line of work, sometimes the kindest act is to end things early. She'll be picked apart by the SCU, her mind documented and studied by government shrinks. We've never seen anything like her before."

"She's sick," I say in a raw whisper.

"I know that, but others won't care. Once they've learned everything they can, she'll be disposed of, quickly and quietly. There's no prison or hospital that could hope to contain her."

"I… I understand."

Enzo's meaty palm lands on my shoulder. "Brooklyn has given you everything. What now? Each day that passes only increases their risk here. Incendia will lose patience and come for them."

"We're concluding our interviews with Patient Seven and Elijah Woods in the morning." Agent Barlow closes her notebook. "We are due to report back to our superiors on Friday. A decision will be made then."

"What about our protection with Sabre?" I bite my lip.

"For now, it remains. We will do our best to ensure a deal is made."

They begin to pack up their supplies, leaving me staring at the blank white wall. I'm still walking away empty-handed. We've spilled our souls and received nothing but empty words in return.

"Hey," Enzo says under his breath. "It's going to be okay, Brooke. We will always keep you and the others safe. That won't change."

"Until they come knocking with handcuffs and straitjackets."

His smile is tight, unhappy. In the many tiring weeks we've hidden out here, I never expected to make friends. Especially with the people we once saw as threats. They welcomed us into their home and gave us hope. This new world we've re-entered has been devastating and surprising in equal measure.

Before the agents can finish packing up their paperwork, our meeting is interrupted by a blaring alarm. Our sessions moved to Sabre HQ last week, once the threat from Incendia became clear to the task force. They quickly changed their tune and wanted the assurance of Hunter's team on hand.

"What's that?" I shield my ears.

Enzo presses the comms in his ear, listening to someone speaking on the end of the line. His face transforms, overcome with concern and urgency. He briefly looks at me before turning to the agents.

"We have a security breach. It could be a false alert, but I don't want to risk Incendia catching wind of your presence. They can never know about this investigation."

The two men sitting behind Agent Barlow and Agent Jonas both step forward, unveiling holsters beneath their pristine grey suits. Their quiet attention becomes determination in a split second. Once packed up, all four agents move in a practised formation towards the exit.

"Stay here," Enzo commands me.

"I can't just sit here! Let me help."

"If Incendia are here, they're here for you. Don't move. I'll get Hunter to send a team up to retrieve you."

Ignoring my protests, he pulls his own gun out and leads the way for the others to follow. Hunter has already vanished from outside the door. I'm left standing in the middle of the interview room like a fucking lemon. I'm not going to sit here and wait for rescue.

Sneaking the opposite way down the corridor, I find the exit door to the stairwell. The fluorescent lights have all switched to dark red, indicating the emergency alert. Blaring drills into my head, but I easily tune it out. After months of white-noise torture, a stupid alarm won't slow me down.

My legs race up the concrete-lined stairwell, all the way up to the level with the temporary apartments. I'm breathing hard by the time I get to the top. The hallway seems undisturbed despite the alarm. Reaching Lucia and Two's door, I hammer on it with both fists until my hands ache.

I nearly fall inwards when it opens.

"Eight?" Lucia's eyes peek around the door.

"It's me. Are you both okay?"

She sags from relief. "We're both here. Two's freaking out. What's happening? Are we under attack?"

"I don't know. Keep the door locked and get in the bathtub. Don't open it for anyone. You still have that gun Hudson stole for you?"

Lucia nods frantically.

"Good. I'll come find you when I know it's safe."

Letting her slam the door in my face, I move to our apartment next. My voice bounces off the walls as I scream for the guys, flying between each empty room like a bat out of hell. Nobody is here. I think Kade mentioned something about a boxing match with the new recruits this evening in the training room.

Fisting my short hair, I try to gain control of my spiralling fear. There's no way Incendia could breach this fortress. It would take an army to get past Hunter's precautions and countless employees, all sworn to defend us. A team of well-paid thugs wouldn't stand a chance.

But a sole person?

That's a possibility.

My heart seizes at the thought. I'm moving fast before I realise it.

Instinct is driving me towards the eighth floor, where the detention cells reside. I first woke up in one such prison. These days, it's home to our favourite psychopath, the affable Professor Lazlo.

Stumbling down the freezing stairwell, I'm sweaty and panting as I get to the detention block. It's eerily quiet on this level, the offices cleared out and abandoned. Nobody comes here. Around several twisting corners, I reach the long stretch of corridor that holds the cells.

I release a breath when I find it also undisturbed. Checking each cell door in turn, nothing looks amiss. It isn't until I reach the final handful of holding cells that the horror reveals itself. One door is busted wide open, the hinges blackened and twisted from the rotors of a spinning saw.

"Lazlo?" I yell inside. "Show yourself!"

Heaving the broken steel slab all the way open, I tentatively step into the room. My vision is dipped in red from the emergency lighting, but that doesn't conceal the message scrawled across the concrete wall in giant, dripping letters. I can taste the metallic tang of blood in the air.

COME HOME, BROOKE.
WE CAN BE A FAMILY AGAIN.

On the other side of the room, a tiny bed is tucked into the corner. An ocean of fresh, sticky blood separates the space. It's everywhere. Enough to fill the world and spill over in a portrait of death.

Well, the saw had two purposes.

This isn't a murder.

It's an execution.

Lazlo lies dismembered in a pool of his own mortality. Flaps of torn skin, muscle and tissue shed more blood, adding to the expanding spill. His arms and legs have been viciously torn from his torso, the bone shattered and jagged.

I suppress a scream as I slide through the cooling liquid, accidentally nudging the remains of his left leg. He's been cut up like meat and methodically ripped apart. It's like fucking artwork. Close enough to study his glassy eyes, they're trapped in an eternal display of agony. I feel oddly relieved.

Nothing looks back at me.

He's as empty as the monsters he created.

Above the remains of his butchered body, another message awaits, written in the same spilled blood. Fitting, really. I do enjoy poetic justice.

YOU TOOK MY CHILDREN FROM ME.
THE PRICE HAS BEEN PAID.

This message isn't for me. Lazlo's corpse stares up at the dripping words with eyes devoid of any life. It would have been the last thing he saw as his pitiful life was stolen, much like he stole so many of our childhoods and futures.

Blind instinct drives me to the barred window. Hunter granted him some daylight, despite the heavy iron cage over the glass that would block any futile attempt to escape. Lazlo still had the privilege of sunshine for his cooperation, which is far more than he ever deserved.

We're high in the sky, with darkness descending upon the evening horizon. I search the ground beneath us, seeing nothing but people going about their business. The world continues to turn as ours grinds to a halt. Glancing at the smaller tower opposite Sabre's monstrosity, the empty roof is laid bare.

Someone awaits, watching for me.

A blood-stained hand offers a slow wave.

"Mum," I whisper against the glass.

She's staring straight back at me, her entire focus trained on the window—almost like she was waiting for me to come and find her. Like a robot, my right hand lifts in a wave. I can't help it. Watching her sick, twisted smile appear still feels like coming home at last.

Her existence is proof that my family was real.

I didn't imagine them, or the happiness I once had.

With an outstretched hand, she points to my left. I let my eyes stray back to the wall, where the message she left for me is gradually becoming obscured as the wet blood spreads.

Come home, Brooke.

Her familiar, coaxing voice whispers through my mind. Only this time, it's real. When I look back, she's gone. I stare at the empty rooftop, her voice in my ears.

We can be a family again.

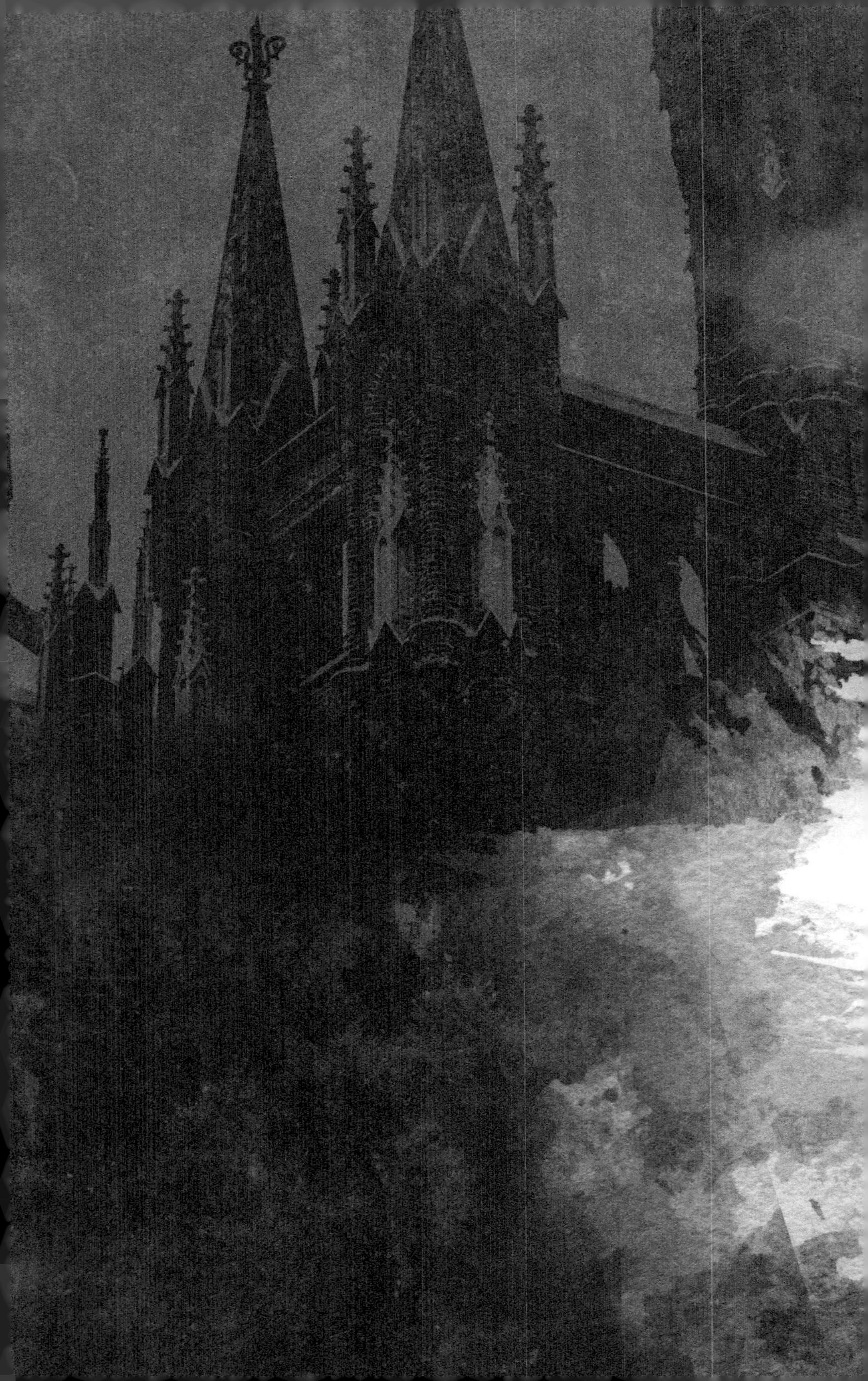

28

SEVEN

Somebody Else - Circa Waves

My fist sails straight into Hudson's face before he can duck and avoid it. I savour his yelp of pain, watching him fall to his knees in the boxing ring. We decided to forgo headgear, so he only has himself to blame for the black eye. I never agreed to pull my punches.

"Dammit, Sev!"

"Too slow," I drone. "Your reflexes are shit."

Spitting blood on the mat, he finds his feet again. "I'm not some psychotic trained killer, so excuse me for taking a hit. You could go a bit easier on me."

"Nobody else will. I'm preparing you for the real world, pretty boy. Patient Delta killed that piece of shit right under our noses. You need to be ready to fight."

"She has a name. That's Brooklyn's mum you're talking about."

"No," I growl at him. "That's the piece of shit who killed my sister.

Next time I see her, you best take our girl away, because I'm gonna cave her fucking head in. Sentiment be damned."

"Good luck breaking Brooke's heart, you moron."

"She has enough people to pick up the pieces."

With a curse, Hudson crouches back in position. This time, his boxing glove manages to connect with my stomach. I barely feel the burst of pain. We've been beating on each other for several hours now; I doubt there's a part of me that isn't bruised from his fists.

"How did she even get in?" Hudson wipes his forehead.

I manage to strike him in the ribs. "We were trained to blend in. Invisible, like phantoms passing through shadows. We didn't exist. Only Augustus's machines were allowed to walk this earth."

"Nobody is that good, not even Lazlo's prized patient."

"You're too cocky. It'll be the death of you out there."

With a snarl, his forehead smashes into mine. I see stars for a moment, shaking my head to clear the haze. The smug son of a bitch looks far too pleased with his headbutt. In retaliation, I deliver a roundhouse kick to his midsection.

"Motherfucker! I need a break," Hudson wheezes.

"You wanna sit around and wait for news like the rest of them?"

Before I can react, his foot sweeps out and catches my ankles. I go down hard and fast, my back smacking into the floor. Breathing becomes difficult as I stare up at his smug grin.

"Not a chance," he fires back. "I'd rather beat the shit out of you."

Offering me a hand up, we return to our vicious sparring. It's another sweaty, bruising hour before our solitude is disturbed. Eight saunters into the training room, wearing her workout gear—a pair of yoga pants and a tight, revealing sports bra. I clip Hudson around the ear when he gets distracted.

"Fuck off!" he bellows.

"Pay attention. I'm not playing a game here."

We beat on each other until Eight slides through the bungee cords, not bothering to wrap her hands or put gloves on. She's eyeing us both with violent anticipation, her body seeming to thrum all over. I haven't heard her speak a single word since Lazlo's body was found.

"Can we help you?" Hudson smarts.

She stretches her arms above her head. "Hunter, Enzo and Theo are in a meeting with the SCU. Kade is doing his obsessive-cleaning thing while Phoenix and Eli finish a bottle of rum. I need a distraction."

"I'm guessing one that doesn't involve talking about what happened."

"Definitely not," Eight retorts.

Undoing the Velcro on my glove with my teeth, I toss it aside. "Come spar with us. But if you step inside this ring, you can't leave, princess. Don't expect us to go easy on you."

"I wouldn't want it any other way."

Hudson frowns at us both. "I can't hit a girl, especially not her."

Eight catches him off guard with a karate chop to the throat. His knees meet the floor for a second time as he coughs and tries not to throw his guts up. She's a fucking savage, especially when angry.

"Feel free to sit it out," Eight offers.

While her most insufferable boyfriend recovers, I box her in with my fist raised in anticipation. I'm glad she doesn't treat me differently for only having one hand. The best thing about Eight is that she embraces every messy, imperfect aspect of us all. Especially the darker parts.

"First to tap out loses?"

I nod at her suggestion. "Hope you're prepared to go down."

In response, she dances towards me on light feet. It's like watching a bloodthirsty ballerina encircling her hopeless prey. I duck and weave, landing a few quick blows to her torso. As I'm bringing my leg up for another kick, someone shoves me from behind, causing me to faceplant.

"Nobody said anything about not playing dirty," Hudson taunts.

I roll onto my back. "Fucking bastard."

"Nice to know our friendship is mutual, asshole."

"Will you two stop flirting already?" Eight complains. "Either fuck each other or quit messing around. You can't expect me to watch this shit and not get ideas."

I catch the hopeful glint in her eye. She looks at us both like we're her fucking dinner. Hudson helps me back up again, but this time, his hand lingers on my back. I lost my shirt a couple of hours ago, and his fingertips seem to caress the hard muscles of my deltoids for a brief second.

"You're playing with fire, blackbird."

Eight leans against the edge of the ring to catch her breath. "I've seen the way you look at each other. Friendship, my ass. Don't act like you're not curious, Hud."

"I'm straight," he splutters.

"Why does that have to come into it? I'm sure Eli thought the same thing. Sometimes people's energies connect. Doesn't mean it has to be labelled or pinned down."

Sauntering towards us, Eight runs a hand down Hudson's defined chest, exposed by the sweaty material of his blue tank top. I watch his throat bob. His eyes are trying to stray over to me as he battles against it.

"You don't even want one little taste?" she taunts.

"Brooke..."

"What if I helped?"

Leaning in, her mouth meets Hudson's without mercy. I stand rock still, his thumb rubbing tiny circles into my back. I don't think he knows that he's doing it. Eight controls their kiss with confidence, taking every ounce of control without giving a single bit back.

When they break apart, Hudson's lips are parted and he's breathing hard. She grabs a handful of his top and uses it to wrench him towards me. We end up chest to chest, with her excited eyes skipping between us both. I duck my head close to hers, stealing my own kiss from her sweet lips.

Hudson watches our tongues duel, heat entering his gaze. When Eight pulls away from me, his fear is obliterated by burning need. I let him come to me, our noses brushing before I can feel the hesitant whisper of his lips on mine. He's waiting for me to cross the finish line.

"Kiss him back," Eight orders me.

I've never been one to deny her darkest desires.

My mouth attacks Hudson's in a furious frenzy. With that final barrier laid bare, he doesn't hesitate to give as good as he gets. There's nothing gentle or tender about our first kiss. It's violent and aggressive, a testament to our loving hatred for the bond tying us together.

Eight's hand strokes my arm, her familiar scent washing between us both. This is still about her. Releasing Hudson's swollen lips, I roughly drag her between us so her tight ass is pressed right up against my cock. Trapped in place, she doesn't protest as we kiss again over her writhing body.

If she doesn't stop moving, I'm going to blow my load long before I'm buried inside her cunt. Hudson's hand twines in my hair, roughly tugging on the long strands. I release a low hiss, biting his bottom lip in retaliation. The taste of his blood in my mouth turns me on even more.

A hand snakes over my hip and down into the soft material of my sweats. Eight's playing a very dangerous game as she slides into my boxers, taking hold of my erect length. Her strokes begin light and teasing, before she's working my shaft from base to tip.

Hudson breaks the kiss to gulp down air. "I've never... uh, you know. Been with a guy."

Swiping the leaking blood from his chin with my index finger, I clean the crimson droplet off with my tongue. He watches every move, his own tongue darting out to lick his lips.

I run a hand over Eight's head. "On your knees, princess. Pretty boy here is shy."

Eight chuckles. "Hudson, shy? Ha. We'll see about that."

She bows before us both, her knees meeting the floor of the boxing ring. Hudson gulps as she unties the drawstring on his workout shorts, dragging them down and freeing the bulge in his boxers. His dick disappears inside her mouth as she greedily takes his full length.

"Fuck, blackbird."

With my hand still on Eight's head, I take control of her movements. She's sucking his cock, but I'm the one in charge. Each pump of her mouth is on my terms. When she gags a little, I push her even further, forcing her to swallow every last inch. I love the way it makes Hudson shudder with pleasure.

Before he can finish inside her mouth, I pull Eight back by her pixie cut. She wipes stray tears from her eyes, still managing to look fucking perfect with a glaze of pre-come on her lips. If there's one thing our girl can do, it's give one hell of a blowjob.

Hudson spares me a look before placing his hands on my shoulders. "Down. You take it now."

Just this once, I'll give him what he wants. Kicking off my remaining clothes without shame, I sit down on the spongy floor of the boxing ring. Eight watches me stroke my length as she peels off her yoga pants, revealing her lack of underwear.

Goddammit, she's too fucking dangerous.

Perfect for a pair of hotheads like us.

Throwing her sports bra aside, she crawls back on her reddened knees. Hudson strips his remaining clothes off and helps guide her forward, so she's kneeling with her face inches from my dick.

"Suck his cock, baby. I want to watch you pleasure him."

"Yes, daddy," Eight echoes, too quick for it to be the first time.

I look between them. Is this a thing? If so, it's fucking hot. Hudson grins, the cocky son of a bitch. I'm about to insult him when Eight's mouth wraps around my length, and all sense leaves my mind. She cups a handful of my balls while going to work, determined to drive me wild.

Kneeling behind her, Hudson buries his face between her legs from behind. Eight's spine arches as he finds her bare pussy. She's trying hard not to get distracted while servicing me, but Hudson's sensual attack is pushing her limits. He licks his glistening lips when he comes up for air.

"Is our girl sweet?" I smirk.

To my surprise, he doesn't back down from the challenge.

"Want a taste, Sev? You only have to ask."

Leaning over Eight's bobbing head, he pulls me back in for another hard kiss. I can taste her salty juices on his tongue as it sweeps through my mouth. Hudson's earlier shyness has long since left the building. We break apart and he winks, looking all too satisfied with this turn of events.

"Now you have to watch me fuck our girl."

I sit back and lift my chin with defiance. "Go right ahead."

Eight's lips tighten around my cock as Hudson surges inside of her. She's barely suppressing a moan, her hands gripping my muscled thighs deep enough to leave nail marks. It's interesting, watching their dynamic. Hudson fucks our girl much like I do, every thrust scarring an irreversible brand into her skin.

My dick hits the back of her throat, and I can't help but growl. Every time Hudson pounds into her, she bites down slightly. The light graze of her teeth against my sensitive flesh is sweet torture. I'm moving my hips in time with her movements, seeking more and more of her compliance.

Unable to hold it in any longer, I feel my climax rise. I want to finish with her tight walls clenching around me, but I'll settle for staking my claim in front of this stubborn asshole. Right before I can finish in her mouth, I pull Eight back by her hair and her eyes widen with surprise.

Fisting my cock, I finish all over her face, covering her in my seed for the entire world to see. Glistening droplets of come drip down her cheeks and lips. She's gasping still, her mouth slightly parted, letting my juices flow into her mouth. I watch with satisfaction as she licks her lips clean.

"Jesus." Hudson watches us both. "That was messed up."

I quirk an eyebrow. "Jealous?"

He can't reach me, so he delivers a punishing spank to Eight's ass instead. She squeals, flashing me an annoyed look. My big mouth is going to get her in some serious trouble now. I can't help but want to punish her more for the shit she pulled the other day.

"Did your girlfriend tell you about the rooftop last week?"

"Seven," she warns.

"What?" I act all innocent.

Hudson's still slamming into her, his grip bruising her scarred hips. Determined to win this fucked-up game of ours, I sit back, stark bollock naked and not embarrassed in the slightest.

"I told her that if she wanted to jump, she could go ahead."

That causes his movements to still, right on the verge of finishing. Eight gasps in pain and frustration, her nails drawing blood from my thighs. He's left her hanging on the edge while his face darkens with anger.

"What?" Hudson utters.

I watch them, far too pleased with myself.

"Ignore him," Eight insists.

"What the hell is he talking about, Brooke?!"

She's ripped from my lap and flipped over by his rough hands. Eight's head lands in my naked lap. Settling between her spread, vulnerable legs, Hudson is free to stare directly into her wide eyes.

"Go ahead," I encourage with a grin. "Tell your boyfriend how you wanted to give up. Tell him that I took you to the edge of a rooftop, and you actually considered jumping off."

"I did not!"

"Stop lying, Eight."

She glowers up at me. "Shut the fuck up, Seven. Last warning."

Her gaze is wrenched back to Hudson by his grip on her chin. There's real anger there, burning in slow, destructive embers. I'm quite pleased with my handiwork. He's even hotter while enraged. Hell, they both are.

"Are we doing this shit again?" Hudson hisses at her. "I've dragged you off a fucking roof once. I won't do it again. We've spent enough of our lives worrying about your death."

"I was never going to jump." Eight bites her lip, but it sounds like the truth. "I just… it's the unknown. I've never feared it before. Now, I have something to lose. I'm terrified of not knowing the future."

Bringing their foreheads together, Hudson's hands move to her exposed throat. Their noses are touching as he inhales every breath she takes. I spot the moment oxygen ceases to enter her lungs. Eight's hands curl into fists as she fights to remain calm, despite being choked.

"My future has meant nothing to me since the day we met," Hudson growls in her face. "I didn't give a damn about anything but you. We belong together, in this world and the next. Where you go, I go."

Eight begins to claw at his crushing hands. Human instinct is a tough nut to crack. To punish her further, Hudson pushes back inside her slick cunt. Her back arches again at the lack of warning. He sets a bruising pace, gliding into her like she's his property—his to hurt and break into pathetic pieces.

"You think death will part us?"

Eight can't answer, her nails tearing his hands to shreds.

"There's no way out of this, blackbird. The Devil wouldn't dare challenge my claim on your soul. Hell will spit you out and back into my arms, where you fucking belong."

I can feel her muscles beginning to tense where our bare skin is touching. She's on the verge of falling apart, even if every instinct is screaming at her to escape and find air to breathe. Hudson won't give it to her without payment. Her complete submission to his will is the price of her release.

"You wanna come, little whore?" he teases her. "Then let's get this straight, once and for all. If we're a motherfucking family, that means we live and die together. No easy exits. No shortcuts."

Her eyelids begin to flutter as her hands tremble. She's going to pass out if he's not careful. At the absolute last second, Hudson releases his hands from Eight's neck. Her next breath sounds excruciating, like breathing underwater. Her skin is already tarnished, turning a nasty shade of purple.

"Come," he demands with a final pump.

The sound that escapes her lips is caught between relief and agony. Hudson's head slumps against her breasts, every taut muscle in his back moving with his rapid breathing. Neither seems able to move as they ride out the waves of their climaxes.

We don't say anything for a long time. Our bodies are wrapped up in each other, spreadeagled across the boxing ring. Eight is staring up at the ceiling, rubbing her sore neck and wincing at the pain. I note that Hudson doesn't bother apologising, nor does she demand he does so.

A throat clearing breaks our post-sex bubble.

"Uh, guys?" Theo stands in the doorway, his eyes averted away from us.

I immediately shove Eight behind me, gritting my teeth against a snarl. If Theo saw even an inch of her bare skin, I'll happily barbecue his eyeballs for dinner.

"What?" Hudson growls, equally annoyed.

"You need to come upstairs." Theo awkwardly rubs the back of his neck. "Hunter wants to speak to you all. It's urgent. Clothes may be a good idea."

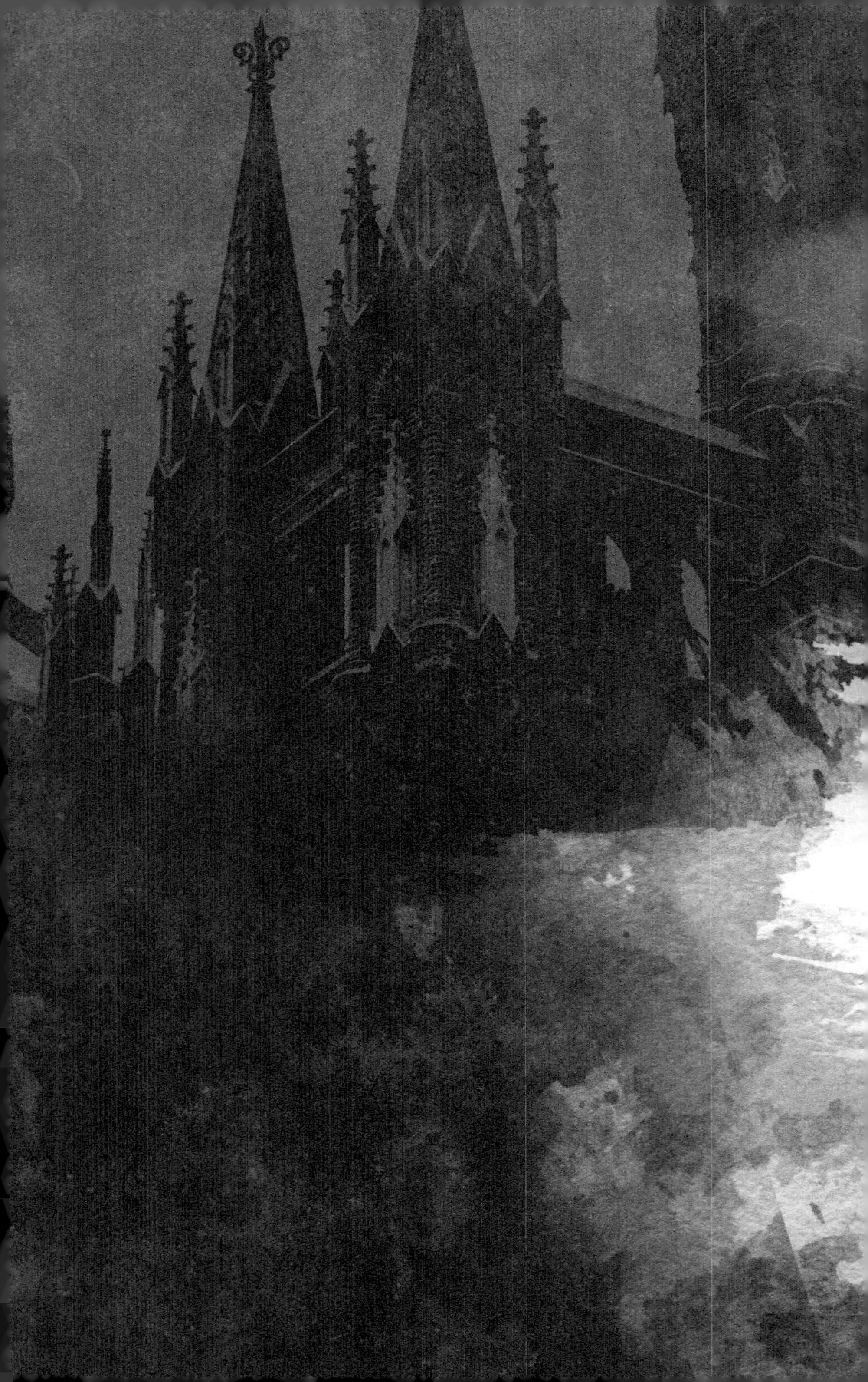

29

BROOKLYN

It's Okay To Be Afraid - Saint Slumber

I yank one of Eli's oversized hoodies over my head, covering the necklace of bruises on my throat. When I spotted them in the bathroom mirror, I couldn't help but stroke the aching flesh with a sick sense of satisfaction.

The voices in my head can't convince me otherwise when I have physical proof of my family's love and twisted devotion.

The walk to Hunter's office is marked by tense, impenetrable silence. Hudson and Seven follow behind me and Theo, both hastily changed into fresh clothing after our… uh, fuck fest. No other word for that toxic fiasco.

"What's the news?" I rasp.

Theo casts me an apprehensive look. "The SCU have made their decision."

"Do you know what it is?"

Rather than answer, he pushes open the huge glass door and beckons for us to enter. I can't help but feel like the hangman is offering us a nice, convenient noose to hang ourselves with. Entering Hunter's office, I take Hudson's and Seven's hands to ground myself.

The others wait inside, all appearing nervous. Kade is propped in the corner, his foot tapping a staccato rhythm. Eli and Phoenix sit next to each other, their entwined hands displayed on the conference table. I kiss both of their cheeks as we pass and find our own seats.

Hunter stands at the head of the table, his arms folded over his perfectly pressed blue shirt. I glance up at his hair. It's loose and untied again. I've come to realise it's a pretty good indicator of his mental state. Right now, he looks ready to burn the entire fucking world down. It's terrifying.

"Now that we're all here, will you answer my question?" Kade sighs.

"Yes, the decision came from above," Hunter concedes. "The task force answers to a higher authority within the Serious Crimes Unit. I'm not familiar with the director, but I've heard he's pretty formidable."

"That wasn't my question. Does Incendia have the SCU in its pocket?!"

"What's happened?" I interrupt with my heart in my mouth.

Releasing his own sigh, Hunter takes the empty seat between Theo and Enzo. None of them can look at us, studying the table instead. I feel the balloon of hope in my chest explode into spectacular pieces.

"The SCU has decided not to proceed with an investigation at this time." Hunter's voice is laden with defeat. "Agent Barlow has handed in her resignation in protest of this decision, along with Agent Jonas."

"They're quitting?" Hudson exclaims. "What the fuck?"

"From what I gather, their superior officer did not agree with the evidence collected. The decision was not theirs to make. After spending three weeks with you all, both felt very strongly that an immediate investigation was needed."

"So why the hell aren't they doing it?" I shout.

"They intend to prosecute." Hunter shakes his head in disgust. "Just not Incendia."

We all fall silent at that bombshell.

"Charges have been filed against Brooklyn for multiple first-degree murders, including Brittany Matthews, Jack Potter, Officer Jefferson and Doctor Augustus. That's without the four-month killing spree. Rio Gonzalez's death is still up for dispute."

"Do I even want to know mine?" Seven drones.

"The list is too long to count."

"Naturally. I'll skip the summary, thanks."

"Kade is facing numerous narcotics charges," Hunter continues. "Along with destruction of private property and charges for inciting the riot. Hudson, Phoenix and Eli stand accused of absconding from custody and participating in the riot. Potentially more if they link guard or patient deaths back to you six."

You could hear a penny drop in the office. I've never seen everyone so equally horrified and stunned into silence, even after all we've been through. Enzo slams his hands down on the table, his face scrunched up. He's turning a brighter shade of red than Hudson did earlier.

"As of tonight, our protection will be rendered illegal and classed as obstruction of justice." Hunter ignores Enzo smashing his chair into the wall. "You will be forcibly removed from the premises, arrested by the SCU, and prosecuted to the full extent of the law."

Kade is the first to find his voice, shaky and uncertain. "What does that mean?"

"Best case? Prison time. Release or parole will be out of the question. For some of you, a psychiatric sentence may be deemed more beneficial. You will be returned to Incendia's care for the rest of your lives."

"Do we get a trial?" Hudson asks.

Hunter shakes his head. "The SCU are in possession of emergency powers granted by the government. High-profile offenders can be dealt with at their discretion, without public involvement. The records will reflect otherwise, but your fates will be sealed the moment they slap the cuffs on."

"That's illegal," Kade argues.

Closing his laptop, Theo removes his glasses to rub his eyes. "So is running a privately funded conspiracy to experiment on and torture the mentally unwell. Doesn't stop Incendia from taking politicians' money and passing their financial endorsement back to our lawmakers."

"You're saying the SCU has been compromised," I summarise.

Hunter meets my eyes. "I'm saying there's nothing else to be done."

"You made promises."

"We all did," Enzo shouts, rounding on his best friend. "This is fucking bullshit, Hunt. We have the resources to take on whatever jackasses the SCU sends here, their warrants be damned. I won't let these kids go without a fight."

"Then we end up in matching cells with them."

"So be it! This isn't right!"

Theo watches his team members argue, his expression beyond bleak. He lost the one thing he cared about in this fight, the person that gave his life meaning and put a smile on his face. It was all for nothing.

"Eight," Seven murmurs behind me. "We need to leave, right now."

"And go where?" Phoenix responds before I can. "They will follow us everywhere. We can't run away, not this time. This is the end of the road."

"You'd give up so fucking easily?" Seven argues.

"You can't punch your way out of this one!"

The crash of a chair hitting the floor interrupts their argument. Eli has backed up into a corner, his hands slammed over his ears. His green eyes are clouded over and far from the strong man he's grown into recently—one brave enough to live, breathe and speak without fear.

"Eli?" I whisper softly.

"W-Won't... b-back... won't g-go... back."

Sliding down the wall, he buries his face in his knees. I'm powerless to stop his dissolution into a trembling wreck, like the scared little boy I found cutting himself in that graveyard last year. It's fucking devastating.

"Nix," I force out. "I can't..."

Taking over from me, Phoenix crouches in front of Eli. I have to look away from their whispered conversation. It hurts far too much to watch him try to pull Eli back from the edge of insanity. Instead, I let rage steel my spine as I face Hunter again.

"Tell us what to do. Give us something."

Hands braced on the table, Hunter hesitates. We stare at each other for several long seconds, locked in our own private conversation. I leave all of my emotions on display. Terror. Hope. Defeat. Exhaustion. Desperation. Fury. Grief. Hatred. I can barely see through the force of them wracking me.

"Hunter," Theo says uncertainly.

"No," he snaps back. "It's a suicide mission."

Standing tall for the first time, Theo replaces his glasses. I've never seen him butt heads with his boss. He's always the obedient lap dog, but not today. This is the final, backbreaking straw. He's had enough.

"The moment they enter the SCU's custody, they're as good as dead," Theo states simply. "That's a suicide mission. You are sending every single one of them to their deaths."

"What else would you have me do?" Hunter throws his hands up.

Theo refuses to back down. "Let them choose their own fates for once."

With his throat bobbing, Hunter's nod signals his defeat. He reaches inside his suit jacket, pulling out a shiny, embossed slice of paper. It looks like an invitation, dipped in luxurious gold ink and calligraphy.

"This arrived a week ago."

He tosses it down the table for me to pick up. Staring at the invitation, I trace the words with my index finger, each letter punching a hole through my numbness. It's addressed to me in handwritten ink.

Incendia Corporation Invites You To Celebrate The Grand Reopening Of Blackwood Institute - An Exclusive Event For Investors And Sponsors.

I can feel the weight of my crimes pressing down on me like an ash cloud after a volcanic eruption. Beneath the grandiose declaration, the same handwriting has left a private message just for me. Bancroft must have written it, but Augustus's dead voice reads the words out.

Brooklyn.

It's time to return home.

Your mother is waiting for her little girl.

Nobody complains as I run for the nearest bin and throw up until my chest burns. With my hands braced on the plastic edges, I watch my tears drip into the rubbish. I know if I turn around, I'll find Augustus waiting for me. I can feel his presence at the edges of my broken mind.

"He wants to draw you out in the open." Hunter stops next to me, a tissue in hand. "I'm sure they have a cover story ready to be printed, the heroic efforts of the SCU praised for stopping a bloodthirsty criminal. The public will celebrate your death and the safety it brings them."

"But we told the truth!" I shout after wiping my mouth. "We fucking told them. It's all a lie, every single, poisonous word they print."

"Money is the truth for people like Bancroft."

"Then what?"

Stepping up next to me, Seven's face is hard. "We end things our way."

I feel the warmth of the others at my back. Kade takes my hand and squeezes his agreement. The gentle caress of Hudson's breath at my neck is all I need from him. Phoenix and Eli come last, stumbling to complete our bruised and battered group.

Eli's barely able to stand, but there's still fierce determination in his emerald eyes. He manages a single, jerky nod that seals our decision. We're all in agreement on one fundamental fact.

Our lives are forfeit right now.

None of us are surrendering willingly.

Incendia has signed our death certificates already; this is just extra time in the eternal playoff for our souls. Hudson was right about one thing—we live and die together, not ripped apart and locked in cells to await the hangman's noose.

"Can you get us to Wales?" I direct my question to Hunter.

Instead, Enzo answers from across the room.

"I'll show you to the damn gates myself. I'm coming with you." He silences Hunter's protests before they can begin. "We made a promise and I never, ever go back on my word."

The two men stare at each other until Hunter breaks. He scrubs his exhausted face several times, savouring a deep, fortifying breath. When he unveils his face again, defeat has been replaced by resolution.

"Alyssa died fighting the system. She believed in the truth."

Theo steps up next, his shoulders set firm. "We honour her wishes by fighting for what's right. I refuse to live in a world where evil wins. If Bancroft goes down, Incendia is weakened."

"We have hours of interviews and evidence to strike the killer blow," Hunter concurs. "The SCU has no idea we had our own cameras rolling. Let's release it to the entire world right now."

The idea of three weeks of evidence being released into the public domain has a clinging chill covering my entire body. I feel fucking sick at the thought of reporters, doctors, pundits, and political commentators hearing about the darkest parts of my life.

"Is there another way?" I ask, defeated.

Hunter shakes his head. "We have to force their hand now. I'm sorry, Brooke."

The others all meet my eyes. Their lives are spelled out in those tapes too, but they are leaving the decision up to me. I don't know if we'll ever know peace again once we do this. But if we don't, our lives will end in the most brutal way imaginable. Incendia will win. I can't let that happen.

"Do it," I command.

Theo nods once, disappearing from the room.

"They didn't believe us before." Phoenix looks fearful. "What's changed?"

"Who would believe the ramblings of a psych patient and some blurry iPhone footage?" Enzo laughs bitterly. "But the sworn testimony of several grown adults, backed up by two SCU ex-employees, and buried by the very people the public trust to defend the law?"

"Nobody can ignore that," I affirm, trying to comfort myself.

Hunter actually smiles. "All we need is one head to turn. The rest will follow. There are good people left in government. We're going above the SCU with this footage, and it will blow them to pieces."

In the office of a man I didn't know two months ago, we seal a pact in the only way we know how. Each person spits into the palm of their hand, like criminals agreeing to a truce. Each handshake is exchanged in turn. When I reach Enzo, he pulls me into a bear hug.

"You'll get that second chance, wildfire," he murmurs into my hair. "I had a sister once. She was full of life and never gave me a moment's rest. I couldn't stop the cancer that ate away at her organs, but I can fight until my dying breath to kill every last son of a bitch that comes for you."

Tears prick my eyes. "You can't give up everything for us."

He holds me at arm's length and scowls. "If one person's life isn't worth risking everything for, then none of this matters. We vowed to fight for justice the day we opened Sabre. I'm doing exactly that."

With another bone-creaking hug, he pushes me back towards the guys. I pretend not to notice the way he clears his throat and subtly wipes under his eyes. The lion-hearted boulder of muscle has a heart of fucking gold, and I love him for it. All of them have done their best by us.

Facing all five guys waiting for my direction—the individual pieces of my heart, my motherfucking family—I say the words I never dreamed of uttering aloud.

"Time to go back to Blackwood Institute."

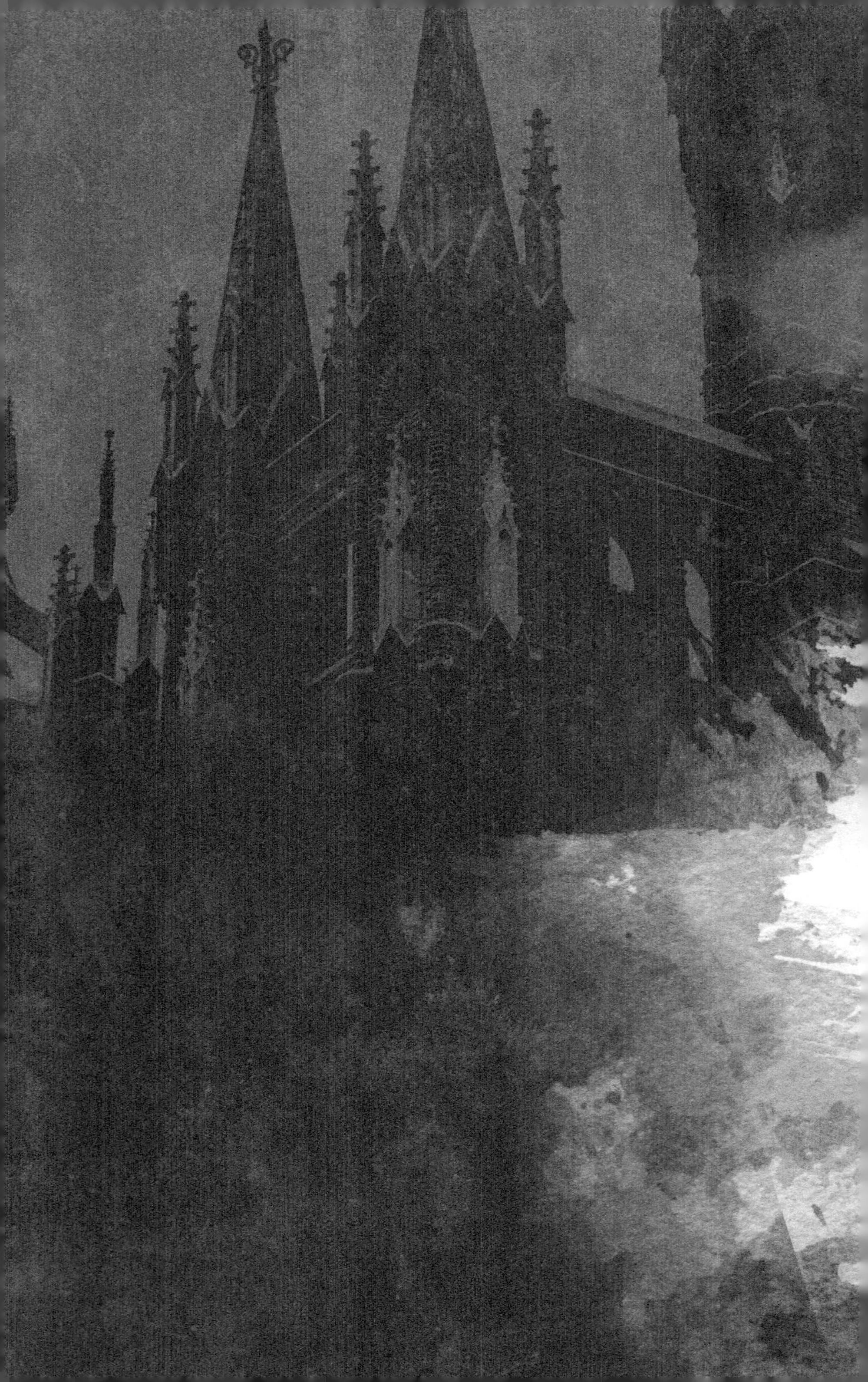

30

BROOKLYN

Wonderful Life - Bring Me The Horizon & Dani Filth

There's something very wrong about driving into Blackwood's car park like normal, law-abiding citizens. No undercover sneaking or clever disguises this time. There's no point in hiding. The SCU's deadline has passed, and Theo offered our lives to the vultures in the media twelve hours ago.

We're fair game now.

There are no more dark corners to hide in.

Hudson pulls the handbrake on the dark, tinted SUV. I'm sitting in the passenger seat, while the other four are crammed in the back. Hunter, Enzo and Theo pull up next to us in a matching armoured company car, giving us a moment to share some final words of wisdom.

I meet Kade's eyes in the mirror. "You look good."

He runs a hand over his perfectly knotted tie, which complements his shirt and trousers. His broken arm is still strapped against his chest.

It figures he'd return to his preppy roots for our final trip to hell. This time, he isn't here to impress anyone but himself.

The rest of us wear our battle armour—ripped jeans and band t-shirts, leather jackets and bad attitudes. There's no point in pretending to fit in with the high-society vampires inside. We're not here for them.

I entered Blackwood as myself.

I intend to return exactly the same way.

"You know, I first came here to prove myself." Kade scoffs at himself. "I was chasing after Hudson's ass like a dog with a bone. All I wanted was to compensate for every shortcoming my father threw in my face."

"You saved us all, Kade. Don't forget that."

"I've brought us right back to our deaths. This is my biggest failure."

"You kept us alive," Hudson grumbles from the driver's seat. "We're not going to second-guess the progress we've all made since leaving this place. Not to get emotional and shit, but I'm proud of us all."

Phoenix savours a final cigarette out the window. "Blackwood broke our spirits, but it couldn't break our family. Two years ago, I never expected to find a life worth living without drugs."

Hudson snorts. "I had no intentions of ever leaving this place, three-year program or not. There was nothing in the world that was worth living for." His eyes meet mine. "Or so I thought."

Staring at Blackwood in the distance, Seven's voice is filled with a warmth that I never thought possible. "Jude came here looking for his life's purpose. I lost myself along the way, but after six years, I think I've found it at last."

The last member of our group is listening in thoughtful silence. Eli's wrapped in the same *Bring Me The Horizon* hoodie he wore when we first met. Then, it was shielding his face from the world and all its terrors. Now, the hood lies back. He has no headphones in. His gaze is clear, firm, unafraid.

"T-Twelve years," he stutters, his voice evening out. "I couldn't s-speak when… came here. Not fucking perfect, but… seen outside w-world now." He smiles to himself. "Scary… but b-beautiful."

Our hands link over the console. I take a moment to meet each of their eyes. My guys. My family. There was a time when I was determined to run far, far away from them. Fear and hatred ruled my life, leaving no room for hope.

"I came here to die," I say with a headshake. "Blackwood was supposed to be my way out. I never expected to find a reason to live, let alone five fucking reasons."

Another hand lays on top of mine, then another. One by one, we all link up, holding on to that final scrap of rebellious hope. None of us will leave this place in cuffs. It's always been ride or die with us—get on the train before it runs you the hell over. I can't love any other way.

This is our last stand, together.

Six misfits against the whole fucking world.

Regardless of what happens, what a tale it will be.

"Nobody gets separated," I remind them all. "We go in together and we leave together, even if it's in body bags. I won't see any of you behind bars. We take Bancroft out, no matter what."

Checking weapons and smoothing our casual outfits, the moment of judgement comes. Hunter, Enzo and Theo wait outside in all black, looking far too much like the spooks they relentlessly train. We're going to stand out, but none of us give a flying fuck.

"Wait," Phoenix blurts. "I, uh. Shit, I'm not gonna beat around the bush. I fucking love you guys." His grin is so much like the cocky bastard that first greeted me. "That's all. We can go now."

Hudson wraps an arm around his neck and messes up his bright-blue hair. "Naw, Nix is getting all soft and weepy. Shall we feed him to Incendia first? Get it over and done with?"

"Dammit," Seven curses. "I was planning that for you, pretty boy. Quit stealing my ideas."

The look Hudson sends him is full of challenging heat.

I stifle an eye roll. "Come on, horny assholes. Let's go die in style."

The car park is packed full of expensive sports cars and far too much money for me to stand. We've arrived fashionably late, so the event should already be in full swing. I can't help but feel slightly sick as we begin the long walk up to Blackwood's gates. I never thought I'd come back here.

By the time we reach the grandiose reception building, cloaked in thick ivy and lit by the full moon hanging overhead, my nausea has been replaced by stone-cold fury. Hunter flashes the invitation and we're barely given a second glance by the security detail.

They've been briefed to expect us.

Bancroft wants his crown jewels back.

Inside, I glance around the familiar reception area. The smell of fresh paint permeates the air from the recent reconstruction. New brocade wallpaper meets identical mahogany panelling to the old entrance. Tasteful artwork, antique vases and gilded mirrors add to the opulence that once turned my stomach.

I feel no different now.

It will be my pleasure to watch it burn all over again.

Kade's gaze is locked on the darkened reception desk, behind a closed shutter. I uncurl his fist to let our fingers entwine. The memories are so close to the surface, I can see them bubbling in his hazel eyes.

"You looked so lost the day you arrived," he whispers. "All I wanted was to hold you."

"I'm glad you latched on and wouldn't let go."

He offers me a crooked smile. "I love you."

"Ditto, Mr Knight."

None of us can stand to look at the repaired offices and treatment rooms down the low-lit corridor. I hate to think of what lies below us. Smouldering ruins have been reborn in a new vision of depravity. No matter what, I won't allow any more lives to be ruined in these hallowed halls.

"Sounds like the party is outside." Hunter checks his gun holster. "I'd say stick to the plan, but at this point, I'm not sure there is one. So, I'll say this. Don't get caught alive."

Enzo chuckles. "Cheery."

Their shoulders bump together.

"We're screwed too, old friend." Hunter shakes his head. "I won't let Alyssa down again."

"The SCU can chase us here and see for themselves what they're enabling," Theo agrees, smoothing his bouncy curls. "Let's go kick some corrupt ass and hope to hell this stupid plan works."

We pass another two guards who note our presence and murmur something into their earpieces. The moment they open the doors for us without a second glance, I know our doom awaits. Outside, bright lights reveal the party in full swing. The once quiet, peaceful quad is bustling with activity.

Benches and picnic tables have been cleared to make way for two huge marquees, the pure-white fabric rustling in the cool breeze. Glimmering lights have been strung to provide a warm ambiance for the circulation of champagne and appetisers on polished, golden plates.

There's even a string quartet, the gentle croon of violins accompanying the hum of laughter and conversation. Guests mill about in floor-length gowns and tailored tuxedos, admiring the grand architecture and impressive surroundings. There isn't a speck of evidence from the fire.

"Stick together." Hunter eyes the crowd. "We're going to check the place out, look for any big fish. The more of Incendia's corrupt officials we document, the easier our jobs will be."

"Be safe," I beg them.

Enzo offers me a dazzling smile. "Don't get into trouble without us."

"Somehow, I think they will," Theo jokes.

Sandwiched between slabs of muscle and defiance, we leave them and head for the upper crusts of society. It isn't long before I start recognising people in the melee. Several familiar faces spot me in turn. I remember the middle-aged, pot-bellied men that Augustus introduced me to at his fundraiser.

"Investors," Kade mutters. "I know a few of them."

"Me too. Keep moving."

Grabbing a glass of champagne from the nearest waiter, I down it in three fast gulps. There's a buzz of whispers around us as we enter the nearest marquee, our hardened expressions and casual clothing betraying us to the stuck-up wankers attending Bancroft's power trip.

Kade guides us towards the pop-up bar at the back, helping himself to a bottle of whiskey before the attendant can say a word. He fills several crystal glasses, and we knock them back, needing the liquid courage. It won't be long before someone finds us.

We wait even less time than expected. This entire parade of wealth and power has been laid out for our benefit. A deliberate throat clear has Kade's unsteady hand hesitating over his glass. I recognise the smug, brutish voice before he says a word.

"Care to pour your father a drink, son?"

The bottle hits the bar with a thud.

"My days of tending to your demands are over," Kade responds coolly.

"Your time in the real world has given you a backbone, has it?"

Huddled together for strength, we turn as a united front to face the infamous Leroy Knight. He's standing a few metres away, dressed in an impeccable suit and blood-red bow tie. His salt and pepper hair has been slicked back to highlight his handsome, ageing face.

There's a willowy blonde woman hanging off his arm, too busy eyeing up the waiter to listen to our conversation. Her satin dress and designer handbag betray her shallow motives. She's just another exploit, one in a long line of people to be controlled.

"Hudson," Leroy greets with a smile. "It's been a long time."

"Not long enough," he grits out.

"Keeping my son on his toes, are you? Only now, he isn't paid to make excuses for you."

"Enough," Kade thunders, stepping forward. "This is between me and you."

Leroy laughs in his face, so loud it's actually unnerving. His date frowns at us all before snagging a fresh drink and making a hasty exit. She's probably off to snort some cocaine in the bathroom before she gets paid for pretending to like this sack of shit.

"Think you're a big man now, do you?"

Kade refuses to cower. "I'm more than the person you taught me to be."

The depraved man I know begins to peek through Leroy's glossy, paparazzi-perfect exterior. He wraps himself in finery and lies, but there's a slavering monster rotting him from the inside out.

"You had one job," he sneers at his son. "Make sure the street rat didn't jeopardise my reputation further. That's it. Eighteen more months and you would've been free to do as you please."

Hudson moves to stand by his brother. "Sorry we derailed your plans. How inconsiderate of us. If you want, I can kiss your ass and pretend I don't want to slit your throat? I did it enough back then."

"That won't be necessary. I've come to realise my efforts have been misguided. Thankfully, I have another child. Once I track your traitorous mother down, I will ensure your sister doesn't repeat your mistakes."

Kade's teeth are bared in a threatening snarl. He looks ready to snap his own father's neck, with or without our help. I doubt he'd hesitate over taking this asshole's life, morals or not.

"Cece won't have to experience your poison," Kade elucidates. "They're never coming back here. You're going to die exactly as you should—humiliated and alone. Then my job here is done."

The crowd parts as a handful of grey-faced, heavily armed guards make their entrance. Leroy taps his concealed earpiece with glee. I'm sure he's being well-compensated for his role in this pantomime. We're surrounded, but not one of us cowers in the face of aggression.

The nearest guard points a gun straight at Kade's face. No tasers or batons, they all pull deadly weapons and train them on every single one of my guys. I'm the only one left without a target on me, so I step forward.

"Why don't you come and give me a proper hello, Patient Eight." Leroy eyes me with interest. "You're looking a little cleaner than the last time I saw you."

"I don't make it a habit to execute wayward employees these days."

"Ah, she speaks! Augustus should've removed your acid tongue when he had the chance. Come along, I tire of your childish games."

Glancing between Kade and Hudson, they both give subtle head shakes. The closest armed guard notices and strides forward, smashing the barrel of his gun into Hudson's temple. I stare at his finger on the trigger, my feet carrying me further forward.

"There we go," Leroy croons. "That wasn't so hard, was it?"

Mentally checking out, I make myself walk straight into his open arms. I can smell the liquor and cigars on his breath as his lips graze my cheek.

"Care to dance, my dear? It is a party, after all."

I lower my voice to a low, sensual croon. "I'd rather cut your dick off with a rusty knife and make you swallow it."

"Such fire, Patient Eight. I am glad your spark hasn't dulled."

His hand clamps around my wrist. He doesn't give me a chance to even say goodbye. I'm dragged through the circular tables and away from the others. Fighting back will only ensure their deaths. I allow my mind to completely empty like it used to, sliding back into the safety of numbness.

When we reach the polished parquet of the dance floor, Leroy pulls me into position. We spin around beneath the light of a chandelier built into the marquee. Champagne and whiskey sour in my stomach at the scent of his aftershave washing over me, laced with imaginary blood.

When I glance at the guys, I find them unmoved.

That's when I realise Seven isn't with them.

"Am I boring you already?" Leroy grips my chin.

"I've had better dancing partners."

He spins us around so we're facing the other way. My lack of submission is beginning to grind his gears; I can see the flames of fury in his eyes. Bancroft still hasn't made an appearance, and I'm beginning to feel antsy.

"You know, impulsivity is your greatest weakness. Not many people would accept an invitation to their own demise, Patient Eight. Things would've been a lot less complicated if we did this a month ago."

I curl my lip at him. "I'm here for Bancroft, not your sleazy fucking ass."

Leroy grunts as he slaps me across the face, hard enough for my head to snap to the side. Licking a bead of blood from my lip, I stare back at him with defiance.

"That all you got, old man?"

"Oh, I have plenty more. I'm on strict orders to be a good boy, though."

"The big, powerful Leroy Knight is on a leash?" I cackle. "How mighty of you."

He merely shrugs. "Like with all good plans, preparation is key. Are you ready for your prize? We can't have a treasure hunt without one."

Leroy roughly turns me around. I'm relieved to see the guys are where I left them, though Seven is still missing. Where the fuck is he? I can't see Enzo, Hunter or Theo either. My heartbeat roars in my ears as Leroy grabs my wrist again, towing me out of the marquee.

Nobody blinks an eye as we're escorted at gunpoint. They all watch with morbid satisfaction. It's like they're trapped in a parallel reality, ignoring the real world slapping them in the face. Many people here will be making millions from Incendia's shady dealings, including the Z Wing program and its valuable recruits.

Humans with no humanity.

We're truly on our own in this theatre of death.

Taken away from the party, darkness invades our surroundings. There are no lights on inside the classrooms. Spooky, seemingly vacant buildings block us on all sides. I realise where we're headed as Leroy's nails dig into my skin. Oakridge dorms await at the end of a cobbled path.

This is where it all began.

It's fitting this should be our end.

Floodlights slam on, momentarily blinding me. As my vision clears, the awaiting scene is a terrifying sight. In front of the carved stone steps that my hallucinations once chased me up, a giant wooden stage has been erected. Great beams stretch upwards, running parallel to the platform raised several feet in the air.

Hanging from the beam, I count five nooses.

Perfectly tied and awaiting a sacrificial neck.

Standing next to his macabre construction, Bancroft watches our arrival with visible joy. He's dressed to the nines in a navy-blue suit and matching velvet bow tie. In the harsh light, I can see Augustus in his features. Sharp and cruel, his entire persona drips with intelligence and authority.

"Good job, Leroy. You might want to make a hasty exit. I have no doubt their reinforcements will be arriving soon. I intend to finish this quickly."

"Indeed," Leroy agrees with a chuckle. "I'll be seeing you soon, old friend. We have another election to win."

Bancroft smiles widely. "Who wouldn't vote for the man that brought these convicts to their doom?"

Leroy's grip on me loosens as his hot, sticky breath meets my ear. "Have fun in hell, darling. He's going to tear you apart. It's been a pleasure."

"Run away," I smart. "Like the coward you are."

Delivering his parting blow, Leroy's eyes narrow as he shoves me hard. I stumble and hit the ground right in front of Bancroft. By the time I crawl onto my knees, Kade's father has scuttled away like the pathetic worm he is, and fascinated investors are crowding around to watch the drama play out.

"Brooklyn West," Bancroft greets. "Or should I say, Patient Eight? We do live in extraordinary times when one body can hold two people. Quite fascinating."

The butt of a gun meets my head, forcing me to cower at his almighty altar of undeserved power. Instead of looking at Bancroft, I watch my guys get escorted up the stairs to the wooden platform. None of them betray any fear in the face of death.

"What is this?" I growl.

"Presumably, you accepted my invitation with some vague notion of ending my life. Can't kill a man at the end of the phone, right? I understand. Vengeance is a powerful motivator."

Forever the fearless leader, Kade takes the first noose. The guard loops it around his neck and tightens the thick rope until he's trapped. My horror increases as each noose is filled with its victim. I never underestimated the risk of coming here, but Bancroft's insanity is far greater than I'd predicted.

"Are you going to murder five wanted criminals in front of hundreds of witnesses?" I ask, playing down my panic. "Even for you, that's a gamble. Loyalties change. People talk. You're being reckless."

"Reckless?" Bancroft laughs loudly. "I've always been a gambling man."

"Your son was too." I let the full force of my hatred shine through my tiny, satisfied smile. "His gamble didn't pay off in the end. I enjoyed watching the blood pour as I twisted the knife in his gut."

Before Bancroft can strike me, my hand snaps up and captures his mid-movement. Rather than scaring him, he looks down at my skin on his with amusement. His grin is seriously unhinged.

"Yet, his legacy lives on," he states with conviction. "You are his greatest creation. I honour my son's hard work by finishing what he started. That begins with removing all temptations from your life."

The nearest guard rests his hand on a built-in lever that holds my entire attention. Bancroft is frowning at the empty fifth noose when the harsh bark of another dickhead foot soldier distracts him. Wherever Seven is, I hope to fuck he has a plan to get us out of this.

"Ah, the final piece of the puzzle." Bancroft claps his hands together in mock excitement. "I believe you two have been reacquainted. Sloppy work at Harrowdean, Miss West. Not your finest hour."

Escorted with a gun at her temple, I feel my world implode as Bancroft's final taunt arrives. Her bald head and gaunt face haven't changed since our silent conversation through blood-stained messages and distant waves. Mum doesn't look at me as she's dragged to Bancroft's side.

"Ah, Patient Delta. Did you find her accomplices?"

"No, sir," her dull voice drones.

"Of course not. While I appreciate Lazlo's impressive work, all things must die. The old is replaced with the new. I no longer have a use for you, Patient Delta, as I have your daughter here now."

That's the exact moment when Mum's eyes snap to mine. Her gaze burns like the air bags that hit my skin in the car crash. Still, she betrays no recognition. I can see the same armour I wrap myself in staring back at me. I've seen proof that she lives within it, a tiny, flickering flame determined to burn bright.

"She will take your place."

Her voice remains flat, complacent. "I understand, sir."

Leaving her standing there, Bancroft returns to me. There's another gun now clasped in his hand. I swallow a bubble of acid as he wraps an arm around my waist, his breath licking against my skin.

"Do you enjoy games, Miss West?"

I refuse to answer.

"I do," Bancroft continues. "So, here's one for you. It's rather simple. I will place this gun in your hand. See? Here we go. Get ready now."

He forcibly uncurls my fingers, positioning the weapon in my hand.

"Your choice is rather simple. On the count of three, a lever will be pulled. Four lives will end. You get to watch the ones you love swing on the end of a noose. Sounds thrilling, doesn't it?"

My eyes connect with Eli's.

His mouth forms the words he cannot say.

Until death do us part.

"You have a chance to save their lives." Bancroft raises my hand until the gun is pointed at my mother. "Kill Patient Delta, and I will let them walk away, unharmed. You will take her place by my side, but they will live. I'll have all charges against them dropped."

His words cause my heart to stop dead.

"Tempting, huh?" he purrs in my ear. "Fail to kill her and I'll gladly take their lives. Your mother will live on. Call it a family reunion. You get to have a parent again, but not without paying the price."

The guard standing behind Hudson kicks his left leg out to illustrate Bancroft's threat. I almost scream as Hudson slips for a brief, horrifying second, the noose tightening around his neck with an awful choking sound. He manages to find his feet again after a scramble, looking blue in the face.

"What will it be, Brooklyn? Your mother or the men who saved your life?"

Bancroft's hands leave mine. I'm left holding the gun alone. It wavers in the air, but I don't lower it. One shot between the eyes and my last remaining parent will return to the grave she should have inhabited twelve years ago. I'll lose her all over again.

If I don't, my family dies.

Either way, the choice rests on my shoulders.

"Tick tock, tick tock," Bancroft leers.

I look over to the guys. I'm on the precipice of that rooftop all over again, despite the passing of time that's bound our souls together. It all comes back to this—death holding us apart. I have nothing to offer this world, but they do. Saving their lives is the only good thing I have left to give.

My finger rests on the trigger.

That's when Mum's mouth opens.

"It's okay," she says softly.

Her voice drags me back into the sordid past, but I'm no longer kicking and screaming. The years melt away in the chasm separating us. We're back on the roof of our crappy, suburban house in rural England. Every morning, we climbed the trellis together, praying it wouldn't break.

Here comes the sun, baby.

Close your eyes and pray for something good.

Why do we pray, Mummy?

For the strength to do good in this life, Brooke.

That's why we put ourselves in the way of beauty.

I can feel the hot sting of tears on my cheeks. Despite the years of torture, conditioning, abuse and neglect, Mum's sunken cheeks are wet too. She touches the tears with wonderment, looking surprised at her own reaction.

She has emotions.

She can feel.

She isn't fucking dead.

The slight upturn of her lips severs my final heartstrings.

"Come on!" Bancroft roars behind me.

For a second, I consider raising the gun to my own head. The familiar crop of shadows that spawns beside my mother halts that thought. Broad shoulders, long legs, and a boyish grin form in my hallucination. Brushing his blonde hair aside, Logan stands next to his murderer.

He glances up at her, even if she can't see him.

"No," I breathe out.

Without a single word, Logan meets my eyes. His strength and devotion pour into me, the warmth in my chest expanding and chasing out the darkness. Standing by our mother's side, I take comfort in the knowledge that she isn't alone. He's waiting to catch her on the other side, where peace awaits.

"I'm sorry, Mummy."

Her lips move in a silent message.

I want to see my boy again.
Let go, Brooke.

Bancroft is screaming at me, but I can't hear him. The threats wash over me like the rolling waves of the ocean. Little details enter my awareness and float away again. The guard's hand is pushing the lever a tiny, warning inch as the countdown begins.

Distant voices and laughter echo from our cruel enablers as they watch the show, like it's some twisted performance displaying what their money created. A flash of chestnut hair enters my periphery before it disappears, leaping back into the dark shadows.

"Please," Mum whimpers quietly.

That's when I realise her plan. The empty shell of my mother wanted me to come tonight. She knew this was the only way to be family again. This cruel world won't give us our happy ending, but perhaps the promise of the next will. After years of torment, she has a chance to escape.

I have to give her that.

I'm the only one who can set her free.

The bullet travels faster than the speed of light. Death is such a quick act for a permanent end. My shot is imperfect from my shaking hand, but it catches her right in the forehead. I squeeze my eyes shut to avoid watching the result. Logan vanishes from sight the moment my mother dies by my hand.

He's waiting somewhere, arms outstretched.

I hope she hugs him and never, ever lets go.

Ears still ringing, it takes a moment for Bancroft's unhinged laughter to register. It's a deep, maniacal cackle that mirrors the sheer insanity of his deceased son. I check the chamber of the gun and find it empty. The sick bastard only gave me a single execution shot. I'll have to do it myself.

The whizz of another bullet cuts off his celebration, slicing through the air with deadly precision. The laughter grating against my skull ceases as the guard holding four lives in his hand is struck, wavering in the air before he plummets in a spray of blood.

Reality shatters and reforms in an instant. The doors to Oakridge slam open, releasing a spray of bullets. Two more guards are caught and fall. When Hunter and Enzo emerge with battle cries, closely followed by Theo, I feel a glimmer of hope. Seven isn't far behind, dropping from a nearby oak tree.

Leaves and branches stir in the wind as it suddenly picks up. My senses are awash with the heavy beat of a helicopter, nearly blowing the marquees over. Bright letters spell out its designation—*SCU*. That's when Bancroft realises he's absolutely screwed.

Two hands latch around my neck, attempting to snap the bone. Sliding back into the welcoming arms of Patient Eight, I break free from Bancroft's hold with practised ease. He stumbles, attempting to regain purchase, but I've already rounded on him. His time has run out.

Terrified eyes meet mine.

Augustus is looking at me through his gaze.

"The game is over," I tell him.

My blow is sharp, brutal. Bancroft's knees crash into the grass as he clutches his head, looking dazed. I could walk away right now. I could spare his life. It will do my future prospects a lot of good. But Augustus taught me a valuable lesson when he ordered the murder of Allison Brunel in the Z Wing.

Fuck the moral high ground.

Never leave a job unfinished.

I can hear Hunter's deep boom over the helicopter as help arrives, but I'm not done. Ignoring them all, I sink my teeth deep into Bancroft's exposed neck. He's powerless to push me away. It takes a decade of hatred and rage to tear into his throat, my mouth filling with hot, coppery blood.

Patient Eight doesn't flinch.

She works in calm, collected silence.

He crashes before me with a thud, jerking as arterial spray paints the grass, along with my entire body. I watch the show with warmth running down my chin. Lazlo, Augustus, Jefferson and Bancroft die together in one body. A monster with many faces bleeds to death in the presence of his crumbling empire.

Voices try to break the violent haze that's descended over me. Enzo is staring down at Bancroft's corpse with a look of triumph, while figures jump from the helicopter and swarm all over us. My brain recognises agents Barlow and Jonas back in their uniforms, where they belong.

I feel absolutely nothing. Not until a hand takes mine, regardless of the blood.

"Brooklyn?" Seven asks warily.

That name is like a hot poker in the chest. It tears a hole in my suffocating shields, letting love and light pour in; so much that my knees buckle and he has no choice but to catch me. I'm enveloped in his coffee scent.

"Brooklyn," he repeats. "Come back, Brooke. The work is done. Patient Eight can rest now. She's finished her last job."

The world is filtering back in with loud noises and frantic shouts. Too many people to count are swarming like ants, including government agents with bright-yellow SCU letters printed across their backs.

They aren't arresting us.

We're not being sedated or trapped in cuffs.

Sponsors and investors are trying to run where they can, but they don't get very far. Designer high heels are tossed aside, and perfect dresses yanked up. I spot a couple of the men from Augustus's fundraiser being pinned to the ground. Our eyes collide briefly. Their fear makes my mouth water.

Guns are pulled and panicked phone calls made, but it does nothing to prevent the inevitable. Agent Barlow is the first one to slap cuffs on a man, yelling into the radio strapped to her chest. I recognise the white-haired dickhead she's arresting. He was there that night at the table, when Augustus boasted about his newest acquisition.

I catch the word *boss* being thrown in for good measure.

She's enjoying every last second of arresting her employer.

"Love!"

"Firecracker!"

"Blackbird!"

Their voices shove that last, clinging tendril of sickness back where it belongs. I blink and take a deep breath, standing back on my own feet. Seven is grinning down at me, his thumb swiping the blood from my bottom lip.

"Nice throat-tearing skills, princess."

I press my lips to his, letting him taste our revenge. "Learned from the best."

He holds my hand as the rest of our family converges in the middle of a war zone. In the light of the helicopter and perfect chaos, our reunion is near delirious. I'm passed around, hugged and kissed, touched and worshipped. Four men saved my life on the rooftop hanging over us.

My debt to them is repaid.

Seven has his revenge, served cold and bloody.

There's no fire and death this time. Incendia's ruin comes in the form of real, tangible justice. For the first time in our lives, the world has sided with us. The truth isn't something that many can afford, but when you're stripped of everything, sometimes it's all you have left.

We told ours.

We braved the world's hatred and judgement.

We won.

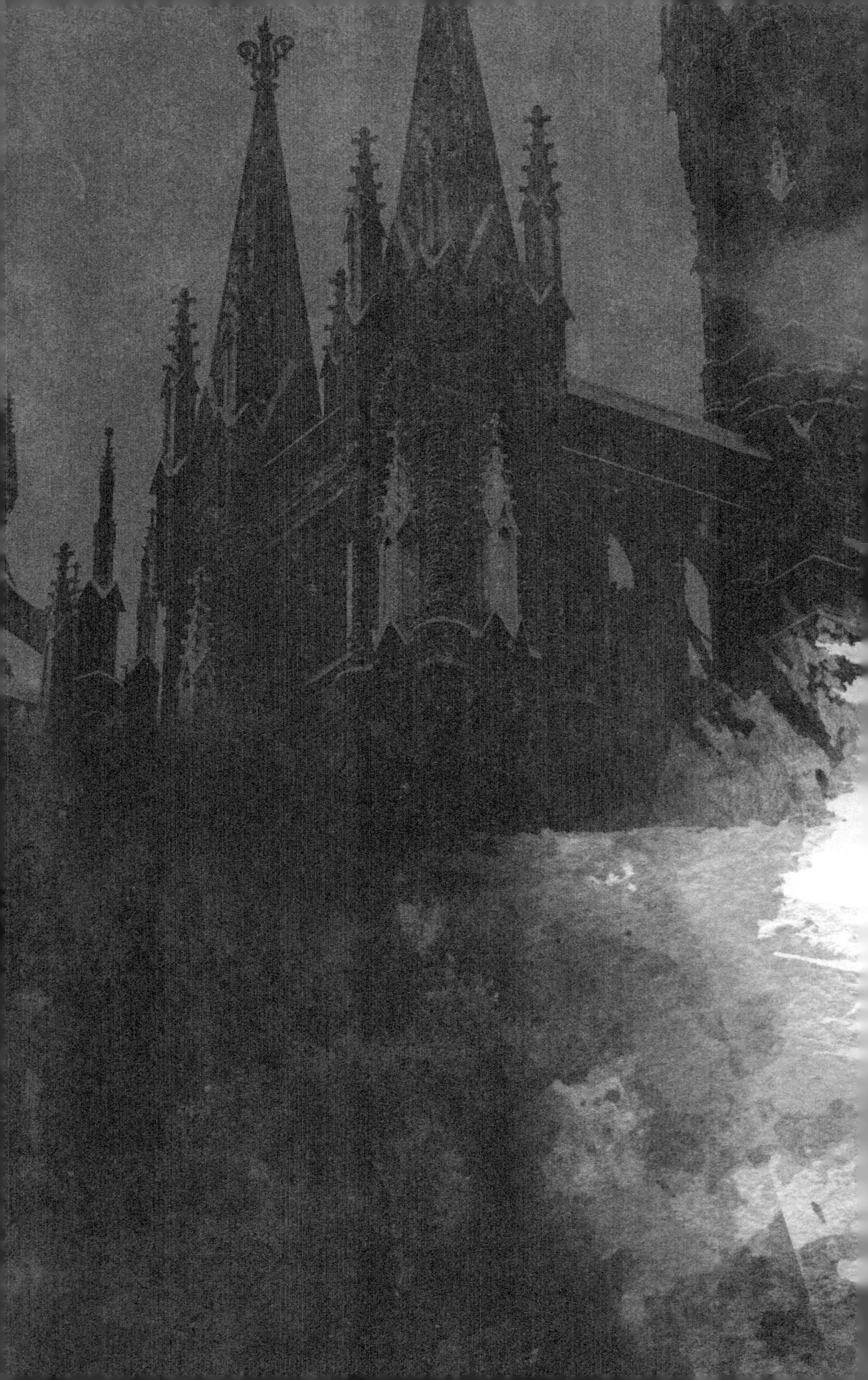

31

ELI

Hope for the Underrated Youth - YUNGBLUD

I entered Blackwood with one certainty—once I stepped through those gates, I would never leave. Each psychiatric unit I inhabited over the years promised recovery and hope after what my father did to me. It took years to find the courage to even be around other people again.

Blackwood was supposed to be my last chance, a final shot at rehabilitation. I was tired. Broken. Scarred. Defeated. A lost, lonely little boy, trapped in the past and unable to move on with the life I had left.

Finding a new family was not on the agenda. I know what families do to you. I still bear the scars to prove it. Those sworn to love and protect us are often the ones most equipped to tear us to shreds, piece by fucking piece.

You never expect to be built up again.

In the darkest of times, light finds its way back in.

We stand as a united front while the cameras flash on our third news conference of the week. Brooklyn's hand is gripping mine tight. In the month since Bancroft's death set the world alight, our private lives have become public property; every last intimate detail unpicked and printed for the world to read.

Sending our sworn testimonies out into the world was a bold move. It's tossed us all from the frying pan and into the fire. Yet, if we hadn't braved that final move, we'd be dead. It was the truth that forced the government to act and realise the SCU was dirty all along.

"This is the final time we will be here before the public," Hunter tells the reporters. "My clients have spent the last month cooperating with law enforcement. They have provided new sworn testimony to investigators. We are grateful to the SCU for reconsidering their position."

"Is it true that you're going to be the new head of service?" a woman asks.

He stifles an eye roll. "That is false. Sabre will be working closely with the SCU following the recent arrest and prosecution of its director. Incendia has many assets that need to be thoroughly investigated for corruption and money laundering."

"Will you volunteer to lead that investigation?"

"Sabre remains my priority. I'm sure the government will choose an appropriate successor. We look forward to working with them for years to come."

Sitting next to him, agents Barlow and Jonas look solemn. Their resignations were quickly halted when news of our stories spread like wildfire. They were the ones who raised the alert and went above the blanket decision made by their director. Now, they're lauded as heroes.

Bancroft knew exactly where to place his own stooge.

Turns out, the director was an old family friend.

One of many in positions of extreme power.

DESECRATED SAINTS

"As the work to dismantle Incendia and the six institutes continues, my team will dedicate all of our resources to seeking justice for the victims." Hunter casts us all a look. "I am requesting privacy for my clients to rest and recuperate. That is all."

Phoenix is squeezing my other hand ferociously tight. We're all connected, needing the reassurance of each other's touch. Enzo stands off to the side, his beefy arms crossed and scowl firmly in place. Nobody would dare go through him to get to us.

We're led from the conference room, blinded by flashing cameras. I rip the microphone off my t-shirt as soon as we're out of sight behind the scenes. This was our final round of questions with the press. The SCU have cancelled all future requests as they officially take over from Sabre.

It will take time, but Incendia is on fire.

The legacy of sorrow is no more.

Each day reveals new levels of corruption—politicians, police officers, members of parliament, the secret service and other turncoats within the SCU. Like dominoes, once one fell, the rest quickly followed. The footage of many public figures and investors watching Bancroft's failed execution was a strong condemnation.

"Head for Theo's office," Enzo instructs.

We gather upstairs in the messy, disorganised space. Theo's sat at his desk, slurping a cup of ramen and watching the live stream far from prying eyes. As we enter, he startles and nearly knocks a cup of coffee over.

"Too slow." Hudson catches the cup easily.

Theo takes it from him with a wince. "It's been a long week. Our public appeal for information has been inundated with ex-patients and detainees coming forward to assist with the investigation."

"From Blackwood?" Brooklyn leans against his desk.

"Harrowdean Manor, Compton Hall, and Priory Lane so far." He frowns at his piece of paper. "More will follow. Incendia's been abusing their privilege for thirty years. Now that the truth is out, people aren't afraid to speak up."

Phoenix snorts. "Snowball effect."

"Not to mention three other facilities decommissioned during the late nineties. Incendia tightened the purse strings, but that didn't erase the evidence. We have hundreds of witnesses ready to go on record."

Hunter strolls in with the two proud agents at his back, finally escaping the reporters. There's something very weird going on with his mouth. I think it's an attempted smile. I had no idea he could do that. The grief that's stained his entire being for so long is absent today.

Agent Barlow deposits her briefcase on one of Theo's cluttered tables. We all gather around as she pulls out thick stacks of paperwork and several ring-bound packets. Each one is placed down in front of us with a meaningful look. I count six legal packets in total.

"Andy, can you take these to Lucia and Patient Two for their signatures?"

Accepting the papers, Agent Jonas offers us all a final smile. The unshakeable government bot has become one of our strongest supporters in the absolute chaos of the last few weeks. All that time spent spilling our guts has earned us something—loyalty and respect. All it took was telling the truth.

Once he's gone to visit the girls in their apartment, Agent Barlow returns her attention to us all. "Are we ready?"

"Everyone's here," Hunter confirms.

One by one, we're each handed a packet of paperwork and a pen. Kade glances between us, a smile tugging at his lips. We've all got one, even Seven. He's frowning at the pen like it's a snake ready to bite his hand off.

"The SCU has been authorised by the prime minister himself to issue a full and unreserved public apology." Agent Barlow meets our eyes. "You have all lost years of your life and suffered irreparable damage. For that, the government takes full responsibility."

Hudson gasps as he scans his packet. "You're dropping all charges?"

"Every single one. No prosecutions will be pursued against you. Any and all crimes committed in Incendia's custody and in recent weeks are being classified as under duress. Nobody is going to prison."

Kade and his brother immediately throw their arms around each other. I'm swept off my feet by Phoenix, his squeal of relief breaking through the shock. We did it. This nightmare is over. Our lives have been given back to us. I've never felt hope like this.

But two of us aren't celebrating.

Seven and Brooklyn stare at each other, clasping identical paperwork.

"Brooke?" Kade frowns at them. "What is it?"

Enzo's head falls as our excitement fades. He can't look at us, nor can Theo. The only one staring straight ahead is Hunter, like he knew this was coming. Tension is rolling off him in waves.

"What Augustus did to you both will go down in history as a heinous violation of human rights." Agent Barlow's smile is tight. "Brooklyn, Seven, the charges against you make for grim reading. We acknowledge the role Incendia had to play in your actions. You're victims, not perpetrators."

"When?" Brooklyn interrupts.

We all glance between them, completely bemused.

"Forty-eight hours. The SCU will release your mother's body. You can bury her before you go."

"What… h-happening?!" I demand.

Everyone startles at the harsh lash of my voice. Brooklyn's eyes slam shut, like she's trying to will herself from this room. It's Seven who answers my question, the papers bunched in his one hand.

"We're being sent to Clearview."

Enzo has to hold Hudson back as he shouts his head off, fists flying. The others filter through expressions of outrage and shock. While they spiral, I approach Brooklyn and cup her cheeks until her eyes open.

"Baby girl?"

"It's okay," she whispers to me. "We aren't safe out there."

"This isn't a prison sentence," Hunter chips in. "You've both been to hell and back. This is your chance to get better. Doctor Richards is taking over as the new head of clinical operations. He wants to help you."

Brooklyn tears her gaze from mine. "What about Zimmerman?"

"He's on his way to a lifelong prison sentence for aiding and abetting the Z Wing program for over a decade. We've connected over thirty transfers into Augustus's care from Clearview, under his direction, for the purposes of human experimentation."

"And you want to send her back to that fucking place?" Hudson rages.

"The facility is being repurposed to support victims of Incendia's institutes. They will be receiving state-of-the-art, real psychiatric care."

"That's exactly the sales pitch we all received," Phoenix adds angrily. "We've heard it all before."

A heated argument breaks out. None of them are paying attention to the determination that's brewing like storm clouds on Brooklyn's face. She lays her hands on top of mine, savouring the tiny glimpse of the lives we could have. It's floating away again, but not out of sight.

"I need to sort myself out before I can be the woman you all deserve." Her eyes beg me to understand. "There's still so much rage inside of me. So much hurt. I can't start a new life until I fix what's broken."

She slips from my grasp before I can attempt to protest. I don't need to scream and rave though. This is her decision, on her terms, for the first time in her entire life. She's choosing to face this sickness head-on. I think that's fucking brave.

"I'll do it," Brooklyn declares.

Agent Barlow nods, offering her the papers again. "Clearview will help those affected by Incendia's Z Wing program. You're not a prisoner there. These people want to help you. I suggest you let them."

Ignoring the continued shouting, Brooklyn signs her life back over to the state with a sigh. Freedom is postponed, and our separation is now set in stone. Hudson turns his back before he hurts someone, fisting his black hair. Brooklyn doesn't approach him, looking to Seven instead.

"I'm not going to leave you on your own," he submits. "We can't live out in the real world like this. I want to be the man Alyssa died searching for. Not just… Patient Seven."

Brooklyn touches his arm. "We'll do it together. Our family will wait for us."

Nodding, Seven takes the pen and signs on the dotted line. That's when the arguing and shouting stops. Kade looks on with bleak acceptance, seeming to realise he can't take this decision away from them. Phoenix holds my hand for strength, his gaze stuck on Brooklyn's face.

Hudson is the last one to turn around. "You can't do this."

"I have to," Brooklyn responds gently. "For us."

Unable to stay away, Hudson walks straight into her arms. His face buries in her neck to hide his despair from us. Kade and Phoenix circle around them in a huge group hug, leaving me to hang back.

I'm too busy staring at the name Seven has signed in black and white, sealing an eternal promise to the one person who deserved to see this day. His eyes connect with mine before he offers me a tiny, hopeful smile.

Jude Farlow.

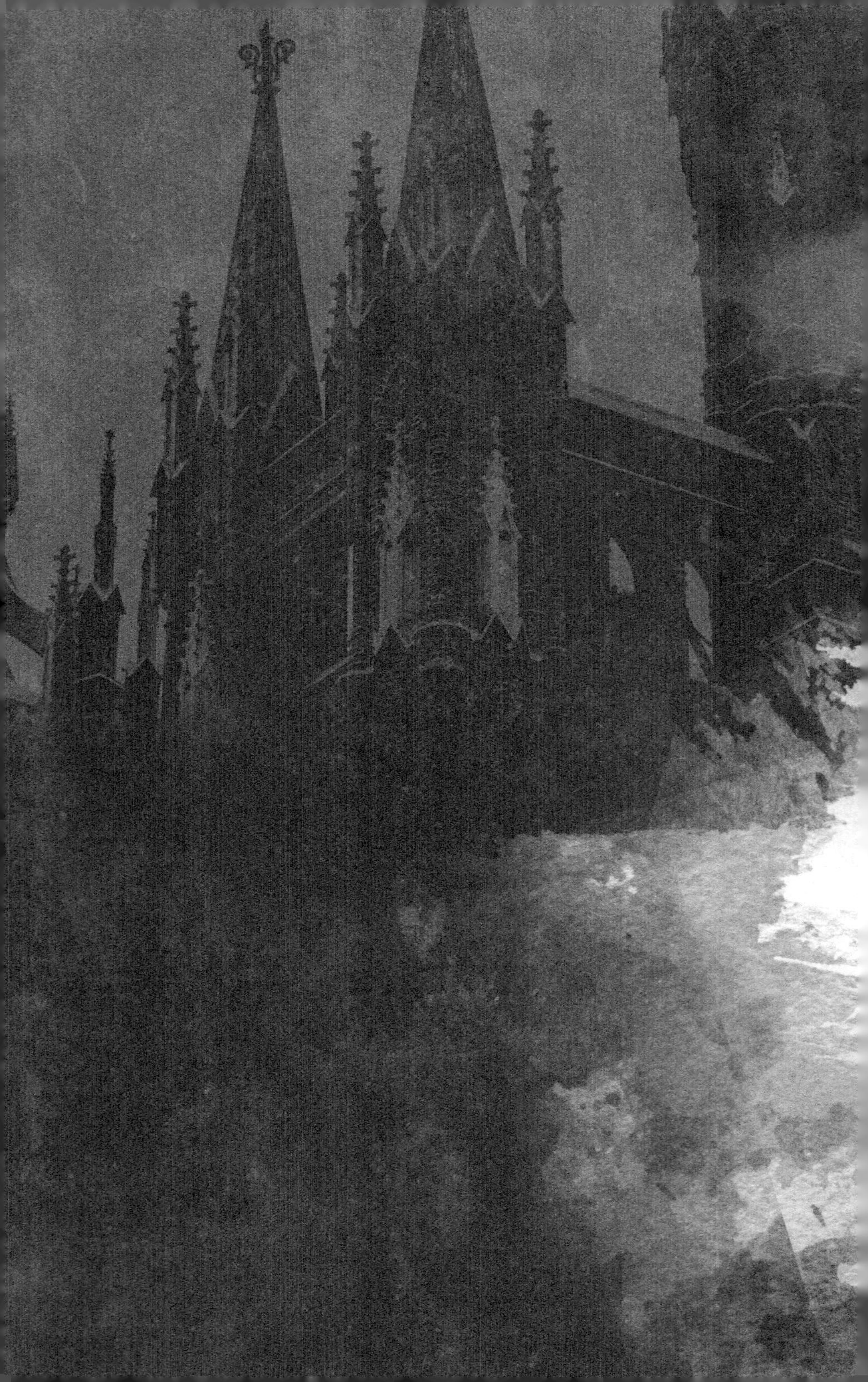

32

BROOKLYN

Hurricane - Dream on Dreamer

This journey ends where it began—on a sandy hill in Northern Scotland, far from the world.

I stare at the blazing rays of the autumn sunset. The light washes over me in a comforting cloud, pink and orange hues painting a perfect picture. I'm standing here on my last night of freedom, doing what Mum would've wanted me to.

Deep down, I know she's here too.

They all are. My dead family.

Next to me, a six-foot hole has been dug deep into the sand. Hudson insisted on doing it for me. I wanted to bury her next to the spot where, months ago, I put Logan's ghost to rest. I couldn't let go of the polaroid photos then. They've followed me through years of pain, death, and turmoil.

Standing at my mother's peaceful graveside, I clasp those photos in my hands now. My tears splash against the faded, creased faces staring back at me from the past. Clearview, Blackwood, Sabre, here. They've lived through it all with me.

The beautiful, tragic memory captured in permanent ink has haunted me for so long. The beach stretched out in summer sunshine. My small body was being swung between my parents while Logan captured the candid photos. Their smiles were bright and full of love. There were no dark shadows in my eyes.

We were happy. Free.

Untainted by sickness and evil.

Swallowing my grief, I kiss my father's face first. His soft, grey eyes radiate love back at me. With his family in his arms, he was at his happiest. Even if that was his undoing in the end.

"I forgive you, Daddy. You can rest now."

With an arm slung around her husband's neck, the unbroken version of my mother looks vastly different to the person I killed. She was beginning to disintegrate then, but the shell that returned to me was truly broken.

"I'm so fucking sorry," I whisper to her. "Pulling that trigger was the hardest thing I've ever done. I wanted you to rest, Mummy. You deserve to rest."

"Brooklyn? You ready?" Hudson prompts.

Nodding through my tears, I kiss her face. "I have to get better for my family now. They need me, Mum. I can't join you. I have to find a way to live. One day, I'll see you all again."

That should be it, but there's one more person I have to kiss goodbye. I can't let go of all my pain until one final corpse is laid to rest. The little blonde girl swinging between her parents had no clue what was coming her way. She died, too.

"So many people hurt you," I admit, studying my childhood self.

"Nobody kept us safe. I've spent so many years trying to kill myself, I forgot to live. I may not be the same person I used to be, but I promise to live for both of us now."

With my final goodbye complete, I watch the polaroids flutter in the air. Sinking down into the sandy hole, they hit the wooden coffin that Kade sourced from the local town.

With a fortifying breath, I turn to face the family I found in the darkness. I lost the people I loved. Not everyone is lucky enough to have a second chance to belong, but I am. All five of them gave that to me.

Hudson's standing next to the grave, a shovel in hand. Behind him, Phoenix and Eli are wrapped up in each other. I drink in the reassurance of their presence. Lastly, Kade and Teegan stand at the back. He's holding her arm while she offers me an encouraging smile.

They're all here. Back at the rented cottage we found our temporary peace in, Hunter, Enzo and Theo are waiting for us. I appreciate their respect for my privacy. All my vulnerabilities are on display right now.

"Brooke?"

I feel Seven's hand slide into mine. He was standing on the cliff's edge, studying the violent sea. With him by my side, I am complete. Every single person I care about is here. Safe. Healthy. Whole. Fucking free.

"I'm ready," I say calmly.

Pressing a kiss to my hair, Seven joins Hudson, shoving sand in the hole with one hand. I stand at the edge of the grave until it's filled all the way in. They smooth the sand over together, concealing my mother's empty body in the rugged beauty of the coastline.

I was prepared for a shadowy figure to appear, but my mind conjures no such horror. Hunter's well-paid shrink started me back on medication. Doctor Richards is actually very kind and amicable, content to sit in silence for hours until I'm ready to talk.

He's preparing for our arrival at Clearview tomorrow morning. Then, our long road to recovery will begin. It promises to be a hell of a bumpy ride.

Clearing her throat, Teegan approaches me next. I let her arms wind around me in one of her signature tight hugs. She penetrated my lonely bubble from day one with her quirks and awkward charm. I couldn't imagine a world without her in it as my best friend.

"I'm gonna come see you all the time," she whispers in my ear. "I'll bring you old records and band t-shirts. Maybe the odd cigarette if I can hide them in my bra."

My laugh is wet, teary. "You have a life to live too."

"Friends don't bail when one of them gets locked in the loony bin. Been there, done that. Got the fucking t-shirt." She pulls back to hit me with a dazzling smile. "When you get out, we'll drink beer and put the whole goddamn world to rights."

"Promise?"

She sticks out her pinky finger. "I promise, crazy bitch. I'll give you guys a minute. See you inside?"

Our fingers link and seal our promise. With a final wink, she begins the long walk back to the cottage. I'm left with the intense stares of five broken, defiant men. Four don't want me to go. One is as batshit crazy as I am. We have to be the most fucked-up family on this earth.

"I don't know what to say to you all."

Despite everything, their strangled laughs match mine until we're all gasping and fighting tears. Kade takes the lead and approaches me, a knowing smile on his lips. I happily walk into his embrace, avoiding his broken arm.

"We told you, love. You're ours, in this life and the next."

Hudson clears his throat, his eyes shining. "Always and forever, blackbird."

"You couldn't get rid of us even if you tried," Phoenix says proudly.

Emerald eyes meeting mine, Eli points to his jean-covered hip. His lips move silently, reserving our macabre promise for the intimacy of silence. Some things shouldn't be said aloud.

"Until death do us part," I mouth back.

A gentle hand lands on my shoulder.

"This is our last night outside for a while," Seven points out. "What do you want to do, princess?"

I watch Hudson approach him, their shoulders brushing. Despite everything, he's still being fucking shy. Seven rolls his eyes before taking his hand from my shoulder and snatching Hudson's instead. Kade smothers a laugh at their antics.

"I want a happy memory to hold on to."

Phoenix's face lights up with a devious idea. He tears his sweatshirt over his head, despite the freezing, almost wintery temperature. We all watch in bemusement as his shoes go flying next.

"Last one in the ocean has to wash the dishes."

Then he's gone, sprinting down the steep sandbank and yelling his head off. It's a split second before Eli follows, unable to be parted from his blue-haired soulmate. I watch the pair of idiots go, shedding even more clothes on their way down to the water.

"I fucking hate washing up," Hudson blurts.

He shoves his lips against Seven's briefly before kissing me with feverish need. We're both left standing there as he takes off after the other two, his black t-shirt landing in a nearby shrub.

"He is quite possibly the laziest human on this planet," Seven grumbles, toeing off his shoes. "We can't let them win, princess. It sets a dangerous precedent."

In a blur of long hair and bared teeth, he gives chase. Hudson's fast, but Seven is a whole other breed. They collide halfway down the sandbank and end up wrestling all the way to the bottom, landing in a steamy tangle. I watch four naked blurs head for the crashing waves.

Kade sighs. "Seeing my brother's naked ass wasn't on my list of priorities for today."

"Looks like we're the sore losers."

He grips my chin, exposing my lips to his. "I don't mind washing up. I'll take the forfeit. It's worth it, so I can do this."

Mouth slanting against mine, I melt into the kiss. Kade doesn't fight to consume me like the others; his battle for my soul has long since ended. I belong to him in every single fucking way a person can be owned. Breaking the kiss, his hazel eyes bore into mine.

"Come back to us, love. I have far too many plans for you to let this sickness win."

I stroke his cheek with my thumb. "I promise, I'll come back to you. I lost my entire family to the darkness buried inside of us. You have too, in your own way. That ends right now."

"I don't care how long it takes, Brooke. Let me worry about tracking my piece-of-shit father down. By the time you come back, I'll have his head mounted on a spike."

"Be careful, Kade. He's dangerous."

"So am I. Enough about him. This is our last night together."

Our foreheads meet as our souls collide. I rest my hand over his thudding heartbeat, and Kade does the same. The organ in his chest is thumping steadily, with the certainty he's always exuded.

Kade can't be my safe place anymore.

I have to find that within myself now.

"Take care of them," I murmur. "Keep my family safe."

"Until my dying breath. We'll be here waiting when you're ready."

Our fingers entwined, we slip and slide down the sandbank. The other morons are already naked and in the sea, whining about cold water.

I let Kade run in first, sticking to the shallow water to avoid getting his plaster-cast arm wet. He barely dodges Hudson's attempt to dunk his head underwater.

On the shoreline, I look up at the night's sky. The sun has given way to clear stars and sparkling constellations, unburdened by pollution or clouds. My heart thuds in my chest. Once, twice, three times. Reminding me once and for all that I stayed alive for a reason.

"Watch over them, Logan. Lord knows, they need it."

I don't need his ghost to respond to me. My brother has always been there, even when I can't see him. He'll protect my guys until Brooklyn West can return, alone in her body.

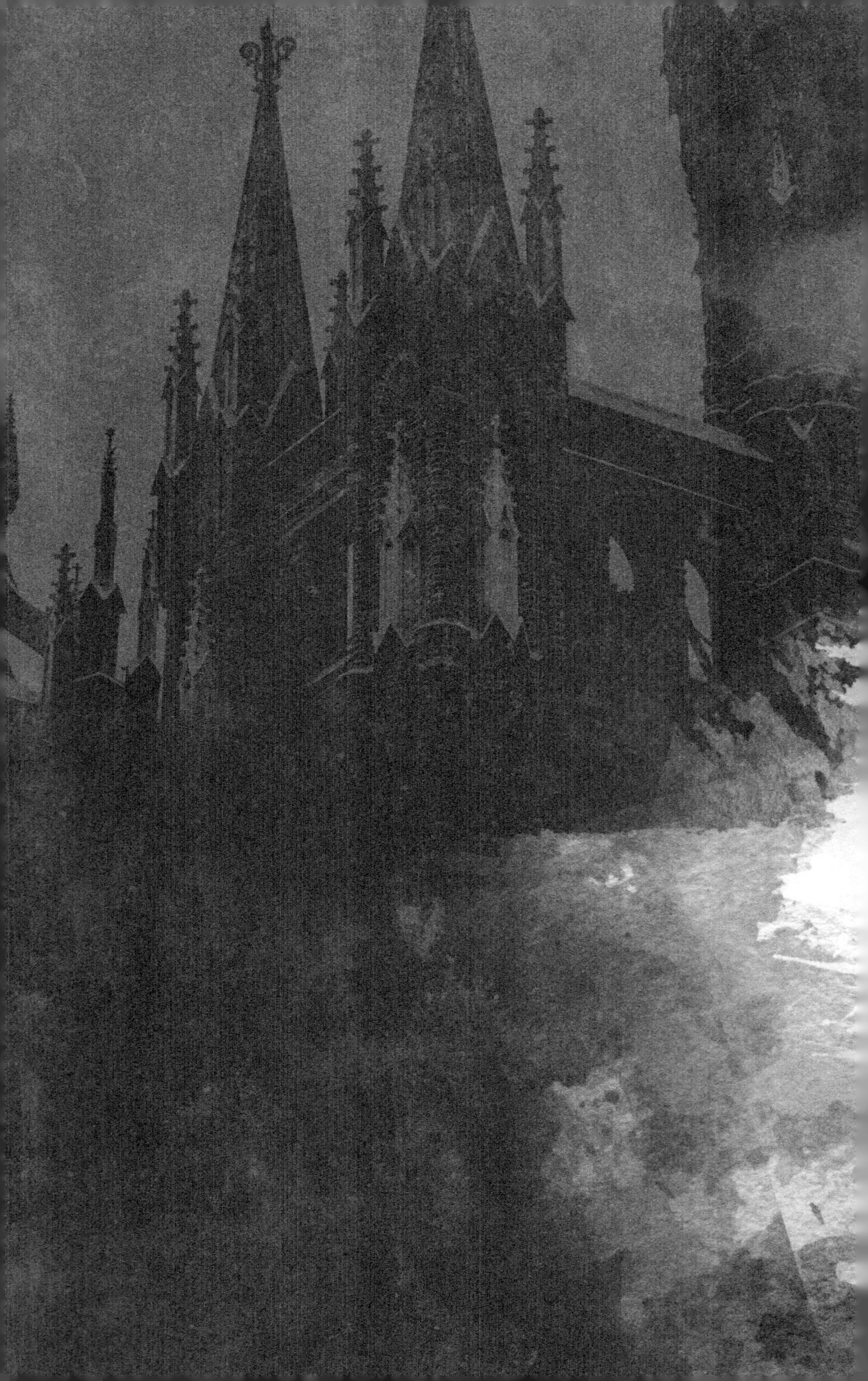

HUDSON'S LETTER

Hey, blackbird.

Bear with me I'm new to this letter-writing shit, but you made us all promise to do it. I want you to have something to hold on to outside of visitation and phone calls I'm writing this from the cottage. You've been gone for approximately twelve hours I tried to hold out for longer, but I need to feel close to you.

I know why you had to do this

It fucking hurts, but I want you to be happy and healthy

This is the only way to do that.

When I met you, my life was spiralling out of control. I was so fucking lonely, Brooke. The world is big and empty when you're sixteen, homeless and abandoned by those who are supposed to love you unconditionally. You were exactly the same as me

But you gave my life back to me

I hurt you, baby I hurt you so fucking much

Yet, you stayed until the very last second, until not even our love could hold the remains of our relationship together. I had to leave, Brooke It killed us both, but now, I'm glad. I finally understand why it happened. You said it yourself. We had to break apart to fall together.

I wanted a second chance.

Blackwood gave that to us.

The world looks different now. Hope isn't something I'm familiar with. We've been sitting around since you left, talking about what happens next. I don't know if we have the answer to that question yet. Kade's father is still out there. The world will be chewing over our stories for a very long time. You're gone.

The one thing I do know for certain?

I'm yours.

Irrevocably.

Forever.

Settle in and write me back, baby. I'll be there at the first chance I get to hold you again.

I love you more than life. You're my blackbird, but our girl.

Hud xx

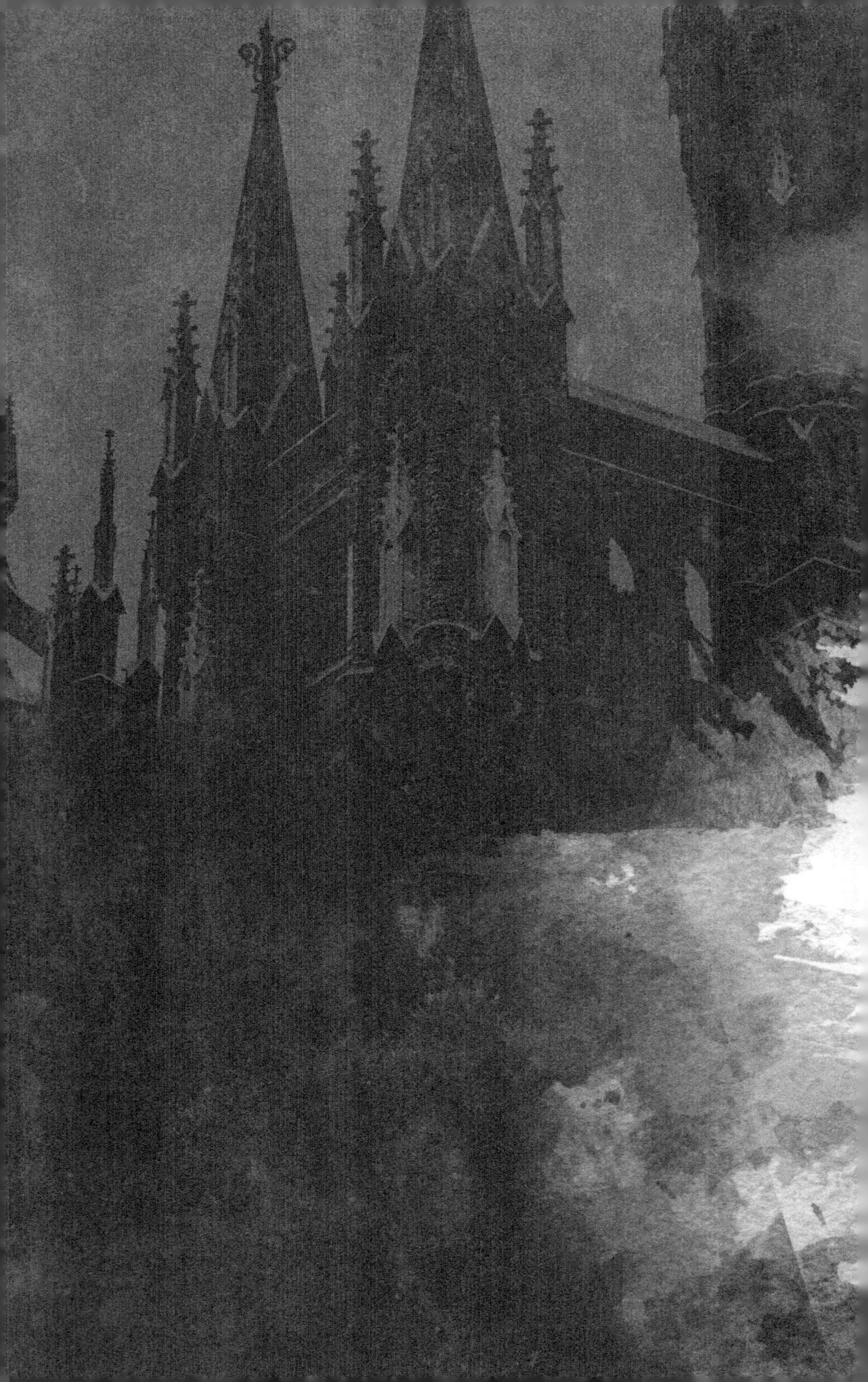

PHOENIX'S LETTER

Firecracker.

Happy six months inside!

That shouldn't be something to celebrate, but after seeing the change in you recently, I'm inclined to think we should mark the occasion. Thanks for the origami paper crane you gave me last visitation. It hangs from the ceiling in our bedroom now. I'm still recovering from the shock of discovering you doing art therapy. Thanks for that heart attack.

The apartment back at Sabre is empty without you.

You should fucking be here.

I started my volunteer program last week. Took a few months to straighten it out given our newfound fame, but the rehab manager is a decent bloke. I'm going to be talking to the kids about gang-related crime and addiction, apparently. The two things I know better than drugs themselves. Ironic, huh?

I'm trying to right the wrong I've inflicted.

I need a new purpose in this world.

Eli got accepted to study remotely at King's College, London. He was over the fucking moon, Brooke. I wish you could've seen his face. All those history essays of mine he wrote have paid off. The scholarship is pretty generous too. He's talking as well. Little bits here and there. His new speech therapist is a fucking saint.

What else?

I haven't seen Nana. She knows I love her, but I can't go back there

I don't want that life anymore. The day she steps down and retires properly, perhaps we can have a relationship again. Until then, this is the right thing to do for me.

Charlie's grave is peaceful.

She's beneath an apple tree.

Got another formal apology from the government for her death. They just keep on coming as more information leaks out. The case is still developing, even six months later. Each week there's a new arrest. More evidence. Victims coming forward. Hunter, Theo and Enzo are still working around the clock to get that justice they promised Alyssa.

She would be proud of them, I think.

I'll be there next week, firecracker. Until then, I'm enclosing a kiss in this letter.

Forever yours,
Nix

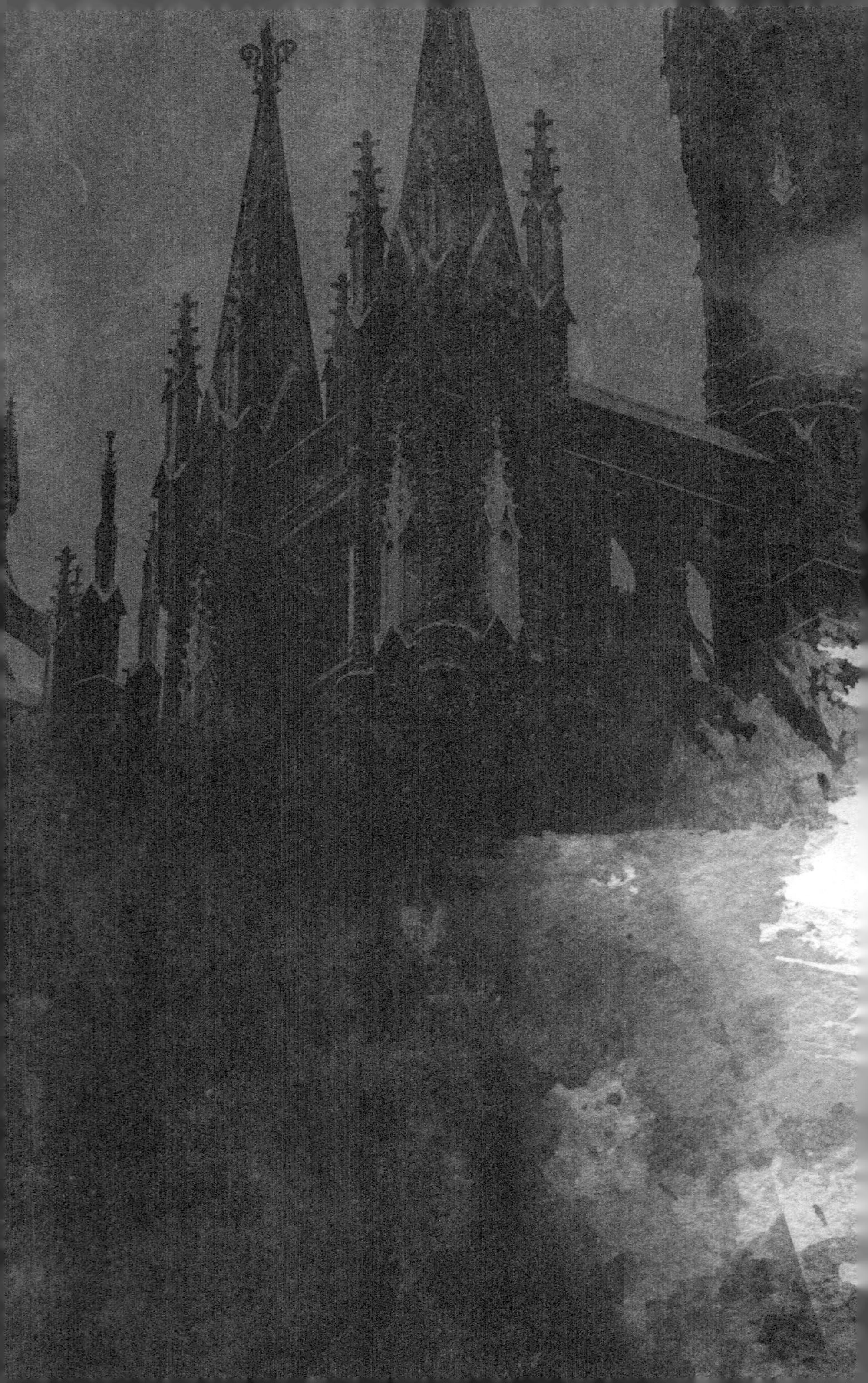

KADE'S LETTER

Hi love,

Happy birthday, Brooklyn.

I hope Seven's spoiling you in there today. We tried to get visitation, but Richards is insistent on not bending the rules. After eighteen months of this, you would think he'd lighten up. I know you had a relapse and things were rough for a while, but still.

You don't need to be afraid of telling us this stuff.

This road you're on isn't easy.

But you're not on it alone.

We've officially been working at Sabre for ten months. It's gone so quickly. Hudson's slotted right into Enzo's new division. He's been in Priory Lane and Compton Hall, documenting any last bits of evidence before the demolition begins. It's given him purpose, I think. Protecting others like you and Seven.

I'm still searching for my father.

We had a hit on one of his offshore accounts a few weeks back. The information Mum provided has left no dark corners for him to hide in. It'll take some time, but we will find him. In the meantime, she's started working again. Opened an art gallery down

south in the village she moved to. She sends her love.
　Cece graduated from university after taking a break.
　She's off to law school in the US next month.
　We're all okay. Still here. Nothing's the same without you. I thought we'd get used to it, but your absence never leaves us. We moved into the new house, just outside of the city. Hunter's fortress with the guys is a few miles away. They got a dog too. Adorable little thing. Should we get one? I think we will when you get out.
　Your room is ready for when you come home. Phoenix and Eli decorated it in all sorts of ridiculous colours, just forewarning you.
　I'm not rushing you. I know you need more time to get better, and this isn't an overnight fix. It's important for you both to be in there, getting the help you need. I'm still holding you to that promise, though.
　Come back to us, love.
　Our family isn't complete without you here.
　Until next time our lips will meet.
　I love you.
　Yours,
　Kade x

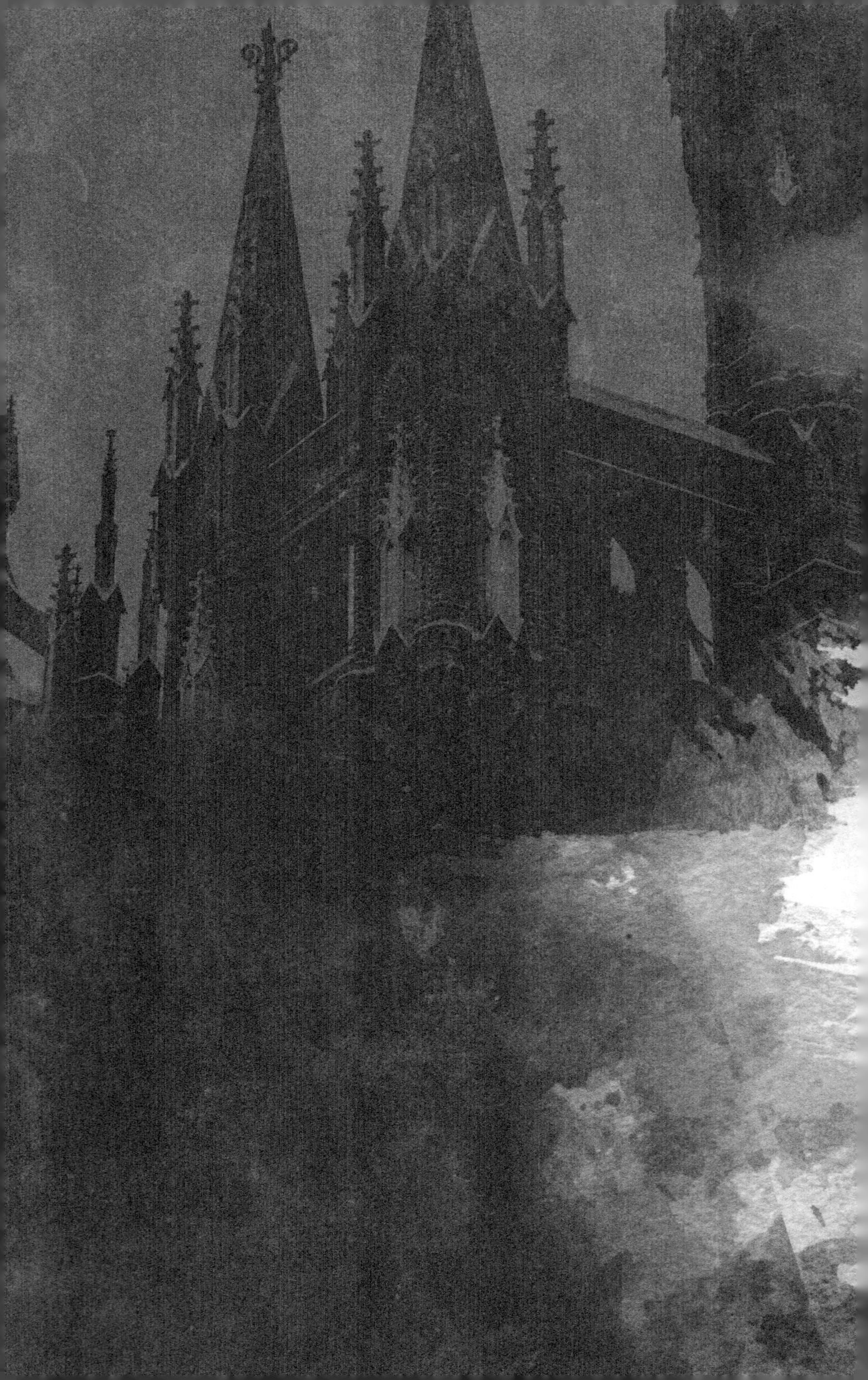

ELI'S LETTER

To Brooke,

This is the first letter I've written to you. This feels scarier than speaking—putting pen to paper. I can't hide behind closed lips in a letter. But today marks two years since you left. I figured it's time I put my fears aside and do this.

So, hi, baby girl.

It's me. Your Eli.

I miss you so fucking much. It hurts most at night. Phoenix is usually snoring while I stay up, unable to sleep. When I look at the sky, I wonder if you're watching the stars too. It makes me feel close to you, knowing we're looking at the same constellations.

I'll take whatever scraps I can get.

I passed my exam last week. The uni course is going really well. I love history, but the political science minor is becoming my favourite. I know, sad.

Watching Incendia being pulled apart and its illegal anatomy examined has inspired me to understand the world around me. I didn't see it for so long. This is the longest I've been out in the world since... well, you know when.

It's still weird writing my own essays, instead of

Phoenix's or yours. He likes to poke me or blare loud music when I'm working, just for old times' sake. But without you, our smiles don't last. Our relationship is empty without you in the middle.

    I'm going to call you this week. When I first started speech therapy last year, Karen made me write a list of goals. It felt stupid at the time. Calling you for a long, meaningless chat about everything and nothing at the same time was number one. I've been practising in the mirror like a fucking dork ever since.

    I think I'm ready now.

    Get ready, beautiful.

    We'll be back in a couple of weeks to see you again. You looked so tired last time. Get some sleep, baby girl. I know it's fucking hard, this recovery bullshit. I'm going through it with you from the outside world. We can compare notes soon.

    The first time we met, you said that having a quirky brain isn't a bad thing.

    Remember that now.

    You took this scared little boy and made him whole again. I'll love you until my very last breath, and even that won't stop me. Donec mors nos separavit. Touch your scars right now. I'll do it too. Can you feel me there?

    I can feel you.

    Fuck, Brooke. Come back soon.

    I love you.

    Your Elijah. X

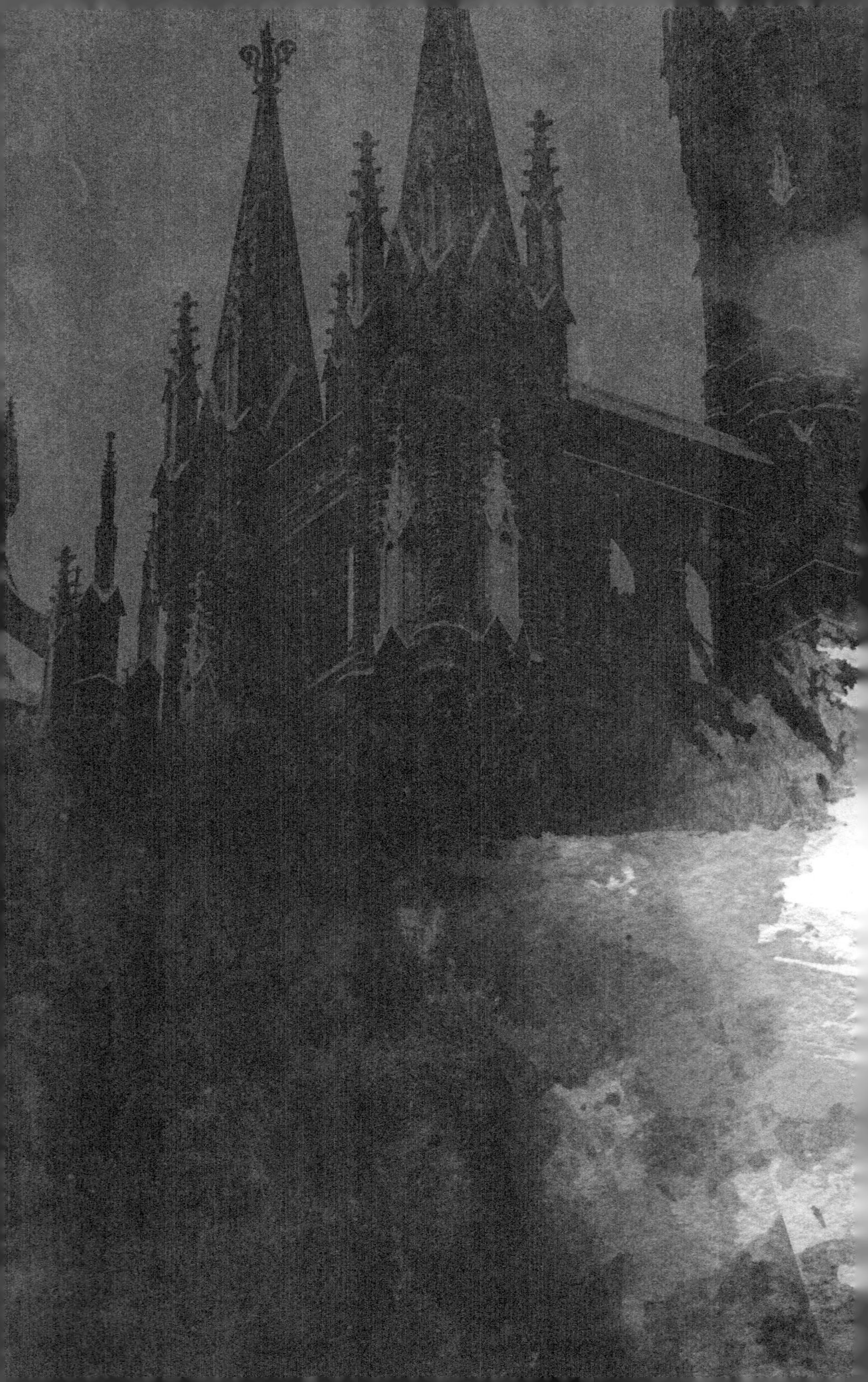

EPILOGUE

JUDE - 3 YEARS LATER

Bad Life - Sigrid & Bring Me The Horizon

Hefting the duffel bag over my shoulder, I take a final glance around the small bedroom. Plain walls and linoleum floors meet anti-ligature bed sheets and a distorted, plastic mirror. Even after all this time, the precautions of a standard psych ward remain. It's been a hell of a ride to get here.

Today is a special day.

After 1095 days, I am being discharged.

Flicking off the fluorescent overhead light, I turn my back on the four walls that have listened to my fears, hopes, nightmares and sobs for the last three years. Endless nights when I felt like giving up, throwing in the towel and letting death take me to peace at last.

So many times, I wanted to succumb to the person inside my head that kept us both alive for all this time. It was a constant battle to remain in the driver's seat of my own life. Nobody could reconstruct my identity for me. I had to do it all myself, piece by painstaking piece.

I owe my life to Patient Seven.

But Jude Farlow is walking out of here, tall and fucking proud.

Strolling down the quiet corridor of Clearview's mixed ward, I make a beeline for the nurses' desk. The other patients are eating lunch, giving us some time to say our goodbyes. Living with the same doctors, nurses, and orderlies for three years grants you a certain bond.

"Jude!"

Behind the desk, Nurse Holly waves me over. She's bouncing up and down on her toes, clutching a piece of paper in her hands. I drop my bag and steal it from her.

"Is this what I think it is?"

"Yes!" she shouts. "I passed the interview. I'm off to medical school."

We exchange high fives as I scan the confirmation letter again. It looks a lot like the one I received a decade earlier, starting me on a path that I never would've believed at the time. I even helped her prep for the interview, happy to be doing something useful.

"Congratulations. Told you!" I grin at her.

Her smile drops slightly. "I know I should be happy to see the back of you, but I'm gonna miss your handsome face around here. It's been a long three years, eh?"

"Careful," a voice interrupts. "She'll be asking for your number next. I don't have time to go back to art therapy instead of beating her up for trying to steal you."

I don't have to turn around to know Brooklyn is approaching. She smells like oil paint and the cheap soap the hospital provides to wash paintbrushes with. Scarred arms wrap around me from behind as her lips graze my neck.

"Damn, busted." Nurse Holly snickers. "I'm old enough to be his mother, Brooke. But I'm flattered you think I could pull such a charming gentleman."

The two women embrace, squeezing each other tight. I watch Brooklyn subtly wipe her eyes when they break apart again. Nurse Holly doesn't bother hiding her emotions. She's played the maternal role since our first day, even as the ward matron. Despite her big heart, she runs a tight ship here.

"Got everything, kids? Doctor Richards should be here to escort you out in a moment. He's just signing off the discharge papers and checking your travel arrangements."

Brooklyn double checks her suitcase before throwing her old leather jacket on. We're granted a moment of privacy as Nurse Holly bustles off to track the doctor down. Nestling herself into my side, Brooklyn lets out a contented sigh that obliterates three years of tedious therapy and painful separation.

"Your sister used to let us raid that vending machine before group therapy." She points towards the machine at the end of the corridor. "The least disruptive patient was awarded with a snack of their choice."

"Isn't that blackmail?"

"Or good crowd management."

I scan the empty recreation room where each night, patients gather to watch the approved selection of movies. We never ended up there often. There's a courtyard outside, protected by a high-security fence, not unlike Blackwood.

Beneath the floodlights and thick cloud coverage, we spent many nights planning our future. Not just mine and Brooklyn's though. There are four other lives caught in this spider's web. After a long time apart, their lives are about to begin too.

"Will you miss it here?" she hums.

"No," I answer easily. "I can be grateful for surviving Clearview without missing it. This place was my first posting when I qualified. I was never supposed to live within these walls."

"I'll miss the sedatives." Brooklyn snorts at her shitty joke. "The real world is a hell of a lot more complicated than this place. We're jumping from a fishbowl into a giant fucking ocean."

With nobody watching, I press my lips to hers. "I won't let you drown, princess. We're gonna swim as far from the past as we possibly can. This is the beginning of the rest of our lives."

"No kissing in my ward, you hooligans!"

We break apart at the sound of Doctor Richards' voice. He's a grey-haired, stout man with an acid-tongue and fierce devotion to his work. Not to mention the world's most eclectic fashion taste.

Today, he's wearing his pink slip trousers—bright, lurid fuchsia. All discharge orders are printed on pink hospital paper. It's his little way of celebrating each life that he's saved.

Doctor Richards claps his hands together. "Let's get this show on the road, shall we? I have four very impatient men camped out in my car park. Anyone would think I'm running a B&B in here."

"A B&B would have better food," Brooklyn teases.

He grins at her, pulling his well-worn smile lines taut. "You can eat everything you want now, Brooke. Do think of us poor, tortured souls surviving off beans on toast when you're living the high life."

With an eccentric flourish that matches his wacky personality, Doctor Richards officially signs our lives back over to… us. I hold the discharge papers in my hand, needing to verify they're real. His smile is understanding.

"Are you ready to face the big, bad world?"

Both picking up our belongings, we follow him through the ward's complex security system. Nurse Holly waves from the back office where she's fixing a cuppa, tears shining in her eyes. I knew she wouldn't wave us off. Saying goodbye is hard for the staff too. People who work in mental health are fucking underrated.

Brooklyn grasps my hand tight as we leave gleaming corridors and treatment rooms behind. The exit awaits, real and terrifying. Life begins on the other side of those doors.

"I understand you're off on a trip." Doctor Richards inspects us both over his spectacles. "I'll be in touch when you return. It's important we keep things up with regular check-ins and continued therapy."

He seems taken aback when Brooklyn drops her bag and throws her arms around him. After a second's hesitation, he hugs her back with a little chuckle. This man has quite literally saved her life these past three years. Mine too, one excruciating step at a time.

"Keep this one in line, Brooke. He's a troublemaker."

"I will, doc. See you soon."

Leaving the man that pieced our minds back together behind, I hold the door open for Brooklyn. She ducks beneath my arm, tears already soaking her cheeks. At the bottom of the wide marble steps that lead to Clearview Psychiatric Unit, a huddle of misfits impatiently waits.

Eli is the first to spot us. Beneath his trimmed head of curls, he removes a pair of sunglasses to reveal his incandescent happiness. Tugging on Phoenix's shirt sleeve, he points up at us. His strong, unwavering shout is the biggest change.

"Brooke! Jude!"

That's all it takes to free Brooklyn from her startled daze. She flies down the steps and drops her suitcase in a frenzied blur. Phoenix moves so fast, his chin-length, green hair waves in the autumn air. They collide somewhere in the middle, a tangle of limbs and gasping cries.

Watching them with a pleased smile, Hudson picks up her discarded suitcase. I meet him at the bottom of the marble steps, my own heart exploding with anticipation. He grabs a handful of my grey t-shirt and drags me close until our chests collide.

"Could've got my bag for me too," I say with a smirk.

"Hey, ladies first. I ain't your damn butler."

Then his mouth smashes into mine. We reunite in a battle of teeth and tongue, fuelled by the unquenchable thirst that drives our intense connection. My relationship with Hudson isn't like Phoenix and Eli's close bond. They adore each other. Hudson loves to hate me. He fucks with the same rage that brought us together.

Kade is the last to join our group. His glasses are long gone after he had laser eye surgery last year. Working at Sabre in the intelligence department has led to far too many accidents, especially smashed lenses during an active operation. He slaps my back, grinning from ear to ear.

"Nice haircut, man."

I run a self-conscious hand over my newly cut hair, buzzed on the sides while leaving some strands for Brooklyn to play with late at night. "Thanks. Figured it's time for a fresh start."

Next to us, Brooklyn is still being suffocated by the terrible twosome. She breaks Phoenix's demanding kiss long enough to shoot us all an apologetic look. He's struggled the most with irregular visitation and forced distance. I doubt he'll be letting her leave his sight any time soon.

"I thought you were working today?"

Phoenix strokes her platinum hair, marvelling at the long length. "Change of plan, firecracker. The kids can live without me for a while. This was too good to miss."

He finally surrenders her to the brothers waiting for their reunion. Hudson picks Brooklyn up in his broad, tattooed arms, twirling her around. He looks happier than I've ever seen him in the four long years of our messed-up family. She studies the new tattoos marking his throat and neck, tracing the dark ink.

"Is Hunter's salary feeding your addiction, Hud?"

"Gotta spend my money on something, blackbird." Hudson places her back down, scanning her from head to toe. "If you think this is a lot, wait until you see my back."

"He's gone full thug life." Kade opens his arms wide. "Come here, love. Why am I always the afterthought?"

She throws herself into his welcoming embrace. "Because I know you'll always be here to catch me, Kade. No matter how long it takes, it's always you. That's why."

"You feel so fucking good. Welcome home."

With our reunion complete, Eli leads the way to the awaiting vehicle parked nearby. Where I expected some slick company car that the brothers pilfered from Sabre, something else entirely awaits. There's a cherry-red VW camper van in the car park. It's been painstakingly restored to perfection.

Brooklyn stops in her tracks.

"Um, what the fuck is that?"

Hudson steals her, their lips smacking loudly. "That is our home for the next three months."

Reaching inside the vinyl-covered cab, Phoenix pulls a giant paper map from the dashboard. He spreads it out across the bonnet, revealing layers of sharpie marks, pins and post-it notes. An entire route across Europe has been obsessively mapped out and thoroughly researched.

"Did Kade get a boner planning this shit to the last detail?" I whisper to Hudson.

He nods with an eye roll. "Even used Theo's new surveillance drones to check out the local hostels for bad vibes. Enzo had to give him a formal warning, even though he couldn't stop laughing."

Gathered around the crazy map, we all study the route that will guide the next months of our lives. Phoenix is taking a break from the rehabilitation centre, while the brothers are on sabbatical from their jobs back at Sabre. Eli's final year of university doesn't begin until after Christmas, when he'll finish his degree.

There's nothing ahead of us but the open road.

Endless possibilities and, for once, a bright future.

Loading up the camper van, Hudson and Kade flip a coin for the driver's seat. I can already see them butting heads every fucking day on this road trip. Phoenix and Eli crawl in the back, already snuggling and sharing headphones like an old married couple.

I stand next to Brooklyn, waiting for her to move.

She turns to look back at Clearview.

"Sev?"

The old nickname doesn't wound me. It slips out from time to time, and it's a welcome reminder. While Jude has walked free, he's infinitely stronger for the pieces of Seven that he took into his heart forever. I can't erase my past and, in all honesty, I don't want to. I'm alive because of it.

"Yeah, princess?"

"What if she comes back?" Her voice lowers. "Eight?"

Trapping her against my chest, my lips meet her ear. "I will always love Patient Eight. Seven loves her too. But Brooklyn West is my future. Jude's future. We'll face it together with our family at our side."

She bites her lip, still uncertain.

"You love me. Real or not real?"

It's a silly coping strategy, something Doctor Richards taught us both in therapy. Our memories get tangled and confused, blurred by trauma. The past we shared and the pain we endured are important. It led us here, to freedom and salvation. We have to remember that. It all meant something.

"Real," I murmur back. "Always real."

Brooklyn looks up at me, hope shining in her grey eyes.

"Yeah, me too. Let's get the fuck out of here."

THE END

Hunter, Theo and Enzo will return in...

CORPSE ROADS
A DARK, CONTEMPORARY RH DUET SET IN THE SAME WORLD AS BLACKWOOD INSTITUTE

Read on for a sneak peek.
Your favourite heathens will make several cameos.

SNEAK PEEK
HUNTER

Crunching the disposable coffee cup in my hand, I toss it into the bin and settle back in the leather chair. A steady thump behind my eyes threatens to distract me from filing this stupid incident report.

"That bad, huh?" Enzo chuckles.

"You could always file your own damn report."

"You're the bossman, not my area."

I stack the papers and crack my neck. "I seem to remember all of us raiding that warehouse, dickhead. Would it kill you guys to do some paperwork?"

"If we had some new leads, we could be doing more important things than filing paperwork."

I spread my hands, indicating to the walls of my office, plastered in crime scene photographs, maps and reports. "You know something I don't? We've been at a dead end for weeks. Until another victim turns up, we're screwed."

"Since when do we wait for the bodies to pile up?" Enzo frowns.

"Since we've been three steps behind Britain's most notorious serial killer for the last six months, and there is still no end in sight."

Abandoning my seat, I pace beside the lengthy conference table to expel some of my frustration. Loosening my tie, I run a hand over my slick, brown ponytail and growl in frustration. Enzo is my best friend and second in command, but he sure as hell knows how to get under my skin, even after over a decade of working together.

"We have other clients to be getting on with."

"None more pressing than this," he points out, his boots propped up on the table. "The SCU is clueless, Hunter. They can't solve this without us."

"They can't solve this with us, dammit."

Joining me, Enzo lays a heavy hand on my shoulder. "We have a better shot at it together. Plus, the retainer fee is too good to give up now. Let's go back to evidence. Take another look."

I turn back to the master board we have set up on the back wall of my office, spiralling into organised chaos. Each victim in the last five years has their own place, with all of the information and autopsy reports spread out. Tiny red cord connects anything relevant.

"Eighteen girls in five years." Enzo runs a hand over the dark scruff on his chin.

At well over six foot six and two hundred pounds of pure muscle, he's the enforcer to my stratagem and planning. Enzo is a scary motherfucker to all but those who know him best—my team. We're proudly known as the finest investigators and most prestigious private security firm in England.

After a tumultuous twelve years in the business and several high-profile cases in recent years, we've reached new heights. Expanding into new premises was necessary after our team doubled in size. While we run the main divisions, our trusted subordinates are working to build new areas of the firm.

"Too many lives," I agree, an unbearable weight on my shoulders.

We were drafted to the case last year by the Serious Crimes Unit. Despite undergoing a full reconstruction and new in-house regulations to protect against corruption, they're seriously slacking with this case. Even after our work whipping them into shape, the fumbling fools took one look and swiftly surrendered all responsibility.

They prefer to sign extortionate cheques than continue wrestling with the impossible. We take on government contracts regularly, but this has proven to be beyond anything we imagined. The victims are all the same—young, brown-haired girls from working-class backgrounds. All brutally murdered, raped, and carved with religious iconography.

"You hear from Theo on those traffic reports?" Enzo muses.

"He's still working on it. The last girl went missing nearly two months ago. No body yet. Perhaps she's still alive."

"You really believe that?"

Meeting his intelligent amber eyes, I shake my head. This man knows my thought processes better than I do at times. We've worked together for so long, our minds and bodies are completely in tune. Building Sabre up to the reputable firm that it is today has taken absolutely everything from us. Even loved ones.

"She's dead. But why no body?"

He tugs a picture down from the wall to examine it closer. "Something's changed. Maybe the killer was spooked? Or they're dragging it out this time. Who knows?"

"She'll turn up eventually. They all do."

My blasé attitude towards discussing death should disturb me, but honestly, it's self-preservation at this point. We've handled many messy cases since dismantling Incendia Corporation several years ago, though none quite on this scale.

I've seen things that I'll never forget and suffered for it, but I still go to sleep every night knowing we've done our best to make the world a safer place.

"Perhaps we should revisit the last victim; maybe we missed something," Enzo suggests, replacing the photograph of the missing woman.

"We picked that crime scene apart, along with the SCU. There was nothing to report, clean as a fucking whistle. We're not dealing with an amateur here."

We lapse back into tense silence, studying various reports and brainstorming for new ideas. It isn't until the door to my office slams open that we startle back to the real world. We're both far too accustomed to losing ourselves in death and destruction.

The blur of blonde curls and a bright-blue flannel reveals our techie and third team member, Theodore. He drops his laptop on the table and straightens his usual graphic t-shirt, this one depicting some complex mathematical symbol that worsens my headache. It's rare that he makes an appearance outside of his computer lab these days.

"It's a miracle." Enzo smirks.

"Are we sure he's real and not a mirage?"

Frowning at us both, Theo slides his phone from his pocket and hands it over to me, mouthing the word Sanderson. Great, that's the last thing I need. The SCU is breathing down our necks for results they can't find themselves. I should've taken that place over when I had the chance.

"Rodriguez," I greet.

"You're a hard man to track down, Hunter."

"Apologies. We were in a meeting."

Sanderson snorts like the annoying bastard he is. This man is the definition of a middle-aged pencil pusher, happy to dole out the dirty work while he keeps his hands clean.

"I got somethin' for ya."

Pinching the bridge of my nose, I force some patience. "Be more specific."

"Next victim has turned up. Meet me at the hospital, half an hour."

"Same MO? Body dumped and carved up?"

"Nah," Sanderson answers grimly. "She's alive."

The line goes dead. I toss Theo's phone back to him, my mind spinning with possibilities. Relaying the information to the others, they both look equally stunned. I refasten my tie and grab my car keys from the desk, already racing against the clock.

My desperation to get this fucking case behind us overrules any misgivings I may have about working with a man like Sanderson. We need results. I'm done facing victims' families with zero answers.

Enzo grabs his leather jacket as Theo's eyes bounce around the room, like he expects me to drag him along too. Fieldwork is not his forte.

"Keep working on those camera feeds. We'll take care of the SCU."

"Call me if you need backup," he offers.

"We'll be fine. See you at home?"

He mumbles, refusing to agree with me. The bedroom we set up for him when we bought the luxurious townhouse in outer London remains untouched, even five years later—though that wasn't when our problems started. Theo pulled away from our group the day he lost his reason for existing.

Meeting Enzo in the garage, we greet a handful of employees on the way to our blacked-out SUV. Everyone defers towards us, their heads lowered with respect. After dismissing them, we climb in and set the navigation for the hospital. It won't take long to get there from Sabre's HQ.

"We'll catch this sick bastard," Enzo states, mostly to himself.

"I hope you're right. This case is starting to get to me."

Both smoothing emotionless masks into place, we leave no room for weakness. It's a professional necessity, something we aren't always the best at. Enzo is far worse than me, a complete sucker for a sob story. He's adopted many strays into Sabre's ranks over the years.

Heading out, we prepare to face our first live victim. Only this time, I hope it will be the last.

Pre-Order: mybook.to/SS1

PLAYLIST

Be Invited - The Twilight Singers
Died Enough For You - Blind Channel
Out Of The Black - Royal Blood
Give - You And Me At Six
Crazy - Echos
Time Changes Everything - The Plot In You
Doomed - Bring Me The Horizon
Left alone - Zero 9:36
You Are Everything - Holding Absence
PSYCHO - Aviva
Lost - Ollie
Kerosene - Vanish
Lust - Saint JHN & Janelle Kroll
Summer Set Fire to the Rain - Thrice
Birdcage - Holding Absence
Lost - The Hunna
Pretty Toxic Revolver - Machine Gun Kelly
Me & My Demons - Omido and Silent Child
Lydia - Highly Suspect
RIGGED - The Plot In You
Reset Me - Nothing But Thieves

Hurts Like Hell - Fleurie
Teresa - YUNGBLUD
Fourth of July (Remix) - Fall Out Boy
Casual Sabotage - YUNGBLUD
DiE4u - Bring Me The Horizon
Youth - Cleopatrick
Heat Waves - Our Last Night
Somebody Else - Circa Waves
It's Okay To Be Afraid - Saint Slumber
Wonderful Life - Bring Me The Horizon & Dani Filth
Hope for the Underrated Youth - YUNGBLUD
Hurricane - Dream on Dreamer
Bad Life - Sigrid & Bring Me The Horizon

ACKNOWLEDGEMENTS

Well, it's surreal to say the least to be typing these words. The end. At last, the final Blackwood Institute book… is done and dusted. What a wild fucking ride.

People always ask authors where they get their ideas from. Brooklyn's story came from my own struggles with mental health and childhood trauma. I wrote her character in a flurry of pain, attempting to understand my own road to recovery.

In the two years since she first came to me, I've undergone my own journey. I'm so proud of the character growth in these three books. But even more so? I'm proud of the person I've grown in to while writing them. This feels like a good place to acknowledge that.

While Brooklyn learned to forgive herself, I cried and ached right along with her, battling the same darkness. We both got there in the end.

This is the part where I thank the army of people helping me. You know the drill. These people are fucking incredible and deserve their due.

As always, Kristen. Blackwood is your world as much as it is mine. Thank you for being here since the very first words, every painful step of the way. I'm so proud of our babies. Donec mors nos separavit, wife.

Lauren, I never expected to find a best friend on another continent. You've been my arc reader, then my beta, proofreader, editor, now my soulmate. I couldn't do any of this without you.

To the best PA, momager and most dedicated friend around, Julia. It's been a crazy two years since we met. Many books, wild signings, hugs and tears later, I'm so thankful to have you in my life.

Mackenzie - my editor and all-round star! Thank you for taking these massive, messy scripts and making them sing. The madness in my brain appreciates all your hard work.

And of course, my beta reader extraordinaire, Kerrie. I'd be lost without you too! Along with the other incredible authors and friends that keep me going: Dani, Lilith, Rosa, Zoe, Sam, Lola. I'm so blessed to have you all.

We can't forget my amazing street and ARC teams too, for all their enthusiasm and dedication to my words. Your help has changed my publishing forever and I love you all dearly.

Finally, I need to say a huge thank you to everyone out there buying my books. Every ounce of blood, sweat and tears I pour into these books are for you!

I'm so excited to see what the next steps of my writing journey brings. Stay tuned, y'all. We're just getting started.

Love always,

J xxx

ABOUT THE AUTHOR

J Rose is an independent dark romance author from the United Kingdom. She dabbles in both the contemporary and paranormal genres, writing emotionally impactful stories that tackle real world issues.

She's an introverted bookworm at heart, with a caffeine addiction, penchant for cursing, and an unhealthy attachment to fictional characters.

Feel free to reach out on social media, J Rose loves talking to her readers!

For exclusive insights, updates, and general mayhem, join J Rose's Bleeding Thorns on Facebook.

Business enquiries: j_roseauthor@yahoo.com

Come join the chaos. Stalk J Rose here…

www.jroseauthor.com/socials

NEWSLETTER

Want more madness? Sign up to J Rose's newsletter for monthly announcements, exclusive content, sneak peeks, giveaways and more!

www.jroseauthor.com/newsletter

ALSO BY J ROSE

www.jroseauthor.com/books

The Redeemed
If You Break
When You Fall

Blackwood Institute
Twisted Heathens
Sacrificial Sinners
Desecrated Saints

Standalones
Departed Whispers
Forever Ago
Drown in You

Sabre Security

Corpse Roads (November 26th)
Pre-Order: mybook.to/SS1
Skeleton Hearts (Coming 2023)

Printed in Great Britain
by Amazon